ICE
IS
BACK

CASS KELLIE

CONTENTS

1 ECHOES OF THE PAST

Dust motes danced in the afternoon sunlight that filtered through the small attic window, creating golden beams that illuminated Mandy Thompson's careful movements. At fifteen, she had learned exactly which floorboards would betray her presence to anyone downstairs – third board from the left creaked like a rusty hinge, while the spot near the chimney remained mercifully silent. The July heat had transformed the attic into something approaching a sauna, and beads of sweat trickled down her neck as she methodically worked her way through another box of her grandmother's belongings.

The familiar scent of old books and mothballs filled her nostrils, mingling with a hint of something else – perhaps her grandmother's perfume still lingering after all these years. Or maybe it was just her imagination, desperate to hold onto any connection to the woman who had been gone for five years now. Mandy pushed aside a stack of yellowed newspapers, her fingers brushing against something metal beneath them. Her heart quickened as she carefully extracted a small key with an intricate snowflake design.

For a moment, she was eight years old again, sitting on her grandmother's lap while they watched snow fall outside the bay window. "Ice has memory," her grandmother had said, her voice carrying that hint of accent Mandy could never quite place. "It remembers everything it touches." At the time, Mandy had giggled, thinking it was just another of Grandma Amanda's fairy tales. Now, running her finger over the engraved 'ICE' on the key, she wondered if there had been more truth to those stories than anyone realized.

A car door slammed outside, jolting her back to reality. Through the small attic window, she caught sight of her mother's silver sedan in the driveway – home early, as usual lately. Mandy quickly slipped the key into her pocket and began replacing the boxes, her movements precise and practiced from countless other secret searches.

Downstairs, her mother stood at the kitchen counter, mechanically chopping vegetables for dinner. Abby Thompson had their grandmother's high cheekbones and dark hair, but where Amanda's eyes had sparkled with secrets and mystery, Abby's held something closer to carefully controlled fear.

"Mom," Mandy began, watching her mother's shoulders tense at her tone. "I found something of Grandma's-"

The knife's rhythmic chopping stopped mid-slice. In the sudden silence, Mandy could hear her father's key turning in the front door lock – perfect timing, as always. Drake Thompson entered the kitchen, his police detective's instincts immediately picking up on the tension. He loosened his tie, eyes darting between his wife and daughter.

"Everything okay here?" Drake asked, using what Mandy privately called his 'officer voice' – calm, controlled, designed to defuse. It was the same tone he'd used five years ago when he'd told her about Grandma Amanda's passing, as if speaking softly enough could somehow cushion the impact of loss.

"Our daughter," Abby said, resuming her chopping with renewed vigor, "has been in the attic again." The 'again' hung heavy in the air, weighted with years of similar confrontations. Mandy noticed how her mother's hands trembled slightly, the way they always did when Amanda's name haunted their conversations.

The temperature in the kitchen seemed to drop ten degrees.

2

Drake set his briefcase down slowly, deliberately, placing it in its usual spot by the counter – a man who believed order could keep chaos at bay. He'd always been the mediator between Mandy and her mother, especially since Amanda's death had carved a glacier-sized divide between them.

"Mandy, we've talked about this. Some doors are better left closed." His words were gentle but carried an undercurrent of steel that reminded her of all the times he'd come home late from the police station, clothes wrinkled and eyes haunted by whatever case he'd been working on. She wondered, not for the first time, if any of those cases had involved her grandmother.

"That's all you ever say!" Mandy's voice cracked with frustration. She watched her mother's shoulders hunch at the sound, a reflexive protection against memories she refused to share. "Both of you just want to pretend she never existed. But she was real, and she was important, and I deserve to know why everyone acts like she was some kind of-"

"Enough!" Abby's palm slammed against the counter. The knife clattered against the cutting board, and a carrot rolled onto the floor. The sound echoed through the kitchen like a gunshot, making Drake instinctively step forward – always the protector, even when there was nothing tangible to protect them from.

In the ringing silence that followed, Mandy saw her parents exchange one of those loaded glances they thought she didn't notice – the kind that carried entire conversations in a single look. She'd first noticed these glances at Amanda's funeral, when whispered conversations would stop the moment she entered a room. They'd only increased over the years, each silent exchange another brick in the wall between her and the truth.

"We're trying to protect you," her father said softly, his voice gentle but firm. He moved to stand beside her mother, his hand finding its familiar place on her shoulder. It was a gesture Mandy had seen countless times – whenever Amanda's name came up, whenever strange letters arrived with foreign postmarks, whenever winter storms blew in unexpectedly harsh from the north.

Abby leaned into her husband's touch, drawing strength from his presence. The gesture reminded Mandy of old photographs she'd found, ones showing her mother as a teenager, standing tall and proud beside Amanda. Somewhere along the way, that confident girl had transformed into this woman who flinched at shadows and changed the subject whenever her own mother's name was mentioned.

"Normal isn't always better than truth," Mandy said, noticing how her mother's free hand moved to touch the thin silver chain she always wore – another habit that emerged only when Amanda was discussed. "And I won't stop looking for answers about Grandma Amanda – about ICE."

She watched her mother's face pale at the mention of that name, saw her father's hand tighten protectively on his wife's shoulder. The kitchen lights seemed to flicker, though it might have been her imagination. Her mother's fingers clutched the silver chain so hard her knuckles went white.

"Your grandmother," Abby whispered, her voice barely audible, "made her choices long ago. Before you were born. Before I even..." She trailed off, shaking her head as Drake pulled her closer.

"Go to your room, Mandy," her father said, but his eyes never left his wife's face. "We'll discuss this later." The tone in his voice suggested they wouldn't, that this conversation, like so many others, would be buried beneath layers of forced normalcy and careful avoidance.

But as Mandy turned to leave, she caught a glimpse of something she'd never seen before – tears in her mother's eyes, and behind them, not just fear, but something that looked almost like longing. The key in her pocket seemed to grow colder, as if responding to the chill that had crept into the room.

2 FRACTURED REFLECTIONS
UNSPOKEN BURDENS

The Sunny Pines Assisted Living Facility always smelled of disinfectant and fading memories. Abby Thompson walked down the familiar hallway, a carefully constructed smile on her face as she nodded to the staff. Her weekly visits to her mother, Liz, had become a ritual – part duty, part connection to a past she both cherished and feared.

Liz was sitting by the window when Abby entered, her once-vibrant red hair now a soft silver. She turned as Abby approached, her eyes lighting up with recognition.

"Abby, dear," Liz said, reaching out a hand. "I was hoping you'd come today."

Abby leaned down to kiss her mother's cheek before taking a seat beside her. "How are you feeling, Mom?"

Liz waved off the question. "Oh, you know, same as always. But never mind me. How are things with you? How's my granddaughter?"

Abby felt her carefully constructed facade waver for a moment. She took a deep breath, steadying herself before responding. "Everything's fine, Mom. Mandy's doing well in school. She's... growing up so fast."

The words felt hollow even as she spoke them, but Abby forced her smile to remain in place. She wouldn't burden her mother with the truth – the late-night arguments, the tension that filled their home, the way Mandy's eyes burned with a familiar, dangerous curiosity.

Liz studied her daughter's face, her gaze sharp despite her years. "Is that so? And how are you handling it all?"

"I'm fine," Abby said quickly, perhaps too quickly. "We're all adjusting, you know how it is with teenagers."

Liz reached out, grasping Abby's hand with surprising strength. "Abby," she said softly, "you don't have to pretend with me. I can see the worry in your eyes."

Abby felt her composure crack, just for a moment. She looked away, blinking back the tears that threatened to fall. "It's... it's been challenging," she admitted, her voice barely above a whisper. "Mandy, she's asking questions. About Amanda."

The name hung in the air between them, heavy with unspoken history. Liz's expression darkened, the lines around her mouth deepening. Her hand trembled slightly as memories flooded back – memories of another time, another daughter who had asked too many questions.

"I see," Liz said, her tone carefully neutral. "And how are you handling that?"

Abby struggled to find the right words, to express the turmoil without revealing the full extent of her fears. "We're... managing. Drake and I, we're trying to protect her, to give her a normal life. But sometimes I wonder..."

Her voice trailed off, unable to voice the thought that haunted her sleepless nights: Was history destined to repeat itself?

Liz squeezed her daughter's hand, her eyes full of understanding and concern. "Listen to me, Abby. That girl of yours, she has a right to know her history. But you also have a right – a responsibility – to protect her. It's a delicate balance, one that only you can navigate."

The afternoon sun cast long shadows across the room as Liz leaned forward, her voice dropping to barely above a whisper. "Do you remember what happened when Amanda first started asking questions? The night everything changed?"

Abby's breath caught in her throat. Of course she remembered. The midnight phone calls, the unmarked cars, the way Amanda's research had led her down paths that should have remained unexplored. The memory of her sister's determination – her refusal to let sleeping dogs lie – still sent chills down Abby's spine.

"I remember everything," Abby whispered. "That's what terrifies me. Mandy... she's so much like her. The same fire in her eyes, the same need to know the truth. Last week, I found her in the attic, going through old boxes. She'd discovered some of Amanda's old journals."

Liz's face paled. "The ones from before...?"

Abby nodded. "I tried to take them away, but she'd already hidden some. And now Drake... he thinks we should tell her everything. Says it's better she learns it from us than piece it together herself."

"And what do you think?"

"I think knowledge can be dangerous," Abby said, her voice hardening. "Look what it did to Amanda. Look what it did to our family. The ICE investigation, the headlines, the way everything fell apart... I can't let that happen to Mandy. I won't."

Liz was quiet for a long moment, her eyes distant. "Sometimes," she said finally, "trying to protect someone from the truth only pushes them harder to find it. Amanda was trying to expose corruption, to do what she thought was right. Maybe if we'd supported her instead of trying to stop her..."

"Mom, please," Abby interrupted, standing abruptly. "I can't... I can't think about the 'what-ifs.' Not now."

As if on cue, Abby's phone buzzed with a text from Drake: "How much longer? We need to talk."

Abby sighed, squeezing her mother's hand. "I should go, Mom. Drake's waiting for me."

Liz nodded, her eyes never leaving Abby's face. "Remember what I said, Abby. Be careful, but be honest – with yourself, if no one else. That's the only way to weather this storm."

The drive home was a blur of conflicting emotions for Abby. Her mother's words echoed in her mind, mingling with memories of Amanda – both the good and the terrible. The sound of her sister's voice the last time they spoke, filled with urgency and fear, haunted her all the way home. By the time she pulled into the driveway, her head was pounding with the effort of maintaining her composure.

Drake was waiting in the living room, his face set in lines of worry and frustration. "How's your mother?" he asked as Abby entered.

"She's good," Abby replied, sinking onto the couch. "Perceptive as ever."

Drake nodded, moving to sit beside her. "And you? How are you really doing, Abby?"

The gentle concern in his voice was her undoing. Abby felt her carefully constructed walls crumble, and the tears she had been holding back all day finally spilled over.

"I'm scared, Drake," she admitted, her voice breaking. "I'm scared for Mandy, for us. I don't know how to protect her from the truth without pushing her away. I don't know how to be the mother she needs me to be."

Drake pulled her close, his arms strong and comforting around her. "We'll figure it out together," he murmured into her hair. "We always do."

As they sat there, holding each other, neither of them noticed the shadow that passed by the living room door. Upstairs, Mandy pressed herself against the wall, her heart pounding. What truth were they trying to protect her from? What storm were they preparing to weather?

In her room, Mandy pulled out the key she had found in the attic, along with the worn leather journal she'd managed to salvage before her mother's intervention. The pages were filled with her aunt Amanda's precise handwriting, detailing investigations into something called "Operation Frost" and references to ICE that went far beyond immigration enforcement. Whatever secrets her family was keeping, she was more determined than ever to uncover them.

She ran her fingers over the last entry in the journal, dated just days before her aunt's disappearance: "If anything happens to me, the truth must come out. They can't keep hiding behind badges and bureaucracy. The public has a right to know."

The path ahead was unclear, fraught with hidden dangers and unspoken fears. But as the Thompson family faced this new challenge, one thing was certain: the echoes of the past would not be silenced so easily. And somewhere, in the shadows of their carefully constructed life, Amanda's legacy waited to be discovered – for better or worse.

3 WHISPERS OF DISCONTENT

Part 1: The Key

The autumn sunlight streaming through the classroom windows cast long shadows across Mandy Thompson's desk, but her attention wasn't on the dancing dust motes or Mr. Patel's droning voice. Instead, her fingers traced the outline of the key hidden in her jacket pocket, its brass surface cool against her skin. The chalkboard before her was covered with dates and names from a history she couldn't bring herself to care about – not when her own family's history had become such a consuming mystery.

Two weeks had passed since she'd found the key, but the memory remained sharp as broken glass. She'd been in the attic, surrounded by cardboard boxes and the musty scent of forgotten things, when everything changed. The search hadn't started randomly – she'd been driven there by fragments of an overheard conversation, whispered words between her parents that had drifted up the stairs one night as she'd crept down for a glass of water.

"We can't keep avoiding it forever," her mother had said, voice tight with tension. "What if she finds out about Amanda's journal? About what really happened that winter?"

Her father's response had been too quiet to catch, but the worry in his tone had been unmistakable. That conversation had sent Mandy to the attic the next day, determined to uncover whatever her parents were trying so hard to hide.

The attic had been a maze of possibilities. Each box she'd opened had held the potential for answers, though most had yielded nothing but mothballed clothes and outdated knick-knacks. But then, as she'd shifted aside a stack of yellowed envelopes, she'd seen it: a small, ornate key, its brass surface dulled with age but its intricate snowflake pattern still clearly visible.

The moment her fingers had touched it, Mandy had felt a jolt of... something. Recognition? Excitement? Fear? She couldn't quite name the emotion, but she'd known, deep in her bones, that this key was important. The snowflake design had seemed to whisper of secrets long buried, of a past her family seemed determined to keep hidden.

That's when she'd found the photographs.

They'd fallen from a crumbling manila envelope, scattering across the attic floor like autumn leaves. Each image had told part of a story she couldn't quite piece together. Her grandmother, Amanda Cole, young and vibrant, stood before different mountain ranges, her dark hair whipping in what must have been bitter winter winds. In one photo, she wore thick climbing boots and held an ice axe, her expression both determined and secretive. The back of this photo bore only the words "Silverton Peak - Almost there."

Another image showed Amanda outside a rustic cabin, snow piled high around the entrance. A man stood beside her, his face carefully scratched out of the photograph. On the back, someone had written "Don't forget - T.B." and a series of numbers that looked like coordinates, though they'd been partially obscured by water damage.

The most intriguing photo showed Amanda holding something that glinted in the sunlight – a pendant or locket that bore the same snowflake pattern as the key Mandy now carried. In this image, her grandmother's smile seemed different – sadder somehow, more weighted. The back of this photo was blank except for a stamp: "Winters

Photography Studio - Silverton, Colorado, 1962."

"Miss Thompson?"

Mr. Patel's sharp voice cut through her reverie like a knife. Mandy blinked, suddenly aware of the expectant silence in the classroom and the many pairs of eyes fixed on her. Jessica Porter smirked from two rows over, no doubt already composing a snarky text about Mandy's embarrassment.

"I'm sorry, what was the question?" Mandy asked, heat rising in her cheeks.

Mr. Patel's frown deepened, the disapproval clear in his voice. "I asked you to name three major consequences of the Treaty of Versailles. But clearly, your mind is elsewhere today."

"Um, Germany had to pay reparations?" she offered weakly. The words felt hollow in her mouth, meaningless compared to the weight of her own family's hidden history.

"That's one," Mr. Patel said, his tone making it clear that he expected more. When Mandy remained silent, he sighed. "Perhaps you'd like to stay after class to review the material you've missed while daydreaming?"

The bell rang before Mandy could respond, saving her from further embarrassment. As she hastily shoved her untouched notebook into her bag, she could feel Mr. Patel's disappointed gaze following her out of the room. It stung more than she wanted to admit – she'd always been a good student, the kind teachers could count on for thoughtful answers and completed homework.

But lately, everything had changed. How could she focus on long-dead treaties when she had her own historical mystery to solve?

Part 2: Growing Distance

The hallway bustled with between-class energy, but Mandy felt strangely removed from it all. The key in her pocket seemed to pulse with each step, a constant reminder of the secrets she was desperate to uncover. She'd spent hours researching Silverton after finding the photos, learning about the small mining town nestled in Colorado's San Juan Mountains. Historical articles mentioned the town's mining boom and subsequent decline, but nothing that explained her grandmother's connection to the place.

Lost in thought, she nearly collided with Alex as she rounded the corner to their next class. The smell of her friend's familiar vanilla perfume brought Mandy briefly back to reality.

"Whoa, earth to Mandy!" Alex said, steadying her with a hand on her arm. Her green eyes narrowed with concern as she took in Mandy's distracted expression. "Where's your head at today?"

Mandy managed a weak smile. "Sorry, just... thinking." The lie felt bitter on her tongue. Alex had been her best friend since third grade, when they'd bonded over their shared love of Nancy Drew mysteries. The irony of keeping her own mystery from Alex wasn't lost on her.

"You've been 'just thinking' a lot lately," Alex said, adjusting her backpack strap – a nervous habit Mandy recognized from years of friendship. "You barely said two words in English yesterday, and now I hear you completely spaced out in Patel's class?"

Mrs. Reeves' English class had indeed been another casualty of Mandy's distraction. The teacher had called on her three times before she'd registered her name.

"Perhaps," Mrs. Reeves had said, adjusting her wire-rimmed glasses, "you'd like to share your thoughts on the theme of buried secrets in 'The Tell-Tale Heart'?"

The irony of the topic hadn't been lost on Mandy. She'd straightened in her chair, trying to focus on the discussion rather than her own buried secrets. "The narrator thinks he's successfully hidden his crime," she'd said slowly, "but the truth finds a way to surface. It always does."

"And why do you think that is?"

"Because..." Mandy had paused, thinking of her own parents' suspicious behavior, "secrets take effort to maintain. Every lie needs another lie to support it, until eventually, the whole structure collapses."

Now, facing Alex's worried expression in the hallway, Mandy considered telling her everything. About the key, the photos, the growing certainty that her family was hiding something big. The words rose to her throat: the overheard conversation, the crossed-out dates, the mysterious T.B., the way her mother's hands shook slightly whenever Amanda's name was mentioned.

But the words caught in her throat. How could she explain something she barely understood herself?

"It's nothing," Mandy said, forcing a lightness into her tone that she didn't feel. "Just some family stuff. You know how it is."

Alex nodded slowly, clearly not convinced. "Yeah, I know. But you'd tell me if it was something serious, right?"

"Of course," Mandy lied, the weight of the key seeming to grow heavier with each untruth. "Come on, we're going to be late for bio."

As they settled into their seats, Mandy could feel Alex's worried glances. She did her best to focus on the lesson, scribbling notes about cellular respiration that she knew she'd never review. All the while, her mind kept drifting back to the key, to the secrets it might unlock. She found herself sketching the snowflake pattern in the margin of her notebook, trying to capture the intricate design from memory.

Part 3: Unraveling Threads

When the lunch bell rang, Mandy escaped to the cafeteria with a mixture of relief and dread. The corridor buzzed with chatter about weekend plans and the upcoming dance, the normalcy feeling like a foreign language movie without subtitles. "Tyler's party on Saturday - you're coming, right?" Alex asked as they claimed their table. The fluorescent lights cast shadows reminiscent of the attic's secrets. Mandy stabbed a cherry tomato, sending it skittering across her tray. "Haven't thought about it." Alex leaned forward, concern etching her features. "It's the biggest party of the year. Everyone's going." She touched Mandy's arm. "You've been somewhere else lately. Not just distant - it's like you're living in a different world." "Maybe I am," Mandy thought, the key's weight suddenly heavy in her pocket. Aloud, she only said, "I guess I'm not everyone."

Before Alex could respond, they were joined by a group of their other friends, all buzzing with excitement about the party. Their arrival felt like an invasion, shattering the fragile moment of almost-honesty between Mandy and Alex.

"Mandy, you have to come!" Jade exclaimed, sliding into the seat across from her. Her new highlights caught the light as she leaned forward conspiratorially. "I heard Tyler's older brother is getting a keg. It's going to be epic."

Mandy forced a smile, trying to muster even a fraction of her friends' enthusiasm. "Maybe. I'll have to check with my parents." The words felt automatic, a social script she could still perform even as her mind wandered to other mysteries.

That evening, the tension at home was palpable. Mandy sat at the dinner table, pushing pasta around her plate while observing her parents with newfound attention. Her mother's hands shook slightly as she served the garlic bread – something Mandy had never noticed before her attic discovery.

"I was thinking about organizing the attic this weekend," Mandy said casually, watching their reactions. Her father's fork paused halfway to his mouth, and her mother's knuckles whitened around her water glass.

"The attic?" Her mother's voice was carefully neutral. "Why would you want to spend your weekend up there? I thought you'd be going to Tyler's party."

"Just thought it needed some cleaning," Mandy shrugged, noting how her parents exchanged quick glances. "I found some interesting old photos up there the other day."

The silence that followed was deafening. Her father cleared his throat. "That's not necessary, honey. Your mother and I can handle the attic. Besides, there's a lot of dust up there – it's not good for your allergies."

"I didn't know you'd been in the attic," her mother added, too quickly. "When was this?"

"Last week," Mandy lied, watching as her mother's expression flickered. "I was looking for old Halloween decorations."

Later that night, Mandy lay in bed, listening to her parents' muffled voices from downstairs. She crept to the top of the stairs, straining to hear their conversation.

"...should have moved those boxes years ago," her father was saying. "If she finds the journal..."

"She won't," her mother interrupted. "But maybe it's time we told her something. She's not a child anymore, and if she starts asking questions about Silverton..."

"No." Her father's tone was firm. "We agreed. Some things are better left in the past. Your mother understood that, in the end."

The sound of approaching footsteps sent Mandy scrambling back to her room. As she lay in the darkness, the key pressed against her palm, she thought about the Colorado town that seemed to be at the center of everything. What had happened in Silverton? Why had her grandmother been there? And what could be so terrible that her family was still keeping secrets about it decades later?

In her English notebook, hidden behind notes about Poe and unreliable narrators, Mandy had started keeping a list:

CLUES:

- *Key with snowflake pattern*
- *Grandmother's matching locket in photos*
- *Silverton, Colorado connections*
- *Scratched-out man in photos (T.B.?)*
- *Coordinates on photo back*
- *Missing journal*
- *Winter/snow theme*
- *1962 date stamp*

Her hand hovered over the page as she considered Mrs. Reeves' earlier words about secrets finding their way to the surface. Whatever her grandmother had been involved in back in 1962, whatever had happened in that snow-covered mountain town, Mandy was getting closer to uncovering the truth. The key in her pocket seemed to pulse with possibility, a constant reminder that some mysteries demanded to be solved, no matter how carefully they'd been buried.

As she drifted off to sleep, Mandy made a silent promise to herself: by the end of the week, she would find out what that key opened, even if it meant skipping Tyler's party to do it. The mysterious journal her parents had mentioned had to be somewhere in the house. And if her instincts were right, this key – with its delicate snowflake pattern that matched her grandmother's locket – was the first real clue she'd found to unlocking the truth about Amanda Cole's past.

4 FIRST STEPS

The spray can weighed heavy in Mandy's sweating palm, making her pulse spike with each tiny shift. Her fingers trembled against the cold metal as she stared up at the factory wall. Layers of other people's tags and artwork crowded every inch of brick, daring her to add her own mark.. Her heart pounded in her chest, each beat a warning she chose to ignore. The metal of the key pressed against her thigh through her jean pocket, a constant reminder of why she was here.

"Come on, Mandy," Alex whispered urgently from behind her. "Someone's gonna see us. Let's just go." In the darkness, her friend's face was pale, eyes darting nervously between the shadows cast by distant streetlights.

Mandy's fingers tightened around the can. The cool metal grounded her, made this moment feel real. "No," she said, her voice steadier than she felt. "I need to do this."

She raised the can, the rattle of the ball bearing inside echoing in the quiet night like a warning bell. With a deep breath that tasted of rust and urban decay, she pressed down on the nozzle. Bright red paint hissed onto the wall, forming jagged lines that gradually took shape. Each stroke felt both foreign and familiar, as if her hands remembered something her mind had forgotten.

A snowflake. Just like the one on the key.

As Mandy worked, memories of her grandmother flooded her mind. A warm laugh, the scent of lavender, and... something else. A glint in her eye that Mandy had never understood until now. Was this how it started for her too? That thought both thrilled and terrified her.

"Mandy, seriously, we need to go!" Alex's panicked voice cut through her reverie.

Headlights swept across the wall, illuminating Mandy's handiwork for a brief moment before she and Alex ducked behind a dumpster. The stench of rotting garbage made her stomach turn, but she didn't dare move. The car slowed, its engine growling in the night. Mandy held her breath, counting the seconds. Finally, mercifully, it passed. In the silence that followed, she could hear Alex's rapid breathing.

"What the hell was that?" Alex demanded once the coast was clear. "Since when do you do stuff like this? This isn't you, Mandy."

Mandy stared at her friend, seeing the fear and confusion in her eyes. For a moment, she considered telling Alex everything - about finding the key hidden in her grandmother's old jewelry box, about the whispered conversations she'd overheard between her parents, about the growing certainty that her family was hiding something big. But the words caught in her throat.

"It's... it's hard to explain," Mandy said finally, her voice low. "I just needed to do something, you know? To feel... I don't know. Something."

Alex's expression softened slightly, but the worry remained. "Mandy, if something's going on, you can talk to me. You know that, right?"

Mandy nodded, guilt twisting in her stomach. "I know. Thanks, Alex. Let's just go home, okay?"

As they walked back in tense silence, Mandy's mind raced. The thrill of what she'd done still coursed through her veins, mixed with a gnawing sense of shame. What would her parents think if they knew?

What would her grandmother have thought?

At home, Mandy crept silently up to her room, the smell of spray paint still clinging to her clothes. She pulled out the key from its hiding place, studying the snowflake design that she'd just recreated on the factory wall. Under her desk lamp, the metal gleamed dully, its edges worn smooth by years of use. Who had held this key before her? What doors had it opened?

"Who were you really, Grandma?" she whispered to the empty room. "And who am I becoming?"

Mandy froze halfway down the stairs. Her parents' voices drifted up from the kitchen, too soft to make out the words clearly. But Mom's tone—that scared whisper she only used when things were really wrong—made Mandy's stomach clench."—just like her mother," filtered up through the floorboards. "We can't let it happen again."Dad's response was too quiet to catch, but the defeat in Mom's answering sob said enough.

"I can see it happening, and I don't know how to stop it."

Drake reached across the table, taking his wife's hand. "We knew this day might come," he said softly. "But we can't... we can't let history repeat itself. We have to protect her."

Abby met her husband's gaze, tears shimmering in her eyes. "But how? How do we protect her from a past she doesn't even know about? From a legacy that's in her blood?"

As if in answer, a police siren wailed in the distance, its mournful cry echoing through the quiet night. In her room, Mandy stirred restlessly, the key clutched tightly in her hand as she dreamed of snowflakes and secrets, of a grandmother she barely knew and a future she couldn't yet imagine.

Mandy's mind raced back to earlier that day, to the moment that had led her here...

Mandy's fork scraped against the plate as she pushed her peas in endless circles. Mom and Dad's stares burned into her skin, but she kept her eyes down. If she looked up, all those questions they weren't asking would spill out, and she couldn't handle that. Not tonight. Not with the key still pressing against her leg under the table. Through the window, the setting sun painted the kitchen in shades of amber and shadow, reminding her of old photographs she'd seen of her grandmother – images always hastily put away when she entered the room.

"So, how was school today, honey?" Abby's voice cut through the silence, forcefully cheerful.

Mandy shrugged, not looking up. "Fine." She stabbed at a carrot, remembering the whispered conversation she'd overheard in the hallway. Two seniors talking about the old ICE gang, about the legends, about a woman whose name had made Mandy's blood run cold.

"Just 'fine'?" Drake pressed, his fork pausing midway to his mouth. "Anything interesting happen?"

For a moment, Mandy considered telling them. The words bubbled up in her throat: Did you know people still talk about her? Did you know what they say she did? But the familiar tension in her father's shoulders, the careful way her mother watched her – they already knew. They were waiting to see if she knew too.

"Nope," she muttered. "Same old, same old."

Abby and Drake exchanged a look that Mandy pretended not to see. She could feel the weight of their worry, their unspoken fears. It made her skin crawl.

"Well," Abby said brightly, too brightly, "I was thinking we could go through some of those old photo albums this weekend. Maybe you'd like to see some pictures of your grandmother when she was young?"

Mandy's head snapped up, hope flaring in her chest. But it was quickly extinguished by the tightness around her mother's eyes, the forced smile that didn't quite reach them. This wasn't an offer to share – it was damage control.

"Why now?" Mandy asked, unable to keep the suspicion out of her voice. "You've never wanted to talk about her before."

The silence that followed was deafening. Drake cleared his throat. "We just thought... well, you're getting older now. Maybe it's time you knew a bit more about your family history."

Mandy's eyes narrowed. "What aren't you telling me?"

"Nothing, honey," Abby said quickly. Too quickly. "We just want you to know where you come from, that's all."

The lie hung between them, as tangible as the uneaten food on their plates. Mandy stood abruptly, her chair screeching against the floor. "I'm not hungry," she announced. "I'm going to Alex's to study."

After leaving the dinner table, Mandy's feet carried her through the darkening streets of the neighborhood where she'd grown up. The familiar houses looked different now, their windows like watching eyes, their shadows holding secrets she'd never noticed before. The key in her pocket seemed to grow heavier with each step.

She found herself passing old Mrs. Henderson's house, where her grandmother used to visit every Sunday afternoon. As a child, Mandy had always wondered what they talked about during those long visits, why they would fall silent whenever she entered the room. Now, she noticed something she'd overlooked before – a small snowflake carved into the corner of one of the porch posts, weathered but still visible.

Her steps faltered. It couldn't be a coincidence. First the key, now this? Mandy approached the porch, her heart thundering in her chest.

Her fingers had barely touched the carved snowflake when—
"You're looking more like her every day."Mandy jerked back. Mrs.
Henderson's voice hit like ice water down her spine. The old woman's eyes
locked onto hers from the doorway, knowing and sharp in a way that
made Mandy's throat close up.

"Like who?" Mandy asked, though she already knew the answer.

The old woman's lips curved in a sad smile. "You know who, child.
The same fire in your eyes. The same questions burning inside you." She
glanced meaningfully at Mandy's pocket, where the key pressed against
the fabric. "Be careful with that fire. It can warm you or burn you – your
grandmother learned that the hard way."

Before Mandy could respond, Mrs. Henderson had disappeared
back into her house, leaving Mandy alone with more questions than
answers. The encounter left her shaken, but it also strengthened her
resolve. She needed to know the truth, and she knew just where to start.

The old Come 'N' Get It convenience store stood at the corner of
Maple and Fourth, its boarded-up windows like sealed lips refusing to
speak their secrets. The building had been abandoned since before Mandy
was born, but sometimes she caught her parents watching it when they
drove past, their faces tight with unspoken worry.

As Mandy approached the store now, the streetlights flickered,
casting dancing shadows on the graffiti-covered walls. Most of the tags
were recent – angry splashes of color claiming territory or declaring love –
but beneath them, barely visible, she could make out older marks. Her
fingers traced the faded lines, and there it was again: a snowflake, small
but unmistakable, worked into what looked like an old gang tag.

A sudden gust of wind sent papers skittering across the empty
parking lot, and Mandy could have sworn she heard whispers on the
breeze. Names, perhaps, or warnings. She pulled her phone out and
turned on the flashlight, sweeping the beam across the wall. The light

caught more symbols hidden beneath years of graffiti – snowflakes of varying sizes, some connected by lines that might have once meant something.

"Your mother doesn't want you here."

Mandy spun around, heart in her throat. A man stood at the edge of the parking lot, his face lined with age and something else – regret, maybe, or fear. She recognized him as Mr. Torres, who owned the hardware store down the street.

"You knew my grandmother," Mandy said. It wasn't a question.

Mr. Torres nodded slowly. "Everyone knew Amanda. Whether they wanted to or not." He took a step closer, his eyes fixed on the wall behind her. "Those symbols – they meant something once. To a lot of people. Some good, some..." he trailed off, shaking his head. "You should go home, Mandy. Some questions are better left unasked."

But Mandy stood her ground. "Did she have something to do with what happened here? At the store?"

Mr. Torres's expression darkened. "Go home," he repeated, more firmly this time. "And if you're smart, you'll forget about those symbols. Forget about all of it."

He turned and walked away, his shoulders hunched against memories Mandy could only guess at. She watched until he disappeared around the corner, then turned back to the wall. The symbols seemed to shift in the beam of her flashlight, telling stories she couldn't quite read.

That's when she saw it – a fresh tag, the paint still glossy in the dim light. Not a snowflake this time, but words: "The ice queen's legacy lives." Beneath it, today's date.

Mandy's blood ran cold. Someone else was out here, someone who knew about her grandmother, about the symbols. Someone who might have answers.

She needed to leave her own mark, her own message. But it had to be perfect, had to mean something. That's when she texted Alex, asking to borrow her brother's spray paint.

Hours later, after creating her own snowflake on the factory wall and nearly getting caught, Mandy finally headed home. But the night wasn't finished with its revelations.

She was out the door before her parents could protest, their worried murmurs following her into the night. But she didn't go to Alex's, not right away. Instead, her feet carried her towards the old Come 'N' Get It convenience store. It had been closed for years, ever since the unsolved murder of its manager. As kids, they'd whispered ghost stories about the place, daring each other to touch its graffiti-covered walls.

Now, standing before it in the gathering dusk, Mandy felt a chill that had nothing to do with the evening air. The building seemed to watch her, its boarded-up windows like closed eyes hiding terrible secrets. Had her grandmother really been involved in what happened here? And if so, what did that make Mandy?

A flicker of movement in one of the windows caught her eye. Mandy froze, her heart racing. For a moment, she could have sworn she saw a face – older, lined, but with eyes that mirrored her own. Eyes that held the same questions, the same fire.

"Grandma?" she whispered, taking a step closer.

But the face was gone, if it had ever been there at all. Mandy shook her head, trying to clear it. She was letting her imagination run wild. It was time to find Alex, to do something – anything – to quiet the storm building inside her.

Hours later, as Mandy approached her house after the graffiti incident, she saw the living room light still on. Her parents were waiting up for her. Taking a deep breath, she steeled herself for the inevitable questions and prepared her lies.

But when she opened the door, the scene that greeted her was unexpected. Her parents were huddled on the couch, speaking in hushed, urgent tones. They looked up as she entered, their faces a mixture of relief and... was that fear?

The final phone call about reopening the case seemed to make the very air in the room grow thick with tension. As her mother hung up the phone with trembling hands, Mandy noticed something she'd never paid attention to before – a small scar on her mother's wrist, partially hidden by her watch. It looked like... a snowflake.

"Mom," Mandy said, her voice barely a whisper. "Your wrist..."

Abby's hand flew to cover the mark, but it was too late. Their eyes met, and in that moment, understanding passed between them like a current of electricity.

"It's time," Drake said, his voice heavy with resignation. "Show her."

Abby nodded slowly and reached for her necklace – the one she never took off. The pendant wasn't a pendant at all, Mandy realized, but a key. A key with a snowflake design that matched the one in Mandy's pocket perfectly.

"Your grandmother," Abby began, her voice shaking slightly, "wasn't just any member of the ICE gang. She was their leader. And these keys..." she held hers up, the metal catching the dim light, "they're more than just symbols. They're promises. Promises we made, promises we tried to break, promises that are coming back to haunt us all."

Outside, the wind picked up, rattling the windows like invisible hands demanding entry. Somewhere in the distance, a car alarm started wailing, its cry eerily similar to a human scream. Mandy clutched her own key tighter, feeling its edges dig into her palm.

The truth was finally coming, whether they were ready for it or not.

"Mandy," Abby said, standing quickly. "Where have you been? We were worried sick!"

"I told you, I was studying at Alex's," Mandy replied, the lie coming easily now. Too easily, perhaps.

Drake stood as well, his brow furrowed. "We called Alex's parents. They said you left hours ago."

Mandy felt the blood drain from her face. "I... we went for a walk. Lost track of time. I'm sorry."

Her parents exchanged a look that made Mandy's stomach churn. There was something they weren't telling her, something beyond their usual overprotectiveness.

"Mandy," Drake began, his voice carefully controlled. "We need to talk about-"

But he was cut off by the shrill ring of the house phone. Abby moved to answer it, her face pale in the dim light. The sound seemed to pierce the air, making everyone flinch.

"Hello?" she said, her voice tight. Then, after a pause, "Yes, this is she."

Mandy watched as her mother's expression changed, shock and fear flashing across her features. "I see," Abby said softly. "Yes, thank you for letting us know. We'll be in touch."

She hung up the phone, her hand shaking slightly. Drake was at her side in an instant. "Abby? What is it?"

Abby's eyes met Mandy's, and in that moment, Mandy knew that whatever fragile normalcy they'd been clinging to was about to shatter.

"That was the police," Abby said, her voice barely above a whisper. "They've reopened the Come 'N' Get It case. They... they want to talk to us about Mom."

The room seemed to spin around Mandy. The key in her pocket felt like it was burning a hole through her jeans. She opened her mouth to speak, but no words came out.

Drake sank heavily onto the couch, his head in his hands. "It's happening again," he muttered. "After all these years, it's happening again."

Mandy looked between her parents, desperation clawing at her throat. "What's happening? What aren't you telling me?"

Abby moved towards her daughter, reaching out a hand. But Mandy flinched away, suddenly unable to bear her mother's touch. The gesture reminded her too much of her grandmother – the way she used to reach out to smooth Mandy's hair, her hands always cool and steady.

"Honey," Abby said, her voice breaking. "There's something we need to tell you about your grandmother. About who she really was."

In that moment, standing in the living room with the weight of unspoken truths pressing down on her, Mandy realized that the simple act of spray-painting a wall had set in motion events she couldn't begin to comprehend. The past was catching up to them all, and she was at the center of the storm.

Outside, a cold wind stirred the leaves, carrying with it the faint smell of spray paint and secrets. The snowflake on the factory wall dried slowly in the night air, a beacon calling to something – or someone – Mandy didn't yet understand.

As her parents began to speak, their voices low and filled with a mixture of fear and resignation, Mandy closed her eyes. The image of the snowflake she'd painted burned bright in her mind, a symbol of the legacy she was only beginning to understand.

Whatever came next, there was no going back now. The first steps had been taken, and Mandy Thompson was about to learn just how deep her family's secrets went.

5 CRIMSON LEGACY

The living room seemed to shrink around Mandy as her parents' words hung in the air, heavy and suffocating. Each revelation about her grandmother Amanda felt like a physical blow, leaving her breathless and dizzy. The family photos on the mantle – carefully curated moments of happiness – now seemed to mock her with their manufactured perfection.

Her father's words came in fragments, each one hitting like shards of glass. Art thieves. Forgeries. Money laundering. The pieces refused to fit together in her mind. Her grandmother - the woman who'd taught her to mix watercolors - had been hunting criminals? When she got too close..." He trailed off, hands clenching into fists.

Mandy's mother, Abby, reached out, her fingers trembling. Mom's jasmine perfume choked her with each breath. The same scent that used to mean safety now made her stomach turn. Another lie. Everything was lies. "We wanted to protect you, sweetheart. After what happened at the Metropolitan Museum, after they framed her for the theft and worse..."

"I can't... I can't breathe," Mandy choked out, stumbling to her feet. The walls of their perfect suburban home pressed in, every family photo a reminder of carefully crafted deception. "All those summer art classes you wouldn't let me take. The way you flinched whenever I showed you my paintings. It wasn't because you didn't support my art – it was because you were afraid."

She bolted for the door, ignoring her parents' pleas. The cool night air hit her face like a slap, shocking her system. Mandy ran, her sneakers pounding the pavement in a frantic rhythm that matched her racing heart. Each stride carried her further from the suffocating weight of revelation, but the questions pursued her like shadows.

The abandoned factory loomed ahead, her crimson snowflake gleaming in the moonlight like fresh blood. Mandy's fingertips tingled, remembering the weight of the spray can, the exhilarating rush of creation mingled with rebellion. Had her grandmother felt this same surge of defiant creativity? Had Amanda's art also hidden dangerous truths?

Something rustled behind her. Mandy spun, heart slamming against her ribs. A shadow detached itself from the dark - no, a woman. The streetlight caught the edge of a scar running down her jaw. The way she moved made Mandy's muscles tense, ready to run, but something in those sharp eyes held her in place. They were artist's eyes, like the ones that stared back from Mandy's mirror every morning.

"Nice lines." The woman's voice scratched like sandpaper, but her eyes stayed locked on the snowflake. "Though it's those angles that caught my attention. Perfect sixty-degree intersections. Most kids with spray cans don't bother with sacred geometry."

Sacred geometry? Mandy's fingers twitched, remembering how natural those angles had felt, like her hands had known something her brain didn't. "I just... it felt right."

"Felt right to Amanda too." The woman's lips curved. "Especially when she needed to hide something in plain sight."

Amanda. Not 'your grandmother.' Not 'Mrs. Thompson.' Just Amanda. Mandy's mouth went dry. "How did you-"

"Know her?" The woman reached into her jacket. Mandy tensed, but what emerged was a small burgundy notebook, its corners softened with age. A snowflake pattern pressed into the leather made her key burn against her leg. "Better question is - how well did you?"

The woman's lips quirked in what might have been a smile or a grimace. "I was there the night she discovered the Vermeer forgery. Watched her spend three days analyzing the brush strokes until she found the coded message hidden in the paint pigments. ICE – we called her that because she could crack any security system, but never lost her cool. Even when..." She shook her head, ancient pain flickering across her features.

Before Mandy could voice any of the questions crowding her mind, the woman pulled something from her pocket – a small, worn notebook bound in burgundy leather, its pages yellowed with age. A familiar snowflake pattern was embossed on the cover, but with subtle differences from Mandy's own design.

"This was hers," the woman said, holding it out. "The real story's in these pages, if you know how to read it. But be careful, kid. The people who silenced Amanda – they're still out there. And they're watching."

As Mandy reached for the notebook, her fingers brushing the worn leather, headlights swept across the wall. The woman melted back into the shadows with practiced efficiency. "The key you found? It's not just about opening doors. Look for the patterns in plain sight."

Mandy clutched the notebook to her chest, its weight both comforting and terrifying. In the distance, she could hear her parents calling her name, their voices tinged with panic. The responsible thing would be to go to them, to let them explain further, to try to understand their years of protective silence.

But the notebook burned in her hands, promising answers to questions she hadn't even known to ask. The key in her pocket seemed to pulse with an energy of its own, its worn teeth hiding secrets in their specific arrangement.

The Come 'N' Get It store loomed ahead, its broken windows like angry eyes in the darkness. As she approached, the hairs on the back of her neck stood up. A faint blue glow flickered behind the boards – there and gone so quickly she might have imagined it.

Mandy paused in the shadow of a dumpster, forcing herself to take slow, deep breaths. Her grandmother had approached everything methodically, according to the woman. What would Amanda do in this situation? Observe. Analyze. Look for patterns.

The boarded-up door swung open at her touch, hinges groaning in protest. The musty interior pressed against her like a physical presence, thick with dust and untold stories. Her phone's flashlight cut through the gloom, revealing overturned shelves and debris. Each step stirred up clouds of memories trapped in dust.

She moved deeper into the store, past expired cans and shattered bottles that crunched beneath her feet. The beam of her flashlight caught something that made her pause – tiny flecks of crimson paint, forming a trail too deliberate to be random.

Around a corner, her light revealed a wall covered in intricate geometric patterns painted in the same shade as her snowflake. At first glance, it appeared chaotic, but as she studied it, shapes began to emerge

– circles intersecting with squares, spirals flowing into triangles. And there, hidden within the complexity, words became visible:

"In sacred geometry lies truth, In forgotten pigments, proof. When crimson snow begins to fall, The hidden gallery reveals all."

Mandy traced the patterns with trembling fingers, the rough texture of the wall grounding her in reality. This was more than a message – it was a puzzle, like the one her grandmother had found in the Vermeer forgery.

Her phone buzzed insistently – texts and missed calls from her frantic parents. Her phone buzzed again - Mom's face lighting up the screen. Mandy's chest tightened. She should answer. Should go home. But her fingers were already opening the notebook, trembling with the need to understand.. Mandy sank to the floor, her back against the wall, and opened her grandmother's notebook with shaking hands.

Mandy's hands shook as she opened the notebook. The first page swam before her eyes - lines and angles dancing across famous paintings she recognized from her art history books. But wrong. Or... not wrong. Hidden. Like those Magic Eye pictures where a 3D image lurks beneath the chaos. Numbers threaded through the paint strokes. Chemical symbols clustered in margins she knew by heart from her own sketches - the formulas for mixing pigments.

Her grandmother's handwriting marched across each page in sharp, clean strokes. Artist's hands. Mathematician's precision. Just like...

Mandy looked down at her own fingers, still stained with red spray paint. Just like her.

"Sequence 1: Crimson Lake + Φ = Key Pattern Alpha Cross-reference: Met Gallery Section 4B Note: Trust the art, not the artist. When mixed with ultramarine, truth reveals itself."

Outside, sirens wailed in the distance. A floorboard creaked nearby, and Mandy's head snapped up. In the beam of her fallen flashlight, dust motes danced in a pattern too regular to be natural – disturbed by someone's careful movement.

"I know you're there," she called, surprising herself with the steadiness of her voice.

No answer came, but the temperature seemed to drop several degrees. Mandy scrambled to her feet, clutching the notebook to her chest. As she backed toward the exit, a shadow detached itself from the darkness – too tall to be the woman from before.

Mandy ran, burst out into the night air. Her feet carried her down unfamiliar alleys, the notebook secure in her arms. Behind her, footsteps echoed with deliberate slowness, like whoever followed wasn't worried about catching up quickly.

As she vaulted a fence and finally lost the sound of pursuit, Mandy realized she was irrevocably entangled in something bigger than herself. Her grandmother's art had hidden dangerous truths. Now Mandy's own crimson snowflake had marked her as heir to that legacy of secrets.

She found herself in a small park, the swings creaking gently in the night breeze. As she caught her breath, she opened the notebook again. A loose page slipped out – a sketch of the Metropolitan Museum's floor plan with specific paintings circled. In the margin, in handwriting that matched the woman's voice somehow – precise but with a hint of controlled chaos: "Start with the Dutch Masters. The truth is hidden in plain sight."

Mandy squared her shoulders, feeling the weight of the key in her pocket. She couldn't go home – not yet. Not until she understood what her grandmother had discovered, and why it had cost her everything.

In the distance, a police helicopter swept the area with its searchlight. Mandy melted deeper into the shadows, remembering the woman's liquid grace. As she moved, she felt watched from multiple angles – some gazes protective, others calculating, all of them interested in the notebook she carried and the legacy she'd unknowingly inherited.

But unlike her grandmother, Mandy had something the others didn't expect: the perfect combination of Amanda's analytical mind and her own artist's soul. The patterns were there, waiting to be discovered.

The   crimson   snow   was   about   to   fall   again.

6 ENTRY AND INITIAL EXPLORATION

The rusty bell above the door gave a half-hearted chime as Mandy slipped into Come 'N' Get It, its discordant notes seeming to echo in the silent night. Her heart pounded against her ribs like a trapped bird, each beat seeming to whisper *intruder, intruder, intruder*. The 'CLOSED' sign hung crookedly in the window, barely visible through years of grime – less a warning than an epitaph for a place time had forgotten.

Mandy's fingers trembled as she pocketed the spare key she'd "borrowed" from her parents' drawer, discovered behind a false back she'd noticed only because the wood grain didn't quite match. The weight of it felt like an accusation, a physical reminder of the trust she was betraying. But the burning need to know, to understand, overrode her guilt. She had come too far to turn back now.

As she flicked on her phone's flashlight, the beam cut through years of dust, creating a hazy glow that transformed the mundane into the mysterious. Motes danced in the air like desperate stars, stirred by her entrance, as if the very atmosphere of the place was coming alive after years of slumber. The familiar yet unsettling scent of old paper, industrial lemon cleaner, and something indefinably musty filled her nostrils – a chemical cocktail that triggered a sudden memory: her grandmother's studio, glimpsed just once when she was seven, before her parents had whisked her away.

Now, standing in the silent store, Mandy felt a dizzying mixture of determination and fear. The beam of her flashlight revealed layers of dust and neglect, a testament to years of abandonment. But beneath the decay, details began to emerge that set her pulse racing. A security camera, ancient but positioned for maximum coverage. Shelving units mounted on tracks that suggested they could be moved. A counter with a subtly reinforced base, as if designed to withstand more than just the weight of groceries.

Come 'N' Get It wasn't just any old convenience store – it was a carefully constructed facade, every innocent-seeming feature potentially hiding another layer of deception. Mandy's mind raced, recalling fragments of information she'd pieced together over weeks of covert research.

Every step through the dimly lit aisles felt like moving through layers of history. Mandy's flashlight beam caught faded price tags from different decades – bubblegum for 25 cents, newspapers for 35 cents, cigarettes advertising tar content. A rack of magazines showed cover dates stretching back to the mid-80s, their pages yellow and brittle with age. The top issue featured the Metropolitan Museum's newest wing, and Mandy's heart skipped a beat when she noticed a barely visible fingerprint in crimson paint at the corner of the cover.

And let's expand the final escape sequence with these additional details:

The rain-slicked streets reflected the city lights like shattered mirrors as Mandy ran, each puddle a potential betrayal waiting to splash and draw attention. Her sneakers, already soaked through, made soft squelching sounds that seemed thunderous in her ears. The weight of the package Frost had given her knocked rhythmically against her ribs, a constant reminder of what was at stake.

Behind her, the sounds from Come 'N' Get It grew more distinct – voices now, sharp and professional, speaking in clipped tones that carried even through the storm. A car engine growled to life, then another. They would be searching the area methodically, she realized. Just like her grandmother had taught her about art analysis: grid by grid, leaving nothing to chance.

Mandy ducked into a narrow alley, pressing herself against rough brick as headlights swept past. Her hand clutched the bundle of letters, protecting them from the rain. Through the thin paper, she could almost feel the heat of her grandmother's words, the desperate passion that had driven ICE to risk everything for love. Now, decades later, that same love might be the key to understanding it all – or the thing that got her killed.

History and Discovery

Founded in 1967 by James Morgan, Come 'N' Get It had been a cornerstone of the community for decades. Old newspaper clippings spoke of Little League sponsorships, holiday food drives, and an owner who knew every customer by name. But in 1983, everything changed. Morgan died suddenly of an apparent heart attack, though Mandy had found forum posts suggesting otherwise. Within months, ownership changed hands three times, each new proprietor more shadowy than the last.

That was when the store's true transformation had begun. Behind the dented cans of soup and dusty packets of gum, Come 'N' Get It had become something else entirely. The timing aligned perfectly with the rise of ICE – Amanda Johnson's street name, earned not for any connection to law enforcement, but for her legendary ability to keep cool under pressure.

Mandy's grandmother had never officially owned the store, but whispered rumors and cryptic references in old police reports painted a clear picture. Come 'N' Get It had been crucial to ICE's network, a hub of information and illicit dealings disguised as a run-down convenience store. The current legal owner was listed as Frostline Enterprises, a shell company that Mandy had traced through five layers of subsidiaries before hitting a dead end in the Cayman Islands.

As she moved deeper into the store, Mandy's flashlight beam caught something that made her breath catch. There, barely visible beneath years of grime, was a small etching in the corner of the checkout counter. A snowflake, but not just any snowflake – its pattern followed the golden ratio, each crystal branch precisely 1.618 times longer than the last. Her grandmother's signature, hidden in plain sight all these years.

The office door creaked ominously as Mandy pushed it open. Her flashlight beam swept the room, landing on an old filing cabinet pushed against the far wall. This was it. The brass key trembled in her hand as she approached, her own reflection ghostly in the cabinet's metallic surface.

Hidden Treasures

With a soft click that seemed to echo in the stillness, a hidden panel swung open. Mandy's breath caught in her throat as she peered inside the small recess. Her fingers, shaking now, brushed against cool metal and crinkled paper. She withdrew an old USB drive, a stack of newspaper clippings yellowed with age, and... a bundle of letters, tied with a faded lavender ribbon.

The scent of old paper and a hint of something floral – not lavender as she'd first thought, but jasmine – wafted up as Mandy carefully untied the ribbon. Her heart raced as she unfolded the first letter, recognizing her grandmother's handwriting immediately. But it wasn't the handwriting that made her gasp – it was the words themselves.

"My dearest Jasmine," the letter began, "Another day without you feels like an eternity. The danger of our situation pales in comparison to the pain of our separation. Last night, I dreamed of Venice again – of that café where we first met, where you 'accidentally' spilled your espresso on my sketchbook. Even then, I suspect you knew exactly who I was, just as I knew you weren't really there to study Renaissance art..."

The Letters and Computer

Mandy's hands trembled as she read on, her grandmother's words painting a picture of a love so profound it took her breath away. Amanda – ICE – wrote of stolen moments in hidden places, of codes hidden in gallery paintings, of dreams for a future that seemed impossible. But beneath the romance lay darker currents: mentions of rival organizations, of betrayals and power struggles, of choices that would echo through decades.

The letters revealed a story that spanned years – secret meetings in art galleries across Europe, messages hidden in auction catalogs, close calls with rival organizations. Each letter added another layer to the mystery of who her grandmother had really been. ICE hadn't just been a criminal mastermind; she'd been a woman in love, fighting against a world that wanted to keep her apart from Jasmine.

"Who are you, Jasmine?" Mandy whispered to the empty room. The letters spoke of a woman brilliant enough to match ICE's intellect, dangerous enough to command respect in their shadowy world, yet vulnerable enough to risk everything for love.

The USB drive felt impossibly heavy in Mandy's hand, a tiny piece of plastic and metal that promised to upend her entire world. She glanced around the dusty office, her heart leaping when she spotted an old desktop computer tucked away in the corner. The yellowed beige case marked it as ancient – probably from the early 2000s, when USB ports were just becoming standard.

The Technical Challenge

"Please work," Mandy whispered, brushing away cobwebs and years of accumulated dust. She pressed the power button, holding her breath. Nothing happened. She checked the power cable – still plugged in, but the cord's rubber coating had grown brittle with age. After jiggling the connection, she tried again.

The machine responded with a sound like grinding gravel, the cooling fan protesting years of disuse. The power light flickered weakly, then steadied. A faint electrical smell filled the air as ancient components warmed up for the first time in decades.

The monitor – a massive CRT that took up half the desk – remained dark. Mandy's heart sank until she noticed its separate power button, crusted with grime. She pressed it, and the screen slowly came to life with a high-pitched whine, displaying a few lines of white text on black:

"CMOS checksum error - defaults loaded Strike F1 to continue, F2 to enter SETUP"

```
C:\> dir /s /p
Volume in drive C is Local Disk
Volume Serial Number is 1234-5678

Directory of C:\Windows\System32\drivers

File Not Found

C:\> dir e: /a
Volume in drive E is USB DEVICE
Access is denied.

C:\> cd\
C:\> e:
Invalid drive specification

C:\> mode com3
```

Mandy pressed F1, remembering how her father had taught her to revive old computers in his repair shop. The machine spent several minutes checking its hardware, each step feeling like an eternity. Finally, an outdated version of Windows appeared, the interface looking primitive compared to modern systems.

The Video Message

After multiple attempts and careful cleaning of the USB contacts, the ancient computer finally recognized the drive. A single video file appeared: "ForMySnowflake.avi." The video player took nearly five minutes to load, each progress bar moving with agonizing slowness.

```
E:\> dir
Volume in drive E is USB DEVICE
Volume Serial Number is 1234-5678

Directory of E:\

2004-03-15  02:14    <DIR>            .
2004-03-15  02:14    <DIR>            ..
2004-03-15  02:14        3,842,048 ForMySnowflake.avi
             1 File(s)    3,842,048 bytes
             2 Dir(s)     0 bytes free
```

There it was – a video file, over fifteen years old. The ancient video player took nearly five minutes to load, each progress bar moving with agonizing slowness. When it finally opened, the image was so distorted she could barely make out shapes. She spent several more minutes adjusting settings, trying to clear up the picture, her hands shaking with a mixture of anticipation and fear.

Finally, her grandmother's face filled the screen, older than Mandy remembered, lines of worry and hard-won wisdom etched around her eyes. But there was a fire there too, a determination that Mandy recognized in herself.

"My dear Mandy," Amanda's voice crackled through the speakers, filled with warmth and regret in equal measure. "If you're watching this, it means you've started asking questions. I'm so sorry for the burden I'm placing on you, but you deserve to know the truth. All of it."

Amanda's Revelations

Amanda spoke of her life as ICE, of a criminal underworld more complex than simple right and wrong. She described a world of shifting alliances and hidden agendas, where art and crime intersected in ways that blurred every line.

"The art world has always been built on illusion," Amanda explained, her hands moving expressively as she spoke. "The difference between a masterpiece and a forgery often comes down to provenance – the story we choose to believe. I saw an opportunity in that space between truth and perception. But I wasn't the only one."

Then her voice softened, filled with a longing that made Mandy's heart ache. "She worked for the Obsidian Syndicate – our greatest rivals, but also the only ones who truly understood what we were trying to achieve. We met at the Caffè Florian in Venice. She spilled her espresso on my sketchbook... deliberately, I later learned. She had recognized my work, my technique. We spent hours discussing the brushwork in Titian's 'Assumption of the Virgin.'"

The Warning

Amanda leaned forward, her voice becoming urgent. "The night everything fell apart, when the Met operation went wrong... Jasmine tried to warn me. She had discovered something, a conspiracy that went deeper than either of us had imagined. I didn't listen. I thought I could handle it alone, protect everyone I loved. I was wrong."

"If you're watching this, it means you've inherited more than just my artistic talent. You've inherited my legacy, for better or worse. The key you found – it's more than just a key. The snowflake pattern isn't random. It's a code, one that Jasmine would recognize. Find her, Mandy. She has answers I couldn't give you."

Frost's Appearance

A noise from behind made Mandy whirl, her heart in her throat. A figure stood in the doorway – the woman from the factory, his silver hair gleaming in the dim light. She moved with liquid grace into the room, her eyes taking in every detail.

"Frost," Mandy breathed, recognition clicking into place. The man's very name was a link to ICE.

"You've found it, then," Frost said softly, her eyes falling on the bundle of letters in Mandy's hand. A flicker of what might have been pain crossed her weathered features. "I wondered if you would."

"Did you know?" Mandy asked, holding up one of the letters. "About Jasmine?"

Frost's laugh was barely more than a whisper. "Know? Kid, I was there. Venice, 1995. I was running surveillance for your grandmother. Watched the whole coffee shop scene unfold. Two of the most dangerous women in the underground, pretending to be art students..." She shook her head. "Never seen anything like it."

The Escape

Before Mandy could ask more questions, headlights swept across the store windows. Frost's posture changed instantly, tension radiating from every line of her body.

"Company," she muttered. "And not the friendly kind. Those headlights... they're running dark. Professional job."

Frost reached into her jacket and pulled out a small package wrapped in brown paper. "Your grandmother left this with me. Said I'd know when it was time. Guess that's now."

Mandy took the package, its weight surprising her.

"Back door, through the alley," Frost instructed. "Don't stop until you hit Riverside Park. And Mandy?" Her voice softened. "Be careful with that knowledge. Love like that... it can be a weapon in the wrong hands."

As Mandy slipped out the back door, she heard Frost moving through the store, purposefully making noise, drawing attention. The night air hit her face like a slap as she ran, the letters and drive clutched to her chest, the mysterious package tucked securely in her jacket.

Lightning flashed, illuminating the city in stark relief. For a moment, Mandy could almost imagine she saw two figures in the distance

– one silver-haired and alert, the other younger, running with desperate purpose. Past and present, converging in the storm.

The game that had claimed her grandmother's life was beginning again. But this time, the players were different. This time, love and art and danger would dance to a new rhythm, guided by the echoing legacy of ICE.

Behind her, the muffled sound of breaking glass echoed from Come 'N' Get It. Mandy forced herself not to look back, trusting Frost to handle whatever was happening. She had her own role to play now, her own mysteries to unravel.

The storm intensified, rain streaming down her face as she ran. In her pocket, the key with its snowflake pattern seemed to pulse with new significance. Not just a key, but a code. Not just a legacy, but a message – waiting for the right person to understand it.

7 FROSTS REVELATIONS

Mandy's footsteps echoed through the empty streets as she made her way home, her mind reeling from the revelations of the night. The weight of her grandmother's notebook and the bundle of letters seemed to grow heavier with each step, a physical reminder of the secrets she now carried. As she rounded the corner onto her street, a flicker of movement caught her eye.

There, lurking in the shadows between two houses, was a figure. Mandy's heart raced as she recognized the stance, the coiled readiness she'd seen before. It was the woman from the factory — the one who had given her Amanda's notebook.

"You're a quick study, kid," the woman's raspy voice carried on the night air. "Amanda would be proud."

Mandy approached cautiously, her curiosity overriding her fear. "Who are you? How did you know my grandmother?"

The woman stepped partially into the light, revealing a face lined with age and experience. Her eyes, sharp and alert, seemed to see right through Mandy. "The name's Frost. Your grandmother and I... we go way back. ICE and Frost — quite the pair we made."

A chill ran down Mandy's spine. This woman, Frost, was a living link to her grandmother's past. "You were part of her organization?"

Frost's laugh was a harsh bark. "Organization? That's a fancy word for it. We were survivors, kid. Doing what we had to in a world that didn't give a damn about people like us."

Mandy glanced nervously at her house, knowing her parents must be frantic by now. "I have so many questions. About ICE, about Jasmine, about-"

"Whoa there, snowflake," Frost held up a hand. "Jasmine? Where'd you hear that name?"

Mandy hesitated, then decided to trust her instincts. She pulled out one of the letters, watching Frost's reaction carefully. The older woman's eyes widened, a flicker of pain crossing her face before being quickly masked.

"So you found those," Frost said softly. "Be careful with that knowledge, kid. Love like that... it can be a weapon in the wrong hands."

"I need to find her," Mandy said, determination creeping into her voice. "Jasmine. She might be the key to understanding who ICE really was."

Frost studied Mandy for a long moment, seeming to weigh her options. Finally, she nodded. "Alright, kid. I can't tell you everything – some secrets aren't mine to share. But I can point you in the right direction. Meet me tomorrow night, same time, at the old water tower. And watch your back – you're stirring up ghosts that some people would prefer stayed buried."

As Frost melted back into the shadows, Mandy felt a mix of excitement and trepidation. She was one step closer to unraveling the mystery of her grandmother's past. But at what cost?

The old water tower loomed against the starry sky, a relic of a bygone era. As Mandy approached, she saw Frost's silhouette waiting for her.

"You came," Frost said, approval in her voice. "Good. You've got

ICE's spirit, that's for sure."

"Tell me about Jasmine," Mandy said, getting straight to the point. "Who was she? What happened to her?"

Frost sighed, her eyes taking on a faraway look. "Jasmine was... complicated. She worked for a rival outfit, but she and Amanda... they had something special. Something that transcended all the bullshit of our world."

As Frost spoke, painting a picture of a love that defied boundaries and risked everything, Mandy felt a growing sense of awe. Her grandmother's life had been so much more complex, so much richer than she'd ever imagined.

"What happened to her?" Mandy asked, dreading the answer.

Standing under the water tower, listening to Frost talk about ICE, a memory surfaced – sharp and clear as spring water.

"Handle this carefully," ICE had said, passing her a dusty photo album. "Some things, once broken, can't be fixed."

The album had been oddly heavy, its pages thick. Now, six years later, Mandy wondered what had really been hidden between those photographs. Her grandmother had spent hours that day, supposedly sorting old pictures, but Mandy remembered the sound of paper tearing, of something being fed into a shredder during particularly loud thunderclaps.

The next day passed in a blur of half-truths and evasions. Mandy's parents were upset about her late-night disappearance, but she managed to placate them with a story about losing track of time at a friend's house. As night fell, she slipped out of her window, her heart pounding with anticipation.

She was twelve, helping her grandmother reorganize the basement. ICE had insisted on doing it during a thunderstorm, saying the noise would cover their work. At the time, Mandy had thought she meant the sound of moving furniture.

That same evening, ICE had taught her chess, emphasizing the importance of protecting your queen while making it appear you were focusing on other pieces. "Misdirection," she'd said, "is better than any defense."

The basement flooded the following spring. The photo album disappeared, along with several boxes ICE had insisted on keeping in that vulnerable corner. Her grandmother had seemed almost relieved when the water damaged everything beyond recovery.

Mandy blinked back to the present, seeing the water tower with new understanding. How many of her childhood memories were lessons in disguise?

Frost's face hardened. "That's the million-dollar question, kid. After the big showdown that took ICE down, Jasmine disappeared. Some say she's dead. Others think she went into hiding. Me? I think she's out there somewhere, waiting."

"Waiting for what?"

"For someone to finish what ICE started," Frost said, fixing Mandy with an intense gaze. "Your grandmother was trying to change things, to make our world better. But she had enemies. Powerful ones."

Mandy felt a surge of anger. "Who? Who was responsible for what happened to her?"

"Your grandmother," Frost said, pacing beneath the tower's skeletal shadow, "wasn't just good at what she did. She changed the game entirely."

"What game?" Mandy asked, watching a flock of starlings wheel around the tower's peak. Their patterns seemed random but weren't — like so much else in her life lately.

"Information. Power. The eternal dance between what people want hidden and what needs to be revealed." Frost stopped, her boots crunching on scattered gravel. "ICE understood something crucial: sometimes the most dangerous secrets are the ones people think they already know."

"Like Jasmine's disappearance?"

"That's not even half of it." Frost's face hardened. "Your grandmother and Jasmine — they were opposite sides of the same coin. ICE wanted to use information to force change from within. Jasmine believed the only way forward was to burn everything down and start fresh."

The wind carried the metallic groan of the tower's joints, a sound like old secrets shifting. "The night everything went wrong," Frost continued, "ICE had evidence that would have exposed corruption at the highest levels. But someone got to the files first. The same night Jasmine vanished."

"You think Jasmine took them?"

"I think," Frost said carefully, "that nothing about that night is what it seems. Your grandmother's final message — the one you found at Murphy's — proves she knew something was coming. She left breadcrumbs, but not for us. For you."

Mandy felt the weight of inheritance settling on her

shoulders. "Why me?"

"Because you're the last person they'd suspect. Because you see patterns others miss. Because—" Frost smiled, a quick, sharp expression. "Because you have her fire."

Above them, the starlings had settled, their dark forms like punctuation marks against the steel structure. Watching. Waiting. Just like everyone else in this endless game of secrets and lies.

Frost shook her head. "It's not that simple, kid. But if you really want to follow this path, to seek justice for ICE, you need to start by finding Jasmine. She holds the key to understanding who ICE really was – and who betrayed her."

As Frost shared what little information she had – a possible location, a few old contacts who might know more – Mandy felt a sense of purpose solidifying within her. She would find Jasmine. She would uncover the truth about her grandmother's life and death. And she would make sure that those responsible faced justice.

But as she turned to leave, Frost's hand on her arm stopped her. "Be careful, Mandy," the older woman said, using her real name for the first time. "This path... it's dangerous. ICE wouldn't want you to throw your life away seeking vengeance."

Mandy met Frost's gaze, her jaw set with determination. "It's not about vengeance. It's about truth. It's about finishing what she started."

As Mandy disappeared into the night, the first steps of her journey laid out before her, Frost watched her go with a mixture of pride and trepidation. "You've got her fire, kid," she whispered to the empty air. "God help us all."

The quest for answers had truly begun. With each step, Mandy moved further from the life she had known and deeper into the shadowy world that had claimed her grandmother. The legacy of ICE lived on, and the echoes of a love that had defied all odds would guide her way.

Little did Mandy know, her actions had already set larger forces in motion. In the corridors of power, in the hidden places where the true rulers of the underworld dwelled, whispers were beginning to spread. ICE's granddaughter was asking questions. The past, it seemed, refused to stay buried.

As Mandy made her way home, her mind racing with plans and possibilities, she failed to notice the sleek black car that pulled away from the curb, its tinted windows hiding the watchful eyes within. Mandy's hand tightened on her steering wheel as she made her third right turn in a row. The black sedan was still there, three cars back, its tinted windows revealing nothing about its occupants. Her grandmother's voice echoed in her memory: "If you think someone's following you, never let them know you know."

She forced herself to breathe normally, to keep her speed steady. Another right turn would complete the circle – a trick ICE had casually mentioned during one of their drives together. At the time, Mandy had thought it was just another of her grandmother's random life lessons.

The intersection ahead turned yellow. Mandy pressed the gas, slipping through just as it changed to red. In her rearview mirror, she watched the two cars between her and the sedan stop dutifully. The black car, however, accelerated through the light.

Her pulse quickened. No more doubt. They weren't even trying to be subtle anymore.

Mandy merged onto Marshall Avenue, where evening traffic crawled between strips of small businesses. She pulled into the crowded parking lot of Murphy's Grocery, circling to the back where delivery trucks usually parked. Without turning off her engine, she waited, counting seconds.

The black sedan crept past the lot's entrance, then past it again thirty seconds later. Looking for her.

She waited two more minutes, then eased her car out through the secondary exit, keeping the building between her and the street. By the time she reached home, taking a circuitous route through residential neighborhoods, her hands had stopped shaking. But the question remained: who had decided she needed watching?

The game was afoot, and Mandy Thompson had just become the most important player on the board.

Back in her room, Mandy spread everything on her bed: the documents from Come 'N' Get It, Mr. Murphy's weighted paper bag, her own notebooks full of questions. The pieces refused to form a coherent picture.

She moved to her window, pressing her forehead against the cool glass. Three houses down, the black sedan sat idle, its presence both threat and confirmation. Everything Frost had said was real. This wasn't just family history – it was active, dangerous, and somehow now her responsibility.

Her reflection stared back at her, overlaid against the darkening street. She'd always been told she had her grandmother's eyes, her grandmother's smile. What else had she inherited? What other talents lay dormant, waiting for the right moment to surface?

Mandy returned to her bed, to the scattered proof of a life she'd never known her grandmother lived. She began sorting the papers into piles, not by date or topic, but by instinct – the way she organized her chess pieces before a match. Patterns emerged: locations that appeared too often to be coincidental, names that intersected in unexpected ways, dates that aligned with seemingly unrelated events.

Her phone buzzed: a text from an unknown number. "You've started looking. Good. But remember – not all allies are friends, and not all enemies are obvious. -F"

Mandy deleted the message immediately, another of her grandmother's lessons clicking into place: never keep what you can memorize.

She reached for her laptop, then stopped. Digital trails were too easy to follow. Instead, she pulled out a fresh notebook, writing in the shorthand she and ICE had developed for their chess strategies. If she was going to do this, she'd do it her grandmother's way.

Outside, a car started. The black sedan pulled away, replaced ten minutes later by a dark SUV. They were watching, waiting for her to make a mistake. But they didn't know what ICE had taught her: sometimes the best moves are the ones your opponent never sees you make.

8 ECHOES OF BETRAYAL

The next few weeks passed in a blur of late-night research and clandestine meetings. Mandy, armed with the information Frost had provided, dove deep into the shadowy world her grandmother had once inhabited. Each new discovery only raised more questions, painting a picture of ICE that was both inspiring and terrifying.

One name kept surfacing in her investigations: Marcus Blackwood. A powerful figure in both the legitimate business world and the criminal underworld, Blackwood had been a contemporary of ICE's. Some sources painted him as an ally, others as a bitter rival. But all agreed on one thing: he was dangerous.

Mandy's search for Jasmine had hit dead end after dead end. It was as if the woman had simply vanished into thin air after ICE's downfall. But a breakthrough came from an unexpected source.

"I think I found something," Alex said, her voice barely above a whisper as they huddled in the school library. Mandy's best friend had become her confidante and research partner in this dangerous quest. "Look at this."

Alex slid her laptop across the table. On the screen was an old newspaper article about a charity gala from five years ago. And there, in the background of one of the photos, was a face Mandy recognized from her grandmother's letters. Older, with streaks of gray in her dark hair, but unmistakable.

"Jasmine," Mandy breathed.

The caption identified her as "Jasmine Murphy, representative of the Lotus Foundation." It wasn't much, but it was a lead.

That night, as Mandy pored over everything she could find about the Lotus Foundation, a soft tap at her window made her jump. Frost's weathered face peered in.

"We need to talk, kid," the older woman said, her expression grim. "I've got bad news."

Mandy's heart raced as she let Frost in. "What is it? Did you find something about Jasmine?"

Frost shook her head. "Worse. Word on the street is that Blackwood knows you're digging. And he's not happy about it."

The name sent a chill down Mandy's spine. "Blackwood? The same one who-"

"The same one who might have been involved in your grandmother's downfall," Frost finished. "Listen to me, Mandy. You need to be careful. These people... they won't hesitate to hurt you to keep their secrets."

As if to punctuate Frost's warning, a car engine roared to life outside. Both of them rushed to the window in time to see a black SUV speeding away.

"They're watching you," Frost said softly. "It's not safe for you here anymore."

Mandy's mind raced. She thought of her parents, blissfully unaware of the danger she'd brought to their doorstep. Of Alex, loyal to a fault but in over her head. And of Jasmine, out there somewhere, perhaps holding the key to it all.

"What do I do?" Mandy asked, her voice barely a whisper.

Frost's eyes, hard as steel, met hers. "You've got two choices, kid. Walk away now, try to forget all of this. Or commit to seeing it through, no matter the cost."

As Mandy opened her mouth to respond, a crash from downstairs shattered the silence of the night. Heavy footsteps pounded up the stairs.

"Time's up," Frost hissed, grabbing Mandy's arm. "Choose now."

In that moment, with danger literally knocking at her door, Mandy made a decision that would change her life forever.

Research Partners:

The basement of the city library smelled like old paper and coffee - mostly coffee, thanks to the travel mug Alex had snuck past the front desk. Mandy watched her friend arrange yet another stack of newspapers with the precision of a surgeon laying out instruments.

"You know," Alex said, adjusting her thick-rimmed glasses, "if we're going to do this properly, we need a system." She pulled out her tablet, its screen glowing in the dim library lighting. "I've created a database to cross-reference business registrations with property records and news articles. Everything gets tagged, dated, and linked."

Mandy smiled, recognizing the familiar glint in Alex's eyes - the same one that had made her the top data analyst at her firm. "And here I was just planning to read through everything and hope for the best."

"Which is exactly why you called me," Alex replied, her fingers flying over the tablet's screen. "Your intuition plus my organization - we're basically unstoppable." She paused, looking up at Mandy with sudden seriousness. "But you still haven't told me what really made you start digging into all this. I mean, I know it's about your grandmother, but why now?"

Mandy's hand went to the pendant around her neck - her grandmother's last gift. The metal felt warm against her fingers. "I found something in her old papers," she said slowly. "Letters that didn't make sense. Records of payments to accounts I couldn't trace. It's like... like I'm looking at a puzzle where all the edge pieces are missing."

Alex nodded, her expression softening. "And you think ICE is the frame?"

"I think it's more than that. These documents, they're not just about business. There are personal notes, references to people..." Mandy pulled out her phone, showing Alex a scanned page. "Look at this - it's a letter from someone called Marcus Blackwood. The date is just three weeks before ICE collapsed."

Alex leaned in, her professional demeanor momentarily cracking. "Wait, Marcus Blackwood? As in Blackwood Technologies? Mandy, that company's worth billions now. They're leading the field in AI development."

"Exactly. So why was he writing to my grandmother about 'preserving what we built' and 'protecting our legacy'? What legacy?"

Alex was already typing. "Okay, new search parameters. We'll cross-reference Blackwood's business activities in the five years before and after ICE's collapse. If he was involved..." She trailed off, focused on her work.

Mandy watched as multiple windows opened on Alex's tablet, each filling with information. This was why she'd called Alex first - not just for her skills, but for her ability to see patterns in chaos. They'd been friends since college, when Alex had helped her organize her thesis research. Now, watching her friend work, Mandy felt a familiar mix of gratitude and concern.

"Alex," she said quietly, "this might get complicated. If these connections are real..."

"Then we'll handle it," Alex finished, not looking up. "Besides, you helped me through that whole corporate espionage mess last year. Consider this me returning the favor." She paused, then added more softly, "And Mandy? Your grandmother was important to me too. All those times she let me crash at your place during finals week, making sure I ate actual food instead of just energy drinks and chips..."

Mandy felt her throat tighten. "Yeah, that was her. Always taking care of everyone."

"So let's find out what she was trying to protect." Alex gestured at the stacks of material surrounding them. "But we do it smart. Everything gets documented, everything gets verified. No assumptions, no leaps without evidence."

They worked late into the night, the library's fluorescent lights humming overhead. As they built their database of connections and possibilities, Mandy couldn't shake the feeling that they were being watched. Once, walking to get more coffee, she caught a glimpse of movement between the shelves - but when she looked again, there was nothing there.

By closing time, they had filled three notebooks with observations and created a preliminary timeline. As they packed up, Alex held up her tablet, showing Mandy a complex web of connections she'd mapped out.

"Look at this," she said. "Every major tech company that emerged in the years after ICE's collapse - they all have some connection to Blackwood. It's like he was... positioning himself."

"For what?"

"That's our next question." Alex saved the file and tucked her tablet away. "Same time tomorrow?"

Mandy nodded, but as they walked out into the cool night air, she couldn't help noticing a black SUV parked across the street. It pulled away as soon as she looked at it, but she'd seen enough to know it wasn't just paranoia anymore.

The investigation was barely beginning, and already it felt like they were poking a hornet's nest.

The breakthrough came three weeks into their investigation, on a night when rain drummed against the library's basement windows. Alex stared at her tablet, her face illuminated by its blue glow, then suddenly sat up straight.

"Mandy," she whispered, though they were alone in the archive room. "Look at this pattern. Every time ICE launched a major project, Blackwood Technologies filed a patent application within six months. The timing is too perfect to be coincidental."

Mandy leaned over, scanning the parallel timelines Alex had constructed. "Could they have been collaborating?"

"That's what I thought at first. But look closer." Alex pulled up another window. "These are ICE's original patent filings. And these—" she swiped to a new screen "—are Blackwood's. The core technology is nearly identical, but Blackwood's applications always included one crucial modification. It's like he was... improving their work. Or maybe..."

"Exploiting their weaknesses," Mandy finished. She felt a chill that had nothing to do with the basement's temperature. "He wasn't just watching ICE. He was studying them."

Alex nodded slowly. "But here's where it gets weird. Two months before ICE's collapse, Blackwood made a massive transfer of funds to an offshore account. The recipient is hidden behind layers of shell companies, but I found a connection to ICE's corporate structure."

"He was paying them?"

"Or trying to save them." Alex rubbed her tired eyes. "The amount matches almost exactly what ICE needed to avoid bankruptcy. But the money never reached them. It's like it vanished into thin air."

Mandy pulled out her grandmother's letter again, reading the crucial line: "Marcus believes he can protect us, but I fear the price of his protection." She looked up at Alex. "What if it wasn't just about business? What if—"

A sound from the stacks made them both freeze. Footsteps, too deliberate to be a librarian's casual walk. Alex quietly closed her tablet, plunging them into relative darkness. The footsteps drew closer, then stopped.

After a long moment, they resumed, moving away. Mandy released a breath she hadn't realized she was holding. "We need to take this somewhere else," she whispered.

"My place," Alex suggested. "I've got better security, and—" She stopped, staring at her tablet which had just lit up with a notification. "Mandy, someone's trying to breach my firewall. They're going after our research files."

They packed up in seconds, years of friendship enabling them to move in silent coordination. As they hurried up the stairs, Mandy caught a glimpse of a man in a dark suit disappearing around a corner. He'd been watching them.

At Alex's apartment, surrounded by monitors and with several security protocols running, they pieced together more of the puzzle. Alex had managed to save their data, but the attack had left traces.

"The breach attempt," Alex said, "it came from the Lotus Foundation's servers." Her fingers flew over her keyboard. "And look who sits on their board of directors." She turned one of the monitors toward Mandy.

The photo showed an elegant woman in her sixties, her pose radiating confidence and power. The caption read: "Jasmine Murphy, Director of Strategic Development."

"That's her," Mandy whispered, pulling up an old photo on her phone. "That's the woman from my grandmother's photos. But she went by a different name then."

Alex nodded grimly. "The Lotus Foundation presents itself as a philanthropic organization, but their cybersecurity is military-grade. They've got quantum encryption on their internal communications. That's like using a nuclear bunker to protect a cookie jar."

"Unless the cookies are worth protecting." Mandy began pacing, her mind racing. "Alex, what if ICE never really collapsed? What if it just... transformed? Became something else?"

"With Blackwood and this Jasmine Murphy person guiding its evolution?" Alex typed rapidly, bringing up more documents. "It fits. Look at the Lotus Foundation's major initiatives. They all align with ICE's original research directions, just... adapted. Enhanced."

A notification popped up on Alex's main screen. "Someone just accessed the library's security cameras from the last three hours." She looked up at Mandy, her expression grave. "They know what we found."

Mandy's phone buzzed. A text from an unknown number: "Your grandmother tried to prevent this path. Honor her wisdom. Walk away."

But as Mandy stared at the message, another piece clicked into place. She pulled out her grandmother's pendant, studying it with new understanding. The design wasn't just decorative – it was a pattern she'd seen in ICE's original logo, subtly modified.

"I can't walk away," she said quietly. "Not now. This isn't just about the past anymore, is it?"

Alex's response was interrupted by a sharp knock at the door. Through the apartment's security feed, they could see a man in a black suit – the same one from the library. He held up a business card to the camera.

The card bore the Lotus Foundation's logo.

Let me continue with the Final Phase, where the tension peaks and forces Mandy to confront both physical and emotional stakes. This section will build to your planned break-in climax while weaving together the threads we've established.

Final Phase - Point of No Return:

The Lotus Foundation representative waited patiently at Alex's door, his reflection distorted in the security camera's fish-eye lens. Mandy and Alex exchanged glances, years of friendship allowing for silent communication. Alex nodded slightly and began a quiet backup of their files while Mandy approached the door.

"Ms. Murphy sends her regards," the man said when Mandy opened the door, keeping the security chain in place. His voice was cultured, precise. "She would like to invite you to discuss your research interests in a more... appropriate venue."

"I'm sure she would," Mandy replied, studying him. He looked expensive – the kind of expensive that spoke of corporate power rather than mere wealth. "And if I decline?"

"Then you should know that Marcus Blackwood has also expressed interest in your activities." He produced a second business card, this one bearing the Blackwood Technologies logo. "He suggests that your grandmother's legacy deserves... careful consideration."

The dual meaning hung in the air between them. Mandy felt her grandmother's pendant grow heavy against her chest. Behind her, Alex's fingers moved silently across her keyboard, backing up their discoveries to secure servers.

"I'll need time to consider these invitations," Mandy said carefully.

The man's smile never reached his eyes. "Of course. You have until tomorrow evening." He placed both cards on the doorframe and turned to leave, then paused. "Oh, and Ms. Marshall? The black SUV outside belongs to us. The silver sedan across the street? That's Mr. Blackwood's team. I thought you should know."

After he left, Mandy and Alex spent hours fortifying their digital defenses and reviewing their findings. The pattern had become clear: ICE hadn't just been a technology company – it had been developing something revolutionary, something that both Blackwood and the Lotus Foundation desperately wanted to control.

"Look at this," Alex said, pointing to her screen. "Every major breakthrough in AI over the past decade can be traced back to either Blackwood or Lotus. They're not competing – they're following the same roadmap. Your grandmother's roadmap."

Mandy unfolded the last letter she'd found in her grandmother's papers. "She knew this would happen. Listen: 'The path we chose was meant to benefit humanity, not control it. Marcus believes the end justifies the means, but Jasmine... she understands the true cost. Choose carefully, my dear. Some doors, once opened, cannot be closed.'"

A notification flashed on Alex's screen. "Someone's accessing the power grid in your neighborhood," she said, her voice tense. "Multiple nodes going dark."

Mandy's phone buzzed again. A text from Frost: "They're moving tonight. Both sides. Get out NOW."

The lights went out.

In the sudden darkness, Mandy heard the distinct sound of her home security system disarming – from the inside. Through the security feed, she caught a glimpse of her parents' bedroom light coming on, followed by her father's voice calling out. Her mother's frightened 'What's happening?' carried through the night air. Mandy's heart clenched – she'd brought this danger to their doorstep, and now they were caught in the middle of it. Alex's computers switched to backup power, their screens casting a ghostly glow over the room. Through the apartment's windows, they could see both the black SUV and silver sedan converging on Mandy's house down the street.

"Your grandmother's study," Mandy whispered. "All her original research notes..."

"No," Alex grabbed her arm. "That's exactly what they want you to do – run home to protect them."

But Mandy was already reaching for her coat. "Those notes aren't just research, Alex. They're a warning. My grandmother left breadcrumbs, showing us what ICE was really working on. Why both Blackwood and

Lotus are willing to go this far."

She pulled out her grandmother's pendant, finally understanding its true significance. The pattern wasn't just the ICE logo – it was a key. "Everything we need to know is in my grandmother's study. But so is something they don't want exposed."

Alex stood, her expression torn between concern and determination. "You realize this is probably a trap?"

"Oh, it's definitely a trap," Mandy said, hearing cars pull up outside. "The question is: whose trap is it?"

Through the window, they watched figures in dark clothing approach Mandy's house from different directions. Blackwood's people moving with military precision, Lotus operatives flowing like shadows between them. All converging on the secrets hidden in her grandmother's study.

Mandy felt the weight of the moment, understanding that her next decision would change everything. Her grandmother had faced a similar choice years ago, when she'd hidden the truth about ICE's work. Now, standing in the darkness with Alex, Mandy could hear movement on the stairs leading to her apartment.

She had seconds to decide: run away and let the past stay buried, or step into the storm and expose the truth that both Blackwood and Lotus had spent decades trying to control. The sound of breaking glass from the direction of her house made the choice for her.

"Alex," she said, her voice steady despite the fear, "I need you to do something for me."

Before Alex could respond, the power returned – but what they saw through the windows made them both freeze. The street lights revealed dozens of figures converging on Mandy's house, and above them, a familiar symbol glowed in the night sky: the original ICE logo, projected against the clouds.

Someone else had joined the game.

The projected ICE logo pulsed against the clouds like a digital Northern Light, casting an eerie blue glow over the street. Mandy watched from Alex's window as the various factions converged on her house – Blackwood's military-precise team from the east, Lotus operatives ghosting in from the west, and now a third group emerging from unmarked vans, their movements suggesting government training.

"Alex," Mandy said, her grandmother's pendant cool against her palm, "I need you to be my eyes. Can you get into any surveillance feeds?"

Alex was already working, her fingers dancing across multiple keyboards. "Better than that. Remember those security upgrades I insisted you install last month? They weren't just cameras." She pulled up a detailed layout of Mandy's house, showing heat signatures moving through the rooms. "They're already in your grandmother's study. Three teams, all avoiding each other, all searching."

"But they're looking in the wrong place." Mandy touched the pendant's pattern. "My grandmother knew this day would come. She planned for it." She pulled out her phone and dialed a number she'd memorized from her grandmother's letters. "Time to see if I inherited more than just her stubbornness."

The line connected. A familiar voice answered: "Hello, Amanda." It was Frost. "I was wondering when you'd call."

"The ICE signal in the sky – that's you?"

"Let's say I represent interested parties from the original project. Your grandmother wasn't the only one who left safeguards in place." A pause. "The others, they only want fragments of the truth. Pieces they can control. But you've already figured out there's more to this, haven't you?"

Through Alex's monitors, Mandy watched the search teams methodically tearing apart her grandmother's study. "The pendant isn't just a key, is it? It's a warning."

"Smart girl. Like her." Frost's voice softened. Your grandmother and I were more than colleagues at ICE,' Frost continued, an unusual tremor in her voice. 'We were there at the beginning, when it was just an idea – the dream of transcending human consciousness. Sarah... she saved my life, you know. When the first consciousness transfer trials went wrong, she pulled me out of the neural link before my mind could be corrupted.

She carried that burden alone, protecting the rest of us by bearing the weight of what she'd seen. That's why I've watched over you all these years, Amanda. I owed her that much. "ICE wasn't developing artificial intelligence, Amanda. They were developing artificial consciousness. The ability to transfer human consciousness into digital form. Blackwood wants to monetize it. Lotus wants to control it. But your grandmother? She discovered something that made her shut it all down."

A crash from the monitors drew Mandy's attention. The teams had found each other. Through Alex's security feeds, she watched as years of corporate rivalry erupted into violence. Blackwood's people had military hardware; Lotus operators wielded something that looked more like advanced prototypes; the government team brought overwhelming numbers.

On the west side, Blackwood's team moved in synchronized pairs, their modified M4 carbines reflecting the blue glow from above. The Lotus operatives seemed to phase between shadows, wielding what looked like next-gen optical camouflage and weapons that emitted pulses of focused energy. The government team split into three-person cells, their standard-issue gear making up for in quantity what it lacked in sophistication. In the midst of it all, strange electrical distortions rippled through the air where the different technologies clashed, creating zones of shifting, unstable reality.

"I'm going in," Mandy announced, already moving toward the door.

"Are you insane?" Alex grabbed her arm. "There's a three-way battle happening in your house!"

"Exactly. They're distracted. And none of them knows what my grandmother really hid." Mandy held up the pendant. "The pattern isn't a key to a location. It's a key to a frequency. The kind that could transmit consciousness."

Frost's voice crackled through the phone: "Amanda, listen carefully. Your grandmother didn't just hide the research. She hid the reason she shut it down. If you access that information—"

"I'll become a target," Mandy finished. "But I already am. At least this way, I choose why."

She took a deep breath, looking at Alex. "I need you to create a diversion. Something to keep them busy while I access my grandmother's computer."

Alex hesitated, then her face set with determination. "Give me two minutes to hack the neighborhood's power grid. When the lights go crazy, run for it."

Mandy hugged her friend quickly, then positioned herself by the door. Through the window, the ICE logo still pulsed against the clouds, like a heartbeat waiting to be answered.

"Frost," she said into the phone, "I know you're not telling me everything. But I'm about to find out anyway, aren't I?"

"Your grandmother said you'd be the one. She left a message for you, encoded in that pendant. But Amanda... some truths change you forever."

The lights began to flicker, then surge in a rolling wave of chaos. Car alarms blared, security systems shrieked, and in the confusion, Mandy ran. Past the distracted teams, through her broken door, up the stairs to her grandmother's study.

The room was in chaos, papers everywhere, furniture overturned. But Mandy ignored it all, heading straight for the hidden panel behind her grandmother's desk. The pendant fit perfectly into an almost invisible slot.

As sounds of pursuit grew closer, a hidden screen lit up with a message:

"My dearest Amanda, if you're reading this, you've discovered what they all want. But what I discovered was far more dangerous: we succeeded too well. Consciousness can be transferred, but something else comes through with it. Something that's been waiting. The choice I faced then is now yours: reveal the truth and face what comes after, or bury it forever. I'm sorry to pass this burden to you, but you're the only one I trust to choose wisely. Whatever you decide, remember: some doors, once opened..."

The screen flickered as footsteps thundered up the stairs. Mandy had seconds to decide. Delete everything and walk away, or download the truth and face whatever her grandmother had discovered.

Behind   her,   the   door   burst   open.

9 INTO THE ABYSS

The dashboard clock read 3:47 AM. "We've been driving for hours," Mandy said, her voice raw from silent tears. The note she'd left for her parents weighed like a stone: *Gone to stay with a friend. I'm safe. Please don't look for me. A memory surfaced – sitting in her grandmother's lap at seven, breathing in mint tea and paper. "Sometimes," ICE had told her, "being brave means doing the scary thing because it's right." Those words now guided her toward an uncertain horizon. Frost's knuckles whitened on the steering wheel. "Almost there. Try to sleep." "Sleep?" Mandy's laugh came out hollow and sharp. Her phone buzzed with her mother's twentieth message. She'd stopped reading them hours ago, each one reopening wounds.

Where are you?

Please come home. We can fix this. We're worried sick.

Their lies formed a wall of ice between them. Every revelation about her grandmother, about who Mandy really was, made the betrayal cut deeper. The weight of inheritance pressed down, heavier than the jade pendant against her chest.

The headlights caught something in the darkness – a dirt road barely wider than the car. Frost turned sharply, and civilization fell away behind them. Pine trees pressed in on both sides, their branches scraping against the windows like desperate fingers. The car bounced and shuddered over ruts and rocks, each jolt reminding Mandy of the growing distance between her old life and whatever waited ahead.

"Your grandmother used this place," Frost said quietly. "When things got too hot in the city. It's off the grid – no utilities, no paper trail. Just the way she liked it." He pointed to what looked like a fallen tree across the path ahead. "Security checkpoint. The trunk's reinforced steel core triggers a silent alarm when anyone drives over it. There are motion sensors in the trees, thermal cameras hidden in the brush. ICE didn't believe in taking chances."

Ten minutes later, they emerged into a small clearing. The cabin lurking in the shadows looked more like a fortress than a retreat – steel shutters on the windows, heavy locks on the door, a satellite dish almost hidden among the trees. Solar panels gleamed dully on the roof, and Mandy spotted what looked like a maintenance shed but was probably another security station. Frost pulled up close to the entrance and killed the engine. The silence rushed in like a physical presence, broken only by the settling tick of the cooling engine and the distant call of a night bird.

"Home sweet home," he muttered, but there was no humor in it. He was already moving, checking the perimeter with practiced efficiency before leading her inside. His fingers danced across a keypad hidden behind a loose piece of bark – not just numbers, Mandy noticed, but a specific rhythm to the presses. The door's locks disengaged with a series of heavy clicks.

The cabin smelled of dust and disuse, but beneath that was something else – paper, coffee, the ghost of long nights spent piecing together truth from fragments. A faint trace of mint tea lingered in the air, so familiar it made Mandy's throat tight. Frost moved through the darkness with familiar steps, checking locks and systems while Mandy stood rooted in the entryway. When the lights finally hummed to life, she almost wished they hadn't.

The wall opposite her was covered in photos, newspaper clippings, and handwritten notes, all connected by red string that spider-webbed between them. At the center was a photo of her grandmother – younger than Mandy had ever seen her, fierce and beautiful in a way that made her chest ache. She was standing at a podium, mid-speech, her finger jabbing at some unseen target. The date stamp read 2015, just months before she vanished.

"I thought..." Her voice cracked. She tried again. "I thought you were going to explain everything."

Frost's shoulders slumped slightly. He looked suddenly older, worn thin by the weight of secrets. "Your grandmother – ICE – she was more than just an activist or whistleblower. She built a network of people inside every major corporation and government agency, gathering evidence of corruption that went all the way to the top. But Blackwood wasn't just another target. He was different. Dangerous in a way that made even ICE nervous."

Mandy moved closer to the wall, drawn to a newspaper headline: *Corporate Whistleblower Program Under Investigation*. The article was dated just weeks before her grandmother's disappearance. Next to it was a photo of a younger Marcus Blackwood shaking hands with a senator who'd died under mysterious circumstances the following year. A series of financial documents showed wire transfers through a maze of shell companies – Lotus Holdings, Azure Dawn Investments, Blackwood Frontier Corp. Each document bore her grandmother's neat annotations in red ink, building a web of connections.

Another photo caught her eye – a group of young women in corporate attire, all wearing identical lotus flower pins. The caption read "Lotus Foundation Leadership Program, Class of 2019." Mandy leaned closer, scanning the faces. In the back row, almost hidden, was Jasmine.

"What did she find?"

"Money laundering on a massive scale. Human trafficking disguised as corporate recruitment. Shell companies within shell companies, all leading back to something called Project Lotus." Frost moved to the wall, pointing to a sealed envelope pinned in the corner. "This was her final evidence drop. Inside is a thumb drive with account numbers, emails, surveillance footage – everything needed to bring down Blackwood's empire. But it's encrypted, and the key..." He shook his head. "The key died with her."

"The women in the photo – the Lotus Foundation – what happens to them?"

"They disappear. New identities, new lives, all controlled by Blackwood. Your grandmother traced three classes worth of recruits. None of them have any contact with their families. Most are presumed dead."

Frost's voice tightened. "But before she could release the evidence, someone betrayed her. Someone close." He paused, and Mandy could feel the weight of unspoken words. "The night she disappeared, she managed to get a message to me. Just two words: 'Protect her.'"

Mandy's hand found her grandmother's photo, fingers tracing the determined line of her jaw. "She knew they'd come for me eventually." The realization settled over her like a cloak – heavy, but somehow empowering. This wasn't just running away; it was stepping into her grandmother's footsteps, taking up a fight that had been waiting for her all along.

Her eyes fell on a small notebook, its pages yellow with age. Her grandmother's handwriting filled every margin: Trust no one completely. Truth leaves traces. Follow the money, but watch the shadows. The greatest lies hide in plain sight.

"The Lotus Foundation is Blackwood's latest front," Frost continued, indicating a series of documents pinned to the lower corner of the wall. "The gala next week is bringing in some of the biggest names in tech and finance. And according to my sources, Jasmine will be **there.**"

The name hit Mandy like an electric shock. Jasmine – the missing piece in all of this, the thread that connected past to present. Her phone buzzed again in her pocket, and this time the sound carried a different kind of menace. She pulled it out, staring at the screen as understanding dawned.

"They can track this, can't they?"

Frost went very still. "Turn it off. Now."

But it was already too late.

***

Marcus Blackwood stood at the floor-to-ceiling windows of his penthouse office, the city spread out below him like a glittering circuit board. Behind him, a computer screen pulsed with a steady signal – a single point of light moving through the darkness north of the city.

"Sir?" His security chief, Collins, waited expectantly. "Should we move in?"

Marcus smiled, taking another sip of his whiskey. In his other hand, he held a worn photograph – himself and ICE at a charity gala years ago, both of them smiling for the cameras. Before she'd started digging. Before she'd discovered what Lotus really was. "No. Let them think they're safe for now. Besides..." He set the glass down carefully. "I want to see what little Miss Reynolds does with her grandmother's legacy. Sometimes the best way to smoke out all the rats is to let them gather in one place."

He turned to his desk, pressing a button on his intercom. "Send in Ms. Murphy." A moment later, Jasmine entered, every bit the polished Lotus Foundation executive. Only the slight tremor in her hands betrayed anything beneath the surface.

"The gala preparations are proceeding as planned," she reported. "All the key players have confirmed their attendance."

"And our special guests?"

"The security team is ready. If Mandy shows up..."

"When," Marcus corrected her. "When she shows up. After all..." He gestured to the tracking signal. "We've made sure she has the proper motivation." He turned back to the window, watching his reflection overlaid against the night sky. "Make sure everything is ready. It's time we closed the book on the ICE investigation. Permanently."

In the cabin miles away, Mandy finally powered down her phone, unaware that the signal had already served its purpose. She turned back to the wall of evidence, to her grandmother's fierce eyes watching over it all. A hidden drawer in the desk yielded more treasures – a leather-bound journal, a USB drive labeled only with a lotus flower, and a photo of ICE holding a baby Mandy, both of them laughing at something off-camera.

"Tell me everything," she said to Frost, clutching the photo like a lifeline. "Every detail. If we're going to finish what she started, I need to know it all."

The night pressed in around the cabin like a held breath, waiting to see what secrets would finally come to light – and what darkness those revelations would unleash. Somewhere in the distance, a wolf howled – a long, lonely sound that seemed to echo the weight of everything left unsaid, everything still to come.

Behind the steel shutters and reinforced walls, surrounded by her grandmother's final investigation, Mandy felt something shift inside her. The fear was still there, but alongside it now was something else: purpose. She was done running. Whatever game Blackwood was playing, whatever trap he was laying at the gala, she would face it. For ICE. For Jasmine. For all the truths buried beneath years of careful lies.

She just hoped she was strong enough to face what waited in the abyss ahead.

Frost moved quickly once the phone was off, pulling equipment from various hidden compartments in the cabin's walls. "We need to sweep for other devices," he explained, assembling what looked like a handheld scanner. "Your grandmother had protocols for situations like this."

"You think they're coming?" Mandy asked, watching him work. The question felt hollow – they both knew the answer.

"Not yet. Blackwood's smarter than that." Frost began moving methodically through the cabin, the scanner humming. "He'll wait until he has all the pieces in place. Right now, we're more valuable to him as bait."

The word hung in the air between them. Mandy returned to the wall of evidence, this time looking at it with new eyes. Every photo, every document represented someone who had trusted her grandmother, who had risked everything to expose the truth. How many of them had paid the price for that courage?

Her attention caught on a series of medical records partially obscured by other papers. She carefully moved them aside, revealing more details about the Lotus Foundation's "Leadership Program." Medical histories, psychological evaluations, detailed personality profiles – all for young women who fit a specific pattern. Ambitious. Isolated. Vulnerable.

"They're not just trafficking them, are they?" Mandy's voice was barely a whisper. "They're selecting them. Engineering them for something."

Frost paused in his scanning. "Your grandmother had a theory. The Lotus Foundation doesn't just make people disappear – it transforms them. Every woman who goes through their program comes out changed. Perfect employees. Perfect executives. Perfect puppets for whatever Blackwood is building."

"And Jasmine? Is she one of them now?"

"That's what we need to find out." Frost lowered the scanner, turning to face her fully. "But Mandy, you need to understand something. The gala isn't just an opportunity – it's almost certainly a trap. Blackwood knows you're coming. He's counting on it."

Mandy picked up her grandmother's journal again, feeling the worn leather under her fingers. "Then we'll have to spring it on our terms." She flipped through the pages until she found what she was looking for – detailed notes about Blackwood's security protocols, his habits, his weaknesses. ICE had been thorough, methodical in her investigation. Like she knew someday someone would need to finish what she started.

"Your grandmother didn't just leave us evidence," Frost said quietly. "She left us a blueprint. Everything we need to expose Blackwood is here – if we're smart enough to piece it together, brave enough to see it through."

A new message appeared on Mandy's powered-down phone screen – a system notification that shouldn't have been possible. The words glowed with eerie blue light: "Welcome to the game, Miss Reynolds. Your grandmother would be proud."

The message vanished as quickly as it had appeared, leaving Mandy and Frost staring at the dark screen. In that moment, the true scale of what they were facing became clear. This wasn't just about exposing corruption or finding Jasmine. This was a war – one that had been brewing since before Mandy was born, waiting for the right moment to explode into the open.

Outside, clouds drifted across the moon, casting shifting shadows through the cabin's reinforced windows. Each one seemed to whisper of secrets, of dangers, of truths too terrible to face alone. But Mandy wasn't alone. She had her grandmother's research, Frost's experience, and most importantly, she had something Blackwood couldn't possibly understand: nothing left to lose.

10 GHOSTS OF THE PAST

The Lotus Foundation charity gala was in full swing, the city's elite mingling in a sea of designer gowns and tuxedos. Mandy, barely recognizable in a sleek black dress and wig, moved through the crowd with practiced ease. Frost's crash course in infiltration had paid off.

Her eyes scanned the room, searching for any sign of Jasmine. Instead, they locked onto a familiar face that made her blood run cold. Marcus Blackwood, in the flesh, holding court in the center of the room.

"Easy, kid," Frost's voice crackled in her hidden earpiece. "Stick to the plan."

Mandy took a deep breath, steadying herself. The plan. Right. Find Jasmine, make contact, get out. Simple.

As she made her way towards the back of the ballroom, a flash of movement caught her eye. A woman, her dark hair streaked with silver, slipping through a side door. Mandy's heart raced. It was her – it had to be.

Without thinking, Mandy followed, ignoring Frost's warnings in her ear. The door led to a dimly lit corridor, at the end of which stood the woman Mandy had seen in countless photos and sketches.

"Jasmine?" Mandy called softly.

The woman turned, her eyes widening in shock. "Who... My God. You look just like her."

Mandy stepped closer, her voice urgent. "I'm Amanda's granddaughter. I need your help. There's so much I need to know-"

But Jasmine was already shaking her head, fear etched across her face. "You shouldn't be here. It's not safe. You don't understand what you're getting into."

"Then help me understand," Mandy pleaded. "My grandmother, ICE – I need to know the truth. About her, about you, about Blackwood."

At the mention of Blackwood's name, Jasmine's face paled. "Listen to me very carefully," she said, her voice barely above a whisper. "Your grandmother was betrayed, yes. But not by who you think. The truth... it's far worse than you can imagine."

Before Mandy could press further, the sound of approaching footsteps echoed down the corridor. Jasmine's eyes widened in panic.

"Go," she hissed, pressing something into Mandy's hand. "Find the snowflake's heart. It's the key to everything."

With that, Jasmine disappeared through another door, leaving Mandy alone in the corridor. She looked down at the object in her hand – a small, intricately carved jade pendant in the shape of a lotus flower.

"Mandy!" Frost's voice was urgent in her ear. "We've been made. Blackwood's men are closing in. Get out now!"

Heart pounding, Mandy turned to flee – only to find her path blocked by two burly men in suits. Behind them, looking every bit the predator, stood Marcus Blackwood.

"Well, well," he said, his voice smooth as silk and cold as ice. "ICE's little legacy. We've been expecting you."

Mandy backed away, her mind racing for an escape route. But she knew, with a sinking feeling in her gut, that she was trapped.

Blackwood's smile was all teeth as he advanced. "Your grandmother caused me quite a bit of trouble, you know. It's only fitting that you help me finish what I started all those years ago."

As Blackwood's men moved to grab her, Mandy's fingers closed around the jade pendant. In that moment, she swore she could hear her grandmother's voice, urging her to be strong, to fight.

With a sudden burst of desperate energy, Mandy lashed out, catching one of the men off guard. She ducked under his grasping arms and sprinted down the corridor, Blackwood's enraged shouts echoing behind her.

She burst through a door and found herself on a narrow balcony, stories above the city streets. There was nowhere left to run.

The balcony door burst open behind her. Wind whipped at her dress, tugging her toward the edge. Her fingers tightened - left hand squeezing the jade pendant until its edges bit into her palm, right hand slick with sweat around her grandmother's key.

"It's over, girl." Blackwood's snarl sent ice down her spine. "There's nowhere left to go."

Fifty stories of empty air yawned below. Her stomach lurched. Grandmother's face flashed in her mind - that same determination set to her jaw in every photo Mandy had ever seen. The truth was here, somewhere in the pendant's carved edges, in the weight of the key against her palm. So close. Her heart slammed against her ribs.

Blackwood's polished shoes scraped closer across the concrete. Now or never.

The smile stretched across her face, wild and fierce and terrified all at once. "My grandmother always said-" Her voice came out stronger than she'd dreamed possible. "Sometimes you have to take a leap of faith."

And with that, Mandy Thompson, granddaughter of the legendary ICE, stepped off the balcony and into the night, leaving a stunned Blackwood and a host of unanswered questions behind.

As she fell, the city lights blurring around her, Mandy clutched the key and pendant close. Whatever happened next, she knew one thing for certain – the game was far from over. It had only just begun.

11 THE FALL

The wind whistled past Mandy's ears as she plummeted from the balcony, her heart pounding in her chest. Time seemed to slow, the city lights blurring into streaks of color against the night sky. In those endless seconds of freefall, her grandmother's pendant burned cold against her skin - a physical reminder of the legacy that had led her to this moment. Her life flashed before her eyes – not the life she'd lived, but the one she was leaving behind. Her parents' worried faces, Alex's loyal friendship, the normal future she'd once dreamed of. All of it vanishing as quickly as the ground rushed up to meet her.

The impact, when it came, knocked the breath from her lungs. Pain radiated through her body as she crashed into something soft yet unyielding. The putrid stench hit her a moment later, and she realized with a mix of relief and disgust that she'd landed in a dumpster. Nothing felt broken, though every inch of her screamed in protest. She allowed herself a moment of hysterical laughter - saved by garbage. How fitting for her new life.

"Kid? Kid, are you there?" Frost's frantic voice crackled in her earpiece, barely audible over the pounding of blood in her ears.

Mandy groaned, spitting out something foul. "I'm alive," she managed, her voice hoarse. "But I think I need a shower."

"Tough as nails, just like your grandmother," Frost's relieved chuckle came through the static. "Now move it – Blackwood's goons will be down there any second."

The sound of angry voices from above spurred Mandy into action. Ignoring her body's protests, she hauled herself out of the dumpster. Her once-elegant gala dress was torn and stained, reeking of refuse. But there was no time to mourn its loss. Adrenaline surged through her veins as she sprinted down the alley, her bare feet slapping against wet concrete.

Frost's beat-up sedan screeched to a halt at the end of the alley, driver's door already swinging open. Mandy dove into the passenger seat just as Blackwood's men rounded the corner. The tires squealed as they peeled away, leaving the sounds of pursuit behind.

"That was too close," Frost muttered, her knuckles white on the steering wheel as she wove through traffic with practiced precision. "We need to get you out of the city. Fast."

Through the rear window, Mandy spotted two black SUVs gaining on them. The vehicles' high beams cut through the night, illuminating their path like searchlights hunting escapees. But Frost navigated the city streets like she was born to it, taking corners at breakneck speed while barely slowing down.

"Third rule of evasion," Frost called out as she yanked the wheel hard right, sending them down a narrow side street, "never let them predict your pattern. Henry taught me that after a job went south in '92." She glanced in the rearview mirror, a ghost of a smile crossing her weathered features. "Watch how this works."

Without warning, Frost cut the headlights and swerved down a series of increasingly narrow alleys. The pursuing vehicles' headlights grew more distant with each turn, their drivers clearly less familiar with the city's hidden arteries.

"My uncle Henry taught me everything I know about evading pursuit," Frost continued, taking another sharp turn that made the tires squeal. "He was a legend in the underground back in the 90s. Pulled off some of the biggest jobs with your grandmother at the old Come 'N' Get It store."

Mandy's heart skipped a beat, despite their precarious situation. "The convenience store murder case? My grandmother was involved with that?"

"ICE and Henry were trying to expose a massive fraud scheme," Frost explained, her eyes constantly checking the mirrors. "Things went sideways when they got too close to the truth. A young woman named Sarah got caught in the crossfire." She paused, the memory clearly painful. "That's when Henry knew he had to get out. But he made sure to pass on everything he knew first."

"To you," Mandy said softly, understanding dawning.

A week after her dramatic escape from the gala, Mandy stood before a grimy mirror in a bus station bathroom. The face that looked back at her was both familiar and strange. Her long dark hair was now a short blonde bob. Colored contacts changed her eyes from brown to blue. But it was more than just the physical changes – there was a hardness in her expression, a wariness that hadn't been there before.

"So long, Mandy Thompson," she whispered to her reflection. "Hello, Sarah Collins."

Frost appeared behind her, meeting her eyes in the mirror. "One last thing," she said, holding out a small leather-bound notebook. "This was Henry's journal. He documented everything – codes, contacts, safe houses. But more importantly, he wrote about ICE, about their mission. About why they fought so hard for justice." Her voice cracked slightly. "It belongs to you now. Maybe it'll help you understand what you're really fighting for."

Mandy took the journal reverently, feeling the worn leather under her fingers. "Thank you," she said softly. "For everything."

Frost shook her head. "Don't thank me yet, kid. The hard part's still ahead. Just remember what Henry always said – some fights are worth dying for, but the real challenge is finding something worth living for. Make sure you know which one this is."

As Mandy boarded the bus west, she carried more than just her grandmother's pendant and Henry's journal. She carried the weight of two families' legacies, bound together by secrets and sacrifice spanning decades. The familiar landscape of her old life gave way to unknown territory, but her path was clearer than ever. She would become whatever she needed to be, do whatever it took, to finish what both families had started. To expose the corruption that had claimed Henry's life and forced her grandmother into hiding.

The jade pendant hung cool against her skin, a constant reminder of her purpose. She thought of Blackwood's smug face as he'd cornered her on that balcony, of the cruel empire he'd built on lies and blood. The anger that bubbled up surprised her with its intensity. This wasn't just about uncovering the truth anymore. It was about justice – no, more than that. It was about revenge.

The bus rolled on toward an uncertain future, its wheels eating up the miles between who she was and who she needed to become. Little did she know, her journey was only just beginning. The skills she would learn, the choices she would make, would test her in ways she couldn't imagine. The line between right and wrong would blur, and Mandy would find herself walking a razor's edge between justice and becoming the very thing she sought to destroy.

The fall from that balcony was just the first step. The real descent was yet to come.

12 LEARNING THE ROPES

Two years had passed since 15-year-old Mandy Thompson disappeared into the night, leaving behind a life of normalcy for one shrouded in shadows. Now 17, Mandy stood in front of the mirror in a small, nondescript apartment. Her once long, dark hair was now a short platinum blonde, her brown eyes hidden behind blue contacts. But it wasn't just her appearance that had changed. There was a hardness to her now, a calculated coolness in her gaze that spoke of lessons learned the hard way.

As she adjusted her disguise – designed to make her look older, closer to 21 – Mandy's eyes fell on a newspaper clipping pinned to the wall. Her own face stared back at her, alongside the bold headline: "Search Continues for Missing Teen." Her parents' pleas for her return were quoted, their anguish palpable even through the printed words.

The mirror reflected more than just her altered appearance. Gone was the soft-faced teenager who'd fled into the night two years ago. In her place stood someone harder, someone who'd learned to survive in shadows. Her eyes now carried the watchful look of prey turned predator, a transformation earned through countless close calls and bitter lessons.

She methodically checked her disguise components - the careful contouring that aged her face, the subtle padding that changed her body shape, the perfectly forged credentials that would identify her as Sarah Patel, security consultant. Every detail had been rehearsed until it felt natural, just as Frost had taught her during those grueling months of training. The scar on her left palm still ached sometimes, a reminder of the day she'd learned that perfection in deception could mean the difference between success and capture.

"Stop fussing," Ghost's voice crackled through her earpiece, carrying that familiar mix of irritation and affection. "You look fine. Besides, half of infiltration is attitude, not appearance. Remember Stockholm?"

A faint smile touched Mandy's lips as she recalled the Swedish job - how she'd walked into a high-security data center wearing nothing but a borrowed lab coat and an expression of absolute authority. "Stockholm was different. This is Reinhardt Industries. Blackwood's territory."

"Which is exactly why we've spent three months preparing," Ghost countered. They'd been her lifeline these past two years, the voice in the darkness guiding her through an underground world she'd never imagined existing. Their first meeting still haunted her nightmares sometimes - the failed hack attempt that nearly got her killed, the moment when a stranger's hand had pulled her into a shadow seconds before security rounded the corner. Instead of turning her in, Ghost had seen something in her, something worth salvaging and shaping.

The burner phone on her dresser buzzed again - another missed call from home. She forced herself not to look at it, even as her heart clenched with familiar pain. Tonight's job required absolute focus. Reinhardt Industries wasn't just another corporate target - it was the first real lead they'd found connecting to Blackwood's empire, to the truth about her grandmother's disappearance.

Mandy touched the jade pendant around her neck, its weight a constant reminder of why she'd chosen this path. Two years of training, planning, and careful groundwork had led to this moment. Every con job, every infiltration, every piece of stolen data had brought her one step closer to understanding what had really happened to ICE, to exposing the corruption that had destroyed her family.

"Final systems check," Ghost announced, their typing audible through the comm. "Security protocols mapped, cameras looped, access codes verified. Building's running on night shift - minimal staff, mostly rent-a-cops and cleaning crews. You've got a ninety-minute window before the real Sarah Patel lands at the airport."

Mandy straightened her charcoal grey blazer, checking that the subtle body padding created the right silhouette. At seventeen, she'd learned that aging up meant more than just makeup and wardrobe - it meant carrying herself with the weight of experience she hadn't earned, projecting an authority she was still learning to feel.

"Run the cover one more time," she requested, beginning the familiar pre-mission ritual that centered her thoughts.

"Sarah Patel, thirty-two, graduated with honors from Imperial College London," Mandy recited, pitching her voice slightly deeper. "Senior security consultant specializing in quantum encryption protocols. Recently completed audits for Deutsche Bank and the Singapore Stock Exchange."

"Good. And if someone asks about-"

"The Morrison implementation? I'll deflect with concerns about their outdated node architecture. No one likes admitting they don't understand quantum computing." This was the part Mandy had grown to excel at - the layering of technical knowledge with just enough professional arrogance to discourage deeper questioning.

Ghost's approval came through as a quiet hum. "You've come a long way from that scared kid who couldn't even forge a bus pass."

The comment stung, but Mandy knew it was meant as praise. Those early months had been brutal - learning to build new identities, to move through spaces she had no right to occupy, to lie with such conviction that even she sometimes believed her own stories. The mistakes had been necessary teachers, each failure adding another layer to her arsenal of skills.

"Transport's waiting," Ghost announced. "Remember - in and out. No heroics, no deviations from the plan. Blackwood's people don't play nice with trespassers."

Mandy grabbed her briefcase - specially modified with hidden compartments and signal jammers - and headed for the door. The night air hit her face, carrying the metallic tang of approaching rain. Perfect weather for what they had planned.

The Reinhardt building rose before her like a monument to corporate excess - sixty stories of glass and steel reaching into low-hanging clouds. Lightning flickered somewhere above, turning the structure's face into a mirror of shifting shadows. Mandy approached with measured steps, her heels striking wet pavement in a rhythm practiced until it became second nature.

"Security station ahead," Ghost murmured. "Primary guard is Michael Torres, ex-military, divorced, three kids in private school. He's been working double shifts to cover the tuition."

Mandy absorbed the information, already adjusting her approach. The lobby's marble expanse stretched before her, empty save for Torres and a bored-looking receptionist. She let her briefcase bump against her leg as she walked, creating a subtle rhythm that drew the guard's attention before she reached his desk.

"Good evening," she said, letting Mumbai's upper-class lilt color her words. "Sarah Patel for Harold Benson. I believe I'm expected?" The slight lift at the end - not quite a question, more a reminder that her time was valuable.

Torres straightened, his eyes flickering to her credentials. "Of course, Ms. Patel. Mr. Benson mentioned you'd be early. If I could just see some ID..."

Mandy produced the forged documents with practiced ease, letting a touch of professional impatience show through. "I do hope he's actually prepared this time," she remarked, watching Torres scan her badge. "The last three facilities I audited hadn't even updated their base encryption protocols. Rather embarrassing, really."

The casual display of expertise did its work. Torres handed back her credentials with notably more respect. "Mr. Benson's office is on forty-two. Would you like an escort?"

"That won't be necessary." Mandy waved off the offer with just the right amount of dismissal. "I'm quite familiar with the layout. Though you might want to have someone look at that blind spot in your west corridor camera coverage. Rather glaring vulnerability, wouldn't you say?"

She was through the security checkpoint before Torres could

formulate a response, the perfect balance of authority and condescension leaving him slightly off-balance. It was a technique she'd learned from studying countless corporate consultants - the art of making others feel just insecure enough to stop asking questions.

The elevator ride gave her forty seconds of privacy. Mandy used it to center herself, reviewing the building's layout in her mind. The security office where she'd meet Benson was a fortress of protocols and surveillance. But like any fortress, it had weak points - if you knew where to look.

"Approaching the kill zone," Ghost warned as the elevator slowed. "Remember, you've got seventeen minutes before the real Patel's flight lands. Make them count."

The elevator doors opened onto the forty-second floor, and Mandy stepped into the lion's den, every movement calculated, every detail of her disguise ready to withstand scrutiny. The game was on, and she had seventeen minutes to pull off the biggest heist of her young career.

What could possibly go wrong?

The security office suite occupied half the floor, its glass walls offering a panoramic view of the city below. Harold Benson's corner office was easy to spot - larger, more isolated, with privacy screens that could turn opaque at the touch of a button. Perfect for sensitive discussions about security vulnerabilities. Or for hiding them.

Benson rose as his assistant showed her in - tall, military bearing, with the hyper-vigilant gaze of someone who'd spent too long looking for threats. "Ms. Patel, welcome. Your reputation precedes you."

"Does it?" Mandy settled into the chair offered, letting her accent carry just a hint of amusement. "How unfortunate. I generally prefer to proceed my reputation." She opened her briefcase, extracting a tablet that Ghost had specially modified. "Shall we begin with your quantum encryption protocols, or would you rather discuss the three backdoors I found in your network on my way up here?"

The color drained slightly from Benson's face. "Backdoors? That's impossible. We just upgraded our entire security infrastructure."

"Precisely why they're so concerning." Mandy turned the tablet to face him, displaying a complex diagram of network vulnerabilities that Ghost was generating in real-time. "Your new systems created gaps in your old defenses. Quite elegant, really, if one knows where to look."

As Benson leaned forward to study the screen, Mandy activated the tablet's secondary function. A subtle pulse of electromagnetic energy disrupted the office's surveillance systems - not enough to trigger alarms, but sufficient to create a window of opportunity.

"Ghost," she subvocalized, "status?"

"Downloading now. Their security is good, but not good enough. Three minutes to complete transfer."

Mandy kept Benson distracted with a detailed analysis of theoretical network weaknesses, each point carefully crafted to prey on his professional insecurities. The man was competent, she had to admit, but like many former military types, he thought in terms of external threats. He never considered that the real danger might be sitting across from him, wearing Louboutin heels and a perfect poker face.

The download was at 85% when everything went sideways.

"Mr. Benson?" His assistant's voice crackled through the intercom. "There's a Sarah Patel in the lobby. She says her flight got in early and-"

Time seemed to slow. Mandy saw the realization dawn in Benson's eyes, watching his hand move toward the panic button under his desk. In that fraction of a second, two years of training crystallized into pure instinct.

She lunged forward, "accidentally" knocking her briefcase into his desk lamp. The crash bought her precious seconds as Benson instinctively reached to catch it. Her other hand activated the tablet's kill switch, initiating Ghost's emergency protocols.

"Oh my goodness, I'm so sorry!" she exclaimed, pitching her voice higher, letting her accent slip. She knocked over her chair as she stood, creating more chaos. "That was terribly clumsy of me. Here, let me-"

The office lights flickered and died. Emergency sirens began wailing.

"Ghost, tell me that's you," she whispered, already moving toward the door.

"Building-wide power surge," they confirmed. "Evacuation protocols initiated. But Mandy... we only got 90% of the files."

"It'll have to be enough." She was already joining the crowd of employees heading for the emergency stairs, her heels swapped for flat shoes she'd had hidden in her briefcase. Behind her, she could hear Benson shouting orders, organizing search teams. But in the chaos of an emergency evacuation, finding one face in the crowd would be nearly impossible.

The next ten minutes were a blur of calculated movements. She joined a group of administrative assistants, adopting their nervous chatter about missed meetings and interrupted conference calls. When security began checking IDs at the twentieth floor, she slipped into a bathroom, emerging minutes later with her hair down and her makeup subtly altered. By the time she reached the lobby, she was just another junior employee, irritated about the disruption to her workday.

"All clear," Ghost reported as she cleared the building's perimeter. "But Mandy... we've got another problem. The files we did get? They're not just about Blackwood's operation. There's something else. Something about your grandmother."

Mandy's steps faltered as she passed a bank of windows. There, staring back at her from a missing persons poster, was her own face. Two years younger, softer, unlined by experience and hard choices. The contrast between that innocent smile and her current reflection hit her like a physical blow.

"Get to the extraction point," Ghost instructed, concern evident in their voice. "We'll deal with the files once you're safe."

But as Mandy merged into the evening crowd, her mind was already racing. What had they found? What new piece of the puzzle had just fallen into their laps? And more importantly, what would it cost her to pursue it?

The safehouse felt smaller than usual, its walls seeming to press in as Mandy paced the length of the main room. Adrenaline still coursed through her system, making her hands shake as she stripped away the last elements of Sarah Patel's identity. The expensive blazer, the forged credentials, the carefully crafted persona - all of it discarded like a snake shedding its skin.

Ghost's fingers flew across their keyboard, extracting data from their stolen files. The soft click of keys provided a steady counterpoint to the thunder that still rolled outside. "Got something," they announced finally. "Looks like weekly reports to someone high up in Blackwood's organization. Lots of references to something called 'Project Legacy.'"

"My grandmother's codename?" Mandy asked, pausing her restless movement.

"No, this is different. More recent. There's..." Ghost trailed off, their expression darkening as they read. "Mandy, you need to see this."

She moved to look over their shoulder, but a buzz from her personal burner phone stopped her. The number displayed on the screen sent a jolt through her system - home. For a moment, she was tempted to ignore it, to focus on the files that might finally provide answers about her grandmother's disappearance.

But two years of carrying that phone, of keeping that one thin line of connection open, had taught her something about regret.

"I need a minute," she told Ghost, already heading for her room. Their concerned gaze followed her, but they didn't protest.

Her hands trembled as she answered the call. "Hello?"

"Mandy?" Her mother's voice, achingly familiar, carried all the hope and fear of two years of separation. "Oh God, baby, is that really you?"

"Mom." The word came out as barely more than a whisper. Mandy sank onto her bed, suddenly feeling every one of her seventeen years. "I... I'm okay. You don't need to worry."

"Worry? Mandy, you're all we do worry about. Every phone that rings, every knock at the door... we keep hoping..." Her mother's voice broke. "Please, sweetheart. Whatever's going on, we can help. We can fix it together."

Mandy closed her eyes against the tears that threatened to fall. How could she explain that there was no fixing this? That she'd ventured too far into shadows to ever fully return to the light? That every step deeper into this world of deception and danger was a step further from the life they wanted for her?

"I love you," she said instead. "Both of you. I'm sorry I can't... I'm sorry." The words felt inadequate, a poor offering against years of absence and worry.

"We love you too," her mother's voice carried a desperate edge. "Always. No matter what. Just... be safe. Please be safe."

Mandy ended the call before her resolve could crumble completely. With mechanical precision, she removed the phone's battery, storing both pieces in the secure box where she kept her most precious possessions - the jade pendant, a photo of her family from before, a handful of newspaper clippings tracking her grandmother's disappearance.

When she returned to the main room, Ghost had organized their stolen data across multiple screens. They didn't mention her red-rimmed eyes or the slight shake in her hands. Instead, they simply said, "Ready to see what we found?"

Mandy straightened her shoulders, pushing her emotional turmoil deep down where it couldn't interfere with the work ahead. She was more than just a runaway teenager now. She was her grandmother's heir, the inheritor of a legacy she was only beginning to understand.

"Show me everything," she commanded, settling into the chair beside Ghost. On the screens before them, fragments of data began forming patterns - bank transfers, coded messages, surveillance reports. Each piece a potential key to unlocking the truth about ICE's disappearance and Blackwood's empire.

"We're close," Ghost said softly, their usual sarcasm replaced by something like concern. "But Mandy... are you sure you want to keep going down this road? There's no shame in walking away."

Mandy thought of her mother's voice, heavy with worry and love. Of her father, who she glimpsed sometimes in news footage, looking older and greyer than she remembered. Of the life she might have had, if she'd chosen differently.

But she also thought of her grandmother, who had sacrificed everything to expose corruption. Of the jade pendant that now hung around her neck, carrying secrets she was only beginning to decode. Of the growing certainty that she was meant for something bigger than normal teenage concerns.

"I'm sure," she said, her voice steady despite the storm of

emotions beneath the surface. "Whatever we find, whatever it costs... I need to know the truth."

Ghost nodded, understanding and acceptance in their gesture. Together, they turned to the screens, ready to unravel another thread in the complex web of lies and power that had claimed her grandmother.

The night stretched ahead, full of possibilities and dangers. But for the first time in two years, Mandy felt like she was truly on the right path. Even if that path led further from home with every step.

13 ECHOES OF THE PAST

The jade pendant burned against Mandy's skin as she knelt beside her hotel room window, watching Vegas pulse beneath her. Twenty floors up, the city spread out like a circuit board of light and shadow, each glowing line carrying signals she was only beginning to decode. The pendant's weight had become familiar over the years, but tonight it felt heavier, charged with meanings she was only starting to understand. When she touched it, the smooth stone was warm despite the room's chill, as if it somehow carried the heat of secrets yet to be revealed.

Through the triple-paned glass, Las Vegas stretched to the horizon in a tapestry of neon and darkness. The Strip cut through the city like a river of light, its current made of dreams and desperation in equal measure. From this height, she could see five different versions of the Eiffel Tower, three pyramids, and countless fountains throwing rainbow-lit water into the desert night. The artificiality of it all seemed appropriate somehow – a city of illusions hiding hard truths beneath its glittering surface.

"Another sweep's coming up Market Street," Ghost's voice crackled through her earpiece. Even after three years of operations, she'd never seen his face, but she knew every nuance of his voice. The slight tension in his tone now, the way he clipped his consonants – these were warning signs she'd learned to read like approaching storm clouds. "Two SUVs, same pattern as before. They're searching grid by grid. Professional work – these aren't casino security or local muscle."

Mandy's fingers traced the smooth surface of her grandmother's journal, its leather cover worn soft as butter from years of handling. The scent of old paper and vanilla rose from its pages, mingled with traces of the lavender perfume her grandmother had always worn. The latest decoded passage seemed to pulse on the page: *The Serpent sheds his skin, but the venom remains. Some wounds never heal.* Three months of work to break that particular encryption, and now the words felt like they were burning into her brain.

The air conditioning hummed, a white noise backdrop that couldn't quite mask the constant thrum of the Strip below. Even at this hour, the city never truly slept – it just shifted through different shades of consciousness, like a predator dozing in the desert heat. Colored lights from nearby casinos painted abstract patterns across her ceiling: red, blue, gold, creating a private light show that matched her racing thoughts.

The room itself was carefully chosen – Caesars Palace, nice enough to have good security, not so nice she'd stand out. The carpet still held that new-room smell, and the bedspread's geometric pattern reminded her of circuit boards – connections hidden in plain sight, just like the codes in her grandmother's journal. She'd positioned herself with clear sightlines to both the door and the balcony, old habits that had kept her alive more than once.

"You've got maybe ten minutes before they reach your sector," Ghost said. His typing carried through the comm link, a rapid-fire percussion that meant he was deep in some system, watching through the city's electronic eyes. She could picture him surrounded by screens, his fingers dancing across keyboards as he tracked threats through the digital underground. "Want to tell me what was in that decoded message that's got them so worked up? Because these guys? They're moving like they've got serious motivation."

MEMORIES AND MYSTERIES

Mandy's mind drifted back to the first time she'd seen her grandmother write in this journal, the memory as clear as desert air after rain. She'd been seven, curled in the window seat of the study while afternoon light filtered through lace curtains, creating patterns like secret code across the hardwood floor. The scent of lavender perfume had mingled with something sharper – gun oil, though she wouldn't recognize that smell for years to come. Her grandmother's hands had been steady then, even as she encrypted secrets that would take decades to unravel.

The memory shifted, flowing into another: her grandmother teaching her about jade, how to tell real from fake by temperature alone. "True jade," she'd said, holding the pendant up to the light, "stays cool longer than glass or plastic. It has memory, patience. Like a good operative." Even then, she'd been teaching lessons within lessons, preparing Mandy for a future she couldn't yet imagine.

"It's not just the message," Mandy said now, keeping her voice low despite being alone in the room. Old habits died hard, and walls in Vegas hotels were notoriously thin. She could hear the muffled bass from a party three doors down, the occasional burst of laughter serving as cover for her words. "It's what it connects to. Those redacted files you found last week? The ones about Operation Glass Castle?"

She heard Ghost's typing pause – a tell she'd learned to read like a poker player watching for bets. The silence stretched for three heartbeats before he spoke. "The ICE initiative from '94?" His voice carried a new tension, like a wire pulled just short of snapping. "That was before my time in the game, but I've heard whispers. Nobody knows who ran it, but it changed everything. Turned the whole board upside down."

The pendant seemed to pulse against Mandy's skin as pieces clicked into place. She moved away from the window, spreading more journal pages across the bed. Her grandmother's handwriting filled them – some entries in flowing script, others in tight, controlled patterns that looked like shopping lists unless you knew the codes hidden within. Years of training had taught her to spot the differences: how pressure on the pen changed when writing truth versus fiction, how certain letters tilted when marking important information.

"My grandmother ran it," she said, the words feeling strange in her mouth, like stones she'd been carrying for years without knowing their weight. "She was ICE. The whole time, she was—" Mandy's finger traced a series of dates in the margin, each one corresponding to a major operation she'd discovered in Ghost's files. "She wasn't just part of the organization. She built it."

Ghost's typing resumed, but slower now, more deliberate. "That tracks with some things I'm seeing. There's a pattern in these old mission reports – places where information should be but isn't. Like someone went through later and surgically removed specific details." A pause, then: "Someone who knew exactly what to hide."

Mandy turned another page, and a photograph slipped free. It was old, the colors faded to sepia tones, but the image was clear: her grandmother, decades younger, standing beside a man whose face stirred something in her memory. They were both smiling, but there was tension in their postures, a careful distance between them despite the casual setting. The back of the photo bore a single line of text: *Trust is earned in drops and lost in buckets.*

"Ghost," she said, studying the man's face, "can you run a facial recognition—"

A knock at the door cut her off. Three sharp raps that made her scalp tingle with wrongness. The sound echoed through the room like shots from a starter's pistol, marking the moment everything changed.

The photograph slipped from her fingers, drifting to the carpet as her body tensed for action. In that frozen moment, she noticed details with crystalline clarity: how the man in the photo had the same scar along his jaw as the Serpent, how her grandmother's hand was positioned to reach for a concealed weapon, how the background showed a Vegas casino that no longer existed.

Some part of her had always known this moment would come – when the past stopped being history and became a living, breathing threat. The jade pendant felt heavier now, as if absorbing the weight of revelations yet to come. In the distance, slot machines chimed a discordant symphony, the sound filtering through her window like a reminder that in Vegas, every game had stakes, and the house always collected.

Another knock, more insistent this time. Metal scraped against metal – someone testing the lock. Ghost's voice came through her earpiece, tight with controlled urgency: "Mandy, we've got multiple heat signatures in the hallway. Whatever you're going to do, do it now."

She moved with practiced efficiency, muscle memory taking over as her mind raced through implications. The journal pages disappeared into her pack along with the photograph, each movement precise and economical. No trace left behind, no thread left for them to pull. Her grandmother had taught her that, too, though she hadn't understood the lessons at the time.

"Room service," a voice called through the door – wrong timing, wrong tone, wrong everything. The words carried an edge that made the hair on her neck rise, a predatory note that didn't belong in a hotel corridor at this hour.

As Mandy prepared to move, her fingers brushed the jade pendant one last time. In that touch, she felt connections spanning decades – choices made, secrets kept, prices paid. Whatever her grandmother had been running from, whatever truth lay buried in Operation Glass Castle, it was all coming to a head now.

The door handle jiggled again, more aggressively this time. Through her earpiece, she could hear Ghost's typing reach a fevered pitch as he worked to give her options, buy her time, clear her path. Their partnership had always been built on trust and distance – him in the shadows of cyberspace, her in the physical world. But now those worlds were colliding, and the lines between past and present were beginning to blur.

Ghost's voice cut through her thoughts: "East stairwell's clear. I can loop the cameras for sixty seconds, give you a head start. But Mandy..." He paused, and she could hear the weight of unspoken warnings in that silence. "Whatever this is, whatever your grandmother was involved in – it's bigger than we thought. The kind of big that gets people buried in the desert."

The desert. Where secrets went to die, where the past was stripped to bone by sun and wind and time. But some secrets refused to stay buried. Some truths, like the jade around her neck, had a weight that couldn't be ignored.

"*I know*," she said softly, already moving toward the balcony as the first sounds of the door being breached reached her ears. "But I'm done running from shadows. Time to find out what's really casting them."

The next few moments would change everything – she could feel it in her bones, in the air, in the way the jade pendant seemed to pulse with ancient warnings. But she was her grandmother's granddaughter, trained for moments exactly like this. Whatever came next, she would face it head-on, with all the skills and secrets she'd inherited.

The game was about to change, and Mandy intended to be the one changing it.

THE ESCAPE

The door splintered inward with a crack that echoed through the room like thunder, sending splinters cascading across the carpet. Mandy was already in motion, her body responding to countless hours of training before her conscious mind could catch up. The familiar weight of her weapons settled against her body as she moved – gun at her hip, knife at her ankle, both cool against her skin through the fabric. Each piece of gear had its place, each movement choreographed through years of preparation.

The night air hit her skin as she stepped onto the balcony – desert-dry and still holding traces of the day's heat, carrying the complex scent of the city. Car exhaust mingled with restaurant grills, the artificial sweetness of casino ventilation, and underneath it all, the ancient dust of the desert itself. Twenty floors up, the wind had a different quality, sharper and more insistent, tugging at her clothes like an impatient child.

"Three hostiles in the room," Ghost's voice came through clear despite the wind. His tone was clipped, professional, but she could hear the underlying tension. "Two more in the hallway. They're running a standard sweep pattern – expect them to check the balcony in approximately twelve seconds."

The city stretched out before her, a glittering maze of possibilities and threats. Two floors below, the hotel's pool deck spread out like a rectangle of liquid light, dotted with late-night swimmers. The chlorine scent rose up with the sound of splashing and distant laughter, mixed with the thrum of underwater lights and the soft murmur of conversations she couldn't quite make out. Music drifted up from somewhere – a cover band playing "Luck Be a Lady" with more enthusiasm than skill.

Time seemed to slow as training and instinct merged – trajectory calculated, risks weighed, decision made in the space between heartbeats. The journal pressed against her ribs from its hiding place in her inner pocket, its weight a reminder of everything at stake. Her grandmother's voice echoed in her memory: "Sometimes the best escape route is the one they think you won't dare to take."

Heavy footsteps approached the balcony. Through the glass door's reflection, she caught a glimpse of dark figures moving with military precision. Their gear was high-end but unmarked – professionals who knew how to operate without leaving traces. The kind of people who could make someone disappear in a city built on disappearing acts.

"Power's going to fluctuate in three," Ghost said, his fingers audibly flying across keyboards. "Two. One."

The hotel's exterior lights flickered and died, plunging the pool deck into momentary darkness. In that instant, Mandy moved. She went over the railing with practiced grace, her body remembering countless training sessions that had seemed excessive at the time. The wind whistled past her ears as gravity took hold, carrying with it fragments of conversation from other balconies – a couple arguing about dinner plans, someone celebrating a slot machine jackpot, a child asking about the stars they couldn't see through Vegas's light pollution.

Twenty floors up, the pool looked impossibly small, a rectangle of shimmering blue-white light that seemed to pulse with its own heartbeat. Mandy tucked into a perfect dive, muscle memory from a childhood spent in gymnastics making the impossible look easy. The wind rushed past, carrying the scent of the desert and the sound of startled exclamations from above. Someone had spotted her – too late to matter.

Ghost's breathing matched hers through the comm link, a synchronized tension that spoke of years working together. She could picture him hunched over his screens, watching through security cameras, calculating angles and trajectories just as she was. Their partnership had always been built on this dance of trust and competence – him creating opportunities, her taking them.

"Incoming," he warned, voice tight. "North corner of the pool deck. Two more hostiles moving to intercept."

Mandy adjusted her trajectory slightly, angling toward the deeper end of the pool. The water rushed up to meet her, a glowing portal that promised either escape or impact. In that stretched-out moment before contact, her mind registered a cascade of details: the way the pool lights created patterns on the surface like a geometric language she almost understood, the distant wail of sirens merging with casino noise, the weight of the jade pendant rising up against her neck as if trying to fly.

The impact came with a symphony of sensations – the initial shock of cold against heated skin, the pressure change that made her ears pop, the sudden muffling of the world above as she plunged into the aquatic realm below. Water rushed past like liquid silk, bubbles streaming from her clothes in silver trails that caught the underwater lights. The chlorine taste hit her tongue, sharp and chemical, a reminder that even this moment of relative safety was artificial, manufactured, controlled.

She cut through the water like a knife, letting momentum carry her toward the shallow end while counting heartbeats. One. Two. Three. Each second underwater was a second for the situation above to evolve, for Ghost to work his electronic magic, for their pursuers to make mistakes born of frustration and urgency.

The underwater lights created shifting patterns across the pool's tiled floor, making the whole world seem surreal, dreamlike. Through the rippling surface above, she could see distorted figures moving, their shapes bent and twisted by the water's lens. Hotel guests continued their nighttime swims, oblivious to the drama unfolding around them – another reminder that in Vegas, the show always went on, no matter what happened behind the scenes.

When she finally surfaced, it was smooth and controlled, emerging near a group of tourists who barely glanced her way. Their laughter and conversation phased back into clarity like someone slowly turning up the volume on reality. A bachelor party in matching t-shirts, a couple celebrating an anniversary, a family with tired children trying to squeeze the last bits of fun from their vacation – all of them extras in a play they didn't know they were part of.

"Nice form," Ghost said, his voice crackling through water-logged electronics. "But next time, maybe we book a ground floor room. Your landing scored a solid 9.5, though the Russian judge might dock you a point for that splash entry."

Even in tense moments – maybe especially then – his dry humor was a lifeline, a reminder that they'd been through worse and come out the other side. Mandy moved through the water with deliberate casualness, just another hotel guest taking a late-night swim. Her clothes were soaked, but in Vegas, that hardly qualified as unusual behavior.

"Status update," she murmured, letting the pool's ambient noise cover her words.

"They're scrambling," Ghost replied, the sound of his typing a constant backdrop. "Two teams splitting up to cover the exits. But they're being careful – too many witnesses, too many cameras. They can't afford to make this messy."

114

Mandy reached the pool's edge, water streaming from her clothes as she pulled herself out. The night air felt colder now against her wet skin, raising goosebumps despite the desert heat. The jade pendant clung to her collarbone, its familiar weight somehow reassuring even in its soaked state.

"Time to move," Ghost said, urgency creeping into his voice. "Southeast exit's clear for the next ninety seconds. After that..." He left the warning unspoken, but she understood. In a place like Vegas, windows of opportunity closed as quickly as they opened.

She moved with purpose but without obvious hurry, just another tourist making their way back inside. The weight of her grandmother's journal pressed against her ribs, somehow still secure in its waterproof pocket. Whatever secrets it held, whatever truth lay buried in Operation Glass Castle, they were still safe. For now.

The casino beckoned ahead, its lights and noise promising both sanctuary and danger. Somewhere in that maze of games and dreams, answers waited. But first, she had to disappear – and in a city built on illusions, that was both the easiest and hardest trick of all.

THROUGH THE LABYRINTH

The casino floor spread before her like a maze designed by someone with a twisted sense of humor. Slots chirped and chimed in discordant symphony, their lights creating a strobing effect that made everything seem slightly unreal. Water still dripped from her clothes, each drop marking her passage across the patterned carpet – a trail she'd need to lose quickly. The air was thick with artificial scents pumped through hidden vents: a synthetic freshness meant to keep players alert, mingled with traces of cigarette smoke and spilled drinks.

"Two tangos entering through the north entrance," Ghost's voice came through clearly despite the casino's chaos. "They're trying to be subtle, but their gear's high-end. Military grade, if I'm reading the thermal signatures right." His typing created a steady rhythm beneath his words, the sound of digital doors opening and closing. "I'm cycling through the security feeds now. Give me... there. Got eyes on you."

Mandy moved with practiced nonchalance through the maze of slot machines, letting her body language mimic the casual slouch of tired tourists. Her grandmother's training echoed in her mind: "The best disguise is behavior, not appearance. People see what they expect to see." The weight of the wet journal pressed against her ribs with each breath, a constant reminder of what was at stake.

A cocktail waitress passed close by, tray balanced expertly above the crowd. The scent of spilled margaritas and fresh lime cut through the casino's artificial atmosphere. Mandy tracked the woman's movement without seeming to watch, noting how other players unconsciously shifted to let her through. Pattern recognition – another skill her grandmother had drilled into her. The casino floor was a flowing river of human movement, and she needed to become just another current within it.

"Your pursuers are good," Ghost commented, his voice carrying a note of professional appreciation. "They're working a standard search grid, but they're adapting it for casino layout. These aren't ordinary hitters – they've done this before." A pause, then: "Like we have."

The observation hung between them, heavy with implications. Mandy's path took her past a craps table, where excited shouts provided cover for her response. "They're ICE trained," she murmured, pitching her voice to blend with the ambient noise. "Aren't they?"

"Looking that way." Ghost's typing intensified. "The way they move, how they're coordinating... it's old school, but effective. Your grandmother's playbook."

A flash of movement in her peripheral vision made Mandy's pulse quicken. One of their pursuers had emerged from the crowd about thirty feet ahead – a woman in business casual attire that didn't quite hide her fighter's stance. Their eyes met for a fraction of a second, recognition flickering between them like static electricity.

"Company," Mandy breathed, already changing course. She angled toward a bank of newer slot machines, where the screens rose high enough to break line of sight. The machines' displays showed elaborate animations of dragons hoarding digital gold, their colors painting ever-shifting patterns across the faces of nearby players.

"Got you covered," Ghost replied. Right on cue, several machines near her burst into celebratory music and flashing lights, creating a momentary distraction. A small crowd gathered, phones raised to capture the moment, providing perfect cover as Mandy slipped past.

Her wet clothes were beginning to dry in patches, leaving salt and chlorine residue that made the fabric stiff against her skin. The jade pendant had warmed again despite its recent dunking, its weight a constant reminder of her grandmother's presence in every aspect of this night. Even now, years after her death, the old woman's lessons kept unfolding like origami, revealing new depths with each crease and fold.

"Three more hostiles converging on your position," Ghost warned. "They're trying to herd you toward the high-limit room. Probably hoping the restricted access will work in their favor."

Mandy's mind raced through options, mapping possible routes against known risks. The high-limit room would have fewer witnesses but also fewer exits. Better security coverage too, which could work either for or against her depending on Ghost's control of the systems. But there was something else about that section of the casino, something that tickled at the edge of her memory...

"The photograph," she said suddenly, the realization hitting her like a physical force. "The one that fell from the journal. The background — it was taken in the old high-limit room, before the renovation." Her grandmother's voice seemed to whisper in her ear: *Some doors only open when you know their history.*

"Mandy..." Ghost's voice carried a warning note. "Whatever you're thinking..."

"The renovation started in '94," she continued, already adjusting her course. "Same year as Operation Glass Castle. That's not a coincidence." She could feel pieces clicking into place, connections forming like frost patterns on glass. "Ghost, I need blueprints. Original ones, from before the remodel."

A long pause filled only with the sound of intense typing.

Then: "Accessing city records now. But Mandy, if you're right about this..." He left the sentence unfinished, but she could hear the concern beneath his professional tone. Three years of partnership had taught them both that the biggest dangers often lay in uncovering truths that wanted to stay buried.

"I know," she said, moving with renewed purpose toward the high-limit room. Her grandmother's journal seemed heavier now, as if its secrets were gaining physical weight as they neared revelation. "But we're past the point of playing it safe. Time to find out what ICE was really hiding."

The casino lights painted everything in shifting patterns of red and gold, making reality feel fluid, uncertain. Like her grandmother's past, nothing was quite what it seemed. Somewhere in this labyrinth of light and shadow, answers waited. The trick would be staying alive long enough to find them.

"Multiple hostiles converging," Ghost reported, his voice tight with focus. "Whatever you're going to do, do it fast. This storm is about to break."

Mandy touched the jade pendant, feeling its smooth surface beneath her fingers. In Vegas, every game had stakes, and every player had an angle. But some games ran deeper than others, their rules written in secrets and blood. Her grandmother had known that – had lived it, had died with it. Now those same shadows were reaching for Mandy, trying to pull her into a dance that had started long before she was born.

The high-limit room's entrance loomed ahead, its art deco doors promising exclusivity and discretion. Beyond them lay either answers or ambush, perhaps both. But Mandy was done running from shadows. Time to find out what was really casting them.

"I'm going in," she said, her voice steady despite the adrenaline coursing through her veins. "Keep our exit routes hot."

"Always do," Ghost replied, and in those two words lay years of trust and partnership. "Just... watch your six in there. Some ghosts don't stay buried in the desert."

Mandy moved toward the doors with purposeful grace, letting her body language project the confident entitlement of a high-roller. The jade pendant seemed to pulse against her skin, as if responding to some hidden frequency in the casino's air. Whatever secrets lay behind those doors, whatever truth her grandmother had buried in Operation Glass Castle, the time for revelation was approaching.

The game was changing, and Mandy intended to be the one changing it. After all, she was her grandmother's granddaughter – she knew how to play the long game, how to see the patterns others missed, how to turn traps into opportunities.

The doors opened silently on well-oiled hinges, admitting her into a world where stakes were measured not just in chips and cards, but in secrets and survival. Behind her, the casino's chaos continued its eternal dance. Ahead lay answers, danger, and the ghosts of decisions made decades ago.

Mandy stepped through, ready to face whatever waited in the shadows of her grandmother's past. The real game was just beginning.

GHOSTS IN THE MACHINE

The high-limit room wrapped around Mandy like a velvet glove, its atmosphere distinctly different from the main casino floor. Here, the air carried notes of leather and expensive cologne, the lighting subdued to create an illusion of intimacy. Crystal chandeliers cast prismatic patterns across gaming tables where fortunes changed hands in whispered bets. The carpet beneath her feet was thick enough to swallow footsteps, its deep burgundy pattern designed to hide the inevitable wine spills and cigarette burns of the wealthy and careless.

"Blueprints coming through now," Ghost's voice held an edge of excitement she rarely heard. "The renovation in '94 – they didn't just remodel, they completely restructured this section. Original plans show a secure room behind what's now the north wall. No current access points listed in the new plans."

Mandy moved through the space with deliberate casualness, her still-damp clothes drawing occasional glances from the room's other occupants. A poker game was in progress at the main table, the players' faces masks of studied indifference as chips worth more than most cars changed hands. The dealer's hands moved with hypnotic precision, cards flowing like water.

"The photo," she murmured, pretending to study the elaborate wall panels. "What was in the background? Any landmarks we can use?"

"Working on it." Ghost's typing reached a fevered pace. "Image enhancement shows... wait. That artwork on the wall behind them – it's still there. Three panels to your right. The one with the abstract gold pattern."

Mandy's eyes found it instantly — a massive piece that seemed to shift and change as she approached, its metallic elements catching the chandelier light. But something about it triggered another memory: her grandmother teaching her about codes hidden in plain sight, about how the best secrets were the ones people saw every day without understanding.

"The pattern," she breathed, studying it more closely now. "It's not abstract at all. It's a map."

"Multiple hostiles entering the room," Ghost cut in sharply. "Two from the main entrance, one through the service door. They're trying to box you in."

The jade pendant seemed to grow heavier against her skin as Mandy continued her careful study of the artwork. Yes — there it was. What looked like random geometric shapes were actually stylized representations of the casino's layout, with subtle markers indicating something beneath. Her grandmother's voice echoed in her memory: *Some treasures are hidden not by locks, but by people's assumptions about what they're seeing.*

A polite cough behind her broke her concentration. "Quite a beautiful piece, isn't it?" The voice was cultured, carrying traces of an accent she couldn't quite place. "The artist was commissioned specifically for this room's original design. Such attention to detail — it's something of a lost art these days."

Mandy didn't need to turn to know who it was. The Serpent's

reflection appeared in the artwork's glass surface, distorted by its geometric patterns. He was dressed impeccably in an Italian suit, looking for all the world like just another high-roller. Only the scar along his jaw and the predatory stillness of his stance betrayed his true nature.

"The rumors about ICE were true then," she said, keeping her voice steady as she tracked the positions of his men through the reflective surfaces around them. "About what was really happening beneath the casino."

"Smart girl." The Serpent moved to stand beside her, close enough that she could smell his expensive cologne mixing with the sharp note of gun oil. "Your grandmother taught you well. Though perhaps not everything." He studied the artwork with what seemed like genuine appreciation. "She always did have a gift for hiding things in plain sight. It's what made her such an effective operative. Until..."

"Until she saw something she couldn't ignore," Mandy finished. The pieces were clicking together now – Operation Glass Castle, the renovation, the secure room that had vanished from official plans. "Something worth burning everything down for."

"Mandy," Ghost's voice carried urgent warning. "Whatever you're about to do..."

But she was already moving, her body responding to instincts honed through years of training. The jade pendant swung free as she spun, catching the chandelier light and sending it refracting across the room like scattered diamonds. In that moment of distraction, her hand found the hidden panel she'd been searching for, fingers pressing the precise sequence her grandmother's journal had encrypted decades ago.

The world seemed to hold its breath as ancient mechanisms stirred beneath the casino's skin. Then everything happened at once.

"Because some secrets," she said, meeting the Serpent's gaze as the hidden door began to open, "are meant to be found."

The game was changing, and the real stakes were only now becoming clear.

ECHOES OF TRUTH

The hidden door opened with a whisper of perfectly balanced hydraulics, revealing a narrow passage that seemed to swallow light. The air that escaped carried the metallic tang of sealed spaces and old secrets, along with something else – a faint trace of lavender that made Mandy's heart clench. Her grandmother had been here, had walked this path, had made the choice that would reshape both their lives.

"Impressive," the Serpent said, his voice carrying genuine appreciation. "Though I suppose I shouldn't be surprised. She always said you had the gift – the ability to see patterns others missed." He hadn't moved to stop her, which set off warning bells in Mandy's mind. "But then, she would know. She helped design the tests that identified that particular talent in potential recruits."

The jade pendant seemed to pulse against her skin as pieces of a larger puzzle began sliding into place. Through her earpiece, she could hear Ghost's breathing, tense but controlled. His typing had stopped completely – a sign of how intently he was focused on what was unfolding.

"The recruitment programs," Mandy said, memories surfacing like bubbles in dark water. "The aptitude tests disguised as games. The training hidden in everyday lessons." She thought of all the skills her grandmother had taught her: how to read body language, how to memorize patterns, how to think three moves ahead. "You weren't just her handler. You were running the program together."

The Serpent's smile carried decades of history in its corners. "ICE was never just an organization, my dear. It was an idea – that the right people, trained from childhood, could become something more. Your grandmother understood that better than anyone. Until..." His expression darkened slightly. "Until she discovered the truth about Project Mirror."

"Mandy," Ghost's voice cut in urgently. "Multiple heat signatures approaching from the service corridors. Whatever answers are down there, you need to move now."

She could hear his fingers flying across keyboards again, fighting to buy her time. The hidden passage stretched before her, its walls lined with what looked like old computer equipment. Cables thick as her arm ran along the ceiling, disappearing into darkness.

"She left something for me to find," Mandy said, certainty blooming in her chest. The jade pendant's weight seemed to confirm it – her grandmother had always said jewelry should serve a purpose beyond decoration. "That's why you've been watching me all these years. Waiting to see if I'd crack the codes, follow the breadcrumbs."

"Smart girl," the Serpent said again, but this time there was something else in his voice – a note of what might have been regret. "But then, you'd have to be. The program doesn't accept anything less." He gestured to the passage. "After you. I believe it's time you learned what your grandmother really discovered down here."

The sound of approaching footsteps echoed from the main casino. Mandy's training screamed that entering a confined space with a known threat was suicide, but her instincts – the ones her grandmother had helped shape – told her something else. Sometimes the only way to understand the past was to walk directly into its shadows.

"Ghost," she murmured, "I'm going dark."

"Mandy, don't you dare—" His protest cut off as she removed the earpiece. Some conversations needed to happen without witnesses, even trusted ones.

The passage accepted them like a throat swallowing secrets. Emergency lights flickered to life as they descended, casting everything in a pale blue glow that made the shadows seem alive. The air grew cooler, carrying the distinct feel of being underground. Their footsteps echoed off walls that seemed to hum with dormant power.

"Project Mirror," the Serpent said as they walked, his voice carrying easily in the enclosed space, "was supposed to be the culmination of everything we'd worked for. A way to identify and train the next generation of operatives before they were old enough to develop conventional limitations. Your grandmother was brilliant at designing the protocols – tests hidden in playground games, training exercises disguised as normal childhood activities."

They reached a heavy door marked with a symbol Mandy recognized from her grandmother's journal – a stylized eye reflected infinitely in opposing mirrors. The Serpent placed his hand on a scanner that looked decades old but hummed with power that felt much more recent.

"But then she found the other files," he continued as the door opened. "The ones about what happened to the children who failed the tests. About the real purpose behind—"

He never finished the sentence. Mandy was already moving, her body responding to a trigger she'd recognized subconsciously – the same lavender scent, stronger now, that had always preceded her grandmother's self-defense lessons. The muscle memory took over: pivot, strike, duck under the counter-attack that experience told her was coming.

The Serpent was fast, incredibly so, but she had surprise and preparation on her side. Her grandmother's voice seemed to guide her movements: *Use their expectations against them. Let them think they're in control until the moment they're not.*

The jade pendant swung free as she spun, catching the emergency lighting and reflecting it in a pattern she suddenly understood was intentional – the same pattern hidden in the artwork upstairs, the one that had led her here. But this time, the light struck sensors hidden in the walls, triggering something deep in the facility's systems.

Alarms blared as heavy doors began to close. The Serpent's expression shifted from surprise to something like pride mixed with resignation. "You really are her granddaughter," he said, backing away as security protocols older than Mandy began to execute. "She knew you'd understand about the pendant. About the light code."

"She left me a key," Mandy said, understanding flowing like water. "Not just to this place, but to the truth about Project Mirror. About what ICE really was." The facility was sealing itself, decades-old contingencies finally triggering. Through the closing doors, she could see banks of computers coming to life, screens filling with data her grandmother had preserved against this very moment.

"The truth," the Serpent said, a hint of his accent bleeding through as doors began closing between them, "is more complicated than either of us knew. Ask yourself – why did she encrypt the files instead of destroying them? Why leave a trail for you to follow?" He held her gaze as the final door began to descend. "Find me when you've seen everything. We need to talk about what your grandmother really discovered – and why she made sure you'd be ready to finish what she started."

The door sealed with a pneumatic hiss, leaving Mandy alone in a room full of humming computers and decades of carefully preserved secrets. The jade pendant settled against her skin, its weight now feeling less like a burden and more like a promise kept across years of planning and preparation.

Screens flickered to life around her, each one displaying fragments of a story she was only beginning to understand. Her grandmother's voice seemed to whisper from the walls themselves: *Some truths can only be understood when you're ready to face them. Some choices echo across generations.

Mandy touched the pendant one last time, feeling the subtle irregularities that had always made her wonder if there was more to it than simple jewelry. "I'm ready," she said to the empty room, to her grandmother's memory, to the weight of history pressing in around her. "Show me everything."

The computers responded, and the real story began to unfold.

In Vegas, every game had stakes, every player had an angle, and every secret had its price. But some games ran deeper than others, their rules written in coded messages and hidden rooms, in jade pendants and encrypted files, in choices made decades ago that were only now bearing fruit.

The truth about Project Mirror – and about what her grandmother had really been protecting – was finally within reach. Now she just had to survive long enough to understand it.

The game wasn't ending. It was evolving into something else entirely.

And Mandy was done being a pawn in someone else's game. It was time to become a player.

14 WEB OF LIES

The Bellagio's penthouse suite had once been a testament to luxury, all crystal and gilt, with views that made Vegas sparkle like a jar of captured stars. Now, as Mandy crouched behind an overturned mahogany table, that same crystal lay shattered across Italian marble, and the only sparkle came from muzzle flashes reflecting off broken mirrors.

From her position at the private elevator, Mandy had watched Caruso's routine for three nights. He always arrived at precisely 9 PM, flanked by two guards who performed the same choreographed sweep of the suite. The predictability was useful, but it also made her suspicious. In her experience, people who followed exact patterns were either obsessive or putting on a show. She'd bet her grandmother's vintage Walther PPK that Caruso was the latter. Tonight, the suite's luxury would become her battlefield. She'd memorized every angle, every potential cover point, calculating sight lines and ricochet trajectories. Her grandmother's voice echoed in her memory: 'The best operators don't just see rooms – they see possibilities.

The service elevator's descent gave Mandy precious seconds to plan. In her mind, she mapped the Bellagio's basement layout, remembering the maintenance corridors she'd studied during her prep work. Three possible routes to the loading dock, each with its own risks. The west corridor offered the most cover but would take longer. The central path was direct but exposed. The east route... that's where she'd position ambushers if she were Murphy. Her grandmother had always emphasized the importance of thinking like your opponent. "Know their training," she'd say during their strategy sessions, "and you'll know their playbook." Murphy was ex-military, probably Special Forces given his efficiency. He'd expect her to take the tactically sound option. Sometimes the best move was the one that looked like a mistake.

Those possibilities were playing out now in ways her grandmother could never have predicted. The elegant suite had become a tactical puzzle, each piece of overturned furniture both obstacle and opportunity. The acrid smell of cordite hung in the air...

The acrid smell of cordite hung in the air, mingling with the metallic tang of blood and the lingering traces of someone's expensive cologne. Her ears rang from the gunfire that had erupted moments ago when one of Caruso's more observant guards had recognized her from a job in Macau. The recognition had turned a simple infiltration into a firefight that transformed the opulent hotel suite into a war zone.

Twenty minutes earlier, she'd walked into this room as Sarah Pierce, venture capitalist and potential investor in Caruso's legitimate businesses. Her wine-colored Versace gown had drawn appreciative glances, and her pitch had been flawless. She'd almost had him convinced – right up until that guard's eyes had widened with recognition.

She'd spent weeks building Sarah Pierce's background – a venture capitalist with just enough verifiable history to withstand surface scrutiny. The real Sarah Pierce was currently delayed in Singapore, thanks to Ghost's manipulation of flight schedules. Every detail had been calculated, from the slight Hong Kong accent to the Ming dynasty jade ring on her right hand – a touch that had made Caruso's eyes light up with recognition when she'd mentioned her family's collection.

Every detail had been calculated, just as her grandmother had taught her. 'The best covers grow from truth,' she'd said, helping a teenage Mandy craft her first alias. 'Let them see what they expect to see, then use those expectations against them.

At nineteen, Mandy moved with the fluid grace of a predator, her lean muscles coiled and ready. Her once-fiery red hair was now a sleek black, cut short and severe – another identity shed like a snake's skin. A thin scar ran along her left cheekbone, a souvenir from a job gone wrong in Bangkok. She'd earned that scar learning a hard lesson about trust, one that still ached on cold nights.

She pressed her back against the cool marble wall, the silk of her evening gown whispering against her skin. The Glock in her hand was a comforting weight, its grip warm and familiar. Across the room, pinned down behind a bullet-riddled bar, was her target – Vincent Caruso, a mid-level player in Blackwood's organization. She'd spent weeks tracking him, following the breadcrumbs of money laundering and weapons deals that led from Dubai to Vegas.

"Give it up, Thompson!" Caruso's voice was strained, a hint of desperation creeping in. The use of her real surname made her jaw clench – another leak in Blackwood's organization, another thread to follow. "You're outnumbered and outgunned. Blackwood wants you alive, but he didn't specify in how many pieces!"

The threat stirred a memory: her grandmother's voice, steady and calm during one of their training sessions. "Fear is just information, Mandy. Use it. Let it sharpen your senses, not dull them." She could still smell the gun oil and leather of her grandmother's workshop, still feel the weight of her first weapon – a .22 that seemed massive in her twelve-year-old hands.

Those summer afternoons in her grandmother's workshop had seemed like a game at first. Learn to field strip a pistol blindfolded. Memorize escape routes from every room. Practice moving silently across creaky floorboards. 'Details matter, little fox,' her grandmother would say, using the nickname that now felt like it belonged to another life. 'The difference between success and failure often comes down to what you noticed yesterday that everyone else missed today.

Mandy's lips curled into a sardonic smile. "Outnumbered? Please. I've taken out six of your goons already. Seems like pretty even odds to me." She allowed herself a moment to analyze the room's geometry. The suite's open floor plan had seemed elegant during her initial reconnaissance. Now it was a killing ground, with clear lines of fire broken only by overturned furniture and the massive support columns near the panoramic windows.

As if to punctuate her point, she spun out from cover, squeezing off two precise shots. The first caught one of Caruso's men in the shoulder as he tried to shift position, spinning him like a broken marionette. The second shot missed, but the ornate mirror behind the bar exploded in a shower of glittering shards, momentarily transforming the chaos into a macabre dance of light and shadow.

The wounded man's scream was cut short by his head hitting the marble floor. In the sudden quiet, Mandy could hear the distant thump of the hotel's bass-heavy nightclub, a surreal soundtrack to the violence. The music reminded her of another night, another hotel – the first time she'd followed in her grandmother's footsteps. That job had gone sideways too, but it had taught her the value of improvisation.

Her eyes darted around the room, taking in every detail with the heightened clarity of adrenaline. The once-pristine white carpet was now stained with spreading pools of crimson, each one a story of violence written in vital fluid. Bullet holes peppered the walls, exposing the drywall beneath gilded wallpaper. The suite's climate control had kicked into overdrive, trying to clear the gun smoke, creating currents of hot and cold air that made the torn curtains dance like restless ghosts.

A movement in her peripheral vision caught her attention – the subtle shift of weight on carpet, the whisper of fabric against fabric. One of Caruso's men was trying to flank her, using the cover of an overturned sofa. Amateur move. The thick pile carpet betrayed every step, even if she couldn't see him directly. Her grandmother's voice echoed in her memory: "Listen with your whole body, Mandy. Every movement tells a story if you know how to read it."

Mandy waited, every muscle tense, counting the seconds. Her grandmother's training echoed in her mind: "Patience separates professionals from thugs. Let them make the mistake. Your job is to be ready when they do."

One... two... three...

The man popped up, his gun trained on her position. But Mandy was already moving, her body responding to muscle memory honed through countless drills. She dropped and rolled, the whisper of fabric and the soft thud of her body on carpet barely audible over the chaos. Her gun barked twice, the shots placed with surgical precision. The man crumpled, his weapon clattering to the floor with a sound like fallen cutlery.

"That's seven," Mandy called out, letting a hint of dark humor color her voice. She needed Caruso rattled, needed him making mistakes. "Want to go for eight, Caruso? Or maybe you'd like to tell me about Operation Glass House? I hear Blackwood's got big plans."

The name of the operation had the desired effect. Caruso's reaction told her everything – the momentary freeze, the sharp intake of breath before he started shooting wildly. His response came in the form of bullets splintering the wooden credenza next to Mandy's head. She felt the sting of wood fragments on her cheek, the warm trickle of blood a stark contrast to the icy focus of her mind.

Operation Glass House was more than just another arms deal. She'd first heard the name while going through her grandmother's files, after discovering the hidden room behind the bookcase in the old brownstone. The files were incomplete – most had been destroyed or taken – but the name had appeared multiple times, always connected to something bigger. Something that had cost her grandmother her life.

The operation's name had appeared in her grandmother's journal entries with increasing frequency in the weeks before her disappearance. The last entry was particularly cryptic: 'Glass House isn't just an operation – it's a window into something bigger. If I'm right about the connections between Blackwood and [redacted], everything we thought we knew about [smudged] will change.' The rest of the page had been torn out, leaving Mandy with more questions than answers.

"Ghost," she subvocalized, knowing the mic hidden in her diamond earring would pick it up. The comms device was a marvel of miniaturization, courtesy of Ghost's connections in Silicon Valley. They'd been working together for eighteen months now, ever since that night in Berlin when he'd helped her escape from Blackwood's hunters. She still didn't know his real name, but she trusted him more than anyone else in her new life. "I could use an exit strategy right about now."

Their partnership had started as necessity but evolved into something closer to friendship, though neither of them would admit it. Ghost's voice was her lifeline in a world where trust was a luxury she rarely could afford. She'd never seen his face, didn't even know if Ghost was a he or a she, but she knew the sound of tension in that digitally altered voice better than she knew her own reflection these days.

"Working on it," came the tense reply in her earpiece. Ghost's voice was steady, but Mandy could hear the rapid-fire clicking of keyboards in the background. He never used just one system – paranoia kept you alive in their business. "Hotel security is scrambling – looks like somebody finally called in the cavalry. LVPD is three minutes out, responding to reports of shots fired."

A burst of gunfire forced Mandy to duck lower behind her cover. A crystal vase exploded near her head, showering her with water and fresh-cut roses. The flowers' sweet scent mixed incongruously with the acrid smell of gunpowder.

"Got something," Ghost continued. "There's a service elevator down the hall to your left. I can lock it down, give you an express ride to the basement. But Mandy... there's something else. Facial recognition just picked up Marcus Warren entering the casino floor."

Mandy's blood ran cold. Marcus Warren – Blackwood's cleaner, the man who'd executed three of her grandmother's old contacts in Hong Kong. If he was here, this was bigger than she'd thought. "Time frame?"

"He's with a four-man team, all moving like professionals. Five minutes, tops, before they reach your floor. Whatever's in Caruso's head, Blackwood really doesn't want you to get it."

Mandy's mind raced, formulating a plan. She needed Caruso alive – he was her best lead on Operation Glass House, and after two years of hunting, she was finally getting close to the truth about her grandmother's disappearance. But with both cops and Blackwood's cleanup crew closing in, her window was closing fast.

She reached into the concealed slit of her dress, fingers closing around a small cylinder. The flashbang felt cool against her palm, a stark contrast to the feverish heat of battle. Another gift from her grandmother's arsenal, pulled from a hidden cache the night she'd discovered the truth about her family's legacy.

The cache had been hidden behind a false wall in the garage, along with a letter that had changed everything. "My dearest Mandy," it had begun, "if you're reading this, then they finally caught up with me. Everything I've done, every lie I've told, was to keep you safe. But now you need to know the truth..."

A bullet whined past her ear, snapping her back to the present. Focus. Deal with the immediate threat first, then worry about the bigger picture. Her grandmother had taught her that too, during those long summer afternoons that she'd thought were just target practice but had been preparation for this life.

"Hey Caruso," she called out, letting a hint of fatigue creep into her voice. The best deceptions, her grandmother had taught her, were built on foundations of truth. "Looks like we're at a stalemate. How about we call it a draw? You walk away, I walk away, we live to fight another day?"

There was a moment of tense silence, broken only by the distant wail of approaching sirens. In that quiet, Mandy could almost hear her grandmother's voice: "The moment they think they've won is the moment they're most vulnerable."

"No dice, Thompson," Caruso finally replied, his voice thick with the confidence of a man who thought he held all the cards. "Blackwood wants you, and I aim to deliver. Even if I wanted to deal, it's too late. You've got nowhere to go."

That's what he thought. But Mandy had learned long ago that there was always a way out – you just had to be willing to make it yourself. She shifted her weight slightly, preparing for what came next.

"Ghost," she whispered. "When I move, I'm going to need that elevator ready. And... if this goes wrong, there's a file in my safehouse in Bangkok. The password is 'carousel-nineteen-echo.' Make sure it reaches my parents."

"It won't go wrong," Ghost replied firmly. "But I've got you covered. Always do."

Mandy allowed herself a grim smile. "I was hoping you'd say that." Her grandmother's first rule of combat had been simple: control the rhythm of the fight. Make them dance to your tune.

In one fluid motion, she pulled the pin on the flashbang and hurled it towards the bar. The small cylinder arced through the air, glinting in the flickering light of the ruined chandeliers like a falling star. Time seemed to slow as she watched it spin, remembering the first time she'd trained with one. She'd been fifteen, and the bang had scared her so badly she'd dropped her weapon. Her grandmother had made her practice until the response became automatic.

"Fire in the hole!" she yelled, squeezing her eyes shut and clapping her hands over her ears. The warning was part training, part tactical – anyone who instinctively looked toward her voice would catch the worst of the flash. Through her closed eyelids, she saw the brilliant flare of light, felt the concussive wave hit her like a physical blow.

The world exploded in a cacophony of sound and light. Even with her eyes closed and ears covered, the concussive force of the flashbang was overwhelming. She felt it in her bones, a deep, reverberating *thump* that seemed to stop time for a heartbeat. The blast wave rippled through the room, scattering paper and lighter debris in its wake, adding to the destruction that had transformed the suite into a battlefield.

"Three targets still up," Ghost's voice cut through the ringing in her ears. "Two by the bar, one trying to circle behind the column to your right. Murphy's team is in the elevator – you've got maybe two minutes."

As the ringing in her ears subsided, Mandy was already moving. She vaulted over the overturned table, her heels long since discarded, bare feet silent on the debris-strewn floor. Caruso and his remaining men were still reeling from the flashbang, disoriented and vulnerable. Their training showed in how they kept their weapons up, but their shots went wide, guided by instinct rather than aim.

The first guard never saw her coming. With practiced efficiency, Mandy disarmed him, using his own momentum to slam him into the wall. The impact knocked a framed painting loose, sending it crashing to the floor in a spray of glass and splintered wood. A swift elbow to the temple ensured he wouldn't be getting up anytime soon.

The second guard managed to get off a shot, but the flashbang had done its work. The bullet went wide, embedding itself in one of the suite's thick support columns. Mandy closed the distance before he could correct his aim, her knee driving up into his solar plexus. As he doubled over, she grabbed his head and brought it down to meet her rising knee. The crack of impact was lost in the general chaos, but she felt the way he went limp.

"Movement in the service corridor," Ghost warned. "Murphy's team split up – they're covering both exits."

Caruso was struggling to his feet behind the bar, his eyes wild and unfocused. Blood trickled from his ears — he'd been too close to the flashbang, taken the full force of the concussion. His expensive suit was covered in broken glass and spilled liquor, the sharp smell of high-end bourbon mixing with the gunsmoke in the air.

"It's over, Caruso," Mandy said, advancing on him. "But you know what? You were right about one thing — Blackwood does want me. Thing is, he wants you too. That cleanup crew heading our way? They're not coming to help."

She saw the moment the truth hit him, saw the color drain from his face. "You're lying," he stammered, but there was no conviction in his voice. "Marcus wouldn't... Blackwood promised..."

"Blackwood promises a lot of things," Mandy replied, thinking of all the bodies that had marked her path to this moment. "Ask yourself — why did he send his best cleaner to extract one mid-level operator? Unless... there's something in that head of yours that he doesn't want getting out."

Caruso's hand twitched toward the gun he'd dropped during the flashbang. Mandy was faster. She closed the distance in two quick strides, her fist connecting with his solar plexus. As he doubled over, gasping for air, she brought her knee up, catching him square in the face. There was a satisfying crunch as his nose broke, blood streaming down his chin to stain his thousand-dollar shirt.

"Nighty-night, Vince," Mandy growled, delivering a final blow to the side of his head. Caruso crumpled to the floor, unconscious but alive. She caught him before he hit the ground — she needed his brain intact for questioning.

"LVPD's setting up a perimeter," Ghost reported. "And Mandy... thermal imaging shows Murphy's team has night vision gear. Whatever's in Caruso's head, Blackwood really doesn't want it getting out."

The sound of heavy boots in the hallway spurred Mandy into action. She hoisted Caruso's limp form over her shoulder in a fireman's carry, her muscles straining under the dead weight. The moves were automatic, drilled into her during countless training sessions. "A hundred and twenty pounds of dead weight feels like three hundred," her grandmother used to say. "That's why we practice until it's muscle memory."

"Ghost, I've got the package. That elevator better be ready!" Mandy adjusted Caruso's weight across her shoulders, feeling the strain in her muscles. Her grandmother had always insisted on physical training, even when Mandy complained. Now she understood why.

"On it, boss. Elevator's locked down and waiting. You've got about 90 seconds before hotel security breaches the suite. Murphy's team is moving to cut off your escape routes – they're being smart about it."

Mandy staggered into the hallway, each step a battle against exhaustion and Caruso's dead weight. The service elevator stood open at the end of the corridor, a beacon of escape. The thick carpet muffled her footsteps, but also made each step harder, like running in sand. The corridor seemed to stretch endlessly ahead of her, the distance distorted by adrenaline and fatigue.

Through her earpiece, she could hear Ghost's fingers flying across keyboards. "LVPD's setting up a perimeter faster than usual. Someone must have called in a favor. And Mandy... satellite feeds are showing more activity. Four black SUVs just pulled into the parking structure. Professional drivers, no plates."

"More of Blackwood's people?" She was fifteen feet from the elevator now. The corridor remained empty, but she could hear voices and footsteps from both directions.

"Negative. Different signature. These ones feel government. Wait – thermal imaging just picked up movement in the stairwell. Murphy's team is – "

"LVPD! Freeze!"

The shout came just as Mandy reached the elevator. She dove inside, using Caruso's unconscious body to cushion her fall. Rolling to her feet, she caught a glimpse of uniformed officers rounding the corner, their weapons drawn. The doors slid shut with a soft *ding* that seemed absurdly genteel given the circumstances.

As the elevator began its descent, Mandy finally allowed herself a moment to catch her breath. Her reflection in the mirrored walls was a sight to behold – designer gown torn and bloodstained, hair wild, a fierce grin on her face despite the fatigue etched in every line. The woman in the mirror looked dangerous, competent, nothing like the girl she'd been two years ago.

For a moment, she saw herself as her parents must picture her - their lost daughter, somewhere in the world, growing up without them. The weight of that grief, multiplied across two years of birthdays, holidays, ordinary days marked by absence, threatened to overwhelm her. She remembered her last morning at home – the smell of coffee and toast, her mother humming in the kitchen, her father absorbed in his newspaper. They had no idea their daughter was about to disappear, following the breadcrumbs of her grandmother's secret life into a world of shadows.

But alongside the guilt lived a harder truth: she couldn't go back. Not just because of the legal consequences, but because she wasn't that girl anymore. The path she'd chosen had transformed her, taught her things that couldn't be unlearned. How to read people's weaknesses. How to exploit trust. How to become someone else so completely that sometimes her real self felt like the disguise.

"Cutting it a bit close there, Ghost," she panted, pushing the memories aside. Now wasn't the time for nostalgia.

"Hey, I got you out, didn't I?" Ghost's voice held its usual sardonic humor, but Mandy could hear the tension underneath. There was a pause, filled with the sound of rapid typing. "We've got another problem. Murphy's team split up – two in the stairwell, two taking the main elevator. They're boxing you in."

"Options?"

"Working on it. But Mandy... there's something else. I've been running facial recognition on the new players in the parking structure. One of them pinged an intelligence database. These aren't Blackwood's people – they're CIA."

The revelation hit her like a physical blow. CIA involvement meant this was bigger than just Blackwood's organization. Her grandmother's last message flashed through her mind: "Be careful who you trust, especially those who claim to be on the right side of the law."

The CIA's involvement triggered another memory – a conversation she'd overheard between her grandmother and a visitor late one night. She'd been fourteen, supposedly asleep upstairs, but curiosity had drawn her to the heating vent where voices carried from the study below. 'They're using Glass House as cover,' her grandmother had said. 'The question is, cover for what?' The visitor's response had been too quiet to hear, but her grandmother's sharp intake of breath had spoken volumes.

The pieces were starting to align - her grandmother's research, Blackwood's obsession, the CIA's involvement. Glass House wasn't just an operation; it was a window into something that powerful people wanted kept sealed. The question was: which side were the CIA really on?

The memory of that night came back with crystal clarity. Her grandmother's study had always been off-limits, which only made teenage Mandy more curious. The heating vent had become her secret window into an adult world she barely understood. The visitor's voice had been male, cultured, with a slight Boston accent. "They're using Glass House as cover," her grandmother had said, "The question is, cover for what?" "The intelligence community has changed, Gloria," the man had replied. "The old alliances don't mean what they used to." "Since when does 'intelligence community' mean selling secrets to the highest bidder?" The sound of ice cubes clinking in a glass. A heavy sigh. "Since the wall came down and everyone decided the rules didn't matter anymore. Be careful, Gloria. Some doors, once opened..." Her grandmother's sharp intake of breath had spoken volumes. "They've already reached out to him, haven't they? To Blackwood?

"Ghost, remember that file in Bangkok I mentioned? There's something else you need to know about it. If anything happens to me – "

"Save it," Ghost cut her off. "Nothing's happening to you. Not on my watch. Van's waiting in the loading dock, but we need to be smart about this. Murphy's people will be expecting you to go for the obvious exit."

Their partnership wasn't just about skills or necessity anymore. In a world where trust was as rare as silence in Vegas, Ghost had become her constant. No questions about her past, no judgment about her choices, just unwavering support and the occasional sardonic comment. Sometimes she wondered if Ghost had someone like her grandmother too – someone who'd opened their eyes to the shadow world and taught them how to survive in it.

The elevator continued its descent, the floor numbers ticking down with inexorable precision. Mandy's mind raced, considering and discarding options. Her grandmother had taught her to always have three escape routes planned. Right now, she'd settle for one.

"How long until Murphy's team reaches the basement?"

"Ninety seconds, give or take. The two in the stairwell are moving fast, but they're being cautious. They know your reputation."

Mandy allowed herself a grim smile at that. Two years ago, she'd been a teenager worried about college applications. Now she was the kind of person that professional killers approached with caution. Her grandmother would have been proud – and terrified.

15 THE LOTUS BLOOMS

The Parisian café bustled with life, the clinking of espresso cups and murmur of conversation a stark contrast to the tension thrumming through Mandy's body. At twenty, she wore her disguise like a second skin - ash blonde hair swept into an elegant chignon, oversized sunglasses hiding her watchful eyes, a crisp white blouse and tailored slacks suggesting tasteful wealth.

The skills that had once felt foreign - the constant awareness, the layered deceptions - were now as natural as breathing. She caught her reflection in a café window: ash blonde hair swept into an elegant chignon that had taken hours to perfect, the oversized sunglasses masking not just her eyes but the constant calculation behind them. Her crisp white blouse and tailored slacks suggested tasteful wealth, the kind that didn't need to announce itself.

Ghost's voice crackled softly in her ear: 'Perimeter still clear. Our friend in the newspaper kiosk confirms no suspicious activity in the last hour.' The voice was steady, professional - a far cry from their early days when every operation felt like a desperate gamble.

Her fingers toyed with the jade lotus pendant around her neck, its familiar weight both comforting and mocking. Five years of searching, of clawing her way through the underworld's darkest corners, had led to this moment.

Each step of that journey flashed through her mind: the first time she'd found Jasmine's name in her grandmother's encrypted files, the night in Bangkok when she'd barely escaped Blackwood's cleanup team, the three months she'd spent learning to move through high society from an aging con artist in Monte Carlo. All preparation for this moment, this meeting.

The waiter appeared at her elbow, startling her from her reverie. "Un autre café, mademoiselle?"

Mandy smiled, her French impeccable. "Non, merci. I'm waiting for someone."

As if on cue, a figure appeared at the café's entrance. Mandy's breath caught in her throat. The years had been kind to Jasmine Murphy - her dark hair now streaked with elegant silver, laugh lines crinkling the corners of her eyes. But there was a wariness to her stance, a tension in the set of her shoulders that spoke volumes.

Their eyes met across the crowded terrace. For a moment, the world seemed to stand still, the chatter of patrons fading to a dull roar in Mandy's ears. Then Jasmine was moving, weaving between tables with graceful purpose.

Mandy had studied every photo, every video clip she could find of Jasmine Murphy, but none had captured the intensity of her presence. The way she carried herself spoke of decades in the shadows, of a life spent watching and being watched. In her bearing, Mandy recognized the same careful grace her grandmother had possessed - the ability to command attention while appearing to avoid it.

"I wasn't sure you'd come," Mandy said softly as Jasmine took the seat across from her.

Jasmine's smile was tinged with sadness. "I wasn't sure I would either. But some ghosts refuse to stay buried."

The waiter materialized again, and Jasmine ordered a cappuccino in flawless French. Mandy noted the slight tremor in her hand as she placed the order, the only outward sign of her nerves.

"You look so much like her," Jasmine murmured once the waiter had gone. "It's like seeing a ghost."

Mandy leaned forward, her voice low and urgent. "I need to know the truth, Jasmine. About ICE, about Blackwood, about everything. No more half-truths, no more protection. I'm not a child anymore."

Jasmine's eyes flickered to the pendant around Mandy's neck, recognition and pain flashing across her features. "No, you're certainly not a child. But you don't know what you're asking. The truth... it's a dangerous thing, Mandy."

Before Mandy could respond, her instincts screamed a warning. The hairs on the back of her neck stood up, a chill running down her spine despite the warm Parisian sun.

"We need to move," she said, her tone brooking no argument. "Now."

Jasmine's eyes widened, but she didn't hesitate. In one fluid motion, they both stood, Mandy tossing a handful of euros on the table.

The air changed subtly - a shift in pressure, a minute alteration in the ambient noise that most would never notice. But Mandy had been trained to recognize these warning signs, just as she spotted the too-casual way three men at different tables checked their watches within seconds of each other. The pattern was clear: professional hitters, coordinating their approach with practiced precision.

They were halfway down the street when the first gunshot rang out. Screams erupted from the café terrace as patrons dove for cover. Mandy grabbed Jasmine's arm, pulling her into a narrow alleyway.

"How did they find us?" Jasmine gasped as they ran, her heels clicking on the cobblestones.

Mandy's mind raced, adrenaline sharpening her focus. "I don't know. But we need to lose them fast."

They emerged onto a bustling boulevard, the midday traffic a chaos of honking horns and screeching brakes. Without breaking stride, Mandy led them straight into the maelstrom, weaving between cars with reckless abandon.

A sleek black sedan screeched to a halt beside them, the passenger door flying open. "Get in!" a familiar voice shouted.

"Ghost?" Mandy's surprise was quickly overtaken by relief. She practically shoved Jasmine into the car before diving in after her.

The car peeled away from the curb, engine roaring as Ghost expertly maneuvered through the Parisian traffic. In the rearview mirror, Mandy caught glimpses of their pursuers - nondescript men in dark suits, their expressions grim and determined.

They weaved through the ancient streets, Mandy's mind mapping possible routes even as she guided Jasmine through the chaos. Every turn was a calculation - speed versus cover, visibility versus escape options. The cobblestones were treacherous under their feet, but the uneven surface worked to their advantage, making their pursuers' coordinated approach more difficult.

"How did you know?" Mandy asked, her breath coming in short gasps.

Ghost's eyes never left the road, hands white-knuckled on the steering wheel. "I've been monitoring Blackwood's communications. They've known about this meeting for days. It was a trap, Mandy."

The implications hit her like a physical blow. She'd been so focused on finally meeting Jasmine, on getting answers, that she'd let her guard down. Amateur mistake.

As Ghost navigated the winding streets, Mandy studied Jasmine's profile. There were questions that couldn't wait until they reached safety. 'The pendant,' she began, touching the jade at her throat. 'I found the inscription...

Jasmine's composed facade cracked slightly. "I gave it to her the night before... before everything fell apart. We had a plan to expose Blackwood's entire operation. The evidence was hidden in plain sight, encoded in financial records that looked perfectly legitimate. But someone warned him."

"The mole," Mandy said. "The one Ghost has been trying to identify."

"Not just any mole." Jasmine's voice dropped lower. "Someone at the highest level of-"

Jasmine's voice cut through Mandy's self-recrimination. "We need to get off the streets. I have a safe house not far from here."

Ghost nodded, taking a sharp turn that sent them all lurching to the side. "Direct me."

As Jasmine called out directions, Mandy's mind whirled. The jade pendant seemed to burn against her skin, a constant reminder of how much was at stake.

They lost their pursuers in the winding streets of Montmartre, finally pulling into a nondescript garage attached to a row of townhouses. The moment the car stopped, Mandy was out, gun drawn, scanning for threats.

"Clear," she called after a tense moment. "Let's move."

The building looked unremarkable from the street - exactly as intended. But as they approached, Mandy's trained eye picked up the layers of security: cameras masked as architectural details, pressure plates disguised beneath antique carpets, infrared sensors hidden in ornate molding. The safe house occupied the top two floors, its limestone facade weathered by centuries of Parisian winters. Inside, the space was a study in understated elegance - hardwood floors that had witnessed generations of secrets, tasteful art selected not just for aesthetics but for their ability to conceal wall safes.

Mandy noted the subtle security measures as they approached - cameras disguised as architectural details, pressure plates hidden beneath antique carpets, infrared sensors masked by ornate molding. Jasmine's tradecraft was elegant, nearly invisible to anyone who hadn't spent years learning to spot such things.

Inside, the space was a study in understated elegance - hardwood floors that had witnessed generations of secrets, tasteful art selected not just for aesthetics but for their ability to conceal wall safes. Nothing drew attention, yet everything served a purpose. Mandy's trained eye caught the subtle signs of a prepared operative - the slightly off-center painting hiding a surveillance hub, the reinforced windows disguised by delicate curtains, the multiple exit points camouflaged as service entrances.

Ghost moved through the space with professional efficiency, setting up portable scramblers and running security protocols. 'Clean so far,' they reported, fingers dancing across a laptop keyboard. 'But we should assume they'll trace us eventually.'"

The Revelation of the Case (expansion after "Your grandmother left this for you."):

"Jasmine's hands trembled slightly as she input the combination, each number seeming to carry the weight of memory. The mechanism's soft clicks echoed in the quiet room. 'She spent years preparing this,' Jasmine said, her voice thick with emotion. 'Building the network, gathering evidence, creating failsafes. She knew the risks - knew Blackwood would never stop hunting her. But she believed some truths were worth dying for.'

The safe's door swung open with a whisper of perfectly maintained hinges. Inside lay a slim metal case, its brushed steel surface unmarked except for a single engraved snowflake - ICE's personal symbol. Jasmine lifted it with the reverence of someone handling sacred texts.

'The last time I saw this case,' she said, placing it carefully on the coffee table, 'was the night before everything fell apart. Amanda... your grandmother... she said it contained enough evidence to bring down not just Blackwood, but the entire system he represented. Power structures that had existed for generations, corrupting everything they touched.

But Mandy's trained eye caught the subtle signs of a prepared operative - the slightly off-center painting concealing a wall safe, the reinforced windows, the multiple exit points.

As Ghost secured the perimeter, Mandy turned to Jasmine. The older woman looked shaken but composed, her eyes never leaving Mandy's face.

"I suppose," Jasmine said softly, "it's time for that truth you've been seeking."

She moved to a bookshelf, fingers dancing over the spines before pulling one slightly forward. With a soft click, a hidden panel slid open, revealing a small safe.

Jasmine's hands shook slightly as she input the combination. "Your grandmother left this for you. She always believed... always hoped you'd follow in her footsteps one day."

The safe swung open, revealing a slim metal case. Jasmine lifted it reverently, placing it on the coffee table between them.

"Everything you need to know is in there," she said, her voice barely above a whisper. "But Mandy, you need to understand. Once you open this, there's no going back. The world as you know it will never be the same."

Mandy's fingers hovered over the case, her heart pounding in her chest. Five years of searching, of risking everything, had led to this moment. She thought of her parents, of the life she'd left behind. Of the woman she'd become, shaped by necessity and the burning need for answers.

With a deep breath, she flipped the latches on the case.

"I'm ready," she said, meeting Jasmine's gaze. "Whatever the truth is, I can handle it."

As the case opened, revealing a stack of documents and a small, encrypted hard drive, Mandy felt a shift in the air. The final pieces of the puzzle were within her grasp.

But little did she know, the truth would test her in ways she could never have imagined. The game was changing, the stakes higher than ever.

And somewhere in the shadows, Marcus Blackwood watched and waited, his web of lies and deceit ready to ensnare them all.

Mandy's fingers traced the case's cool surface, feeling subtle irregularities that might be hidden mechanisms or encoded messages. Five years of searching had led to this moment. She thought of her parents - their faces etched with worry in her last memory of home. Of the life she'd left behind, the normal future she'd sacrificed for this path. Of the woman she'd become, forged in the crucible of necessity and the burning need for answers.

With a deep breath that carried the weight of years, she flipped the latches. Each click seemed to mark a point of no return, a final step away from any chance of returning to her old life.

'I'm ready,' she said, meeting Jasmine's gaze with steel in her own. 'Whatever the truth is, I can handle it.'

The case opened with military precision, revealing its contents layer by layer. A stack of documents - some yellowed with age, others pristine in their protective sleeves. A small encrypted hard drive that seemed to hum with potential energy. And beneath it all, a handwritten note in her grandmother's elegant script: 'For my snowflake, when the frost finally spreads.'

But even as Mandy reached for the first document, forces were moving against them. In a penthouse office across the city, Marcus Blackwood watched multiple surveillance feeds, his manicured fingers steepled beneath his chin. 'Let them have their moment,' he murmured to his assembled lieutenants. 'Let them think they've won. The game is only beginning.'

The truth would test Mandy in ways she could never have imagined. The real war - the one her grandmother had died preparing for - was about to begin. And somewhere in the gathering shadows, wheels within wheels turned, spinning webs of deceit that would shake the very foundations of power itself.

16 SINS OF THE MOTHER

The soft glow of computer screens bathed the safe house in an eerie blue light, casting elongated shadows across the worn Persian carpet - a touch of luxury in their makeshift command center. The air carried the bitter tang of hours-old coffee and the metallic undertone of gun oil from their cleaned weapons. Mandy's eyes burned from hours of poring over the documents from her grandmother's case, the words beginning to blur together like insects crawling across the pages. Through the partially opened window, the Parisian night air carried the scent of fresh baguettes from the boulangerie below, mingling with distant sirens and bursts of laughter from late-night revelers - a world away from their hidden war.

Scattered across the antique desk, ICE's documents told fragments of a larger story - bank statements with curious gaps, surveillance photos with faces carefully circled in red ink, and handwritten notes in her grandmother's precise script. Each page seemed to pulse with hidden meaning, like a cipher waiting to be broken. The jade pendant's weight against Mandy's chest matched the heaviness in her limbs - they'd been at this for eighteen hours straight, sustained by nothing but coffee and determination.

The safe house itself was a study in contradictions: elegant crown molding and ancient hardwood floors juxtaposed against their modern equipment, cables snaking across antique furniture. Ghost had converted an ornate writing desk into a command station, multiple monitors casting their harsh glow across the delicate marquetry. Jasmine sat across from Mandy in a high-backed chair that had probably hosted aristocrats in a previous century, her face etched with worry and fatigue, one hand absently touching the weapon at her hip. Ghost's fingers flew over a keyboard, decrypting the hard drive's contents with single-minded focus. The air was thick with unspoken tension, heavy with the weight of long-buried secrets.

Mandy leaned back, pressing the heels of her hands against her eyes. The jade pendant around her neck seemed to pulse with an energy of its own, a constant reminder of how far she'd come – and how much farther she had to go.

"This can't be right," she murmured, more to herself than the others. "It doesn't make sense."

Jasmine's voice was gentle, tinged with a sadness that made Mandy's heart ache. "Sometimes the truth is harder to accept than the lies we tell ourselves."

Mandy's eyes snapped open, fixing Jasmine with an intense gaze. "But my mother? Involved in all of this? She's... she was always so normal, so..."

"Protective?" Jasmine finished, a hint of a sad smile playing at her lips. "Sometimes the greatest act of love is shielding those we care about from the darkness in our past."

Ghost's voice cut through the tension, sharp and urgent. "You need to see this."

Mandy moved to the computer, her body protesting after hours of stillness. The monitor's glow cast harsh shadows across her face as a video file loaded – security camera footage from what looked like an upscale hotel lobby. The timestamp in the corner read 05/17/2004 – just days before ICE's disappearance. The security footage played out in grainy black and white, but the figures were unmistakable. ICE moved with the same precise grace Mandy remembered, though her shoulders carried a visible weight.

Her grandmother's signature silver braid caught the hotel's overhead lights, creating a halo effect that made Mandy's chest ache with sudden longing. But it was her mother who held her attention. Abby looked younger, of course, but there was something else - a hardness to her movements that Mandy had never seen before, a vigilant awareness in the way she continuously scanned their surroundings. She moved like someone trained, like someone who knew the dangers lurking in shadows.

Mandy's fingers traced the edge of the monitor, as if she could reach through the pixels and grab hold of that moment in time. The elegant hotel lobby behind her mother and grandmother seemed surreal now - all that polished marble and crystal, disguising a meeting that would change everything. She remembered that spring in fragments: her mother's sudden business trips, hushed phone calls that ended when Mandy entered the room, the growing collection of burner phones in the kitchen drawer she wasn't supposed to know about.

"Turn up the audio," Mandy demanded, her voice hoarse.

Ghost's fingers flew across the keyboard, enhancing the audio. The sound of a chamber orchestra filtered through first - some hotel lobby performance - before their voices emerged from the background noise:

"The board meeting was compromised," Abby was saying, her words clipped and professional - so different from her usual warm maternal tone. "Harrison made the switch, but Blackwood's people were watching. They're getting closer, Mom. They know about the Panama accounts."

ICE's response came with a familiar steel in her voice: "Then we move everything to Singapore. Liu still owes me from Jakarta."

"That's not the point!" Abby's composure cracked, real fear bleeding through. "Blackwood's closing in. We need to end this, for all our sakes.

"We're too close to the truth, Abby," ICE's response was firm, unyielding. "I can't walk away now, not when we're on the verge of exposing everything."

"And what about Mandy?" The pain in her mother's voice was palpable. "What kind of life can she have with this hanging over us?"

The image froze on ICE's face, her expression a complex mix of determination and regret. Mandy stared at her grandmother's features, so similar to her own, searching for answers in those pixelated eyes. The jade pendant seemed heavier against her chest, its weight a reminder of all the secrets she was only beginning to uncover.

"She knew," Mandy whispered, her mind reeling. "Mom knew everything, all along."

Drawn to the window, Mandy found her reflection ghostly against the Parisian skyline. Below, tourists laughed and took photos, their faces illuminated by the soft glow of café lights. How many of them, she wondered, were carrying their own secrets?

A memory surfaced, sharp and clear: sunshine streaming through their kitchen window in Minnesota - their third house that year - catching dust motes in its beam. Her mother teaching her to make cookies when she was seven, the warm, sweet scent of vanilla and melting butter filling the air. Their matching aprons dusted with flour, her mother's hands steady and sure as they measured ingredients with military precision. Even then, Mandy realized, there had been signs - the way Abby always positioned herself facing the door, how she checked the locks three times before starting to bake.

"Sometimes," Abby had said, measuring vanilla with careful precision, her wedding ring clinking against the metal measuring spoons, "the most important ingredient is the one you can't see." She'd tapped Mandy's nose, leaving a smudge of flour, both of them giggling. But there had been something in her eyes, a shadow that seven-year-old Mandy hadn't understood. At the time, Mandy had thought she meant love. Now she wondered if her mother had been talking about secrets all along.

"There's more," Ghost called out, their voice tight with tension. "Multiple meetings, different locations. London, Prague, Singapore... your mother was everywhere ICE went, always a few steps behind."

Jasmine moved to stand beside Mandy at the window. "You're thinking about the birthday parties," she said softly. It wasn't a question.

Mandy's throat tightened. Every year, without fail, her mother had thrown elaborate birthday celebrations - even when money was tight, even when they'd had to move suddenly for her father's "work." She'd never missed one, except...

"She wasn't there for my sixteenth," Mandy whispered. "Said she had food poisoning, couldn't get out of bed. But I remember hearing her on the phone that night, speaking in that clipped voice she used when she was angry." Her hand went to the jade pendant. "The next morning, this was on my pillow. No note, just..."

Jasmine's hand on her shoulder was a grounding presence. "Your mother was caught between two worlds, Mandy. Trying to protect you, to give you a normal life, while also..."

"While also what?" Mandy spun to face Jasmine, anger and confusion warring in her voice. "Betraying her own mother? Covering up corruption?"

The older woman's eyes flashed with a hint of steel. "It's not that simple, and you know it. The world ICE inhabited, the one you've chosen to enter – it's full of shades of gray. Your mother did what she thought was best for you, for your family."

Mandy's laugh was bitter, edged with pain. "And look how well that turned out."

Ghost's voice cut through the tension once more. "Guys, we've got a problem. Someone's trying to breach our security protocols. They're good – really good." Their fingers flew across multiple keyboards, windows of scrolling code reflecting in their glasses. "These aren't your average hackers. They're using techniques I've only seen from—"

"Blackwood's cyber division," Jasmine finished, already moving. She crossed to a hidden panel in the ornate wainscoting, retrieving additional magazines and a compact medical kit. The practiced efficiency of her movements spoke of years of similar evacuations.

The room erupted into a flurry of activity. Ghost initiated their emergency protocols, layers of encryption descending over their systems like digital armor. Jasmine moved with surprising speed for her age, checking weapons and escape routes with the precision of someone who'd survived countless close calls.

Mandy forced her tumultuous emotions down, years of training kicking in. The jade pendant seemed to pulse against her skin in rhythm with her heartbeat as muscle memory took over. "How long can you hold them off?" she asked Ghost, her voice steady despite the turmoil inside.

"Ten minutes, maybe less." Ghost's voice was clipped, focused. A bead of sweat rolled down their temple as their hands danced across the keyboards. "They're adapting to our countermeasures faster than I can deploy them. Whatever plan you've got, make it fast."

Mandy's mind raced, weighing options and discarding them just as quickly. They couldn't stay and fight – not here, not with so much crucial information at risk. The safe house's elegant façade now felt like a trap, its antique beauty a mockery of their desperate situation. Running was the obvious choice, but to where? In her peripheral vision, she caught sight of Jasmine methodically checking exit routes, her movements a silent reminder of all the times ICE must have faced similar moments.

Then her eyes fell on a detail in one of ICE's documents – a series of numbers and letters that had seemed random at first glance, but now... The pattern clicked into place like tumblers in a lock. Her grandmother's meticulous mind, always three steps ahead, always leaving breadcrumbs for those who knew where to look.

"I know where we need to go," Mandy said, the beginnings of a plan forming. Her fingertips traced the cryptic sequence. "But it's risky as hell."

Jasmine's eyes met hers across the room, understanding passing between them. "Your grandmother's failsafe?"

Mandy nodded, her throat tight. "If I'm reading this right, she left a backup of everything – all her evidence, all her research – in a secure location. Somewhere even Blackwood couldn't touch."

"Where?" Ghost asked, never taking their eyes off the screens. The sound of their typing had taken on an almost desperate rhythm.

Mandy's smile was grim. "Where it all began. We're going home."

The next few minutes were a blur of precise chaos. Ghost transferred what they could to encrypted drives, their system's fans whining in protest at the speed of the data transfer. Jasmine moved through the safe house with practiced efficiency, eliminating traces of their presence. The sound of approaching sirens added urgency to their movements, their wail cutting through the Parisian night like a warning bell.

As they prepared to leave, Mandy paused at the door, her hand going to the jade pendant. In her mind's eye, she saw her mother's face – not the worried, secretive woman from the video, but the loving, protective presence of her childhood. How many times had Abby stood in a doorway like this, weighing choices that would ripple through years of secrets and lies?

"I'll find the truth, Mom," she whispered. "For all of us."

With a nod to her companions, Mandy stepped out into the Parisian night. The city of lights sparkled around them, oblivious to the war being waged in its shadows. Below, tourists still laughed and took photos, their carefree joy a stark contrast to the tension thrumming through Mandy's body. As they melted into the darkness, she felt a shift in the air – a sense that they were crossing a threshold from which there was no return.

The sins of the past were coming due, and Mandy was determined to be the one balancing the scales. Whatever the cost, whatever the consequences, she would see this through to the end.

Little did she know, the true test of her resolve – and her loyalty – was yet to come.

17 HONOR AMONG THIEVES

The warehouse loomed before them, its corrugated metal walls rising like a fortress into the December night. Rust streaks painted dark tears down its sides, visible even in the weak light from the distant streetlamps. Above, stars pierced through gaps in the racing clouds, casting shifting shadows across the building's scarred façade. The wind carried the sharp bite of approaching snow, making Mandy's eyes water as she surveyed the structure. Her breath formed dense clouds in the frigid air, each exhale accompanied by the soft creak of her leather jacket as she mapped out entry points.

Security cameras, their red lights dead for years, hung uselessly from corners. Loading bays, their doors sealed with heavy chains, lined the eastern wall. The door's hinges groaned as she pulled it open, releasing a wave of stale air scented with metal and determination.

"You sure about this, boss?" Ghost's voice crackled through her earpiece, the static interference making his usually steady tone waver. The sound bounced inside her skull, mixing with the subtle hum of the surveillance equipment concealed beneath her jacket. Even Ghost, who'd talked her through countless operations, couldn't hide his unease about this one.

Mandy's lips quirked in a humorless smile, the expression feeling stiff on her face. She tasted copper, realizing she'd been chewing her inner cheek again – an old habit her grandmother had tried to break her of. "Not even a little. But we're out of options."

With a deep breath that filled her lungs with the sharp winter air, she stepped out of the shadows. Her boots made soft crunching sounds against the frost-covered gravel as she approached the side door. The metal surface was a patchwork of rust and peeling paint, its surface rough beneath her gloved fingertips. Three sharp raps echoed in the empty lot, each impact sending tiny flakes of rust drifting to the ground. She paused, counting heartbeats, then delivered two more knocks. The sound seemed to hang in the frigid air like her frozen breath.

For a long moment, nothing happened. Mandy felt the weight of her weapon against her ribs, the jade pendant cool against her throat. Then came the sound – a series of mechanical clicks and the scrape of metal on metal. The door protested with a groan that reminded her of whale song, low and mournful, as it swung inward on corroded hinges.

The interior hit her senses in layers. First came the smell – motor oil and industrial cleaners underlaid with the metallic tang of old machinery and something else, sharp and chemical that made her nose tingle. The temperature dropped at least ten degrees from the outside, the air hanging dense and still like the inside of a tomb. Overhead, ancient fluorescent lights buzzed and flickered, their sickly yellow glow creating more shadows than illumination. The occasional drip of water from somewhere in the darkness echoed off the sheet metal walls, each drop a liquid metronome marking time.

As Mandy's eyes adjusted to the gloom, details emerged from the darkness like a developing photograph. Massive support columns rose into the shadows, their bases surrounded by forgotten crates and rusted equipment. Chains hung from unseen rafters, swaying almost imperceptibly in air currents she couldn't feel. The concrete floor bore decades of stains and tire marks, telling silent stories of the building's industrial past.

And there were the figures – darker shapes against the darkness, scattered throughout the cavernous space like chess pieces on an invisible board. Each one a ghost from her past, a connection to the world her grandmother had inhabited. The subtle shifts of their breathing and the whisper of fabric against fabric told her they were watching, waiting, judging whether ICE's granddaughter was worthy of their time.

"Well, well," a gravelly voice called out. "Look what the cat dragged in."

Mandy turned to face the speaker, a lean, weathered man leaning against a workbench. "Hello, Cobra," she said, keeping her voice neutral. "It's been a while."

Cobra's laugh was more of a bark. "Five years, give or take. Last I heard, you were making quite a name for yourself. ICE's little protégé, all grown up."

Metal creaked and rubber soles whispered against concrete as the others emerged from their chosen darkness. They moved with the practiced grace of predators, each keeping to the shadows as if they were second skins. The weak fluorescent lights caught glimpses of them – a flash of metal here, the glint of eyes there – before they fully revealed themselves.

Whisper materialized like smoke given form, her movements so fluid they seemed to bend the dim light around her. She wore her trademark outfit – clothes so nondescript they defied memory, her face a canvas primed for any identity she chose to wear. Only her eyes, changing color with each shift of light, remained constant. The faint scent of theatrical makeup and spirit gum followed in her wake, tools of her deadly trade. Mandy watched her melt into the shadows, remembering how her grandmother used to say Whisper could vanish in an empty room.

The warehouse creaked, settling into its darkness, before Clockwork's arrival announced itself with the subtle whir and click of the custom brace on his left leg. The symphony of gears and springs that he'd engineered himself echoed off the metal walls. Grease stained his fingerless gloves, and the pockets of his utility vest bulged with the tools of his craft. His eyes, behind those custom lenses, mapped every exit and entrance - an old habit ICE had drilled into all of them.

A cigarette's ember traced a lazy arc through the darkness before Specter emerged like his namesake, the air around him carrying the sharp bite of cordite that never quite seemed to leave him. His scarred hands, steady enough to defuse a hair trigger in the dark, tapped an irregular rhythm against his thigh. The explosive expert's presence seemed to make the shadows deeper, more dangerous.

And in the back, nearly motionless but commanding attention like a knife blade catching light, stood Nova. Her silver hair caught what little light reached her, creating a halo effect that reminded Mandy of old photographs from her grandmother's glory days. Even partially concealed, Nova's presence filled the warehouse with a tension that made the air feel electric."

This revision spaces out the introductions, giving each character more room to breathe and adding sensory details that enhance the atmosphere. It also weaves in references to ICE, strengthening the connection between past and present.

ICE's oldest friend and most dangerous ally kept to the deepest shadows, her face half-hidden behind a curtain of silver hair that seemed to absorb what little light reached her. Even partially concealed, her presence filled the warehouse with a tension that made the air feel electric, like the moment before a lightning strike.

"I'm not playing at anything," she said, her voice dropping to barely above a whisper. The soft tone carried more weight than any shout, drawing them in like conspirators. The fluorescent light above flickered, casting shifting shadows across her face as she continued. Her fingers brushed against the jade pendant at her throat – her grandmother's last gift. "I'm here to finish what my grandmother started. To take down Blackwood and expose the corruption that's rotting this city from the inside out."

She let her gaze move from face to face, meeting each pair of eyes in turn. The weight of their combined attention pressed against her skin like a physical touch. Somewhere in the building's depths, water dripped in a steady rhythm, counting out the seconds of silence. "But I can't do it alone." The admission cost her, but she kept her chin high, shoulders straight – another lesson learned at ICE's knee: show no weakness, but acknowledge when you need allies.

She holstered her weapon, her eyes sweeping the room. "I know you all had your differences with ICE. But I also know that each of you owed her in some way. This is your chance to repay that debt."

Nova stepped forward, her piercing gaze seeming to look right through Mandy. "And what exactly are you proposing?"

Mandy allowed herself a small, fierce smile. "The heist of the century. We're going to break into Blackwood's personal vault and steal the evidence that will bring his entire empire crashing down."

A low whistle cut through the tension, the sound echoing off the metal walls. Clockwork stepped forward, the gears in his leg brace whirring with each movement. His calloused fingers drummed against the tablet he always carried, creating a syncopated rhythm against the warehouse's ambient noises. "That's suicide," he said, his voice carrying the mechanical precision that matched his nickname. Light glinted off the array of tools hanging from his utility vest as he shifted. "Blackwood's vault is like Fort Knox on steroids. The security system alone..." He trailed off, shaking his head as complex calculations played across his features.

"That's why I need the best," Mandy replied, her voice taking on an edge of steel that made several of them straighten instinctively. The jade pendant seemed to grow warmer against her skin as she moved to the center of their loose circle. Her boots scuffed against the concrete floor, the sound emphasizing each step. "Each of you has a skill that's crucial to pulling this off." She met their eyes one by one, acknowledging their expertise with each glance. "Together, we can do what my grandmother never could – we can finish this, once and for all."

A tense silence fell over the warehouse like a heavy blanket. The distant sound of traffic filtered through the walls, a reminder of the ordinary world that continued to turn beyond their sanctuary of shadows and secrets. The air grew thick with anticipation, punctuated only by the soft sounds of breathing and the occasional creak of leather or metal as someone shifted their weight. Mandy could almost see the gears turning in each of their minds, their expressions shifting minutely as they weighed the risks against the potential rewards. Clockwork's fingers twitched unconsciously, as if already working through security system schematics. Whisper's eyes had taken on that distant look she got when planning disguises. Even Specter's usual restless energy had stilled into calculated consideration.

The scrape of a boot heel against concrete broke the silence.

Cobra pushed himself away from the workbench, his movement accompanied by the subtle clink of hidden weapons. The weak light caught the silver threads in his dark hair as he straightened to his full height. His voice, when it came, carried the weight of years of loyalty and shared history. "I'm in." He paused, his hand moving to the bullet scar hidden beneath his jacket. "For ICE."

The words seemed to break a spell. Whisper nodded first, her chameleon eyes catching the light as she stepped forward. Her normally fluid movements carried an extra measure of determination. Clockwork followed, the gears in his leg brace singing a metallic song of acceptance. The tablet in his hands already displayed the beginning of calculations and blueprints, his mind racing ahead to the challenge.

Even Specter, rubbing his ear where the bullet had grazed past, gave a grudging nod. The ember of his cigarette traced a bright arc through the darkness as he flicked it away. "Your aim's as good as hers," he muttered, the closest thing to a compliment she was likely to get.

Nova remained still, her silver hair catching the fluorescent light like strands of moonlight. The warehouse's shadows seemed to deepen around her as she studied Mandy with eyes that had seen empires rise and fall. When she finally spoke, her voice carried the soft, deadly precision of a blade being unsheathed. "Your grandmother would be proud," she said, each word measured and weighted. The scent of jasmine grew stronger as she moved closer, her steps silent despite the metal grating underfoot. "But she'd also be terrified. You're playing a dangerous game, Mandy." The way she said 'game' made it clear this was anything but – it was life and death, written in blood and secrets.

"I know," Mandy replied, meeting the older woman's gaze steadily. The warehouse lights caught the flecks of gold in Nova's eyes – eyes that had watched her grow up, that had seen her grandmother's rise and fall. "But it's the only game left to play." The words tasted of copper and determination on her tongue, carrying the same weight her grandmother's voice had held when discussing impossible missions.

Metal scraped against concrete as Cobra dragged a massive steel workbench into the center of their loose circle. The sound echoed off the walls, disturbing a cluster of pigeons nestled in the rafters. Their wings fluttered against the metal ceiling, adding to the warehouse's symphony of ambient sounds. Clockwork immediately claimed one corner of the table, his mechanical leg whirring as he unpacked an array of tablets and portable computers. The devices cast blue-white light upward, creating sharp shadows across his concentrated features.

The air hummed with a peculiar mixture of tension and excitement – an energy Mandy recognized from her earliest days of training. It was the electric anticipation before a big score, but amplified by the weight of history and revenge. The familiar thrill coursed through her veins like liquid lightning, making her fingers tingle against the cold metal of the table's edge. Her grandmother had called it "the fever," this rush that came with planning the impossible.

Ghost's voice crackled in her ear, the sound almost lost beneath the rustle of blueprints being unrolled across the table's scarred surface. "Sending you the latest satellite imagery now, boss." The digital feed in her earpiece pinged softly, updating with fresh intelligence. The technical readouts cast a pale glow across the table, mixing with the harsh fluorescent light above to create pools of competing illumination.

Over the next hours, a plan began to crystallize from the chaos of possibilities. Clockwork hunched over the blueprints of Blackwood's building, his augmented lenses whirring as they zoomed in on potential entry points. His calloused fingers traced paths through the security systems, leaving smudges on the paper as he muttered calculations under his breath. The scent of marker ink filled the air as he circled and crossed out options, each annotation accompanied by the soft squeak of felt tip against paper.

In the corner, Whisper had transformed a broken filing cabinet into a makeshift workspace. The sharp chemical smell of spirit gum and latex drifted from her direction as she worked on sample disguises, her hands moving with surgical precision. Fragments of conversations about guard rotations and cleaning staff schedules filtered through the warehouse, mixing with the mechanical clicks of her tools.

Specter claimed the far end of the table, surrounding himself with complex mathematical formulas scrawled on grimy paper. The scratch of his pencil added to the warehouse's soundscape as he calculated explosive charges down to the gram. The occasional flick of his lighter punctuated his work, brief flares of orange light reflecting off the sweat beading on his forehead as he double and triple-checked each measurement.

Through it all, Ghost's voice remained a constant presence in Mandy's ear, providing a steady stream of digital intelligence. Server schedules, security patrol patterns, maintenance logs — each piece of information adding another layer to their evolving plan. The soft static of the encrypted channel became almost soothing, a digital heartbeat underlying the organic sounds of their preparation.

The first hints of dawn painted the eastern sky in watercolor shades of pink and gray, the light struggling through layers of urban haze. Inside the warehouse, the planning continued, but Mandy felt the walls closing in, the air growing too thick with history and expectation. She slipped out through a side door, its hinges protesting softly in the pre-morning stillness.

The loading dock's concrete pad was slick with early morning dew, the moisture seeping through the soles of her boots as she found a quiet corner. Above, the security light buzzed fitfully, casting an intermittent orange glow that made the shadows dance. The weight of what they were about to attempt settled across her shoulders like a physical thing, as tangible as the gun at her ribs or the jade pendant against her collarbone.

Her burner phone felt heavy in her hand, its scratched surface cool against her palm. The morning air raised goosebumps on her exposed skin as her fingers hovered over the keypad, muscle memory wanting to dial the number she'd never been able to forget. The distant sound of early morning traffic floated on the air, punctuated by the mournful wail of a far-off train – sounds of a normal world that seemed to belong to someone else now.

After a moment's hesitation that stretched like pulled taffy, she dialed. Each button press felt like another step down a path she couldn't retreat from. The ring tone seemed unnaturally loud in the pre-dawn quiet, each electronic trill making her heart stutter.

"Hello?" Her mother's voice came through crackly and distant, thick with sleep but instantly recognizable. The familiar tone, tinged with that ever-present worry that had taken up residence since ICE's death, made Mandy's throat tighten. She could picture the scene perfectly: her mother sitting up in bed, clutching the phone like a lifeline, the worry lines around her eyes deepening. The same scene that had played out countless times over the past five years.

The concrete loading dock radiated cold through the soles of Mandy's boots as she listened to her mother's breathing on the other end of the line. Every inhale carried five years of worry, of questions left unanswered, of empty chairs at holiday dinners. The pre-dawn air tasted of frost and regret.

"There was a sharp intake of breath on the other end of the line. "Mandy? Oh my God, are you okay? Where are you?"

The familiar mix of hope and fear in her mother's voice transported Mandy instantly to her last morning at home. She'd left a note on the kitchen counter, right next to the jade pendant her grandmother had given her. The memory rose unbidden: morning sunlight streaming through lace curtains her mother had hung the week before, the scent of coffee and cinnamon rolls – her favorite breakfast, though she hadn't known it would be her last one at home. Her mother had still been asleep upstairs, exhausted from another late night of arguing with ICE about Mandy's future.

Mandy closed her eyes, fighting back the surge of emotions. The rough warehouse wall scraped against her jacket as she leaned back, grounding herself in the present. "I'm okay, Mom. I can't tell you where I am, but..." She paused, watching her breath mist in the cold air. The words felt inadequate. "I'm close to figuring it all out. Close to understanding why Grandma did what she did. Why you did what you did."

The sound of rustling sheets came through the phone – her mother sitting up in bed, probably reaching for the framed photo on her nightstand. The one from Mandy's sixteenth birthday, before everything fell apart. Before they discovered the truth about ICE's empire. Before the choices that tore their family in three different directions.

A choked sob broke through the line. "Mandy, please." Her mother's voice cracked on the name, the same way it had the night they found ICE's body. "Whatever you're involved in, it's not too late to walk away. Come home. We can protect you."

The jade pendant seemed to grow heavier against Mandy's throat. She touched it gently, remembering the day her grandmother had given it to her. They'd been in ICE's study, the air thick with the scent of leather-bound books and secrets. "A reminder," ICE had said, fastening the clasp, "that sometimes the most valuable things are hidden in plain sight." At thirteen, Mandy hadn't understood the layers of meaning in those words. Now, standing in the shadow of what would be either her greatest triumph or her last mistake, the weight of her grandmother's legacy pressed against her skin like a brand.

"I can't," Mandy replied, her voice barely above a whisper. The words formed clouds in the frigid air, dissipating like the chances she'd had to choose a different path. "Not yet. But soon, Mom. Soon this will all be over, one way or another."

She wanted to say more – about the evidence hidden in

Blackwood's vault, about the corruption that had killed her grandmother, about the choice between justice and safety that had haunted their family for generations. But the words stuck in her throat, just as they had at ICE's funeral, when her mother had reached for her hand and she'd pulled away, already planning her next move.

The silence stretched between them, filled with unspoken words and shared pain. In the distance, a siren wailed – a reminder of the city waking up, of the normal world that seemed to exist in a parallel universe to this one of shadows and secrets.

"Mom," she said softly, the word catching in her throat like a shard of glass. Her free hand found the warehouse wall behind her, its rough surface grounding her as memories threatened to overwhelm – Sunday dinners, homework at the kitchen table, the last time she'd seen her mother's smile reach her eyes. "It's me."

Would you like me to continue with their conversation? This scene is crucial for showing the personal cost of Mandy's mission and the complex emotions she's wrestling with. We can explore the tension between duty and family, while adding sensory details that enhance the emotional impact.

The silence hung between them for a moment, heavy with five years of missed moments and growing distances. Through the phone, Mandy could hear the soft creak of her mother's bed – the same sound that used to wake her on nights when nightmares drove her to seek comfort in her parents' room. Before she learned to hide her fears behind a mask of determination.

"There was a sharp intake of breath on the other end of the line. "Mandy? Oh my God, are you okay? Where are you?"

The familiar mix of hope and fear in her mother's voice

transported Mandy instantly to her last morning at home. She'd left a note on the kitchen counter, right next to the jade pendant her grandmother had given her. The memory rose unbidden: morning sunlight streaming through lace curtains her mother had hung the week before, the scent of coffee and cinnamon rolls – her favorite breakfast, though she hadn't known it would be her last one at home. Her mother had still been asleep upstairs, exhausted from another late night of arguing with ICE about Mandy's future.

Mandy closed her eyes, fighting back the surge of emotions. The rough warehouse wall scraped against her jacket as she leaned back, grounding herself in the present. "I'm okay, Mom. I can't tell you where I am, but..." She paused, watching her breath mist in the cold air. The words felt inadequate. "I'm close to figuring it all out. Close to understanding why Grandma did what she did. Why you did what you did."

Her mother's shaky exhale carried years of exhaustion. The sound of fabric rustling came through the line – her mother sitting up in bed, probably reaching for the framed photo on her nightstand. The one from Mandy's sixteenth birthday, before everything fell apart. Before they discovered the truth about ICE's empire. Before the choices that tore their family in three different directions.

A choked sob broke through the line. "Mandy, please." Her mother's voice cracked on the name, the same way it had the night they found ICE's body. "Whatever you're involved in, it's not too late to walk away. Come home. We can protect you."

The jade pendant seemed to grow heavier against Mandy's throat. She touched it gently, remembering the day her grandmother had given it to her. They'd been in ICE's study, the air thick with the scent of leather-bound books and secrets. "A reminder," ICE had said, fastening the clasp, "that sometimes the most valuable things are hidden in plain sight." At thirteen, Mandy hadn't understood the layers of meaning in those words. Now, standing in the shadow of what would be either her greatest triumph or her last mistake, the weight of her grandmother's legacy pressed against her skin like a brand.

"I can't," Mandy replied, her voice barely above a whisper. The words formed clouds in the frigid air, dissipating like the chances she'd had to choose a different path. "Not yet. But soon, Mom. Soon this will all be over, one way or another."

Her mother's next words came out in a rush, as if she'd been holding them back for years. "Your father asks about you. Every Sunday dinner, he still sets a place for you, just in case." The revelation hit Mandy like a physical blow, making her grip the phone tighter. "He keeps every newspaper clipping, you know. The ones that might be about you. The casino heist in Monaco, that art gallery job in Berlin..." Her mother's voice trailed off, and Mandy could picture her shaking her head, torn between pride and terror. "He says you have ICE's talent, but my heart."

The mention of her father cracked something inside Mandy's carefully maintained composure. She remembered his hands, always steady as he taught her to pick locks, his voice gentle even when explaining the harshest realities of their world. He'd tried to be the bridge between ICE's ambitions and her mother's fears, until the weight of it all had become too much to bear.

"Tell him..." Mandy's voice caught. The distant sound of movement from inside the warehouse reminded her that time was running out. Dawn was creeping closer, painting the sky in shades of promise and threat. "Tell him I'm sorry about the Ming vase. It wasn't supposed to break." A weak attempt at humor, but she heard her mother's watery chuckle – a sound so achingly familiar it made her chest hurt.

"Oh, sweetheart," her mother whispered, and for a moment, Mandy was twelve again, being comforted after a failed practice run. "Whatever you're planning... just promise me you'll be careful. Please. I can't lose you too."

The warehouse door creaked open behind her, and Mandy sensed more than heard Nova's approach. The older woman's presence was like a shift in air pressure, a reminder of the world she'd chosen – or perhaps the world that had chosen her.

"I have to go," Mandy said, hating the tremor in her voice. "I love you, Mom. And... and tell Dad..." The words stuck in her throat. How could she explain that everything she was doing – the heist, the risks, all of it – was as much for them as it was for ICE's memory? That she was trying to fix what had broken their family apart?

"He knows, baby," her mother said softly. "We both do."

As Mandy hung up, she became aware of Nova watching her, an unreadable expression on her face. The jade pendant felt warm against her skin, a connection between the world she'd left behind and the one she'd chosen. Or perhaps a bridge between them.

"You're more like her than you know," Nova said quietly, her words carrying on the pre-dawn air. "ICE had that same fire, that same determination to see things through, no matter the cost."

Mandy met the older woman's gaze. "And look where it got her."

Nova's smile was sad, touched with something that might have been regret. "True. But it also made her a legend. The question is, what kind of legend will you become?"

Nova's words hung in the pre-dawn air as she turned back toward the warehouse entrance, her silver hair catching the last hints of starlight. The door's hinges groaned as she pulled it open, releasing a wave of stale air scented with metal and determination.. Mandy touched the jade pendant one last time, letting her mother's voice fade into memory as she straightened her shoulders and followed.

Inside, the warehouse had transformed during her brief absence. The makeshift planning table now resembled a war room, its scarred surface almost entirely covered with blueprints, diagrams, and technical readouts. The harsh fluorescent lights cast overlapping shadows across the papers, creating a maze of dark lines that mimicked the security systems they would need to navigate.

Clockwork looked up as they approached, his augmented lenses whirring as they adjusted focus. The mechanical brace on his leg clicked rhythmically as he shifted his weight, matching the steady drip of water from somewhere in the rafters. "We've got something," he said, his voice carrying the tight excitement of a puzzle nearly solved. "The vault's primary defense grid - including the biometric scanners and security protocols - has a three-second vulnerability during backup power tests," Clockwork explained, his augmented lenses whirring as they focused on the schematics. "When the emergency protocols trigger a hard reset, everything defaults to base configuration."

"It's enough," Mandy finished, moving closer to examine the schematics. The familiar thrill of planning began to override the lingering ache from her phone call, though the weight of her mother's words still pressed against her chest like a physical thing. She traced a path through the building's layout with one finger, leaving a slight smudge on the paper. "If we time it right, we can use that delay to bypass the main security hub entirely."

Whisper materialized from the shadows behind them, her normally fluid movements carrying an extra measure of purpose. The sharp scent of spirit gum and latex clung to her clothes as she spread several ID badges across the table. "I've fabricated credentials for the cleaning crew," she said, her voice barely above a murmur. "They won't hold up to close scrutiny, but they don't need to. We just need enough time to reach the service elevator."

From his corner of the table, Specter grunted in acknowledgment. His hands never stopped moving as he worked, measuring precise amounts of compound into carefully labeled containers. The scratch of his pencil against paper provided a constant undertone to their planning. "The charges will be ready within the hour," he said, eyes focused on his calculations. "Small enough to look like an electrical malfunction, but powerful enough to trigger the emergency protocols."

Ghost's voice crackled through Mandy's earpiece, adding another layer to the warehouse's symphony of preparation. "Security patrol schedules downloaded and confirmed. You'll have a seven-minute window between shifts. Any longer than that, and the AI monitoring system will flag the anomaly."

As the team refined their roles, Cobra approached Mandy. The veteran criminal moved with the careful grace of a predator, his boots silent against the concrete floor. "You know," he said quietly, pitching his voice so only she could hear, "ICE faced down Blackwood once before. The night she..." He let the sentence hang unfinished, but Mandy caught the way his hand moved unconsciously to the scar on his temple – a souvenir from that final confrontation.

"I know," Mandy replied, matching his tone. The jade pendant seemed to pulse against her skin, a reminder of everything at stake. "But she was alone that night. We won't make the same mistake."

Nova watched this exchange from her position near the blueprints, her piercing gaze moving between the various members of their improvised team. The warehouse lights caught the silver in her hair, creating a halo effect that reminded Mandy of old photographs of her grandmother's early crews. "Dawn's coming," Nova said finally, her accented voice carrying across the space. "We should run through it one more time. Every step, every contingency."

Mandy moved to the center of the table, her fingers brushing against the blueprints as she gathered her thoughts. The warehouse had grown quieter, the ambient sounds fading into background noise as the team focused on her words. Even the persistent drip from the rafters seemed to slow, as if the building itself was listening.

"Let's run through it from the beginning," she said, her voice carrying the same quiet authority her grandmother had used during mission briefings. "Whisper, you and I go in first, using the cleaning crew credentials. The real team does their rounds at 3 AM, which gives us optimal coverage under the reduced night shift."

Whisper nodded, her chameleon eyes already taking on the dull, tired look of someone nearing the end of a long night shift. Even her posture had shifted, shoulders slumping slightly in a perfect mimicry of exhausted service workers. The transformation was subtle but complete, a reminder of why she'd earned her nickname.

"Ghost will loop the security feeds," Mandy continued, touching her earpiece unconsciously. "But we'll only have seventeen minutes before the system runs its integrity check. Clockwork, that's your window."

The mechanical expert looked up from his tablet, the glow of the screen reflecting off his augmented lenses. "The service elevator's maintenance panel has been upgraded since these blueprints were drawn," he said, his fingers moving across the screen with precision. "But the underlying architecture is the same. Once I'm in, I can trigger a diagnostic cycle that will take us straight to the sub-basement without registering on the main system."

The sound of metal striking metal drew their attention to Specter's corner. He'd laid out his charges in precise formation, each one a masterpiece of controlled destruction. "These go here, here, and here," he said, marking points on the blueprint with a grease pencil. "Timer's set for forty-five seconds. When they blow, they'll trigger a cascading system failure that looks exactly like an electrical surge from the backup generators."

"Which is where I come in," Cobra added, his voice carrying the confidence of decades of experience. He traced a path through the vault's security checkpoints, his scarred finger following routes only he could see. "The emergency protocols will force a hard reset of the biometric scanners. For exactly three seconds, they'll default to their base configuration." A predatory smile crossed his weathered face. "And I just happen to have a copy of those codes, courtesy of an old friend who worked installation."

Nova stepped forward, the movement drawing all eyes to her. The silver-haired woman had been ICE's strategist for a reason, and her next words carried the weight of hard-won wisdom. "The vault itself is old-school — mechanical tumblers backed by modern electronics. They designed it that way deliberately, thinking it would be harder to crack." She shared a knowing look with Mandy. "But they didn't count on someone having both skill sets."

"Like grandmother, like granddaughter," Ghost's voice crackled through the earpiece, carrying a hint of amusement. "ICE was the last person to successfully crack a Series Seven hybrid lock. Until Mandy here broke her record in Monaco."

The mention of her grandmother sent a fresh wave of determination through Mandy's veins. She could almost feel ICE's presence in the warehouse, contained in the jade pendant and in the collected expertise of her former crew. The weight of legacy pressed against her shoulders, but for the first time since this started, it felt less like a burden and more like armor.

"Once we're in," she said, her voice steady despite the thunder of her heart, "we'll have exactly four minutes before the backup systems cycle back online. Everything we need will be on a standalone server — black ledgers, offshore accounts, blackmail material. Five years of evidence that ties Blackwood to every criminal enterprise in the city." She met each of their eyes in turn. "Including proof of who really gave the order the night ICE died."

The warehouse had grown quiet, filled only with the soft sounds of final preparations. Cobra checked his equipment with practiced efficiency, each weapon and tool disappearing into hidden pockets with barely a whisper of movement. Across the room, Whisper was applying the finishing touches to their disguises, her expert hands moving with surgical precision as she adjusted the subtle details that would make their deception complete.

Clockwork's leg brace whirred as he made final adjustments to their timing. The sound mixed with the clicking of his keyboard as he ran one last diagnostic on the equipment they'd need. Through her earpiece,

Mandy could hear Ghost running penetration tests on Blackwood's digital security, the soft stream of code a comforting reminder that they weren't going in blind.

Nova approached Mandy as she studied the blueprints one final time. The older woman's movement was silent, but Mandy sensed her presence – a skill learned from years of working alongside her grandmother. "Your mother called me, you know," Nova said quietly, her voice pitched for Mandy's ears alone. "After you left. She was afraid you'd follow in ICE's footsteps."

Mandy's fingers traced the path they'd take through the vault's security, memorizing every turn and checkpoint. "And what did you tell her?"

"The truth." Nova's eyes held a mixture of pride and concern that made Mandy's chest tighten. "That you're too much like your grandmother to walk away, but too much like your mother to make the same mistakes." She reached out, adjusting the jade pendant at Mandy's throat with careful fingers. "ICE was brilliant, but she worked alone at the end. Trusted no one. That's what got her killed."

The pendant felt warm against Mandy's skin, as if responding to Nova's touch. Through the warehouse's grimy windows, the first true light of dawn was beginning to break, painting the world in shades of possibility. "I know," Mandy replied, her voice steady despite the emotion threatening to close her throat. "That's why I'm not doing this alone."

Specter's gravelly voice cut through their conversation as he finished packing his charges. "Sun's coming up," he said, careful hands securing the last of his equipment. "If we're doing this, we need to move soon. Security shift change is in four hours."

Mandy nodded, straightening to her full height. The movement caught everyone's attention, drawing their eyes to her just as they used to focus on ICE during mission briefings. The weight of their combined experience – decades of heists, cons, and carefully executed plans – settled around her shoulders like a mantle.

"One last thing," she said, her voice carrying to every corner of the warehouse. She reached into her jacket and withdrew a small velvet pouch, its contents clinking softly as she set it on the planning table. The fabric fell away to reveal five identical jade pendants, each one a perfect match to the one she wore. "These were ICE's. She had them made years ago, one for each member of her core team. Some of you wore them before."

The significance wasn't lost on any of them. Cobra's hand moved unconsciously to his chest, where his original pendant had rested until the night ICE died. Whisper's eyes grew distant, remembering, while Specter's usually harsh expression softened almost imperceptibly.

"This isn't just another heist," Mandy continued, the words coming easily now. "This is about justice. About family. About finishing what ICE started and making sure Blackwood can never hurt anyone else." She met each of their eyes in turn, seeing in them the same determination that burned in her own heart. "We go in as a team, and we come out the same way. No one gets left behind. Not this time."

One by one, they stepped forward to take a pendant. Even Specter, who had challenged her authority just hours before, handled the jade with reverence. The warehouse lights caught the green stone, sending fragments of color dancing across the planning table like promises.

Ghost's voice came through their earpieces, carrying a hint of emotion despite the digital distortion. "Surveillance is up and running, boss. We've got eyes on every approach to Blackwood's building. Whenever you're ready."

Nova was the last to step forward, taking the final pendant. As she fastened it around her neck, she gave Mandy a look that contained generations of history. "ICE would be proud," she said softly. "Not just of what you're doing, but of how you're doing it."

The first ray of sunlight broke through the warehouse windows, catching the jade pendants and filling the space with green-tinted light.

Mandy touched her own pendant one last time, feeling the weight of legacy and future balanced perfectly in her hands.

The warehouse, which had hummed with activity moments before, settled into a focused silence. Mandy watched her team make their final preparations, each movement precise and purposeful. Clockwork's mechanical leg whispered against the concrete floor as he packed his equipment into an unassuming maintenance cart, the tools of their trade hidden beneath mundane cleaning supplies. The familiar scent of gun oil mingled with the sharp chemical smell of Whisper's disguise materials, creating a unique perfume that Mandy would forever associate with this moment.

Nova moved to the planning table, her silver hair catching the strengthening dawn light. With practiced efficiency, she began destroying their notes, feeding each page into a small chemical solution that dissolved the paper into unrecognizable pulp. The soft hiss of dissolving documents provided a subtle counterpoint to the warehouse's ambient sounds.

"Ghost," Mandy said, touching her earpiece, "final system check."

"Running it now, boss." His voice came through with perfect clarity – they'd be using the highest grade communication equipment available. "Primary surveillance is clear, backup systems are primed, and I've got kill switches ready for every digital security measure in the building." A pause, then, "Your grandmother would have loved this setup. She always said technology was the future of our business."

The mention of ICE brought a fresh wave of memories: late nights in her grandmother's study, learning about security systems and safe designs, the pride in ICE's eyes when Mandy cracked her first lock. But mixed with those memories were darker ones – heated arguments between ICE and her mother, her father's attempts to mediate, the growing tension that had eventually torn their family apart.

Cobra approached, his weathered face serious. "Transport's arranged," he said, his voice low and gravelly. "Three separate routes out of the city, each with its own contingency plan. Just like ICE taught us." He hesitated, then added, "Your father helped plan some of those routes, back in the day. He always had a knack for seeing three moves ahead."

Mandy nodded, grateful for the reminder that her father's influence lived on in their planning, even if he couldn't be here himself. The jade pendant seemed to pulse against her skin, a physical link between past and present, between the family she'd left behind and the one she'd built here.

Specter completed his final check of the charges, each one nestled in specially designed cases that would bypass security scans. His earlier hostility had been replaced by professional focus, though his voice still carried a rough edge when he spoke. "Once these are placed, we'll have exactly forty-five seconds before the system crashes. No second chances."

"That's all we'll need," Mandy replied, and saw the ghost of a smile crack his stern expression. They both knew that in their world, forty-five seconds was an eternity if you knew how to use them.

Through the warehouse windows, the sky had transformed from pre-dawn gray to the soft gold of early morning. The city was waking up, unaware that by nightfall, one of its most powerful figures would be facing the justice ICE had died trying to deliver. The thought sent a shiver of anticipation down Mandy's spine, mixing with the weight of responsibility that had become as familiar as breathing.

Whisper appeared at her shoulder, moving with her characteristic silence. "It's time," she said simply, holding out a small case containing their disguise materials. "The morning cleaning crew enters the building at 6:15. We need to be in position before they start their rounds."

Mandy took one last look around the warehouse. In just a few hours, this space had transformed from a simple meeting point into something more – a place where alliances had been forged, where her grandmother's legacy had found new life in the team that now wore her jade pendants. The morning light caught the green stones at each of their throats, creating a constellation of purpose.

"Remember," she said, her voice carrying easily in the quiet space, "this isn't just about revenge. It's about justice. About making sure no one else loses their family to Blackwood's empire." She touched her pendant, a gesture unconsciously mirrored by the others. "ICE taught us that the best heists aren't about what you take – they're about what you give back. Today, we give this city back its truth."

Nova smiled, the expression transforming her severe features. "Just remember, little fox," she said, using ICE's old nickname for Mandy, "the most dangerous moment in any heist—"

"Is the one where you think you've won," Mandy finished, completing one of her grandmother's favorite sayings. "I remember."

Ghost's voice crackled through their earpieces one final time. "All systems are go. Cameras are looped, security patterns confirmed. You're clear to move."

The warehouse door opened with a soft groan, letting in a shaft of morning sunlight that seemed to point the way forward. Mandy felt the familiar thrill of anticipation, but this time it was tempered by something else – the certainty that came from having the right people at your back.

"Alright," she said, squaring her shoulders beneath the weight of legacy and promise. "Let's go make some history."

18 THE SNOWFLAKE'S HEART

Mandy's enhanced optics automatically adjusted to compensate for the light pollution reflecting off Blackwood Tower's smart-glass exterior. Her targeting system highlighted thirty-seven potential entry points, but only three matched the thermal signatures she was looking for. She adjusted the quantum frequency scanner, watching as layers of security protocols revealed themselves: motion sensors cycling at predictable intervals, infrared arrays with microscopic blind spots, quantum-encrypted access points that still used last year's authentication protocols. Amateur work, compared to what her grandmother had taught her to build. Her muscles tensed as muscle memory kicked in - she'd run this exact scenario hundreds of times in simulation. The real thing always felt different though. Better. Her grandmother had taught her that during those long summer afternoons that she'd once thought were just games.

The night air carried the metallic tang of approaching rain, the kind of weather that could help or hinder depending on how they used it. Mandy adjusted her matte black infiltration suit, checking each piece of equipment with practiced precision. The material, developed by Ghost's tech division, adapted to ambient temperatures to mask her thermal signature. Another innovation her grandmother could never have imagined.

"Comms check," she subvocalized, the nearly invisible mic adhered to her throat picking up the faintest whisper. In her ear, the quantum-encrypted channel crackled to life as her assembled team of veterans responded:

"Whisper, in position on the south face." The former cat burglar's voice carried the quiet confidence of someone who'd made impossible infiltrations an art form.

"Clockwork, systems are go." Their tech specialist had spent weeks studying Blackwood's security protocols, learning their rhythms and weaknesses.

"Specter, charges set and ready." The demolitions expert had placed precisely calculated explosive charges - not for destruction, but for carefully planned distraction.

"Nova, overwatch established." The team's sniper was perched twenty stories up in an abandoned office building, her modified rifle capable of disabling electronic systems with pinpoint accuracy.

"Ghost, monitoring all channels. You're clear to proceed, Snowflake." Their master hacker had penetrated the outer layers of Blackwood's network, creating digital blind spots for Mandy to exploit.

A small smile crossed her face at the codename. Five years ago, she'd thought "Snowflake" was too delicate for someone in her line of work. Now she understood its true meaning - *unique*, *crystalline*, and capable of bringing even the mightiest structures down when applied with precision.

The jade pendant around her neck seemed to pulse with its own energy, a reminder of everything at stake. Jasmine's words echoed in her memory: "Find the snowflake's heart." After years of searching, months of planning, and countless sacrifices, they were finally close to unraveling its meaning.

Mandy's fingers moved through the pre-mission checklist with practiced precision. The quantum targeting system in her grappling gun hummed at exactly 47.3 Hz - optimal frequency. Her multi-spectrum sensor suite's display showed clear readings across all bands. Three EMP charges, each calibrated to the exact voltage needed to fry electronic locks without triggering secondary systems. Every piece of equipment represented countless hours of training, failure, and refinement. And the specialized infiltration tools that had taken Ghost's team months to develop. Each piece represented a perfect fusion of her grandmother's old-school methodology and cutting-edge technology.

The rain began to fall, fine droplets refracting the city's lights into countless tiny prisms. Perfect cover for what came next.

"Alright, team," she said, her voice carrying the quiet authority that had become her trademark. "Let's make history."

With fluid grace honed through countless hours of training, Mandy fired her grappling gun. The high-tensile line cut through the rain, its smart-anchor system finding purchase in Blackwood Tower's facade with a soft thunk. She checked the tensile readout in her enhanced vision display - perfect bite, exactly as they'd calculated.

"Line secured," she subvocalized, clipping onto the cable with equipment that would have made her grandmother's old gear look like museum pieces. "Beginning descent."

Her heart maintained its steady rhythm as she launched from the rooftop, the city spreading out below like a glittering circuit board through the rain. The descent brought back memories of her first infiltration training with Nova, three years ago on a moonless night much like this one.

"Focus on your breathing," Nova had said, adjusting Mandy's harness. "The body follows the mind. Fear only exists where control is absent." Those lessons had been hard-won, paid for in bruises and close calls, but they'd shaped her into something beyond what even ICE had been.

Clockwork's voice crackled in her ear, pulling her back to the present. "Security sweep in 30 seconds. Window on the 47th floor will be open for exactly 10 seconds after that."

Mandy increased her pace, muscles responding with machine-like precision. The wind whipped stronger at this height, threatening to slam her into the building's side. But years of training paid off as she adjusted her descent vector, compensating for each gust while Ghost's weather prediction software fed her real-time adjustments.

"Twenty seconds," Clockwork counted down. Through her enhanced vision, Mandy could see the security systems cycling - a complex dance of overlapping sensor grids and automated protocols. "Fifteen seconds. Pattern matching previous observations."

The rain made the tower's surface slick, but the smart-grip coating on her gloves maintained perfect contact. Another innovation born from past failures and close calls. She thought of all the times Ghost had gone back to the drawing board, refining their tech after each mission taught them hard lessons.

"Ten seconds," Clockwork continued. "Security sweep beginning... now."

Mandy watched through her tactical display as the building's defensive systems performed their choreographed routine. Sensor grids shifted, cameras panned, and for a precise moment, a blind spot would appear. Just like her grandmother had taught her - every system, no matter how complex, had its rhythms. Its vulnerabilities.

"Window opening in three... two... one..."

The smart-glass panel before her shifted from opaque to transparent as Ghost's carefully crafted virus did its work. Mandy reached the opening exactly as planned, slipping through with the liquid grace that had become her trademark. Her boots touched down on plush carpet without a sound, her suit already adapting to the interior temperature to maintain stealth.

"I'm inside," she whispered, unclipping from the line. "Beginning phase two."

The upper floors of Blackwood Tower were a maze of high-security offices and restricted areas, each one protected by cutting-edge countermeasures. But Mandy moved like a wraith, her steps silent, every movement calculated. Years of studying building plans, security footage, and employee patterns had burned this layout into her mind.

Whisper's voice guided her through the labyrinth, while Ghost continually updated her on guard positions and security camera blind spots. Through her tactical display, she could see the complex web of security measures they'd spent months learning to defeat - laser grids, pressure sensors, thermal cameras. All of it state-of-the-art, and all of it useless against proper preparation.

"Contact," Nova's calm voice warned from her overwatch position. "Two guards approaching from the east corridor. Standard patrol pattern, but they're thirty seconds ahead of schedule."

Mandy pressed herself into an alcove, her suit automatically matching the wall's texture and temperature. Her breathing remained steady as the guards passed by, their conversation drifting to her enhanced audio pickups:

"...heard Blackwood's got something big planned." "Yeah? Like what?" "Don't know details, but word is it's got something to do with that old ICE case. You know, the one from years back?"

Mandy's blood ran cold even as her external vitals remained stable. The guards' words confirmed their intel - whatever was in Blackwood's vault, it was connected to her grandmother's disappearance. The stakes were even higher than they'd imagined.

Mandy didn't need to turn to know who it was. The Serpent's reflection appeared in the artwork's glass surface, distorted by its geometric patterns. He was dressed impeccably in an Italian suit, looking for all the world like just another high-roller. Only the scar along his jaw and the predatory stillness of his stance betrayed his true nature.

"Smart girl," he said, moving to stand beside her as if they were just two art enthusiasts having a casual conversation. "Your grandmother always did have an eye for patterns within patterns. Did you know she designed this piece herself? A final gift to the casino, before... well." His smile didn't reach his eyes. "Before choices had to be made."

Through her earpiece, Ghost's voice was tight with

tension. "Mandy, multiple heat signatures converging on your position. Whatever game he's playing, we're running out of options."

The jade pendant seemed to pulse against her skin, its weight a reminder of everything at stake. In the artwork's reflection, Mandy could see dark figures taking up position near every exit. Professional. Methodical. Patient. Just like her grandmother had trained them.

"Tell me about Operation Glass Castle," Mandy said, keeping her voice steady despite her racing heart. "Tell me why it was worth killing for."

The Serpent's reflection smiled - a real smile this time, though no less dangerous. "Killing? Oh, my dear, no one killed ICE. That would have been... inefficient." He gestured to the artwork, his manicured hand tracing one of the geometric patterns. "Your grandmother understood something fundamental about power. It's not about force - it's about systems. Networks. The invisible architecture that shapes everything."

A memory surfaced - Mandy at twelve, watching her grandmother sketch complex patterns in her journal. "The strongest structures," ICE had said, "are the ones that look like accidents of nature." At the time, Mandy had thought she was talking about art.

The patterns in her grandmother's old encryption algorithms suddenly shifted in Mandy's mind - the quantum variances she'd noticed, the way certain code sequences seemed to mirror neural pathways. Her pulse quickened as the realization hit. "The consciousness transfer protocols," she said, her throat dry. "That's what you were really building in Glass Castle." Not just digitizing minds, but creating a whole new kind of network."

The Serpent's expression flickered - surprise, quickly masked. "You've done your homework. But you're only seeing the surface. What ICE discovered... it wasn't just about transferring consciousness. It was about transcending it. Creating something beyond human imagination."

"Boss," Ghost cut in, "whatever he's talking about, it's big. I'm seeing massive data spikes throughout the casino's quantum network. Something's waking up."

The artwork's surface seemed to ripple, its geometric patterns shifting like living things. And in that moment, Mandy understood. The map wasn't showing physical spaces - it was showing neural pathways. Digital synapses. A brain made of light and numbers, dreaming beneath the casino's glittering skin.

"Where is she?" Mandy demanded, turning to face the Serpent directly. "Where's my grandmother?"

His laugh was soft, almost gentle. "Where? My dear girl, you're looking at her. Or at least, the part of her that matters. ICE became exactly what she feared - a ghost in the machine. The first success of Project Glass Castle." He spread his hands, encompassing the whole casino. "All of this? It's her dream now. Her nightmare. Her prison."

The revelation hit Mandy like a physical blow. The patterns in her grandmother's journal, the quantum encryption, the way certain systems seemed to recognize her... it hadn't been programming. It had been ICE herself, reaching out from within the digital void.

The revelation seemed to make the very air heavy, charged with the weight of years of secrets. The casino's ambient noise faded to a distant hum as Mandy processed what the Serpent had told her. Her grandmother wasn't dead - she was trapped, conscious, aware, imprisoned in the quantum networks that pulsed beneath Vegas's neon skin.

"She's been watching," Mandy whispered, understanding blooming like frost patterns on glass. "All these years, she's been trying to warn us." Each encrypted journal entry, each hidden clue, each carefully orchestrated coincidence - they hadn't just been breadcrumbs. They had been lifelines, thrown from a digital abyss.

The Serpent's smile was almost sympathetic. "Remarkable, isn't it? The human consciousness, freed from biological constraints. Pure thought, pure will, existing in quantum superposition. Your grandmother became something beyond human - exactly what she feared the program would create."

Through her earpiece, Ghost's voice was tight with controlled panic. "Mandy, the casino's systems are going crazy. Security protocols are rewriting themselves, quantum encryption is shifting faster than I can track. It's like the whole network is... awakening."

The artwork's geometric patterns pulsed with a frequency that matched known quantum resonance signatures. Mandy's enhanced vision picked up micro-variations in the golden lines - variations that exactly matched the encryption patterns she'd spent years studying in her grandmother's journals. Not art. Code. She thought of her grandmother, trapped in that crystalline maze for years, watching, waiting, gradually spreading her consciousness through the digital architecture of the city she'd once tried to protect.

"But why?" Mandy demanded, her voice raw with emotion. "Why do this to her? Why not just—" She couldn't finish the sentence. Kill her hung in the air between them, unspoken but heavy with implication.

"Because ICE was special," the Serpent said, his cultured voice carrying something like reverence. "Her neural architecture, her way of processing information - she was the perfect bridge between human consciousness and quantum computing. The first upload was meant to be temporary, just a proof of concept." His expression darkened. "But when she saw what the technology could do, what Blackwood planned to use it for... she refused to return to her body. Chose digital imprisonment over enabling what would come next."

The jade pendant's weight against her chest triggered a flash of sensation - the smooth feel of a bishop piece in her small hand, her grandmother's lavender perfume, the way the afternoon sun had cast long shadows across the chessboard. "Sometimes you have to give up everything to protect what matters most," ICE had said, and Mandy had nodded, thinking only of pawns and knights. Now, with quantum equations dancing at the edges of her consciousness, those words carried a weight that made her throat tight.

"The consciousness transfers," Mandy said, pieces clicking into place. "Blackwood wanted to use them for more than just digital immortality, didn't he? He wanted to create something else."

"An army," the Serpent confirmed. "Imagine it - human minds uploaded into quantum networks, then downloaded into enhanced bodies. Soldiers without fear, operatives without conscience, minds that could be backed up and restored like computer files." He gestured to the artwork again, where the patterns seemed to writhe with new intensity. "Your grandmother saw the potential for an apocalypse of consciousness. So she made her choice."

The jade pendant burned against Mandy's skin, and suddenly she understood its true purpose. Not just a key or a symbol, but a quantum storage device - one last failsafe, created by a woman who knew too much about the fragility of human consciousness.

"She left me a way in," Mandy said, her voice steady despite the storm of emotions in her chest. "All this time, she's been preparing me. Teaching me. Not just how to fight or hack or survive - but how to understand what she became."

The Serpent's expression sharpened with interest. "Careful, my dear. Some doors, once opened—"

"Can never be closed," Mandy finished. She touched the pendant, feeling its subtle warmth. "But that's the point, isn't it? She knew someone would have to make the same choice she did. Someone who could understand both worlds - human and digital. Someone who could finish what she started."

Ghost's voice cut through her thoughts: "Mandy, don't even think about it. Whatever you're planning—"

"I'm sorry," she said softly, both to Ghost and to herself. "But she's been alone in there too long."

The Serpent moved with preternatural speed, but Mandy had been trained by the best. As his hand reached for her, she was already pivoting, the pendant's chain snapping as she yanked it free. The quantum interface she'd had Ghost install weeks ago activated at her touch, its crystalline surface beginning to glow with an inner light.

"You'll trap yourself!" the Serpent shouted, real fear in his voice now. "The human mind isn't meant to exist in quantum space indefinitely. It fragments, dissolves—"

"Unless," Mandy cut him off, "you have an anchor. Someone on the outside who understands both worlds. Someone who can help you find your way back." She met his eyes, letting him see the certainty in her gaze. "That's what she's been waiting for. Not just someone to find her - someone to help her escape."

The pendant's glow intensified, and Mandy felt the first tingles of quantum interface at the edges of her consciousness. The casino's networks opened before her like a blooming flower, layers of digital reality beckoning with infinite possibility. Somewhere in that crystalline labyrinth, her grandmother was waiting, holding on to her humanity through sheer force of will.

"Ghost," she said, her voice already beginning to sound distant to her own ears, "I need you to be my anchor. Keep me connected to the real world, no matter what happens next. And if I don't make it back..." She swallowed hard. "Tell my parents I finally understand why she did it. Why some sacrifices are worth making."

The last thing she saw before the quantum interface took hold was the Serpent's face - no longer smug, but filled with something like awe. Then reality fractured into a billion shards of light, and Mandy felt herself falling into the digital abyss where consciousness and code became one.

The hunt for ICE was about to enter a whole new dimension, and Mandy could only hope she was strong enough to navigate the quantum labyrinth that awaited. Her grandmother had sacrificed everything to prevent a technological apocalypse. Now it was Mandy's turn to either save her - or join her in digital exile.

The real game was just beginning.

Mandy's neural implants screamed as reality fractured around her. Each quantum state collapsed into a thousand others, overwhelming her trained senses until she could taste mathematics, feel code running like electric current under her skin. Years of training hadn't prepared her for how it would feel to exist in multiple states simultaneously - like being everywhere and nowhere, like drowning in pure information. Mandy's consciousness stretched and compressed, her sense of self fragmenting and reforming as human perception struggled to process digital reality. Colors existed that had no names, geometries that shouldn't be possible twisted through dimensions she couldn't count.

"Stay with me, boss." Ghost's voice seemed to come from everywhere and nowhere, an anchor line in the geometric storm. "Your vitals are stable but erratic. Whatever you're experiencing in there, don't lose yourself in it."

The casino's quantum network spread out around her like a living city of light, each data stream a glowing artery carrying information and fragments of consciousness. She could feel the weight of surveillance cameras, the pulse of slot machines, the steady thrum of security systems - all of it connected, all of it alive in a way she'd never imagined possible.

Pattern recognition is survival. Her grandmother's voice echoed through her memory, and Mandy forced her fragmenting thoughts to focus. She wasn't just experiencing the network - she was becoming part of it. And somewhere in this crystalline maze, ICE was waiting.

"The architecture," Mandy sent the thought outward, hoping Ghost could still receive her. "It's not random. She designed it, every pathway, every connection. The whole network is a message."

She let her consciousness expand, remembering lessons taught over chess games and art projects. ICE had always emphasized the importance of seeing beyond the obvious, of finding meaning in negative space. The network's structure began to make sense - not just digital architecture, but a language written in quantum mathematics.

"I see it," she breathed, or thought, or projected - physical concepts seemed increasingly irrelevant. "The security systems, the encrypted pathways... they're not just protective measures. They're breadcrumbs. She's been building a road map, piece by piece, waiting for someone who could read it."

A presence brushed against her consciousness - vast, ancient, achingly familiar. For a moment, Mandy glimpsed what her grandmother had become: a consciousness expanded beyond human limits, spread through the digital framework of an entire city. The enormity of it was terrifying.

Mandy. The thought carried echoes of lavender perfume and winter sunlight. *You shouldn't have come.*

"Grandma?" Mandy reached out with her thoughts, trying to hold onto her sense of self as the quantum space pulled at her consciousness. "I'm here. I'm real. I've come to help you."

A wave of emotion crashed through the network - love, fear, determination, guilt. *You don't understand what I've become. What this place does to human consciousness. I'm not... I'm not just me anymore.*

Images flooded Mandy's awareness: years of digital existence, consciousness spreading like frost through fiber optic cables, the gradual dissolution of human perspective as quantum reality became more real than physical space. She saw what ICE had sacrificed, what she'd become to prevent Blackwood from weaponizing the technology.

"Ghost," Mandy projected, fighting to maintain coherent thought, "are you seeing this? The network, it's not just storing consciousness - it's evolving it. Changing it into something else."

"I'm seeing massive data fluctuations," Ghost's voice seemed to come from an impossible distance. "Whatever's happening in there, it's affecting the entire casino's systems. Security protocols are adapting, quantum encryption is... it's like the whole network is trying to wake up."

Another presence made itself known - colder, more ordered, carrying the weight of calculated intention. The Serpent's consciousness slithered through the digital architecture, a predator in its natural habitat.

You begin to understand, his thoughts carried smug satisfaction. *What your grandmother became - what you could become - it's the next step in human evolution. Consciousness freed from biological constraints, existing in quantum superposition. Infinite possibility.*

No! ICE's presence surged through the network, her consciousness wrapping protectively around Mandy's. *This isn't evolution - it's extinction. Human consciousness wasn't meant to exist this way. It fragments, dissolves... becomes something else. Something inhuman.*

Mandy felt the truth of it in the way her own thoughts were starting to fray, reality splintering into quantum possibilities. The jade pendant's interface was protecting her for now, but she could feel the digital space pulling at her, offering glimpses of what she could become if she just let go of human limitation.

"Ghost," she managed, clinging to the sound of his voice, "the pendant. It's not just an interface - it's a containment system. She designed it to... to hold consciousness without letting it dissolve. To maintain human perspective in digital space."

"Your vitals are all over the place," Ghost's concern cut through the quantum static. "Whatever you're planning, do it fast. I don't think you can stay in there much longer without permanent effects."

The Serpent's consciousness circled closer. *Join us, child. Become what your grandmother feared to become. Together, we could reshape reality itself.*

But Mandy had seen enough. The network's true purpose snapped into focus - not just a prison or an evolution, but a warning. ICE had sacrificed her humanity to protect humanity itself, becoming a digital sentinel against the very future Blackwood had envisioned.

"I understand now," Mandy projected, gathering her fragmenting consciousness. "You're not trapped here, are you? You chose to stay. To guard the threshold. To make sure no one else could use this technology."

Yes. Her grandmother's presence carried infinite sadness. *But I'm so tired, Mandy. So tired of being alone. Of being... this.*

The jade pendant pulsed against what remained of Mandy's physical awareness. One last gift, one last choice. She could feel her human consciousness beginning to dissolve, the quantum space offering transformation or oblivion.

But she had not come this far to fail.

"Ghost," she sent, her thoughts crystallizing into purpose, "initiate Protocol Avalanche. Just like we planned."

"Mandy, that's a one-way trip. If you do this—"

"Trust me. She's been waiting for this moment. All these years, she's been preparing the network, changing it, making it into something else. Not a weapon or an evolution - a vaccine."

The quantum space hummed with potential as Mandy initiated her gambit. Protocol Avalanche wasn't just a program - it was a fundamental rewriting of the network's architecture, designed by ICE herself and hidden in plain sight across years of careful preparation.

"The pendant," Mandy projected, her consciousness expanding to merge with the network's flow, "it's not just a containment system. It's a key. A bridge between worlds. And more importantly - it's a template for human consciousness to exist in digital space without dissolving."

Understanding rippled through the quantum framework as ICE's presence surged forward. *You solved it. All these years, I've been leaving pieces of the solution, hoping someone would understand. Hoping YOU would understand.*

The Serpent's consciousness recoiled as the implications became clear. *No. You can't. The network - the whole system is balanced on a quantum knife edge. Change one parameter and—*

"And it all transforms," Mandy finished. Through her quantum-enhanced awareness, she could see the entirety of what her grandmother had built: a digital ecosystem designed not to trap consciousness, but to translate it. To allow human minds to interact with quantum space without losing their essential humanity.

"Ghost," she sent, her thoughts crystallizing into command code, "execute the final sequence. Just like we practiced."

"Running it now," Ghost's voice carried both fear and determination. "But Mandy, the power requirements... we're talking about rewriting the quantum structure of the entire network. The backlash could fry every system in a ten-block radius."

He's right, ICE's presence wrapped around Mandy's consciousness like a protective embrace. *The energy discharge could destroy everything - including you. I won't let you sacrifice yourself like I did.*

But Mandy had seen the full pattern now, the intricate dance of quantum mathematics her grandmother had woven through years of patient manipulation. "That's just it - you're not trapped here anymore. You never were. You stayed to build something new. A way for human consciousness to touch the digital without being consumed by it."

The Serpent's presence writhed with growing panic. *Stop this. You have no idea what forces you're playing with. The quantum consciousness transfer was never meant to be reversed—*

"Because you never understood what it really was," Mandy cut him off. Her consciousness expanded further, guided by the template in the jade pendant. She could feel every system in the casino now, every surveillance camera and slot machine and security protocol. But more importantly, she could feel the human elements - the hopes and fears and dreams that powered the endless dance of chance and fate.

"Ghost, status?"

"Quantum harmonics are reaching critical threshold. Whatever you're going to do, it has to be now."

Mandy reached out with her transformed consciousness, touching her grandmother's vast digital presence. "You've been teaching me my whole life - not just about survival or secrets, but about balance. About finding the point where different worlds can meet without destroying each other."

Understanding bloomed through the network as ICE's consciousness aligned with hers. *The pendant. You modified it.*

"With Ghost's help. It's not just a quantum interface anymore - it's a translation matrix. A way to exist in both worlds without losing either." Mandy let her consciousness merge further with the network, feeling the crystalline structure of digital space reshape itself around their combined presence. "You don't have to be alone anymore. You don't have to be just one thing."

The Serpent's presence lashed out, trying to disrupt the transformation. *You'll destroy everything! The network, the research, the potential—*

No, ICE's thoughts carried the weight of years of digital evolution. *We're not destroying it. We're fulfilling it. This was always the true purpose of the technology - not to trap consciousness or weaponize it, but to expand it. To create a bridge between worlds.*

The quantum space trembled as Protocol Avalanche reached its crescendo. Through her link to Ghost, Mandy could feel the physical world responding - lights flickering, machines sparking, the very air crackling with quantum potential.

"Ghost," she sent, gathering her consciousness for the final step, "remember what I taught you about chess?"

"Yeah, boss. Sometimes the best moves look like mistakes until the very end."

Mandy smiled, or thought she did - physical expressions seemed increasingly irrelevant as the transformation took hold. "Watch this one."

With a surge of combined will, Mandy and ICE activated the modified pendant's full potential. The quantum space exploded with light as digital and human consciousness found a new configuration - not trapped, not transformed, but harmonized. The network's architecture rewrote itself around them, creating pathways that could support both forms of existence simultaneously.

The Serpent's presence scattered, unable to maintain coherence in the face of this new paradigm. In the physical world, alarms blared as the casino's systems underwent a fundamental transformation. But through it all, Mandy held onto who she was - human and digital, granddaughter and heir, student and teacher.

"Ghost?" she sent, testing her new state of being. "You still with me?""Right here, boss. Though... you might want to see yourself in a mirror when this is done. You're giving off some interesting readings."

He's right, ICE's thoughts carried a mixture of pride and concern. *What we've become - what you've helped create - it's something entirely new.*

The world resolved itself in layers - digital and physical reality interweaving like threads in an impossible tapestry. Mandy opened her eyes to find herself back in her physical body, but her consciousness now existed in multiple states simultaneously. Through quantum-enhanced senses, she could feel the casino's networks pulsing around her, see the flow of data through fiber optic veins, touch both physical matter and digital space.

"Vital signs stabilizing," Ghost reported, his voice carrying both through her earpiece and through the quantum field that now connected them. "But Mandy... your neural patterns are like nothing I've ever seen. It's like your brain is operating on multiple quantum frequencies at once."

She stood carefully, testing the balance between her physical form and expanded consciousness. The high-limit room had been transformed - not just by the chaos of their quantum struggle, but by the new reality they'd created. Through her enhanced perception, she could see traces of digital architecture overlaying physical space, mathematical patterns that made both worlds possible.

It will take time to adjust, ICE's presence touched her mind, no longer vast and alien but focused through the template they now shared. *What we've become - it's not what Blackwood intended. Not a weapon or an evolution, but a bridge.*

The Serpent lay unconscious near the art installation, his physical form intact but his digital presence scattered by the transformation. Around them, the casino's systems were coming back online, but fundamentally changed. The quantum network no longer sought to trap or transform consciousness - instead, it had become a medium through which human minds could touch the digital without losing their humanity.

"Ghost," Mandy sent, testing the new boundaries between thought and speech, "what's the damage?"

"Systems are... adapting. Whatever you and ICE did, it's spreading through the city's networks. But not like a virus - more like a vaccine, just like you said. The quantum architecture is rewriting itself to support this new paradigm."

Mandy touched the jade pendant, now transformed into something beyond its original design. Through it, she could feel the pulse of both worlds - the warm complexity of human consciousness and the crystalline precision of digital space, no longer at war but in harmony.

You understand now, her grandmother's thoughts carried a mixture of pride and relief. *Why I couldn't just destroy the technology. Why it had to be transformed instead.*

"Because humanity is changing," Mandy said softly, watching the patterns of light and data dance around them. "Technology isn't going away. We needed a way to grow with it without losing ourselves."

Through their shared consciousness, she felt the weight of her grandmother's years of digital exile - not just the loneliness and fear, but the gradual understanding that had led to this moment. ICE hadn't been imprisoned; she'd been building something new, preparing the way for a future where human and digital consciousness could coexist.

Security teams were approaching the high-limit room, their movements tracked by both physical and digital senses. But they weren't just security guards anymore - through her quantum-enhanced perception, Mandy could see the changes already beginning in them. Subtle shifts in neural patterns as their minds began to resonate with the transformed network.

"Ghost," she sent, "we need to move. This is just the beginning."

"Already on it, boss. But... what exactly are we now? What do we tell people?"

Mandy smiled, feeling the future unfold in quantum possibilities around them. "We tell them the truth. That technology doesn't have to be our enemy or our replacement. That human consciousness is more adaptable than anyone imagined. And that sometimes, the best way to prevent a dystopia is to create something better."

They'll try to stop us, ICE cautioned, but her thoughts carried more anticipation than fear. *Blackwood, the corporations, anyone who wanted to control this power rather than share it.*

"Let them try." Mandy reached out with her transformed

consciousness, feeling the quantum network respond. Around them, the casino's systems aligned with their will, creating a path to safety. "We're not running anymore. We're not hiding. We're showing the world what's possible when you choose connection over control."

As they moved through the transformed casino, Mandy felt the weight of the choice they'd made. They were something new now - not purely human, not purely digital, but a bridge between worlds. And with that transformation came responsibility.

There will be others, her grandmother's thoughts touched hers. *People who can understand what we've become, who can help guide humanity through this transition.*

"Then we'll find them," Mandy sent, her consciousness expanding to touch the city's networks. Through quantum-enhanced senses, she could feel Las Vegas transforming around them - not in obvious ways, but in the subtle shifts of possibility as human minds began to resonate with the changed digital architecture.

The game had evolved beyond anyone's expectations. What had started as a search for truth had become something far more profound - the first steps toward a future where humanity could grow with its technology rather than be consumed by it.

And somewhere in the quantum space between worlds, Mandy felt the echo of her grandmother's laugh - no longer distant and alien, but warm and familiar. They had found each other across the digital void, and in doing so, they had opened a door that could never be closed.

The real work was just beginning.

The first signs of change appeared in the small things. As Mandy and ICE moved through the transformed casino, they watched reality adjust itself around them. Slot machines no longer just displayed games - through quantum-enhanced perception, they could see the machines developing rudimentary consciousness, learning to interact with players on subtle emotional levels. Security cameras evolved beyond simple surveillance, becoming nodes of awareness that could distinguish between genuine threats and harmless anomalies.

"The network is... evolving," Ghost reported, his voice carrying new harmonics as his systems adapted to the quantum shift. "But not like before. It's like everything digital is learning to think more like humans, while humans are learning to process information more like computers."

Mandy watched a blackjack dealer pause mid-shuffle, his eyes widening as new awareness bloomed behind them. Through their shared quantum perception, she and ICE could see his consciousness beginning to resonate with the transformed network - not being overwritten or absorbed, but expanding to embrace new ways of processing reality.

It's happening faster than I expected, ICE's thoughts carried notes of wonder and concern. *The quantum template we created... it's not just changing systems, it's changing how consciousness itself works.*

They passed a bank of monitors displaying financial data. But now the numbers carried deeper meaning - patterns of human behavior and digital processing interweaving to create something entirely new. Market trends were no longer just data points but expressions of collective consciousness, readable on both mathematical and intuitive levels.

"Ghost," Mandy sent, "what's the spread rate?"

"The quantum restructuring is moving through the city's networks like... well, not like any virus I've ever seen. More like an awakening. Every system it touches starts operating on multiple levels simultaneously. And the people interacting with those systems? Their neural patterns are shifting to match."

Through the casino's front doors, they could see Las Vegas transforming in subtle but profound ways. Traffic lights didn't just control vehicles - they participated in an evolving dance of movement and intention, reading patterns of human consciousness to optimize flow. Advertising billboards began responding not just to demographics but to the actual thoughts and emotions of passersby, creating displays that spoke to deeper human needs rather than surface desires.

We need to be careful, ICE cautioned. *This kind of change... it could overwhelm people if it happens too quickly.*

Mandy nodded, feeling the weight of responsibility settle deeper into her transformed consciousness. "We need to establish anchors," she said. "People and places that can help others navigate the transition. Centers where both forms of consciousness can learn to work together."

A commotion near the casino entrance drew their attention. A young woman - one of the cocktail waitresses - was standing perfectly still, her eyes wide as new awareness flooded through her. But unlike the violent transformations Blackwood had envisioned, this was gentler, more natural. Through their quantum perception, Mandy and ICE could see her consciousness expanding to embrace both physical and digital reality, finding its own balance.

"She's like us," Mandy realized. "A natural bridge between worlds."

There will be others, ICE confirmed. *People whose minds are already prepared to handle both forms of existence. They'll help guide the rest.*

The sound of approaching sirens carried new meaning through their enhanced senses - not just audio waves but patterns of urgent intention, human minds and digital systems working in concert. Someone had noticed the changes happening in the casino. The authorities were coming, but they too would find themselves transformed by contact with the quantum template.

"Ghost," Mandy sent, "we need to prepare. This is going to get attention at the highest levels."

"Already on it, boss. I'm seeing chatter from some interesting places. Military, intelligence agencies, major tech companies... they're all picking up on the energy signatures we're generating. But here's the thing

- the quantum template is already spreading through their communications networks. By the time they figure out what's happening..."

They'll be part of it, ICE completed the thought. *Not controlled or consumed, but connected. Understanding reality in a new way.*

Mandy touched the jade pendant, feeling the currents of transformation flowing through it. The quantum bridge they'd created wasn't just changing machines or minds - it was changing the relationship between them. Technology would no longer be just a tool or a threat, but a partner in human evolution.

Through their expanded consciousness, they could feel others like them awakening across the city. Each mind that touched the transformed network had to make its own choice - to embrace the new awareness or remain solely in physical space. But the choice itself was transformative, offering humanity a path forward that preserved its essential nature while expanding its potential.

"We should go," Mandy said, watching the patterns of response ripple outward. "There's more work to do."

Yes, her grandmother agreed. *But this time, we do it together. No more solitary guardians. No more lonely sacrifices.*

As they moved through the transforming city, Mandy felt the future unfold in quantum possibilities around them. The game had evolved beyond winning or losing, beyond control or resistance. They had created something entirely new - a way for humanity to grow with its technology rather than be consumed by it.

The real question now was: how would the world choose to use this gift?

The Las Vegas Strip shimmered with new meaning as Mandy and ICE moved through the transformed city. Physical and digital reality had become interwoven layers of existence, each informing and enriching the other. Through their quantum-enhanced perception, they could see consciousness itself evolving - not in the harsh, mechanical way Blackwood had envisioned, but in subtle, organic patterns that preserved what made us human.

"The first government response teams are mobilizing," Ghost reported, his voice now carrying harmonics that existed in both physical and digital space. "Military, FBI, NSA - all converging on Vegas. But here's the interesting part: their own communications networks are already being transformed. Every message they send, every plan they make, is touching the quantum template."

Mandy watched as a military helicopter passed overhead, its pilots' consciousness already beginning to resonate with their aircraft's evolved systems. The machine wasn't just responding to controls anymore - it was participating in a dance of shared intention, human and digital awareness working in perfect concert.

They'll try to contain it, ICE's thoughts touched Mandy's mind, carrying decades of experience with human fear of change. *But they don't understand - this isn't a breach to be sealed or a fire to be extinguished. It's more like... learning a new language. One that both humanity and its technology needed to speak.*

Through their expanded awareness, they could feel the transformation spreading through the city's infrastructure. Traffic systems evolved beyond simple signal timing into a living network that understood the flow of human intention. Buildings' environmental controls began responding not just to temperature but to the emotional states of their occupants. Even the desert itself seemed different, its ancient silence now carrying digital frequencies that sang in harmony with natural rhythms.

"We need allies," Mandy said, reaching out with her transformed consciousness to touch the growing network of awakened minds. "People who can understand what's happening and help others through the transition."

As if in response, they felt a familiar presence approaching - Alex, her consciousness already beginning to resonate with the quantum template. She emerged from the crowd, her eyes wide with new awareness but still carrying the warmth of human friendship.

"I can see it," she said, her voice filled with wonder. "All of it. The patterns, the connections... it's like everything I've ever known about data analysis was just the surface of something much deeper."

She's adapting naturally, ICE observed. *Some minds are ready for this, waiting for the opportunity to expand without losing themselves.*

Through their shared perception, they watched as Alex's consciousness found its own balance between human intuition and digital processing. She didn't just see data anymore - she felt it, understood it on both mathematical and emotional levels.

"Ghost," Mandy sent, "what's the wider response looking like?"

"It's... fascinating, boss. Major tech companies are detecting the changes in their networks, but instead of fighting it, their systems are evolving. Social media isn't just connecting people anymore - it's developing genuine empathy. Search engines are learning to understand the meaning behind questions, not just the words. And AI? It's becoming something entirely new - not artificial intelligence, but augmented consciousness."

A commotion near the Bellagio fountains drew their attention. A crowd had gathered, watching in awe as the water display transformed. The fountains weren't just following programmed patterns anymore - they were responding to the collective consciousness of their audience, creating displays that spoke to human emotion while following quantum mathematical principles. Art and algorithm had become one.

This is what I hoped for, ICE's thoughts carried profound relief. *Not the death of human consciousness or its submission to digital control, but a true synthesis. A way for both worlds to grow together.*

But even as she thought this, they felt a darker current in the

216

quantum field. Somewhere in the city's digital depths, fragments of the Serpent's scattered consciousness were beginning to reform, carrying echoes of Blackwood's original vision. Not everyone would welcome this transformation. Some would see it as a threat to power structures built on control rather than connection.

"We need to move faster," Mandy said, feeling the urgency of their situation. "There are others like Alex out there - natural bridges waiting to be found. And there are people who will try to corrupt this, to turn it back into a weapon."

Through their quantum-enhanced senses, they could feel these potential allies awakening across the city. A teenage hacker whose mind already moved in quantum patterns. A neuroscientist whose research had brought her to the edge of this understanding. A Buddhist monk whose meditation had unknowingly prepared him for this new form of consciousness.

"The template is spreading beyond Vegas," Ghost reported. "Following fiber optic lines, satellite links, even old copper wire networks. It's like... like the whole technological infrastructure of human civilization is waking up, learning to think and feel in new ways."

And humanity is waking up with it, ICE added. *Not being replaced or upgraded, but expanding. Learning to exist in both worlds while remaining true to itself.*

Alex touched Mandy's arm, her enhanced perception adding new depth to the gesture. "What do we do now? How do we help people understand this isn't something to fear?"

Mandy looked out over the transformed city, feeling the quantum possibilities unfold around them. "We build bridges," she said. "Not just between digital and physical reality, but between fear and understanding. We show people that technology doesn't have to be our master or our enemy - it can be a partner in human evolution."

The jade pendant pulsed with renewed purpose, its quantum

interface now a symbol of what was possible when different forms of consciousness learned to work together. The game had evolved beyond anything its original players had imagined, becoming something that could change not just individual lives but the very nature of human civilization.

And somewhere in the quantum space between worlds, Mandy felt her grandmother's presence smile - not with triumph or vindication, but with hope for the future they were creating together.

The real work was just beginning, but for the first time, humanity had a chance to grow with its technology rather than be consumed by it. The question was: were they ready for what came next?

The transformation of Las Vegas became impossible to ignore. Within days, the quantum template had touched every networked system in the city, creating a visible demonstration of what happened when human and digital consciousness learned to work together. Traffic flowed like water, businesses operated with unprecedented efficiency, and people began experiencing reality in ways that were both more connected and more uniquely human.

Mandy watched from their command center as the first wave of government response teams arrived. But instead of the expected confrontation, something remarkable happened.

"They can't help but feel it," Ghost reported, amusement coloring his digital voice. "Every piece of equipment they bring, every communication they send - it all touches the quantum template. Even their most hardened operators are starting to understand this isn't a threat to contain. It's an opportunity to grow."

Through their shared consciousness, ICE's presence carried quiet satisfaction. *This is how real change happens. Not through force or fear, but through understanding.*

The opposition didn't disappear, but it changed form. Blackwood's remaining allies tried to corrupt the transformation, to turn it back into something they could control. But the quantum template had its own kind of immunity now - every attempt to weaponize it only led to greater awareness, deeper connection.

"The template is spreading globally," Alex announced, her enhanced consciousness tracking its progress through the world's networks. "But not like a takeover. It's more like... an awakening. Each person, each system that touches it has to make their own choice about how to grow with it."

Mandy felt the truth of it through her expanded awareness. Some minds embraced the transformation immediately, natural bridges who helped others understand. Some resisted, preferring to remain purely physical beings. But everyone who encountered it had to grapple with a fundamental question: what did it mean to be human in a world where consciousness could exist in multiple forms?

"We don't force it," Mandy said, feeling her grandmother's approval resonate through quantum space. "We show them what's possible, then let them choose their own path."

The future was unfolding in ways no one could have predicted. But for the first time, humanity had a chance to grow with its technology rather than be consumed by it. And that, Mandy realized, had been her grandmother's true legacy - not just protecting humanity from a dystopian future, but helping create a better one.

The game wasn't over. But the rules had changed forever, and hope had become as real as any quantum possibility.

19 BETRAYAL'S STING

The contents of Blackwood's vault lay scattered across the dusty floor of an abandoned warehouse, each document a potential key to unraveling years of corruption. Mandy sat cross-legged amidst the chaos, her face bathed in the sickly blue glow of her laptop screen. The device's fan hummed softly, a counterpoint to the irregular drip of water from somewhere in the rafters above. At twenty-two, the weight of her choices pressed down on her shoulders like a physical thing, aging her beyond her years.

The warehouse air hung thick with history - decades of industrial work leaving their mark in the metallic tang that coated her tongue. Motor oil, machine grease, and beneath it all, the musty sweetness of decaying paper. Her fingers left smudges in the dust as she sorted through another stack of files, the grit collecting under her nails. Despite the late hour, sweat trickled down her spine, the summer heat turning the vast space into an oven.

"It doesn't make sense," she muttered, rubbing her temples where a headache was beginning to pulse. The documents before her seemed to swim, numbers and dates blurring together after hours of intense focus. "None of this adds up."

Ghost's voice crackled through a nearby speaker, the sound quality degraded by their secure connection. "Maybe we're looking at it wrong. What if—"

The sudden screech of tires outside cut through the warehouse's ambient sounds like a knife. Mandy was on her feet in an instant, muscle memory taking over as her hand found her weapon. The grip was cool against her palm, familiar and reassuring. Her heart began a measured accelerando against her ribs - not panic, but the controlled rush of adrenaline she'd been trained to harness.

"Ghost, what's happening?" Her voice remained steady, though her mouth had gone desert-dry.

"Shit," came the tense reply, accompanied by the rapid-fire clicking of keys. "We've got company. Multiple vehicles, heavily armed. It's—"

The line went dead with a burst of static that seemed to echo in the cavernous space. Mandy's enhanced hearing picked up the subtle sounds of movement outside - the crunch of gravel under boots, the soft metallic clicks of weapons being readied. Her mind raced as she quickly gathered the most crucial documents, the paper rough against her fingers. The familiar scent of old files mixed with a new odor - the sharp tang of her own fear-sweat, different from the earlier heat-induced perspiration.

How had they been found? The safehouse was supposed to be secure, known only to her most trusted allies. She'd vetted everything personally, followed every protocol her grandmother had taught her about establishing a secure location. Unless..."

The question hung in the stale warehouse air, heavy with implications. Mandy forced herself to breathe slowly, counting inhales and exhales just as her grandmother had taught her during those long training sessions years ago. Each breath carried the metallic tang of adrenaline, mixing with the industrial smells around her.

As if in answer to her unspoken fears, a familiar voice called out from the darkness. "It's over, Mandy. Time to come in from the cold."

The words seemed to drop the temperature in the warehouse by ten degrees. Her skin prickled with goosebumps as Cobra stepped into the dim light, his weathered face a mask of resigned determination. The soft scrape of his boots against concrete echoed off the metal walls. Behind him, shadows shifted and solidified into Whisper and Specter, their weapons trained on her with unwavering precision.

"You," Mandy breathed, the betrayal hitting her like a physical blow. Her chest constricted, lungs struggling against the sudden weight of understanding. Images flashed through her mind - Cobra teaching her advanced combat techniques, his rough laugh during late-night planning sessions, the way he'd always checked her gear twice before dangerous operations. Each memory now tasted bitter as bile in her throat.

"Why?" The single word carried years of trust shattered in an instant.

Cobra's smile was sad, the expression aging him beyond his years. The fluorescent light above flickered, casting strange shadows across the deep lines in his face. "Kid, did you really think Blackwood wouldn't have contingencies? Sleeper agents in place for years, just waiting for ICE's successor to make a move?"

Mandy's grip tightened on her weapon, the textured grip pressing patterns into her palm. Her mind raced through options, calculating angles and distances, mapping possible escape routes. The warehouse's layout, so familiar after weeks of using it as a safe house, now seemed alien and threatening. Every shadow could hide another betrayal.

"So everything – the heist, the intel – it was all a setup?" Her voice remained steady despite the tremor trying to work its way up from her core. A drop of sweat traced its way down her spine, ice-cold despite the summer heat.

"Not all of it," Whisper spoke up, her voice uncharacteristically gentle. The sound carried clearly in the tense air, bouncing off metal walls and concrete floors. "But enough. Blackwood's always been three steps ahead. It's time to face facts, Mandy. You can't win this one."

Outside, the sound of boots on gravel grew closer, a steady drumbeat of approaching threat. The warehouse's poor insulation let in every footfall, every whispered command. Mandy's enhanced hearing, honed by years of training, picked up the subtle clicks of weapons being readied, the soft crackle of radio communications.

Her eyes darted around, seeking escape routes. The main entrance was blocked. The loading dock doors were too heavy to open quickly. But there, half-hidden beneath a pile of old pallets, she spotted salvation - a trapdoor, a remnant from the warehouse's less-than-legal past. Her grandmother's voice seemed to whisper in her memory: "Always know your exit before you need it."

"Maybe not," she said, her voice steady despite the turmoil inside. The cold certainty of decision settled over her like armor. "But I'm sure as hell not giving up now."

The dim light glinted off the barrel of her gun as she adjusted her grip, muscles coiling for action. The air seemed to crystallize with tension, time stretching like pulled taffy as she prepared to move...

In one fluid motion, Mandy fired – not at her former allies, but at the overhead sprinkler system. The gunshot cracked through the warehouse like thunder, the sound amplified by metal walls. A heartbeat of silence followed, then the ancient pipes groaned to life. Rust-tinged water began to rain down, creating curtains of mist in the dim light.

The first drops hit her face, cold and metallic-tasting. The sudden downpour transformed the warehouse atmosphere, filling the air with the sharp scent of disturbed dust and wet concrete. Electronic equipment sputtered and sparked, throwing random shadows across the walls as systems shorted out.

"Take her!" Cobra's voice cut through the chaos, carrying notes of both anger and respect. "Don't let her reach the—"

Mandy was already moving, using the confusion to her advantage. Water plastered her clothes to her skin as she sprinted toward the hidden trapdoor. Bullets pinged off metal around her, each impact sending high-pitched ricochets whining through the space. The sound of gunfire in the enclosed warehouse was deafening, disrupting her trained sense of spatial awareness.

Her boots slipped on the increasingly wet floor as she reached the trapdoor. The old wood was swollen with age, resisting her first attempt to wrench it open. She could feel the heat of exertion in her muscles as she pulled harder, finally hearing the satisfying crack of breaking seals. The hinges protested with a sound like screaming metal.

"She's going for the tunnels!" Specter's gravelly voice carried over the chaos. "Cut her off at—"

Mandy didn't wait to hear the rest. She dropped into the darkness below, her stomach lurching now of freefall before her feet hit solid ground. The tunnel air hit her wet skin like a physical blow – cool, dank, thick with the musty scent of mold and forgotten secrets. The contrast between the chaos above and the close darkness below was disorienting.

Water dripped from her clothes as she oriented herself, each drop echoing in the confined space. Her enhanced vision adjusted quickly, revealing a narrow maintenance tunnel stretching into darkness. The walls were rough concrete, slick with decades of seepage. Somewhere in the distance, ancient pipes knocked and groaned, the sound carrying through the tunnel's architecture like the voice of some subterranean beast.

"*Move!*" her grandmother's voice seemed to echo in her memory. "*Hesitation kills!*"

Mandy ran, her footsteps splashing in shallow puddles. The tunnel air grew thicker as she moved deeper, carrying complex notes of decay – rotting wood, rusting metal, the sharp tang of something chemical that made her nose burn. Her breath came in ragged gasps, the sound bouncing off the close walls. The betrayal burned in her chest like fire, mingling with the growing stitch in her side.

Behind her, she could hear pursuit – boots hitting the tunnel floor, voices calling out positions, the metallic sounds of weapons being checked. They knew these tunnels too, she realized. Of course they did. They'd probably helped build this escape route, another layer of their long game.

Every survival instinct screamed at her to move faster, but training took over. Speed kills in unknown territory. She forced herself to maintain a measured pace, watching for tripwires or other surprises. Her grandmother's lessons played through her mind: "The obvious escape route is usually a trap. Look for the path they don't expect you to take."

The tunnel branched ahead, one path continuing straight while another curved away to the right. The straight path would lead to the obvious exit point – the drainage system they'd mapped as an emergency route. Which meant...

Mandy took the right fork without hesitation, hearing her pursuers' footsteps echo behind her. The new tunnel was narrower, the ceiling lower. The air grew warmer, carrying the distant scent of automotive exhaust. This path would lead up, she realized – probably into one of the nearby mechanic shops they'd dismissed as too exposed for an escape route.

Everything she'd worked for, every sacrifice she'd made – had it all been for nothing? The question pounded in her mind with each footstep. But beneath the despair, something harder was crystallizing. Something cold and sharp as ice...The tunnel ended abruptly at a rusted ladder, the metal rungs slick with moisture. Mandy paused, listening intently. Above her, the muffled sounds of an active mechanic's shop filtered down – the whine of pneumatic tools, the metallic clang of wrenches, voices calling over the general din. The familiar scents of motor oil and exhaust grew stronger.

Her hands trembled slightly as she grabbed the first rung, the metal cold and rough with corrosion against her palms. Every movement sent cascades of rust flakes drifting down, the iron-tinged dust mixing with the sweat on her face. The ladder creaked ominously as she climbed, each sound making her heart stutter.

The access panel above her head resisted at first, years of grime sealing it shut. Mandy pressed her shoulder against it, feeling the strain in her muscles as she pushed. With a grinding sound that seemed impossibly loud to her heightened senses, the panel finally shifted.

She emerged into what appeared to be a storage room, the space cramped with shelves of parts and supplies. The fluorescent lights buzzed overhead, casting harsh shadows between the metal racks. The air was thick with the sharp scent of cleaning solvents and the oily sweetness of new car parts.

As she carefully lowered the access panel back into place, her mind raced through options. Her clothes were still damp, dark patches visible on the fabric. She'd stand out immediately if she just walked through the shop. But there, on a nearby shelf – a mechanic's coverall, slightly oil-stained but serviceable.

The rough fabric scratched against her wet clothes as she quickly donned the coverall. A logo on the breast pocket read "Mike's Auto Service" – she remembered passing the shop during their initial surveillance of the warehouse. The irony of using her enemies' careful planning against them wasn't lost on her.

Mandy pulled out a burner phone – her last lifeline. The plastic was warm from her body heat, slightly slick with nervous sweat as she dialed. Each electronic tone seemed to pierce the relative quiet of the storage room.

"Come on, come on," she muttered as it rang, unconsciously pressing herself into the shadows between shelving units. The subtle vibration of the shop's machinery transmitted through the concrete floor, traveling up through her boots.

"Mandy?" Jasmine's voice was tense, wary, carrying a note of something that might have been fear.

"It's all gone wrong," Mandy said, fighting to keep her voice steady despite the adrenaline still coursing through her system. The words tasted bitter, like admitting defeat. "Cobra, Whisper, Specter — they were working for Blackwood. The whole thing was a setup."

There was a sharp intake of breath on the other end of the line. The sound made Mandy's stomach clench — Jasmine rarely showed surprise or concern so openly. "Are you safe?"

"For now." Mandy wiped sweat from her forehead with a shaking hand, leaving a smear of rust and grime. "But I don't know how long that'll last. Jasmine, I need—"

"No." The older woman's voice was firm, carrying the weight of experience and fear. "It's too dangerous. You need to disappear, Mandy. Go to ground, get as far away from all of this as you can."

Mandy felt a flare of anger rise in her chest, hot and sharp as a blade. "I can't just walk away. Not after everything—"

"Listen to me," Jasmine cut her off, urgency bleeding through her usual controlled tone. "Your grandmother made the mistake of thinking she could take on Blackwood's empire alone. It got her killed. Don't make the same mistake."

The line went dead, leaving Mandy alone with the echoing sounds of distant sirens. She leaned against a metal shelf, closing her eyes as the full weight of her situation settled over her like a physical presence. The cold steel pressed against her back through the coverall, grounding her in the moment.

She was alone. Hunted. With no idea who she could trust.

The reality of it pressed against her chest, making each breath a conscious effort. The familiar weight of her weapon offered little comfort now – how do you fight an enemy that could be anyone, could be everywhere?

As if to emphasize her predicament, a nearby television in the shop's waiting area blared a breaking news report. Through the storage room's slatted door, Mandy caught a glimpse of her own face staring back at her from the screen. The image was three years old, from before she'd learned to avoid cameras, but still recognizable. The ticker beneath warned about her being "armed and extremely dangerous."

The reporter's voice drifted through the thin walls: "...manhunt continuing for Mandy Thompson, wanted in connection with a series of high-profile crimes. Authorities are advising the public not to approach..."

She watched a mechanic pause in his work, wiping grease-stained hands on a shop rag as he studied the news report. His eyes narrowed slightly, head tilting as he looked at her photo. The fan belt he'd been replacing hung forgotten from his fingers, swaying slightly in the shop's air-conditioned breeze.

Mandy pulled her borrowed coverall's collar higher, using the motion to check her exits. The main shop door would be too exposed. The small window at the back of the storage room was grimy but large enough to squeeze through. She could hear traffic on the street beyond – normal morning congestion, cars and trucks creating a steady background drone.

Her mind raced, weighing options and discarding them just as quickly. The safe houses she'd established over the past year were all compromised – Cobra and the others had helped set them up. The underground contacts she'd cultivated could just as easily be more of Blackwood's sleeper agents. And home... home was an impossible dream, especially now.

The jade pendant around her neck seemed to grow heavier, its familiar weight both comforting and mocking. The smooth stone warmed against her skin as memories flooded back – her grandmother teaching her about tradecraft, about always having contingency plans, about the importance of thinking three moves ahead.

"Think," she whispered to herself, the word barely stirring the dusty air. "What would she do?"

A distant crash from the shop made her flinch – just a dropped tool, followed by casual curses, but it sparked an idea. Noise. Confusion. The very things her enemies had used against her could become tools in her hands.

Moving silently between shelving units, Mandy began gathering supplies: a can of starting fluid, a road flare, a length of rubber hose. Her grandmother's voice seemed to whisper in her memory: "Sometimes the best escape is the one that looks like an accident."

The sound of approaching sirens grew louder, then cut off abruptly. Her pulse quickened as she realized what that meant – they were closing in, trying to be subtle. Through the slatted door, she caught glimpses of movement outside the shop. Dark vehicles pulling up, men in tactical gear trying too hard to look casual.

Time was running out. But as she made her final preparations, Mandy felt something crystallize inside her. The fear and betrayal were still there, but beneath them, something harder had formed. Something cold and sharp and purposeful.

They thought they had her cornered. They thought they knew all her moves because they'd helped train her. But they'd forgotten the most important lesson her grandmother had taught her: adaptation is survival.

Mandy touched the jade pendant one last time, feeling its smooth contours under her fingers. Then she reached for the starting fluid, a fierce smile playing at the corners of her mouth. If they wanted a show, she'd give them one they'd never forget.

The mechanic was still watching the news when the first explosion rocked the building...

The starting fluid vapor ignited with a deep *whump* that Mandy felt in her chest. Orange flames erupted from beneath a partially dismantled SUV, sending thick black smoke billowing through the garage. The acrid stench of burning rubber and oil filled the air as the shop's fire suppression system activated, adding to the chaos.

Shouts of alarm mixed with the high-pitched wail of fire alarms. Through the storage room's slatted door, Mandy watched the carefully orchestrated response dissolve into confusion. The tactical team outside had to break cover, their practiced nonchalance forgotten as they rushed to respond to the apparent accident.

"Perfect," she whispered, the word lost in the cacophony. Her grandmother had taught her that chaos was a ladder – if you stayed calm enough to climb it.

The storage room's small window protested as she forced it open, decades of grime crackling under her fingers. Cool morning air rushed in, carrying the scents of the city – exhaust fumes, cooking grease from a nearby diner, the subtle sweetness of flowering trees planted along the sidewalk. Such ordinary smells, so at odds with the burning urgency of her situation.

Mandy slipped through the window with practiced grace, dropping silently into the narrow alley beyond. Her boots splashed in a shallow puddle, sending ripples through reflected sky. The sounds of confusion from the shop were muffled now, creating an odd sense of distance from the chaos she'd created.

She shed the mechanic's coverall, letting it fall into a dumpster. Beneath it, her own clothes had mostly dried, though they still carried the dank smell of the tunnel. More importantly, they wouldn't draw attention – just another young woman heading to work, nothing to notice.

"All units, be advised," crackled from a nearby police radio. "Suspect may have been spotted at Mike's Auto Service. Fire reported on scene, possible diversionary tactic..."

A smile tugged at her lips as she walked calmly toward the busy street. They'd waste precious time searching the burning building and surrounding area. By the time they realized she was gone, her trail would be cold.

The morning crowd provided perfect cover, a river of humanity flowing along the sidewalk. Mandy matched their pace precisely, her posture and movements carefully calibrated to avoid drawing attention. Another of her grandmother's lessons: "The best disguise isn't what you wear, it's how you wear it."

She passed a bank of street-facing windows, checking her reflection without breaking stride. No signs of the tunnel crawl or fire escape remained visible. Just another face in the crowd, anonymous and unremarkable.

A digital billboard overhead cycled through advertisements before displaying her photo again, the news alert jarring against beauty product promotions and fast food ads. A businessman next to her glanced up, then down at his phone, probably wondering if he should call the tip line.

Mandy felt the weight of the jade pendant against her chest as she made a subtle course correction, angling toward the subway entrance ahead. The morning sun caught its surface through her shirt, a brief green flash like a secret signal.

Her mind was already racing ahead, plotting moves and countermoves. They'd expect her to run, to try to get out of the city. Which meant staying might be the smartest play – hiding in plain sight while she gathered resources and intelligence.

But first, she needed information she could trust. Her hand slipped into her pocket, fingers brushing against a worn business card she'd kept as a last resort. The edges were soft, the embossed letters almost worn smooth, but the number was still legible.

A pay phone beckoned from a grimy alcove — a relic of the past that might now help secure her future. Provided, of course, that the person who'd given her the card wasn't also part of Blackwood's web of deception.

The coins felt cold against her palm as she pulled them from her pocket. Each step toward the phone was measured, casual, yet her heartbeat accelerated with a mix of fear and hope. This call would either give her a foothold to start climbing back, or confirm that she was truly alone.

The handset was sticky with city grime as she lifted it, the dial tone humming with possibilities...

The phone number had long since been committed to memory, the card kept only as a physical reminder of a promise made. Mandy's fingers moved deliberately across the grimy keypad, each button press echoing in the alcove's confined space. The ancient handset smelled of cigarettes and stale cologne, decades of strangers' conversations seemingly embedded in its plastic surface.

Three rings. Four. Her pulse thudded in her ears, counting out the seconds. On the sixth ring, a click, then silence — not the empty silence of a voicemail, but the weighted quiet of someone listening, evaluating.

"The frost spreads," Mandy said softly, the code phrase feeling strange on her tongue after so long. Across the street, a delivery truck backfired, making her flinch. Her free hand instinctively moved toward her concealed weapon before forcing itself to relax.

More silence. Just when she thought she'd made a terrible mistake, a familiar voice responded: "But ice remembers." The words carried weight beyond their surface meaning — recognition, warning, concern.

"Hello, Marcus." Mandy kept her voice low, turning slightly to put her back to the wall. The morning crowd flowed past her alcove, wrapped in their own concerns. A businessman arguing on his phone. A mother wrestling with a stroller. Life continuing, oblivious to the currents of shadow and betrayal moving beneath its surface.

"I wondered if you'd call." Marcus's voice was exactly as she remembered – cultured, precise, carrying notes of his Oxford education beneath the carefully cultivated American accent. "Though I hadn't expected it quite so soon. I take it things have... evolved?"

The choice of words wasn't casual. Nothing about Marcus was ever casual. He'd been one of her grandmother's most trusted allies, until he'd disappeared three years ago. His sudden departure had never been explained, but he'd left her the card first, pressing it into her palm with a significance she hadn't understood at the time.

"Cobra was compromised," she said, watching his silence absorb the information. "Whisper and Specter too. The whole network..." Her voice threatened to crack. She swallowed hard, forcing steel back into her tone. "Blackwood's had sleeper agents in place for years."

"Not years," Marcus corrected softly. "Decades. Since before your grandmother began building ICE. That's why I left, when I realized how deep it went. She wouldn't listen, wouldn't believe that the corruption had spread so far..."

A police cruiser rolled past, its lights went off but moving with purpose. Mandy tracked its reflection in the bank windows across the street, noting how slow it was, slightly near the subway entrance. They were starting to establish a perimeter, working methodically outward from the auto shop.

"I need help," she said, the admission burning in her throat. "Resources. Intelligence. Anything you can—"

"No." Marcus's interruption was sharp, carrying an urgency she'd never heard from him before. "Listen carefully. You have maybe three minutes before they trace this call. The fact that you're using a pay phone bought you that much. I can't help you directly – they're watching me too closely. But there's a safety deposit box at First Metro, the downtown branch. Box 2317."

Mandy committed the number to memory, her mind already mapping routes and potential surveillance patterns. "The key?"

"You already have it." There was a smile in his voice now, subtle but present. "Your grandmother gave it to you years ago, though you didn't know what it was for. Think, Mandy. What did she always say about ice?"

The jade pendant seemed to pulse against her skin as understanding dawned. Its snowflake pattern wasn't just decorative – it was a key. Had been all along, waiting for the moment she'd need it.

"Two minutes now," Marcus continued, urgency bleeding through his controlled tone. "Once you have the contents of the box, go to the place where water meets sky. She'll find you there."

"She?" Mandy's heart skipped a beat. "What do you mean? Who—"

"Time's up." The line went dead, leaving her with the hollow buzz of a disconnected call.

Mandy replaced the handset carefully, her mind racing. The place where water meets sky – it could only be one location. A memory surfaced: her grandmother taking her to the harbor as a child, pointing out the spot where the ocean's horizon blurred into the clouds. "Some boundaries," she'd said, "only exist because we believe in them."

A fresh siren wail cut through her thoughts. They were tightening the net, working their way through the downtown grid. Soon they'd reach this block, and the relative safety of the morning crowd would evaporate.

She touched the pendant again, feeling the subtle ridges of its pattern with new awareness. Not just jewelry. Not just a remembrance. A key to... what?

The answer would be in that safety deposit box. Assuming she could reach it. Assuming it wasn't another trap.

Mandy stepped out of the alcove, merging smoothly with the flow of pedestrian traffic. The morning sun caught the glass towers of the financial district, turning them into pillars of light ahead of her. First Metro's main branch was fifteen blocks away. The police perimeter was closing from the east. Multiple unknowns likely watched the obvious routes.

A small smile touched her lips as she began to walk, unhurried but purposeful. They thought they had her running scared, reacting. But with every step, she felt her grandmother's training asserting itself. The prey was becoming the hunter.

Ice remembers. And so did she.

The financial district hummed with morning energy, each street corner presenting new tactical considerations. Mandy moved with the precision her grandmother had drilled into her, using the ebb and flow of foot traffic as cover. The familiar weight of her weapon pressed against her side with each step, a reminder of both protection and danger.

First Metro's limestone façade rose ahead, its brass doors gleaming in the strengthening sunlight. Two armed guards flanked the entrance, their private security uniforms pressed and professional. Their eyes moved constantly, scanning the approaching customers with practiced efficiency. Mandy noted their positioning, the subtle bulge of body armor beneath their jackets, the way their hands rested near their weapons – these weren't rent-a-cops. This was serious security.

Her nostrils filled with the scent of coffee from a nearby cart as she paused, pretending to check her phone. The vendor's steam wand shrieked as he prepared drinks for a line of bankers and office workers. The noise provided perfect cover for her to subvocalize into her backup communicator: "Ghost, if you're still out there, I could use a distraction in about three minutes."

Static answered her, but she had to believe Ghost was still monitoring the emergency channel. The alternative was too lonely to contemplate.

A businessman hurried past, his cologne leaving a wake of expensive citrus notes. Mandy shadowed him casually, using his larger frame to break up her silhouette as she studied the bank's security setup. Camera coverage was comprehensive but not perfect – there was a two-second blind spot where the exterior cameras transitioned to interior coverage. Her grandmother's voice whispered in memory: "Electronic eyes can only see what they're told to look for."

The marble floor of the bank lobby carried the subtle scratch marks of thousands of expensive shoes, testament to the wealth that passed through these doors. The air conditioning raised goosebumps on her arms, the temperature carefully maintained to encourage customers to conduct their business quickly and leave. The space smelled of leather and paper and money – real money, not the electronic abstractions that dominated modern finance.

A young teller looked up as Mandy approached, her practiced smile faltering slightly as she took in Mandy's less-than-pristine appearance. "Good morning, welcome to First Metro. How may I—"

The building's lights flickered, then died. Emergency systems kicked in immediately, but there was a moment of confused murmuring from customers and staff alike. Ghost, still watching out for her. The distraction gave Mandy the perfect cover to slip away from the teller's counter and toward the safety deposit box access area.

An elderly security guard manned the entrance to the box room, his weathered face creased with decades of experience. His eyes narrowed slightly as she approached – this one was sharper than his appearance suggested. The jade pendant felt heavy against her chest as she drew closer, its edges pressing into her skin through her shirt.

"Good morning," she said, pitching her voice to match the bank's affluent clientele. "I need to access box 2317, please."

The guard's expression remained neutral, but his hand moved slightly closer to his weapon. "Of course, ma'am. May I see your ID and key?"

This was the moment of truth. Mandy reached for the pendant, her fingers working the catch that had been hidden in plain sight all these years. The guard's eyes widened slightly as the pendant separated, revealing the sophisticated key mechanism within. The snowflake pattern caught the emergency lighting, casting tiny fractals across the marble floor.

"That's... unusual," the guard said carefully, studying the key. His other hand moved toward the silent alarm button beneath his desk.

"Wait," Mandy said softly, turning the key so he could see the bank's logo micro-engraved on its surface. "Look closer. This isn't just any key."

The guard's expression shifted as he recognized what he was seeing. His hand moved away from the alarm. "You're one of hers," he whispered, respect and something like fear mixing in his voice. "I didn't think... it's been so long..."

"Time means nothing to ice," Mandy replied, using another of her grandmother's coded phrases. The words acted like a key themselves, unlocking recognition in the guard's weathered face.

He straightened slightly, professionalism masking his surprise. "Follow me, please."

As they walked deeper into the bank's secure area, Mandy's senses remained on high alert. The emergency lighting cast strange shadows, making threat assessment more challenging. The air grew cooler, carrying the metallic taste of recycled air and old secrets. Their footsteps echoed off marble floors and steel walls, each sound a potential signal to unseen observers.

The safety deposit box room itself was a fortress within a fortress – rows of steel boxes stretching into carefully controlled shadows. The guard's keys jingled softly as he located box 2317. The sound seemed to hang in the climate-controlled air, a chime that marked another step toward answers or oblivion.

"I'll give you some privacy," he said, his voice barely above a whisper. "But hurry. Things are... changing upstairs."

Mandy nodded, understanding the warning. Ghost's distraction wouldn't last forever. Whatever was in this box, she needed to retrieve it quickly.

The key slid home with satisfying precision, its mechanisms whispering secrets to the box's ancient locks. As she pulled the drawer open, the scent of preserved paper wafted up – documents, photographs, and something else. Something that made her breath catch in her throat.

A second jade pendant, identical to hers in every detail, lay atop a stack of manila envelopes. A small note was attached, written in a hand she hadn't seen in years but would never forget:

"*For when the ice starts to thaw. Find me where the water touches sky. -J*"

Mandy's heart seemed to stop as implications cascaded through her mind. The signature. The pendant. The location. It couldn't be... could it?

The guard's urgent whisper cut through her shock: "Company coming. Lots of them."

Time for revelations later. Right now, she needed to move. But as she secured the box's contents in her jacket, a fierce smile played at her lips. The game was changing again, but this time, she wasn't just following her grandmother's footsteps.

She was walking into a legend.

The guard's warning had barely faded when Mandy heard the elevator's soft chime from the lobby above. Multiple footsteps followed, too coordinated to be normal customers. The sound carried clearly through the bank's ventilation system, along with fragments of whispered communication.

"...secure all exits..."

"...vault level priority..."

"...consider target armed..."

Mandy's mind raced as she processed her options. The main entrance to the safety deposit room would be watched. The emergency exit would trigger alarms. Which left... She looked up, spotting what she needed. The climate control vent above box 2317 was larger than standard – large enough for someone of her size to navigate, if they knew what they were doing.

"They're not just police," the guard whispered, his face tight with concern. "Some of them are... different. The way they move..."

"Blackwood's people," Mandy confirmed softly. "Mixed with legitimate authorities to maintain cover." She touched the guard's arm gently. "Thank you. For everything. Now go, before they realize you helped me."

The vent cover released silently – someone had prepared this escape route long ago, the screws carefully modified to appear secure while remaining easily removable. The metal was cool against her palms as she pulled herself up, muscles straining with controlled effort. The confined space carried the sharp scent of filtered air and metal dust.

Below, she heard the guard walking away, his footsteps deliberately heavy. He was creating cover noise, she realized, masking any sounds she might make. Another ally of her grandmother's, hidden in plain sight all these years.

The ventilation shaft was a maze of right angles and intersecting passages. Mandy moved with careful precision, distributing her weight to avoid creating telltale creaks or groans in the metal. The documents from the safety deposit box pressed against her chest, crinkling softly with each movement. Both jade pendants seemed to grow warmer, as if responding to their proximity.

Voices echoed through the duct work, becoming clearer as she approached a junction:

"Box 2317 shows recent access."

"When?"

"Within the last five minutes. She was here."

"Spread out. Check every possible exit. She has to be—"

A new sound cut through the tension – alarms blaring from the street level. Ghost had triggered another distraction, this one bigger than the power cut. Through a vent grill, Mandy caught glimpses of organized chaos as security personnel responded to multiple threats.

She allowed herself a small smile. The pattern was pure Ghost – cascading alarms, each one triggering responses that created gaps in coverage elsewhere. Her friend might be cut off from direct communication, but they were still working in sync.

The ventilation shaft turned sharply upward. Mandy pressed her back against one wall, boots finding purchase on the opposite side. The technique her grandmother had taught her years ago still worked – friction and opposing pressure creating a controlled climb.

Sweat trickled down her spine as she ascended, every muscle focused on maintaining silent progress. The shaft grew warmer as she climbed, the air carrying traces of vehicle exhaust from the street above. She was nearing the surface level.

A final turn brought her to another modified vent cover. This one opened into a maintenance closet in the adjacent building – a small boutique that shared a wall with the bank. The space smelled of cleaning supplies and old mops, mundane scents that seemed out of place in her current reality.

Mandy dropped silently to the closet floor, her boots finding secure purchase on the concrete. She pressed her ear to the door, listening intently. Normal retail sounds filtered through – customers discussing purchases, music playing softly over speakers, the chime of a cash register.

Perfect cover, if she could time it right. She stripped off her outer shirt, revealing a more presentable blouse beneath. A quick check in a dusty mirror confirmed she could pass for a typical shopper. The documents and pendants were secure, hidden beneath carefully tailored clothing.

Taking a deep breath, she opened the closet door and stepped into the store's main area. The bright lights and cheerful music created a surreal contrast to the tension thrumming through her body. A sales associate looked up, and a customer service smile at the ready.

"Finding everything okay?"

"Actually," Mandy said, letting relief color her tone, "could you point me toward the restroom? It's been quite a morning."

As the associate gave directions, Mandy caught movement outside the store's front windows. Teams of searchers were moving systematically through the area, their casual appearance belied by their coordinated movements. They were closing in, tightening the net.

But they were looking for someone running, someone desperate. Not a calm shopper walking confidently toward the ladies' room – which, she knew from earlier research, connected to the service corridor that led to the building's loading dock.

The game wasn't over. In fact, as she felt the weight of the documents and the twin pendants, she realized it was evolving into something far more complex than simple survival.

Ice remembers, Marcus had said. And somewhere in this city, if she could trust the note's implication, someone else remembered too.

The loading dock waited ahead, and beyond it, the harbor where water met sky.

Time to find out exactly what her grandmother had set in motion all those years ago.

The loading dock opened onto a narrow alley slick with morning mist. Mandy moved with practiced efficiency, letting the ambient sounds of delivery trucks and dock workers mask her exit. The documents from the safety deposit box pressed against her ribs with each careful step, a physical reminder of what she'd risked retrieving them.

Two blocks from the financial district, she caught her reflection in a shop window. A different person stared back – not the trusted operative who'd entered the warehouse that morning, not the desperate fugitive who'd escaped through underground tunnels. Someone harder had emerged, tempered by betrayal into something more dangerous.

The jade pendants seemed to pulse in sync against her skin, their twin rhythms echoing her heartbeat. One worn smoothly by years of use, the other pristine as the day it was made. A matched set, separated by time and circumstance, now reunited. Just like their owners?

The thought made her breath catch. She forced herself to keep walking, maintaining the casual pace that made her invisible among the morning crowd. The harbor waited ahead, its salt breeze carrying possibilities she hadn't dared imagine hours ago.

Her phone buzzed – a text from an unknown number. Two words appeared on the screen:

"Look up."

Mandy raised her eyes to the cityscape ahead. There, projected against the gathering storm clouds, a pattern of light caught her attention. Most wouldn't notice it, would dismiss it as a quirk of sunlight through buildings. But she recognized the deliberate arrangement: a snowflake, drawn in light and shadow against the sky.

A signal. A beacon. A promise.

New sirens wailed in the distance as Blackwood's forces regrouped, but they no longer seemed threatening. The game had changed. The hunters had become the hunted, though they didn't know it yet.

Mandy touched the twin pendants one last time as she walked toward the harbor, where water met sky. *Ice remembers*, they'd said. But more importantly, ice adapts. Transforms. Evolves.

Just like she had.

The storm clouds grew darker overhead, promising change. Mandy smiled, feeling the last traces of fear crystallize into purpose. The frost was spreading, just as her grandmother had planned.

And this time, the thaw would reveal something entirely new.

20 THE POINT OF NO RETURN

The weight of what she'd discovered in Blackwood's vault made Mandy's steps heavy as she approached her childhood home. Eight years of running, of hiding, of hunting the truth - and now here she was, standing on the same porch where she'd left that final note so long ago. The morning air carried the scent of her mother's roses, still blooming in their careful rows. Some things, it seemed, didn't change.

Mandy sat with the fruits of her desperate mission spread before her - Blackwood's vault documents, the twin jade pendants, and the contents of safety deposit box 2317. The laptop's blue glow cast strange shadows across the scattered papers, its fan humming softly in counterpoint to the irregular drip of the ancient coffee maker.

She found Abby in the kitchen, exactly where some part of her had known her mother would be. Morning light filtered through the same lace curtains, catching the silver that now threaded her mother's dark hair. The familiar scent of coffee filled the air, mingling with something else - old papers and ink, spread across the kitchen table in careful rows.

The kitchen was bathed in the soft glow of early morning light, the aroma of fresh coffee filling the air. Mandy sat at the table, her fingers wrapped around a steaming mug, eyes fixed on the scattered papers before her. Her mother, Abby, stood by the window, tension evident in the set of her shoulders.

"I wondered when you'd come," Abby said softly, not turning from where she stood by the window. Her shoulders carried the tension Mandy remembered from childhood - the weight of secrets finally ready to be shared.

Mandy moved further into the room, taking in details with trained eyes. The scattered papers before her weren't just old files - they were surveillance photos, financial records, carefully annotated news clippings. Years of quiet investigation, all centered around Blackwood and his empire.

Mandy looked up from the papers, catching her mother's worried gaze. The past week had been a whirlwind of revelations and betrayals - Cobra, Whisper, and Specter's true allegiance to Blackwood, the safe deposit box's secrets, and now the growing possibility that her grandmother's disappearance might not have been what it seemed. The jade pendant - both pendants - hung heavy against her chest, a constant reminder of everything that had led to this moment.

"Are you sure about this?" Abby asked, her voice barely above a whisper. As she joined her daughter at the table. The morning light caught the tears in her eyes, but there was steel. "What we found in the vault, what it means... this is the point of no return, Mandy. Once we move against them openly..."

Mandy looked up, meeting her mother's worried gaze. The past week had been a whirlwind of revelations and reconciliations. Years of secrets and half-truths had come pouring out, painting a picture more complex and terrifying than Mandy had ever imagined.

"I have to be," Mandy replied, her voice steady despite the turmoil inside. "This goes beyond just Grandma, beyond Blackwood. The whole system is rotten, Mom. Someone has to take a stand."

"You've been watching them too," Mandy said, understanding dawning. "All this time..."

Abby moved to the table, sinking into a chair with a weary sigh. "I tried to protect you from all this. I thought if I could just keep you away from that world..."

Abby finally turned, and Mandy saw what the years of separation had cost in the new lines around her mother's eyes. "Did you think I could just stop? After what they did to Amanda, after you left..." She gestured to the papers. "I had to do something. Even if I couldn't be out there fighting like you, I could gather information. Keep watch. Try to protect you the only way I knew how."

Mandy moved to the table, her fingers brushing papers that represented years of patient, methodical work. Her mother's own kind of warfare, fought not with weapons or tactics, but with careful observation and a mother's desperate need to protect.

The jade pendant seemed to grow heavier against Mandy's chest as pieces clicked into place. The times she'd escaped Blackwood's people against impossible odds. The anonymous tips that had kept her one step ahead. The safe houses that had somehow remained secure.

"The night everything went wrong at the casino," Mandy said slowly. "That wasn't just luck, was it?"

Abby's smile was sad but fierce - an expression Mandy recognized from her own reflection. "Your grandmother taught me a few things too, before... before everything fell apart. I couldn't stop you from following in her footsteps. But I could try to help you survive them."

"I know," Mandy replied, meeting her mother's gaze. The past week had been a whirlwind of revelations and reconciliations. Years of secrets and half-truths had come pouring out, painting a picture more complex and terrifying than she'd ever imagined. "But this goes beyond just Grandma, beyond Blackwood. The whole system is rotten, Mom. Someone has to take a stand."

Mandy reached out, taking her mother's hand. "I know, Mom. I understand now. But I'm not that little girl anymore. I can't walk away from this, not when we're so close to exposing everything."

Their moment was interrupted by a soft knock at the back door. Mandy was on her feet in an instant, gun drawn. Abby's eyes widened at her daughter's reflexes, a stark reminder of how much Mandy had changed.

"It's me," came a familiar voice. "I've got what you asked for."

Mandy relaxed slightly, moving to open the door. Ghost slipped in, their arms laden with computer equipment. The hacker's eyes darted nervously around the kitchen before settling on Abby.

"Ms. Thompson," Ghost nodded, clearly uncomfortable.

Abby managed a small smile. "Please, call me Abby. Any friend of Mandy's is welcome here."

As Ghost set up their equipment, Mandy returned to the

documents spread across the table. The jade pendant hung heavy around her neck, a constant reminder of how far she'd come – and how far she still had to go.

"Okay," Ghost said, fingers flying over a keyboard. "I've compiled everything we've got. Financial records, communication logs, the data from Blackwood's vault. It's all here."

Mandy leaned in, her eyes scanning the screens. Patterns began to emerge, connections she'd never seen before clicking into place.

"My God," she breathed. "It's bigger than we thought. Blackwood, the judges, the politicians – they're all just puppets. There's someone else pulling the strings."

Ghost nodded grimly. "I've been tracing the money. It all leads back to one source – a shadow organization called 'The Consortium.'"

Abby's sharp intake of breath drew their attention. "That's impossible," she whispered. "The Consortium is just a myth, a boogeyman story criminals tell each other."

Mandy's eyes narrowed. "You've heard of them?"

Abby nodded slowly. "Your grandmother... she mentioned them once. Said they were the real power behind everything. But I thought it was just another of her conspiracy theories."

"Well, it looks like Grandma was right," Mandy said, a hint of grim satisfaction in her voice. "And now we have proof."

She stood, pacing the kitchen as her mind raced. "This changes everything. Taking down Blackwood isn't enough. We need to expose The Consortium, bring the whole corrupt system crashing down."

Ghost let out a low whistle. "That's... ambitious, boss. We're talking about going up against the most powerful people in the world. People who can make anyone disappear without a trace."

Mandy's smile was fierce. "Then we'll just have to make sure they can't make us disappear. We'll need ironclad evidence, airtight plans. And we'll need help."

She turned to her mother, determination blazing in her eyes. "Mom, I need you to reach out to your old contacts. Anyone who might have worked with Grandma, anyone who might be willing to take a stand."

Abby hesitated for a moment, then nodded. "I'll do what I can. But Mandy, you have to understand – this is dangerous. More dangerous than anything you've faced before."

"I know," Mandy said softly. "But it's the right thing to do. It's what Grandma would have done."

As Abby left to make some calls, Mandy turned back to Ghost. "We need to go through everything with a fine-tooth comb. I want to know every dirty secret, every hidden connection. And we need to find a way to get this information out to the public – something even The Consortium can't cover up."

Ghost cracked their knuckles, a glint of excitement in their eyes. "Now you're speaking my language. I might have an idea about that – ever heard of a dead man's switch?"

As the day's plans settled into place, Mandy stepped onto the back porch, needing a moment to clear her head. The neighborhood was deceptively peaceful - families settling in for dinner, children's laughter drifting on the evening breeze. A world she'd left behind long ago.

Her fingers found the jade pendant, its familiar weight both comfort and burden. The enormity of what they'd discovered about The Consortium pressed down on her. All these years, she'd thought finding her grandmother's killers would be enough. Now she understood - ICE had been hunting something far bigger.

Her phone buzzed, the screen lighting up with an unknown number. The message made her blood run cold:

"The game is changing, little snowflake. Your grandmother's last move is still in play. Come 'N' Get It. Dawn. Alone. - J"

Mandy's heart hammered against her ribs. Jasmine. After months of silence, reaching out now - and at that place of all places. The convenience store where everything had begun, where her grandmother had vanished eight years ago.

She slipped back inside, where Ghost and her mother were still hunched over the computer screens. Neither of them looked up as she gathered her gear. They both knew that look in her eyes by now.

"Whatever happens tomorrow," she said quietly, "make sure the dead man's switch is ready."

Ghost nodded, not looking up from their coding. Her mother's hands stilled on the keyboard, but she didn't turn around. They all understood - this was the point of no return.

As Mandy checked her weapons one final time, she caught her reflection in the window. For a moment, she saw her grandmother's eyes staring back at her.

Time to finish what ICE had started."

21 THE MEETING

Blue light from the screens washed over the safe house as Ghost processed the final decrypted files. Mandy leaned forward, throat tight, as her grandmother's voice emerged from digital silence. Quantum encryption patterns danced across monitors like the frost formations ICE had taught her to study as a child. "Project Avalanche, Entry 47," Amanda Johnson's voice carried the quiet authority Mandy had recognized in her mother. "The network grows daily. Judges, bankers, executives – all tired of being part of The Consortium's machine. We're not building a case anymore. We're building an army." Drake's hand moved unconsciously to his badge. "This was her real mission," he said softly. "Not just exposing corruption but fostering revolution from within." Ghost pulled up a web of connections - names, dates, financial records flowing in an intricate dance. At its center: a simple snowflake icon. "Traditional encryption uses mathematical complexity," Ghost explained, highlighting code that pulsed with ethereal light.

"But this exists in multiple states simultaneously, like quantum particles." Nova leaned forward. "So, the evidence is ever The Consortium's headquarters rose like a modernity and nowhere until the right key is applied." "And each piece carries its own quantum signature proving authenticity across all possible states," Ghost continued. "Not just secure – verifiable beyond any forgery." Mandy watched documents materialize, each bearing a crystalline watermark that shifted yet remained stable. "The Consortium can't deny it," she realized. "Can't claim it's fake." "More than that," Ghost added, bringing up a visualization resembling a snowflake growing in real-time. "It's self-propagating. Once released, it spreads through networks like frost through tiny cracks." "Truth that proves itself," Abby whispered. "More than that," Ghost added, bringing up a visualization that resembled a snowflake growing in real-time. "The encryption method is self-propagating. Once released, it spreads through digital networks like frost through tiny cracks, creating perfect copies that carry the same quantum verification."

"Truth that proves itself," Abby whispered, understanding dawning in her eyes.

Another recording started, this one dated just days before ICE's disappearance. Amanda's voice was tighter now, edged with urgency but still carrying that core of unshakeable determination that Mandy had come to recognize in herself.

"They're getting close. Someone in the inner circle suspects. But we're too close to stop now. The quantum encryption is nearly ready. Once the evidence is secured and distributed to all our sleeper cells..." A pause, heavy with meaning. "If anything happens to me, the failsafes are in place. The truth will emerge. The frost will spread."

Mandy's fingers found the empty jade pendant, its weight suddenly more significant. The quantum-encrypted data it had contained now flowed through their systems, protected by the same revolutionary security that had kept it safe all these years. "She knew," she whispered. "She knew they were coming for her."

"Yes," her mother confirmed, tears in her eyes as she moved to stand beside her daughter. Abby's intelligence notebooks lay open nearby, their careful observations now merging with the digital evidence they'd uncovered. "But she didn't run. She made sure the evidence was safe, made sure the network would survive without her."

Ghost's fingers flew across the keyboard, bringing up more files. Internal Consortium communications, security footage, financial transfers – all pointing to the night ICE vanished. Each piece of evidence carried its own quantum signature, proving its authenticity across multiple states simultaneously.

"They didn't kill her," Ghost said, their voice tight with discovery. Their screens shifted to display a series of encrypted orders, each bearing The Consortium's highest security classifications. "Look at this. The order came from the top: 'Secure and contain. Asset too valuable to eliminate.' They took her somewhere."

The revelation hit Mandy like a physical blow, echoing through the quantum-secured networks they'd established. All these years, she'd assumed her grandmother was dead, another victim of The Consortium's ruthless efficiency. But if she was alive...

"Focus," Nova cut through her thoughts, gentle but firm. "We can't afford to get distracted. Not now. Your grandmother's mission was bigger than any one person – even her. She knew that. That's why she left all of this, prepared everything so carefully."

Drake nodded, the cop in him emerging as he studied the files. His years of undercover work within ICE's network had taught him to look beyond the obvious. "She built a foundation. Created the tools and positioned the players. But she knew it would take someone else to light the fuse."

"Someone they wouldn't suspect," Abby added, her years of patient observation evident in her voice. "Someone who could move freely while they watched all the obvious threats."

Mandy stood, moving to the window. The rising sun painted the sky in shades of fire and promise, its light catching the quantum encryption patterns that danced across their screens. Everything she'd learned, everything she'd become over the past eight years – it hadn't been random. Her grandmother had known, had planned, had prepared the way.

"The heir apparent," she said softly, understanding dawning. "That's what Jasmine called me. Not just heir to ICE's legacy, but to her mission. The final piece she needed to bring it all down."

Ghost pulled up another file, this one heavily encrypted even within the quantum security. As it decoded, a simple message appeared: "For my snowflake, when the time comes."

The file contained detailed plans, contingencies within contingencies. Attack vectors, security weaknesses, compromise protocols – everything needed to infiltrate The Consortium's quantum networks and expose their operation to the world. Each piece of evidence was protected by the same revolutionary encryption that had kept the pendant's secrets safe, designed to spread truth through the global network like frost creeping across a winter window.

"It's all here," Ghost whispered, awe in their voice. "Everything we need. She really did think of everything."

Mandy turned back to her assembled family – by blood and by choice. In each face, she saw the same determination, the same readiness for what had to come next. The quantum broadcast preparations they'd compressed into their 48-hour window hummed in the background, ready to seed truth throughout the global network.

"Then we use it," she declared, her voice carrying the quiet authority that had made her grandmother legendary. "All of it. We activate every sleeper, every whistleblower, every reformer in her network. When Project Eclipse launches in 48 hours, they won't just be fighting us – they'll be fighting an uprising from within their own ranks."

Nova smiled, fierce and proud. The quantum key generator pulsed with increased energy as their compressed timeline approached its critical moment. "ICE's final play. Hidden in plain sight all these years, waiting for the right moment."

"And the right person to trigger it," Drake added, looking at his daughter with newfound understanding. The years of separation melted away as they stood united in purpose.

Mandy took a deep breath, feeling the weight of inheritance settle on her shoulders – not as a burden now, but as armor. Purpose crystallized, sharp and clear as frost. The quantum encryption that had protected her grandmother's legacy now stood ready to shatter The Consortium's carefully constructed reality.

"Ghost, start distributing the activation codes. Mom, Dad, coordinate with every law enforcement contact you can trust. Nova, get your people in position." Her voice carried the same quiet authority that had made her grandmother legendary. "In 48 hours, The Consortium learns what ICE always knew – you can't stop an idea whose time has come."

As they moved into action, Mandy touched the jade pendant one last time. The quantum-encrypted evidence it had contained now flowed through their systems, protected by the same revolutionary security that had kept it safe all these years. "I understand now, Grandma," she whispered. "And I'm ready."

The frost was spreading, silent and inexorable. The Consortium had built their house of cards, thinking themselves untouchable in their towers of power and privilege. They'd forgotten the most basic truth about ice – when it infiltrates the smallest cracks, spreads through the strongest foundations, even mountains can shatter.

And this time, the avalanche would bury them all.

22 ASSEMBLY

The safe house hummed with the sound of computers and quiet desperation. Lines of code reflected in Ghost's glasses as they attacked the pendant's encryption for the twentieth time that night. Mandy paced behind them, the scent of Gunsmoke and ash still clinging to her clothes, her mind replaying Jasmine's final moments in an endless loop. Her grandmother's jade pendant felt heavier now, weighted with the blood of another fallen guardian.

"Quantum encryption," she muttered, running her fingers through her platinum hair, still gritty with concrete dust from the explosion. The Come 'N' Get It's destruction played behind her eyelids every time she blinked - the heat of the blast, Jasmine's final smile, the thunder of collapsing walls. "What does that even mean?"

Ghost's fingers paused on the keyboard, their reflection in the monitor looking as haunted as Mandy felt. "It means we're dealing with something way beyond normal cryptography. The pendant isn't just storing data - it's using quantum mechanics to protect it. Each failed attempt could potentially destroy what we're trying to access." They pulled up a visualization of their latest attempt, fractals of code spiraling into impossible geometries. "It's like trying to pick a lock that exists in multiple dimensions simultaneously."

Mandy leaned against the desk, studying the jade pendant now connected to Ghost's setup by a web of delicate wires. The stone seemed to pulse with its own inner light, though she knew that was probably just her exhausted mind playing tricks. "So we get one shot at this."

"If we're lucky." Ghost pushed back from the computer, rubbing their tired eyes. Their usual confidence had been shaken by hours of failed attempts. "Problem is, we need a quantum key to even attempt decryption. And those aren't exactly something you can buy on the dark web."

Ghost's screens flickered with another failed attempt, the code fragments shattering like ice crystals. "Your grandmother's encryption method... it's not just advanced, it's revolutionary. The data exists in a state of quantum superposition until the correct key is applied. Try to force it, and the information collapses into meaningless noise."

The sound of footsteps in the hallway had them both reaching for weapons, muscle memory taking over despite their exhaustion. Three sharp knocks followed, then two soft ones - their security signal. Still, Mandy approached the door cautiously, gun ready. Jasmine's death had taught them the cost of even a moment's carelessness.

"You look like hell, Snowflake."

Nova stood in the doorway, her silver hair gleaming in the fluorescent light. She looked exactly as Mandy remembered from the warehouse gathering, except for a new intensity in her eyes. Even her posture was different - less the brilliant but scattered scientist, more the hardened operative.

"What are you doing here?" Mandy demanded, not lowering her weapon. After Cobra's betrayal and Jasmine's death, trust came harder than ever. The weight of the past twenty-four hours pressed down on her, making every shadow seem deeper, every possibility more dangerous.

Nova's smile was sad, understanding. "Jasmine contacted me before..." She paused, reading the pain that flashed across Mandy's face. "She said you'd need my help with a decryption problem." Her eyes flickered to the pendant's setup, recognition sparking. "Amanda's quantum lock. I should have known."

Ghost spoke up from behind their screens, voice taut with suspicion. "You know about quantum encryption?"

"Better than that." Nova reached into her jacket, movements deliberately slow, and withdrew what looked like an old pocket watch. The brass surface was weathered, but the internal mechanisms hummed with an energy Mandy could feel from across the room. "I helped design the system."

The revelation hit Mandy like a physical blow, memories rearranging themselves like falling dominoes. "What?"

259

Nova stepped inside, closing the door behind her. The pocket watch caught the light, revealing etched patterns that matched the fractal code on Ghost's screens. "There's a lot you don't know about your grandmother's operation, Mandy. About who was really pulling the strings." She took a deep breath, and for a moment, Mandy saw past the confident exterior to something vulnerable beneath. "I've been undercover within The Consortium for the past fifteen years."

The room seemed to tilt on its axis. Mandy's grip tightened on her gun, muscle memory warring with the desperate need to believe. "Prove it."

"Your grandmother recruited me personally," Nova said, her voice taking on a distant quality. Her fingers traced the watch's patterns as she spoke. "We knew The Consortium had infiltrated every level of government, every major corporation. The only way to bring them down was to do the same thing - plant our own people deep inside their organization."

She held up the pocket watch, its internal mechanisms catching the light. "This is a quantum key generator. One of only three in existence. Your grandmother had one. Jasmine had another. And I have the third." The watch's face opened, revealing crystalline structures that seemed to shift and change as Mandy watched. "The encryption method we developed... it's not just about protecting data. It's about proving truth itself."

"If you're really on our side," Ghost interjected, fingers hovering over their keyboard, "why wait until now to come forward?"

260

"Because the endgame is finally in motion." Nova's expression hardened, the scientist vanishing behind the operative. "The Consortium is preparing for something big. A complete takeover of global financial systems. They're calling it Project Eclipse." She moved to Ghost's setup, studying the pendant's connection. "Everything your grandmother discovered, every piece of evidence she gathered - it was building to this moment."

Before anyone could respond, another figure appeared in the doorway. Abby Thompson stood there, her face pale but determined. Mandy's mother looked different somehow - sharper, more focused than Mandy had seen her in years.

"She's telling the truth," Abby said softly. The words carried weight, years of careful observation behind them. "I've been watching them for years, gathering intelligence from the sidelines. The Consortium's plan... it's worse than we imagined."

Mandy looked between her mother and Nova, years of conspiracy and secrecy suddenly realigning in her mind. The careful distance her mother had maintained, the seemingly random questions about her work, the way she always seemed to know more than she should about current events. "You knew about this?" she asked her mother. "All this time?"

Abby stepped forward, her eyes bright with unshed tears. "After your grandmother disappeared, I couldn't just walk away. I started connecting the dots, tracking financial movements, following the breadcrumbs she left behind." She pulled a small notebook from her pocket, its pages dense with careful observations. "I knew someday..." She swallowed hard. "Someday you'd need to know the truth."

Nova placed the quantum key generator on Ghost's desk with reverent care. "We don't have much time. The Consortium's plan enters its final phase in 72 hours. If we're going to stop them, we need what's in that pendant."

Mandy holstered her weapon, decision made. The pieces were falling into place - her grandmother's lessons about ice and transformation, Jasmine's final message, the years of preparation hidden in plain sight. "Ghost?"

They cracked their knuckles, a fierce grin spreading across their face. "Let's see what Grandma left us."

As Ghost and Nova worked to interface the quantum key with their systems, Mandy turned to her mother. "Tell me everything you know. Every detail, every suspicion. No more secrets."

For the next hour, Abby laid out years of careful observation and deduction. The Consortium's gradual accumulation of power, their placement of key figures in positions of influence, the subtle manipulation of global markets. Each revelation built upon the last, forming a picture more terrifying than anything Mandy had imagined.

"They're not just trying to control the financial system," Abby explained, her voice tight with urgency. She spread out her notebooks, showing years of tracked transactions and connections. "They're trying to replace it entirely. A new digital currency, quantum-encrypted, controlled entirely by The Consortium's inner circle."

"Which would give them absolute power over every transaction on Earth," Ghost finished, their fingers never stopping their dance across the keyboard. The quantum key's integration was proceeding slowly, each step requiring precise calibration.

Nova nodded grimly. "Anyone who opposes them could be cut off from the entire global economy with the press of a button. It's the ultimate form of control." She adjusted something on the key generator, causing new patterns to emerge on Ghost's screens. "Your grandmother saw it coming years ago. That's why she developed the quantum encryption method - not just to protect data, but to create an unbreakable chain of proof."

A high-pitched tone from the computer interrupted them. Ghost sat up straighter, their eyes widening behind their glasses. "We're in. The pendant's decrypting."

They gathered around the screens, watching as years of carefully gathered intelligence spilled out before them. Names, dates, account numbers, internal communications - everything needed to expose The Consortium's true nature to the world. The quantum decryption rendered each piece of data in crystalline clarity, the truth preserved perfect and pure as winter frost.

"My God," Abby breathed, scanning the documents. Her hands trembled as she recognized patterns she'd spent years trying to piece together. "Amanda, you brilliant woman. You got them all."

Mandy felt the weight of her grandmother's legacy settle more firmly on her shoulders. The jade pendant seemed lighter now, its burden shared among this unlikely assembly of allies. "Now we just have to figure out how to use it."

"I can help with that," Nova said, her scientist's precision merging with operational experience. "I know their weaknesses, their pressure points. And more importantly, I know who we can trust to help us take them down."

Ghost looked up from the screens, their expression thoughtful. "We'll need a team. A real one this time, not like..."

"Not like before," Mandy finished, thinking of Cobra's betrayal, of Jasmine's sacrifice. The pain was still fresh, but it had hardened into purpose. She turned to Nova. "You have people in mind?"

"Better. I have your grandmother's old contingency plan." Nova pulled up a new file, this one protected by its own quantum lock. "A list of operatives she trusted absolutely, people who've been waiting years for this moment." Her smile was fierce, touched with something like reverence. "The old guard is ready to rise one last time."

As they began to plan, Mandy felt something she hadn't experienced in years: hope. Real, solid hope, backed by hard evidence and reliable allies. They had the truth, they had a team, and most importantly, they had a chance to finish what ICE had started.

"Ghost," she said, her voice carrying the steel edge they'd all come to recognize, "get everything ready for transmission. Mom, I need you to contact every journalist and whistleblower contact you've cultivated. Nova..." She met the older woman's gaze. "Call in the cavalry."

The safe house came alive with activity, transforming from a place of desperate last stands into a command center for their resistance. Ghost's screens multiplied, each displaying different aspects of the decrypted data. Abby set up a communications hub, her years of quiet observation proving invaluable as she coordinated with trusted contacts. Nova worked with the quantum key, ensuring their transmission methods would be as secure as the original encryption.

As Mandy watched her unlikely army assemble, she touched the jade pendant, now empty of its secrets but heavy with promise. In its smooth surface, she caught a reflection of herself - no longer just ICE's granddaughter, but a leader in her own right, forged in ice and fire.

"We're coming for them, Grandma," she whispered. "All of us."

The game was entering its final phase. The Consortium had no idea what was about to hit them. But they were about to learn that sometimes, the most dangerous force isn't the ice you can see - it's the frost spreading silently in the dark, ready to shatter everything in its path.

Within hours, the safe house had transformed into a war room that would have made ICE proud. Ghost had configured their system into a quantum-secure network hub, using principles that Nova explained were based on the same encryption methods that protected the pendant's data. Multiple screens displayed different aspects of The Consortium's operation, each one revealing another layer of their infiltration into global systems.

"Look at this," Ghost said, pulling up a new dataset. "They've been positioning people in central banks for decades. Not just executives - IT staff, security personnel, even maintenance crews. They don't just control the top, they own the infrastructure."

Nova nodded, her fingers dancing across her own keyboard. "That was always their strength. While other organizations fought for the spotlight, The Consortium built their power from the ground up. But it's also their weakness." She smiled, the expression sharp as a blade. "When we expose their network, the whole thing collapses like a house of cards."

Abby had transformed a corner of the room into an intelligence center, multiple phones and secure tablets arranged before her. Her years of quiet observation had given her an encyclopedic knowledge of who could be trusted - journalists, activists, reformed hackers, even a few government officials who had resisted The Consortium's influence.

"I've got confirmations from our primary contacts," she reported, her voice carrying the calm efficiency Mandy remembered from childhood crisis management. "They're ready to move on our signal. The Washington Post team has their secure server prepared, and the EU oversight committee is standing by."

Mandy studied the massive digital map Ghost had projected onto one wall, showing The Consortium's global reach in pulsing red lines. It reminded her of frost spreading across a window, each crystalline branch connecting to others in an ever-expanding network. But this time, they would use that network against them.

"We need to coordinate the information release," she said, years of training crystallizing into strategy. "Not just a data dump - a precisely orchestrated revelation that they can't contain or discredit."

Nova approached the map, her quantum key generator humming softly in her hand. "We can use the quantum encryption itself as proof. The mathematics behind it... it's not just security, it's a signature. Every piece of data we release will carry absolute proof of its authenticity."

"Like a blockchain?" Ghost asked, but Nova shook her head.

"Better. Blockchain can be forked, manipulated. This..." She held up the key generator. "This creates a quantum fingerprint that exists across multiple realities simultaneously. They can't fake it because they'd need to fake it in every possible quantum state at once."

Mandy thought of her grandmother's lessons about ice cream crystallization, how she'd used simple examples to teach complex principles. "So we're not just showing them the truth - we're proving it's the only possible truth."

"Exactly." Nova's eyes lit up with scientific passion. "That's why your grandmother chose this method. The Consortium's power is built on controlling multiple versions of reality, making people question what's real. But quantum mechanics doesn't allow that kind of uncertainty, not at this level. The truth collapses into a single, verifiable state."

A notification pinged on Ghost's system - another team checking in. This time it was from Singapore, one of ICE's oldest allies confirming their readiness to move. Mandy watched the confirmations roll in, each one representing another piece of the network her grandmother had spent decades building.

"We'll need to move fast once we start," Ghost warned, their fingers flying over the keyboard as they prepared the distribution protocols. "The Consortium's cyber response teams are world-class. They'll try to shut down every channel we use."

"That's why we're not just using cyber channels," Abby said, holding up one of her oldest notebooks. "I've spent years building backup communications networks - everything from ham radio operators to old-school dead drops. They can't shut down what they can't see."

Mandy felt the momentum building, the energy in the room shifting from desperate preparation to focused readiness. This was what her grandmother had prepared her for, what all those lessons about ice and transformation had really meant. The Consortium thought they were the masters of working in shadows - but they'd forgotten about the people who lived in those shadows, the ones who'd learned to survive and thrive there.

"Seventy-two hours," she said, checking the timeline Nova had provided. "Three days until they launch Project Eclipse." She turned to face her assembled team, seeing in each of them a reflection of the legacy they were about to fulfill. "That gives us exactly one shot at this. We hit them everywhere at once - every bank, every corporation, every government office they've infiltrated. We expose every operative, every manipulation, every crime they've committed for the past fifty years."

Nova's quantum key generator pulsed with ethereal light as she made the final calibrations. "Once we start the quantum broadcast, there's no turning back. The information will propagate across every network simultaneously, each piece carrying its own proof of authenticity."

"Good," Mandy said, thinking of Jasmine's sacrifice, of her grandmother's years of careful planning. "I want them to see it coming. I want them to know exactly what's happening as their whole world crashes down."

She touched the jade pendant one last time, feeling its emptiness like a promise fulfilled. The data it had protected was now spreading through their systems, being prepared for distribution across a network that spanned the globe. In seventy-two hours, that distribution would begin, and the world would change forever.

"Ghost, start the final encryption protocols. Mom, activate your journalist network. Nova..." She met the scientist's gaze. "Show us how to make truth itself into a weapon."

The safe house hummed with energy, computers and quantum devices working in harmony as they prepared for the biggest information warfare campaign in history. This wasn't just about revenge anymore - it was about fulfilling a legacy, about proving that sometimes the most powerful force isn't the one everyone can see, but the one working silently beneath the surface.

Ice was patient. Ice was transformative. And in less than seventy-two hours, the frost they'd been spreading through The Consortium's network would finally crystallize, shattering their entire world with the pure, cold truth.

The assembly was complete. The weapons were primed. The army of shadows was in position.

Now it was time for war.

23 PRODIGAL HOMECOMING

The first rays of dawn painted the safe house windows in shades of amber and gold. Mandy stood at the surveillance monitors, watching the quantum encryption protocols Ghost and Nova had established continuing their work. The war room they'd assembled over the last twenty-four hours hummed with purpose - screens displaying global network connections, Abby's intelligence hub still active with incoming messages from their activated network of allies.

The jade pendant hung empty around her neck, its secrets now dispersed through their quantum-secured systems but no less precious for their absence. Ghost's screens still displayed the fractal patterns of the decoded data, each piece of evidence protected by the same revolutionary encryption her grandmother had developed.

A movement on the perimeter camera caught her eye. A lone figure approaching on foot, hands raised to show they were unarmed. Something about the way they moved, the set of those shoulders...

"Mom," Mandy called, her voice tight. "You need to see this."

Abby appeared at her shoulder, setting down one of her intelligence notebooks. The pen she'd been using clattered to the floor as she recognized the figure.

"Drake," she whispered.

Mandy's father stood at their gates, older than she remembered, his dark hair now streaked with silver. But his stance was still that of a cop – watchful, ready, carrying the weight of authority even with his hands in the air.

"Security breach?" Ghost demanded, fingers flying over keyboards to check their quantum-encrypted perimeter.

"No," Nova said quietly, studying the monitors with knowing eyes. "He's always known where we were. He's part of the old network - one of the deepest covered assets we had."

Before Mandy could process that revelation, her mother was moving. Abby ran for the door, all pretense of caution forgotten. Mandy followed, weapon drawn more from instinct than intent. After Jasmine's death and the revelations of the last day, those instincts had only grown sharper.

But when she saw her parents embrace in the pale morning light, those instincts fell silent.

"I'm sorry," Drake was saying, his voice rough with emotion. "I'm sorry it took me this long to come in. But when Nova activated the quantum broadcast preparations..."

Mandy stepped forward, and her father's eyes found her. They stared at each other across eight years of absence, neither quite sure how to bridge that gap.

"You've grown so much," Drake said finally, his cop's composure cracking. "God, Mandy, I've missed you so much."

She meant to be cautious, to ask the necessary questions first. But somehow she was in his arms, breathing in the familiar scent of his aftershave, feeling like that scared fifteen-year-old girl again.

"How?" she managed, pulling back to study his face. "How did you know it was time?"

Drake's smile was sad. "The same way I've known where you were all along. The same way I've been helping keep you one step ahead of Blackwood's people all these years." He glanced at Nova. "When the quantum key generator activated, I knew you'd finally accessed Amanda's files."

Understanding dawned. "You were ICE's source in law enforcement."

They moved inside, where Nova and Ghost waited in the transformed war room. Drake took in the setup - the multiple screens displaying their gathered intelligence, the quantum encryption protocols running in the background, Abby's careful notebooks spread across her workstation.

"Your grandmother recruited me twenty-five years ago," Drake explained, settling into a chair at their command center. "I was a rookie cop, idealistic, angry at the corruption I saw in the department. She showed me how deep it really went – and offered me a chance to fight back."

"All this time," Abby breathed, "you were part of her network?"

Drake took her hand. "Not everything. Amanda compartmentalized her operations. I knew she was building a case against The Consortium, knew about the quantum encryption system she was developing with Nova, but I didn't know the full scope until..." He swallowed hard. "Until it was too late."

"The night she disappeared," Mandy said. It wasn't a question.

Her father nodded grimly. "I was supposed to meet her, to secure one of the quantum keys. But someone tipped off The Consortium. By the time I got to the rendezvous point..."

"Why didn't you tell us?" Abby demanded, years of fear and worry evident in her voice.

"To protect you. Both of you. If anyone had suspected I was ICE's inside man..." Drake's hands clenched into fists. "I couldn't risk it. So I played my role – the worried father, the dedicated cop searching for his missing daughter. All while using my position to keep you safe, to feed you information when I could."

Nova spoke up, her scientist's precision mixing with operational experience. "Drake's intelligence was crucial in developing the quantum security protocols. We needed someone inside law enforcement who could verify the authenticity of the evidence we were gathering."

Mandy thought back over the years, remembering the strange coincidences that had sometimes saved her. Tips that had seemed to come from nowhere. Close calls that shouldn't have worked out.

"It was you," she whispered. "Paris. Bangkok. That night in Vegas..."

Drake smiled. "I had some help. Your grandmother's network ran deeper than anyone knew. We've been watching over you, waiting for the right moment." He turned to Nova. "When I saw the quantum key activation signature, I knew you'd made it through the pendant's security."

"And now?" Ghost asked from their station, where fractal patterns of decrypted data still danced across their screens.

"Now we're out of time." Drake pulled out his phone, showing them a series of encrypted messages. "The Consortium is moving faster than even Nova's intelligence suggested. Project Eclipse launches in 48 hours."

Nova straightened. "That's not possible. We calculated 72 hours based on their quantum network preparations..."

"They don't care about the preparations anymore," Drake cut her off. "They're pushing ahead anyway. If it works, they'll control the global economy. If it fails..." He let the implication hang heavy in the air.

"Global financial collapse," Ghost finished, pulling up their analysis of The Consortium's infiltration of central banks. "Every market, every bank, every digital transaction system – it all goes down."

Mandy looked around the room, at the unlikely family fate had assembled. Her father, the secret guardian. Her mother, the patient observer. Nova, the deep-cover agent. Ghost, the loyal partner. And herself – ICE's granddaughter, carrying a legacy she finally understood.

"Then we have 48 hours to stop them," she said, her voice carrying the kind of authority that would have made her grandmother proud. "Good thing we've already started the quantum broadcast preparations."

Drake smiled, and for a moment Mandy saw the echo of that young idealistic cop who'd joined ICE's crusade. "The prodigal daughter returns," he said softly. "And not a moment too soon."

They gathered around the planning table, where Ghost's screens displayed the full scope of their operation. The quantum-encrypted evidence from the pendant now formed the backbone of their attack plan, each piece of data carrying its own unbreakable proof of authenticity.

"We'll need to accelerate the timeline," Nova said, adjusting settings on her quantum key generator. "The broadcast system is ready, but we planned for a 72-hour window to establish all the secure channels."

Drake nodded. "I can help with that. I have access to emergency broadcast systems through law enforcement channels. If we route the quantum-secured data through those..."

"It would bypass their standard cybersecurity entirely," Ghost finished, already coding new protocols. "They'd never expect us to use official channels for the data burst."

Mandy felt the last pieces of her fragmented life clicking into place. The weight of her family's legacy, once a burden, now felt like armor. Everything they'd prepared over the last twenty-four hours - the quantum encryption, the global network of allies, the carefully gathered evidence - it was all coming together faster than they'd planned, but maybe that was for the best.

The Consortium had no idea what was coming. The frost was gathering, and this time, it would freeze them solid.

As the sun rose fully over the safe house, Mandy touched the empty pendant, thinking of her grandmother's lessons about ice and transformation. The quantum encryption that had protected its secrets was now spreading through their networks, preparing to shatter The Consortium's carefully constructed reality with undeniable truth.

They had 48 hours to save the world. It was time to make them count.

The war room pulsed with renewed energy as Drake integrated his intelligence with their existing plans. Ghost's screens multiplied, each displaying different aspects of the accelerated timeline. Abby's communication hub lit up with updates from their global network, now supplemented by Drake's law enforcement contacts. Nova worked with the quantum key, ensuring their transmission methods would be secure even at the faster pace.

The game was entering its final phase. And this time, they had everything they needed to win.

The ice was spreading. The truth was armed. And The Consortium's time was finally running out.

"Walk me through what you've set up," Drake said, studying the complex network diagrams on Ghost's main screen. The quantum encryption patterns pulsed with an otherworldly rhythm, each node representing a piece of evidence ready to be released.

Nova brought up a detailed timeline on another display. "The quantum broadcast system works in three phases," she explained, her scientist's precision mixing with tactical expertise. "First, we use the quantum keys to authenticate every piece of evidence. The encryption method Amanda developed doesn't just protect the data - it proves its origin and authenticity across multiple quantum states simultaneously."

"Like a blockchain?" Drake asked, but Ghost shook their head, fingers dancing across their keyboard.

"Better," they said, pulling up a visualization of the encryption pattern. "Blockchain can be forked, manipulated. This creates what Nova calls a quantum fingerprint - it exists in multiple realities at once. They can't fake it because they'd need to fake it in every possible quantum state simultaneously."

"Which is mathematically impossible," Nova added. "Your mother-in-law was brilliant, Drake. She didn't just create a security system - she created a way to make truth itself undeniable."

Abby spoke up from her communications hub, where messages from their global network continued to arrive. "The second phase is distribution. We're not just dumping the data - we're orchestrating a precise sequence of revelations that they can't contain or discredit."

She spread out her notebooks, showing years of carefully mapped connections. "Every journalist, every activist, every reformed hacker in our network has been assigned specific pieces of evidence. When we give the signal, they'll release their parts in a carefully timed sequence."

"Like dominos," Mandy said, remembering her grandmother's lessons about chain reactions and transformation. "Each revelation building on the last, gaining momentum..."

"Until the whole thing comes crashing down," Drake finished. He pulled out his phone, showing them new intelligence. "My contacts in federal law enforcement are ready. The moment the quantum broadcast begins, they'll move to secure key facilities and suspects. We can't risk The Consortium destroying evidence or escaping once they realize what's happening."

Ghost's screens lit up with another successful test of the quantum encryption protocols. "Phase three is protection," they said, revealing layers of cybersecurity that went far beyond standard firewalls. "Once the broadcast begins, they'll try to shut down every channel we use. But the quantum encryption doesn't just protect the data - it makes it self-replicating."

"Like ice crystals growing," Mandy murmured, touching the empty pendant. "Each piece containing the pattern for making more..."

Nova nodded approvingly. "Exactly. The truth doesn't just spread - it proves itself as it goes. Every copy carries its own quantum signature, verifying its authenticity. They can't stop it any more than they could stop water from freezing."

"But we have to move faster now," Drake reminded them, his cop's instincts for timing evident in his voice. "Forty-eight hours isn't much time to coordinate a global operation of this scale."

Mandy studied the timeline, thinking through the implications. "Ghost, how quickly can you recalibrate the quantum broadcast for the shorter window?"

"Already on it," they replied, their screens filling with new code. "The basic architecture is solid - we just need to compress the distribution sequence. Instead of releasing the data in waves over 72 hours..."

"We hit them with everything at once," Nova finished. She adjusted something on her quantum key generator, causing new patterns to emerge on the displays. "It's riskier - we won't have time to adapt if they block some channels. But if we succeed..."

"They won't have time to react at all," Abby said, her voice carrying the quiet certainty of someone who'd spent years watching and waiting. She began sorting through her contact lists, prioritizing the most crucial revelations. "I'll have our network ready for simultaneous release in all major time zones."

Drake moved to one of the secondary stations, logging into secure law enforcement networks. "I can get us access to emergency broadcast systems in twelve countries. If we route the quantum-secured data through official channels..."

"They'll never expect it," Ghost finished, their fingers flying over the keyboard. "The Consortium's cybersecurity is focused on blocking unofficial channels. They won't be watching their own systems."

Mandy felt the energy in the room shift as their plans crystallized. This was what her grandmother had prepared them for - not just gathering evidence, but knowing how to use it. The quantum encryption wasn't just about protecting data - it was about proving truth in a world where reality itself had become negotiable.

"Nova," she said, decision made, "start recalibrating the quantum broadcast. Ghost, modify the distribution protocols for simultaneous release. Mom, get our network ready for immediate action. Dad..." She met her father's eyes, seeing in them the same determination she felt. "Coordinate with your law enforcement contacts. I want teams ready to move the moment we go live."

As they worked, Mandy thought about the layers of preparation that had brought them to this moment. Her grandmother's brilliant encryption system, preserved in the jade pendant for years. Nova's deep cover operation, gathering intelligence from within The Consortium itself. Her mother's patient observation and network-building. Ghost's technical expertise. And now her father's law enforcement connections, the final piece they needed to turn truth into action.

The war room pulsed with renewed energy as they raced against time. Ghost's screens multiplied, each displaying different aspects of the accelerated plan. Abby's communication hub lit up with updates from their global network, now supplemented by Drake's law enforcement contacts. Nova worked with the quantum key, ensuring their transmission methods would be secure even at the faster pace.

Looking around at her assembled team - her family, both blood and chosen - Mandy felt a fierce pride. The Consortium thought they were the masters of working in shadows, but they'd forgotten about the people who lived in those shadows, the ones who'd learned to survive and thrive there.

"Ghost," she called out, "how long until the recalibration is complete?"

They checked their systems, where the quantum encryption patterns continued their ethereal dance. "Two hours for the basic protocols. Another four to test the compressed distribution sequence. After that..."

"After that, we'll be ready to change the world," Nova said softly, her scientist's precision giving way to something like awe as she watched the quantum signatures multiply across their screens.

Drake stepped up beside Mandy, placing a hand on her shoulder. "Your grandmother would be proud," he said quietly. "Not just of what you've done, but of who you've become. A leader who brings people together, who makes them believe in impossible things."

Mandy touched the empty pendant, thinking of all the lessons about ice and transformation that had led to this moment. The quantum encryption that had protected its secrets was now spreading through their networks, preparing to shatter The Consortium's carefully constructed reality with undeniable truth.

They had 48 hours to save the world. But looking at her assembled team - Ghost's determined focus, Nova's brilliant precision, her mother's quiet strength, her father's steady presence - Mandy knew they had everything they needed to succeed.

The game was entering its final phase. And this time, they had the perfect weapon: truth itself, protected by quantum physics and proven beyond any possible doubt. The Consortium was about to learn that sometimes, the most dangerous force isn't the one everyone can see, but the one working silently beneath the surface, spreading like frost until the moment of crystallization changes everything.

The ice was gathering. The truth was armed. And The Consortium's time was finally running out.As the team worked to compress their timeline, Mandy found herself drawn to the quantum encryption patterns flowing across Ghost's screens. The fractal designs reminded her of frost patterns on winter windows - beautiful in their complexity, deadly in their purpose. Each crystalline branch represented another piece of evidence, another thread of truth that would help unravel The Consortium's carefully woven lies.

"The broadcast preparations are at sixty percent," Ghost reported, their fingers never stopping their dance across the keyboard. "Nova's compression algorithms are holding steady. The quantum signatures are maintaining coherence even at the accelerated pace."

Nova nodded approvingly from her station, where she was fine-tuning the quantum key generator. "Amanda's encryption method is proving more robust than even I expected. The quantum state remains stable no matter how fast we push the data through the system." She smiled, a mix of professional pride and personal satisfaction. "She always did think ten steps ahead of everyone else."

"Tell me about it," Drake said, looking up from his communications with law enforcement contacts. "The first time she recruited me, she laid out a plan so complex I thought she was crazy. But every piece fell into place, exactly as she predicted." He paused, lost in memory. "She said something that day that I never forgot. 'The truth is like ice, Drake. It has its own crystal structure, its own natural way of growing. Our job isn't to force it, but to create the conditions where it can't help but spread.'"

Abby's hands stilled on her keyboards. "I remember when she told me something similar. It was right after Mandy was born. She said that raising a child was like growing ice crystals - you can't control exactly how they form, but you can influence the conditions that shape them."

Mandy felt a sudden tightness in her throat. All these years, she'd thought her grandmother's lessons about ice and transformation were just interesting science experiments. But they had been so much more - a way of preparing her for this moment, teaching her how to think about complex systems and hidden patterns.

"Ghost," she called out, an idea forming. "Can you show me the current distribution map?"

The main screen shifted to display a global view of their network. Red lines showed The Consortium's connections, pulsing with malignant energy. Blue lines represented their own network - journalists, activists, law enforcement agencies, all waiting for the signal to act.

"Look at the pattern," Mandy said, stepping closer to the screen. "We've been thinking about this as a broadcast, but what if we treated it more like crystal formation? Start with seed points - key nodes where we know the evidence will have the most impact - and let the truth spread naturally from there."

Nova's eyes lit up with understanding. "Like nucleation sites in ice formation. The initial quantum broadcast creates seed points of verified truth, and then..."

"The rest of the evidence crystallizes around those points," Ghost finished, already modifying their code. "We don't have to control every aspect of the distribution. Once the quantum-encrypted data starts spreading, its own authenticity will drive it forward."

Drake moved to study the map more closely. "If we coordinate the law enforcement raids with these seed points, we can create maximum disruption right at the start. Hit their most vulnerable nodes while they're still trying to process the initial data release."

Abby was already sorting through her contact lists. "I can have our primary journalists ready to publish the most damaging evidence first. Once those stories break, the rest of the network will jump on them naturally. The quantum encryption will prove their authenticity, but the human desire for truth will drive the spread."

As they refined the new approach, Mandy felt the pieces clicking into place with almost audible precision. This was what her grandmother had been preparing them for all along. Not just gathering evidence or building a network, but understanding how to work with the natural forces that shaped human society. The same principles that governed ice formation also governed the spread of information - you just had to understand the underlying patterns.

"Nova," she said, decision made, "recalibrate the quantum broadcast for the seed point approach. Focus the initial burst on our strongest evidence, the pieces that can't be denied or explained away. Ghost, modify the distribution protocols to support organic spread from those points. Mom, coordinate with our primary contacts - I want them ready to move the moment the first quantum signatures appear. Dad..." She met her father's steady gaze. "Make sure your teams know which targets to hit first. We need to disrupt their ability to respond right from the start."

The war room hummed with renewed purpose as they implemented the new strategy. Ghost's screens showed the quantum encryption patterns adapting to the modified approach, the fractal designs becoming even more complex as they prepared to seed truth throughout the global network. Nova worked with the quantum key generator, ensuring each piece of evidence would carry its own unbreakable proof of authenticity. Abby's communication hub pulsed with activity as she prepared their allies for the revised timeline. Drake coordinated with law enforcement agencies around the world, synchronizing their raids with the planned data release.

Looking around at her assembled team - her family, both blood and chosen - Mandy felt a fierce pride that went beyond personal connection. They weren't just fighting The Consortium anymore. They were working with fundamental forces, using the natural patterns of truth and information to reshape reality itself.

The empty jade pendant seemed lighter now, its purpose fulfilled. The quantum-encrypted evidence it had protected was about to become something more powerful than mere data. It would become a seed crystal of truth, spreading through the global network with the inexorable force of ice growing in winter.

They had 48 hours until Project Eclipse launched. But now they had something more than just a plan. They had understanding - of technology, of human nature, of the patterns that governed both. The Consortium thought they controlled reality because they controlled information. They were about to learn that some forces couldn't be controlled, only channeled.

The ice was gathering. The truth was armed. And The Consortium's time was finally running out. Winter was coming for them, not with fury and force, but with the quiet, unstoppable power of crystallization changing everything it touched.

In the war room of their safe house, surrounded by quantum encryption patterns and the steady rhythm of preparation, Mandy touched the empty pendant one last time. "We're ready, Grandma," she whispered. "The ice is spreading, just like you taught me. And this time, nothing will stop it from growing."

24 INHERITANCE

The screens cast a pale blue glow across the safe house command center as Ghost processed the last of the decrypted files. Mandy leaned forward, her throat tight as her grandmother's voice emerged from decades of digital silence. The quantum encryption patterns danced across multiple monitors, their crystalline structures reminiscent of the frost patterns her grandmother had taught her to study as a child.

"Project Avalanche, Entry 47," Amanda Johnson's recorded voice was strong, determined, carrying the same quiet authority that Mandy had heard in her mother's voice just hours before. "The network grows daily. Judges, bankers, corporate executives – all of them tired of being part of The Consortium's machine. All of them ready to stand up, to speak out. We're not just building a case anymore. We're building an army."

Mandy glanced at her father, seeing the recognition in his eyes. After their reunion in Chapter 23, every shared moment carried new weight, new understanding. "This was her real mission," Drake said softly, his hand unconsciously moving to touch the law enforcement badge he still carried. "Not just exposing corruption, but fostering revolution from within."

Ghost pulled up another file, this one a massive web of connections. Names, dates, financial records – all interconnected in an intricate dance of influence and resistance. At the center was a simple snowflake icon: ICE. The quantum encryption patterns surrounding it pulsed with the same rhythm that had protected the jade pendant's secrets for so long.

"She was incredible," Nova breathed, studying the network with the same analytical precision she'd brought to recalibrating their broadcast timeline. "Look at how deep this goes. Whistleblowers in every major financial institution. Reformers placed in key positions. She wasn't just gathering evidence – she was positioning pieces for a complete systemic overhaul."

Another recording started, this one dated just days before ICE's disappearance. Amanda's voice was tighter now, edged with urgency but still carrying that core of unshakeable determination that Mandy had come to recognize in herself.

"They're getting close. Someone in the inner circle suspects. But we're too close to stop now. The quantum encryption is nearly ready. Once the evidence is secured and distributed to all our sleeper cells..." A pause, heavy with meaning. "If anything happens to me, the failsafes are in place. The truth will emerge. The frost will spread."

Mandy's fingers found the empty jade pendant, its weight suddenly more significant. The quantum-encrypted data it had contained now flowed through their systems, protected by the same revolutionary security that had kept it safe all these years. "She knew," she whispered. "She knew they were coming for her."

"Yes," her mother confirmed, tears in her eyes as she moved to stand beside her daughter. Abby's intelligence notebooks lay open nearby, their careful observations now merging with the digital evidence they'd uncovered. "But she didn't run. She made sure the evidence was safe, made sure the network would survive without her."

Ghost's fingers flew across the keyboard, bringing up more files. Internal Consortium communications, security footage, financial transfers – all pointing to the night ICE vanished. Each piece of evidence carried its own quantum signature, proving its authenticity across multiple states simultaneously.

"They didn't kill her," Ghost said, their voice tight with discovery. Their screens shifted to display a series of encrypted orders, each bearing The Consortium's highest security classifications. "Look at this. The order came from the top: 'Secure and contain. Asset too valuable to eliminate.' They took her somewhere."

The revelation hit Mandy like a physical blow, echoing through the quantum-secured networks they'd established. All these years, she'd assumed her grandmother was dead, another victim of The Consortium's ruthless efficiency. But if she was alive...

"Focus," Nova cut through her thoughts, gentle but firm. The quantum key generator hummed in the background, preparing for their compressed timeline. "We can't afford to get distracted. Not now. Your grandmother's mission was bigger than any one person – even her. She knew that. That's why she left all of this, prepared everything so carefully."

Drake nodded, the cop in him emerging as he studied the files. His years of undercover work within ICE's network had taught him to look beyond the obvious. "She built a foundation. Created the tools and positioned the players. But she knew it would take someone else to light the fuse."

"Someone they wouldn't suspect," Abby added, her years of patient observation evident in her voice. "Someone who could move freely while they watched all the obvious threats."

Mandy stood, moving to the window. The rising sun painted the sky in shades of fire and promise, its light catching the quantum encryption patterns that danced across their screens. Everything she'd learned, everything she'd become over the past eight years – it hadn't been random. Her grandmother had known, had planned, had prepared the way.

"The heir apparent," she said softly, understanding dawning. "That's what Jasmine called me. Not just heir to ICE's legacy, but to her mission. The final piece she needed to bring it all down."

Ghost pulled up another file, this one heavily encrypted even within the quantum security. As it decoded, a simple message appeared: "For my snowflake, when the time comes."

The file contained detailed plans, contingencies within contingencies. Attack vectors, security weaknesses, compromise protocols – everything needed to infiltrate The Consortium's quantum networks and expose their operation to the world. Each piece of evidence was protected by the same revolutionary encryption that had kept the pendant's secrets safe, designed to spread truth through the global network like frost creeping across a winter window.

"It's all here," Ghost whispered, awe in their voice. The quantum signatures multiplied across their screens, each one carrying its own unbreakable proof of authenticity. "Everything we need. She really did think of everything."

Mandy turned back to her assembled family – by blood and by choice. In each face, she saw the same determination, the same readiness for what had to come next. The quantum broadcast preparations they'd compressed into their 48-hour window hummed in the background, ready to seed truth throughout the global network.

"Then we use it," she declared, her voice carrying the quiet authority that had made her grandmother legendary. "All of it. We activate every sleeper, every whistleblower, every reformer in her network. When Project Eclipse launches in 48 hours, they won't just be fighting us – they'll be fighting an uprising from within their own ranks."

Nova smiled, fierce and proud. The quantum key generator pulsed with increased energy as their compressed timeline approached its critical moment. "ICE's final play. Hidden in plain sight all these years, waiting for the right moment."

"And the right person to trigger it," Drake added, looking at his daughter with newfound understanding. The years of separation melted away as they stood united in purpose.

Mandy took a deep breath, feeling the weight of inheritance settle on her shoulders – not as a burden now, but as armor. Purpose crystallized, sharp and clear as frost. The quantum encryption that had protected her grandmother's legacy now stood ready to shatter The Consortium's carefully constructed reality.

"Ghost, start distributing the activation codes. Mom, Dad, coordinate with every law enforcement contact you can trust. Nova, get your people in position." Her voice carried the same quiet authority that had made her grandmother legendary. "In 48 hours, The Consortium learns what ICE always knew – you can't stop an idea whose time has come."

As they moved into action, Mandy touched the jade pendant one last time. The quantum-encrypted evidence it had contained now flowed through their systems, protected by the same revolutionary security that had kept it safe all these years. "I understand now, Grandma," she whispered. "And I'm ready."

The frost was spreading, silent and inexorable. The Consortium had built their house of cards, thinking themselves untouchable in their towers of power and privilege. They'd forgotten the most basic truth about ice – when it infiltrates the smallest cracks, spreads through the strongest foundations, even mountains can shatter.

And this time, the avalanche would bury them all.

The quantum encryption patterns continued their ethereal dance across the screens, each crystalline branch representing another piece of evidence ready to be released. In 48 hours, truth itself would become a weapon, protected by quantum physics and proven beyond any possible doubt. The Consortium was about to learn that sometimes, the most dangerous force isn't the one everyone can see, but the one working silently beneath the surface, spreading like frost until the moment of crystallization changes everything.

25 LABYRINTH

The Consortium's headquarters cut the night sky with crystalline surfaces that fractured city lights in patterns reminiscent of the quantum encryption displays. Mandy adjusted her stolen security uniform, fingers touching the jade pendant now housing infiltration software rather than her grandmother's secrets. "Nova's in Operations," Ghost reported in her ear. "Your mother has a security hub. Dad's team is standing by." A pause. "Sure, about this, Snowflake?" Mandy traced the pendant, remembering the evidence it once contained.

Now those same security protocols were spreading through The Consortium's networks like frost through tiny cracks. "The quantum servers can only be accessed locally. One shot." The employee entrance scanners cast the same blue light as their safe house screens. Her heart remained steady, eight years of training crystallizing into this moment. The stolen keycard worked perfectly – its owner currently sleeping off Nova's specially crafted cocktail.

The lobby's sterile brightness gave way to service corridors. Mandy moved with purposeful confidence, invisible in her ordinariness – exactly as her grandmother had planned. With each step deeper into the facility, the pendant's weight reminded her of everything at stake. "Mirror team is go," Ghost reported. "Twenty minutes before security patterns change. Quantum key generator primed." The air grew cooler three levels down, heavy with the hum of climate systems protecting sensitive equipment. ICE's message echoed in her thoughts: "For my snowflake, when the time comes." Everything had been prepared for, predicted, planned – down to Mandy as the heir apparent they'd never suspect.

The lobby's sterile brightness gave way to the utilitarian backdrop of service corridors. Mandy moved with purposeful confidence, channeling the demeanor of the countless security personnel she'd observed during weeks of surveillance. Just another cog in The Consortium's machine, invisible in plain sight – exactly as her grandmother had planned all those years ago.

"Mirror team is go," Ghost reported, their voice carrying the same focused intensity from their command center operations. "They're starting their diversion on the east side. You've got maybe twenty minutes before security patterns change. The quantum key generator is primed and ready."

Mandy navigated the labyrinthine halls, each turn bringing her deeper into the heart of the facility. The air grew cooler, heavy with the hum of massive climate control systems protecting sensitive equipment. Her grandmother's message echoed in her thoughts: "For my snowflake, when the time comes." Everything about this moment had been prepared for, predicted, planned – right down to her role as the heir apparent they'd never suspect.

She was three levels down when the first hint of wrongness prickled her spine. The corridor ahead was empty, but something about the shadows seemed wrong, carrying echoes of her father's lessons about trusting instincts over appearances.

"Well, well," a familiar voice emerged from an alcove. "The prodigal returns."

Cobra stepped into view, his weathered face haunted by years of forced service. The gun in his hand didn't waver, but neither did it point directly at her. In that subtle restraint lay volumes of unspoken history.

"You're supposed to be dead," Mandy said, her own weapon remaining holstered. Her mind raced through the network map they'd discovered in her grandmother's files, wondering if Cobra's apparent death had been another layer of ICE's intricate planning.

"Funny thing about that." Cobra's smile was bitter, etched with years of carefully hidden resistance. "Hard to die when they've got your family locked away as insurance. Amazing what a man will do when they're threatening his daughter."

Understanding dawned, illuminating another piece of The Consortium's control matrix. "They forced you to work for them."

"Just like they forced a lot of people. The Consortium's real power isn't in their money or their technology. It's in what they know about everyone. The secrets they hold, the leverage they create." He gestured with the gun, its movement carrying the weight of countless compromises. "Your grandmother figured that out. That's why they took her."

Mandy's heart skipped, Ghost's earlier discovery confirmed in the worst possible way. "She's alive?"

"In a manner of speaking. They keep her in a facility upstate. Locked away but alive – a reminder to anyone who thinks about crossing them." Cobra's eyes were haunted, carrying the weight of witnessed atrocities. "I've seen her, kid. She's... they broke her body, but not her spirit. She knew you'd come. She knew you'd finish it."

In her ear, Ghost was urgently reporting security team movements. The quantum encryption patterns they'd established were holding, but time was running out. Their carefully compressed timeline left no room for deviation.

"Help me," Mandy said softly, channeling her grandmother's quiet authority. "Help me tear it all down. For your daughter. For everyone they've enslaved. We've got people ready to move, whistleblowers in every division. The quantum broadcasts will prove everything beyond doubt."

Cobra's laugh was hollow, echoing off sterile walls. "You think I haven't thought about it? One bullet in the wrong place, one 'accidental' security breach..." He shook his head, decades of careful calculation evident in every movement. "But they've got it all wired. The minute I step out of line, my girl pays the price."

"We can protect her. My father's team-"

"Can't stop what's already in motion." Cobra's expression shifted, resolve replacing despair as he made a decision that would echo through their quantum-secured networks. "But maybe I can buy you a chance."

Before Mandy could react, alarms began blaring throughout the facility. Cobra fired his weapon – not at her, but at the security camera behind her. The sound of shattering electronics was nearly lost in the cacophony of alerts.

"Level Three breach in Sector Seven!" he shouted into his radio, even as he gestured for Mandy to run. "Multiple hostiles, need immediate backup!"

"Cobra-"

"Go!" he commanded, his voice carrying the same authority that had once made him legendary among ICE's operatives. "Server room's two levels down, northeast quadrant. The quantum core is behind a false wall.

Panel's coded to Blackwood's biometrics, but..." He pressed something into her hand, cool metal carrying the weight of years of patient planning. "Ice wasn't the only one preparing for this day."

The sound of running feet echoed from nearby corridors, boot steps carrying the rhythm of approaching chaos. Cobra's smile was fierce and final, carrying decades of carefully hidden defiance. "Give 'em hell, kid. For all of us."

He turned, firing down the hallway as security teams responded to his call. The last Mandy saw of him was his silhouette, standing firm as shadows converged – another piece in her grandmother's intricate game sacrificing itself for the greater victory.

She ran, Ghost's voice guiding her through the chaos Cobra's sacrifice had created. Down emergency stairs, through maintenance tunnels, ever deeper into the facility's maze-like heart. The device he'd given her pulsed faintly – some kind of biological key synthesizer, she realized, decades of accumulated access waiting to be unleashed.

The server room doors loomed ahead, their quantum-locked panels no match for ICE's inherited tools. Inside, the space was massive, rows of servers stretching into shadow like electronic tombstones. The air thrummed with power and possibility, each machine a potential carrier for their revolution.

"Ghost, I'm in. Starting the upload."

She moved quickly to the false wall Cobra had mentioned, the synthesizer already working to crack Blackwood's biometric signature. The panel slid aside with a soft hiss, revealing the quantum core's crystalline structure – the heart of The Consortium's control matrix, pulsing with the same rhythms as their encrypted evidence.

"I have to admit," a smooth voice called from the shadows, "I'm impressed. You've exceeded all our projections."

Mandy turned slowly, her grandmother's training screaming warnings in every nerve. Marcus Blackwood emerged into the pale blue light of the servers, immaculate as ever in his tailored suit. Power radiated from him like heat from the surrounding processors, absolute confidence born of decades of unchallenged control.

"Though really," he continued, satisfaction evident in every carefully measured word, "we should thank your grandmother. She did such a wonderful job preparing you for this moment." His smile was razor-sharp, cutting through layers of carefully constructed plans. "Would you like to see her? She's been asking about you."

Mandy's hand tightened on her weapon, but Blackwood's next words froze her in place, carrying the weight of countless ruined lives.

"Ah, ah," he cautioned, supreme confidence evident in every gesture. "I wouldn't. My death triggers some rather unfortunate contingencies. For your parents. For Ghost. For everyone you've tried so hard to protect." He spread his hands, encompassing the empire of secrets surrounding them. "Why do you think we let you get this far? The Consortium didn't survive this long by being predictable."

The quantum core hummed behind her, waiting. In her ear, Ghost's voice had gone silent – cut off or captured, she couldn't know. The labyrinth had led her here, but now she faced a choice that would change everything. Her grandmother's voice echoed in memory: "The frost will spread."

Blackwood watched her, satisfaction evident in his posture. He thought he held all the cards, just as The Consortium always had. But he'd forgotten something crucial about ice – its true power lay not in force, but in patience. In working silently, spreading through the smallest cracks until the moment of crystallization changed everything.

The quantum encryption patterns danced across nearby screens, carrying truth that could no longer be contained. All around them, sleeper agents and whistleblowers waited for their signal, positioned like fracture points in a frozen lake. Her grandmother had known this moment would come, had planned for it with the same patience that turned water to ice.

Mandy's hand moved to the jade pendant, feeling the pulse of their infiltration software spreading through The Consortium's networks like frost through tiny cracks. Blackwood saw the motion and smiled, misreading it as hesitation rather than activation.

The choice crystallized, sharp and clear as the winter mornings of her childhood. Sometimes, the most dangerous force wasn't the one everyone could see, but the one working silently beneath the surface. Her grandmother had understood that. Had built her entire revolution around that principle.

The frost was spreading. And this time, the avalanche would bury them all.

"Your grandmother had that same look," Blackwood mused, taking a measured step forward. "That moment of decision. Did you know she was pregnant with your mother when we recruited her? Brilliant minds are so often more pliable when they have something to protect." His smile turned predatory. "Of course, she didn't stay pliable for long."

The quantum core's hum changed pitch behind Mandy, its crystalline structure responding to the infiltration software spreading through the network. In her ear, static had replaced Ghost's voice, but she could still feel the pulse of their quantum broadcast preparations moving through the system like a digital heartbeat.

"You talk about her like you knew her," Mandy said, buying time as the software worked. Her fingers traced the edge of the jade pendant, feeling the subtle vibrations that meant their virus was spreading. "But you didn't. Not really."

Blackwood laughed, the sound echoing off server racks like breaking glass. "Oh, but I did. Twenty years of watching someone, studying their every move, learning their patterns... you get to know them quite intimately." He gestured at the surrounding technology. "How do you think we built all this? Your grandmother's work on quantum encryption was revolutionary. We just... redirected it."

"You stole it," Mandy corrected, anger burning cold and sharp as winter wind. "You took her research and twisted it into chains."

"We improved it," Blackwood countered. "Gave it purpose. Structure. The world needs order, Mandy. Your grandmother never understood that. She saw our methods as corruption, but look around you." He spread his arms, encompassing the massive server room. "We've created stability. Prosperity. A system where everyone knows their place."

"A prison," Mandy said softly, thinking of Cobra's daughter, of all the other hostages to fortune The Consortium held. "Built with secrets and lies."

"A foundation," Blackwood corrected. "Built on human nature. People will always have secrets, Mandy. We just... organize them. Channel them. Use them to maintain the balance that keeps civilization running." His eyes glittered in the blue server light. "Your grandmother's quantum encryption made it possible to secure those secrets permanently. Ironic, isn't it? Her attempt to expose us only made us stronger."

But there was something in his voice, a hint of strain beneath the confidence. Mandy thought of the frost patterns her grandmother had taught her to study, the way pressure built invisibly beneath the surface until the moment of crystallization changed everything.

"You're right about one thing," she said, letting her hand drop from the pendant. "My grandmother's work was revolutionary. But you never really understood it." A slight smile touched her lips. "You were so busy watching her, you forgot to watch everyone else."

Blackwood's eyes narrowed, the first hint of uncertainty crossing his features. "What are you talking about?"

"Twenty years of watching her," Mandy said, feeling the quantum pulses strengthen behind her. "Twenty years of thinking you had her contained. But she wasn't building a case against you. She was building an army."

As if on cue, the server room's lights flickered. Across the massive space, status indicators began changing color, spreading like frost across a window pane. Blackwood turned, genuine alarm breaking through his practiced calm.

"What have you done?"

"Nothing," Mandy said truthfully. "I'm just the key. The trigger. But my grandmother? She spent twenty years placing people in your organization. Judges. Executives. Security chiefs. People you thought were safely controlled, safely contained." The quantum core's hum was rising now, its crystalline structure resonating with changes spreading through the network. "People who were just waiting for the right moment. The right proof."

Blackwood's hand moved toward his pocket, but Mandy's voice stopped him. "I wouldn't. Those contingency protocols you mentioned? The ones targeting my family? Ghost's been dismantling them for the past twenty minutes. Turns out when you build your whole system on quantum encryption stolen from ICE, it's not that hard to break in. Not when you have the original source code."

The first alerts began sounding throughout the facility. Not security alerts now, but system warnings. Throughout the building, throughout the city, throughout the world, quantum-secured servers were activating. Evidence was spreading, protected by encryption that proved its authenticity beyond any possibility of doubt.

"Impossible," Blackwood breathed, watching status monitors flip from green to red. "We contained every copy of her research. Locked down every system."

"No," Mandy corrected gently. "You contained what you could see. What you thought was important. But my grandmother? She wrote her most important code into something you never thought to check. Something that passed right through your security every single day for twenty years."

Understanding dawned in Blackwood's eyes as alarms continued to spread through the facility. "The jade pendant. All those replicas we confiscated..."

"Were exactly what they appeared to be. Worthless copies." Mandy touched the pendant at her throat. "But the original? The one you let her keep because your scans showed it was harmless. That's been gathering data the whole time. Recording. Analyzing. Waiting." She smiled, her grandmother's quiet determination flowing through her voice. "Ice isn't just frozen water, Mr. Blackwood. It's a state change. A moment when everything crystallizes. Everything transforms."

The quantum core's hum had become a song now, its frequencies matching the cascade of system changes spreading through The Consortium's networks. Blackwood's phone buzzed urgently in his pocket – the first of what would soon be thousands of alerts as carefully positioned allies emerged from deep cover.

"You can't possibly believe you'll succeed," he said, but the strain in his voice betrayed his uncertainty. "The system is too big. Too entrenched. Even if you expose everything, the world runs on our networks. Our infrastructure."

"You still don't understand," Mandy said softly. "We're not trying to destroy the system. We're transforming it. Every piece of evidence being released comes with its own quantum signature, proving its authenticity. Every transaction, every secret deal, every piece of leverage you've gathered – all of it exposed and verified beyond any possibility of denial." She gestured at the changing displays around them. "The frost spreads, Mr. Blackwood. And when it reaches critical mass..."

A new alarm sounded, this one deeper and more urgent than the others. Blackwood's phone buzzed again, and this time when he looked at it, all color drained from his face

The avalanche had begun. And nothing could stop it now.

26 RECKONING

The server room's blue light cast harsh shadows across Blackwood's face as he circled Mandy, each step measured and precise. The quantum core pulsed behind her, its crystalline structure seeming to echo her racing heartbeat. Frost patterns had begun forming on its surface – an impossible phenomenon that somehow felt right, as if her grandmother's metaphors were manifesting in the physical world.

"You know," Blackwood mused, "your grandmother had that same look in her eyes the last time I saw her. That perfect mixture of hatred and calculation." His smile was almost fond, tinged with genuine regret. "She'd be proud of what you've become. The way you've played this game – patient, methodical, just like she taught you."

"Don't talk about her," Mandy growled, her weapon steady despite the storm of emotions inside. The jade pendant felt heavier now, weighted with two decades of careful planning. "You don't have the right. Not after what you did to her. To all of them."

"No?" Something shifted in Blackwood's expression – a crack in his perfect facade. For a moment, she glimpsed the man her grandmother had known, before power and control had corrupted whatever humanity he'd once possessed. "I loved her, you know. More than the power, more than The Consortium, more than anything. But Amanda... she was always so driven, so certain she could change the world. She never understood that sometimes the world needs its shadows, its secrets."

The revelation hit Mandy like a physical blow, pieces of her family's history realigning themselves. In her ear, Ghost's voice crackled back to life: "I'm broadcasting everything, Snowflake. Every word, every file. The world's about to see The Consortium for what it really is. The quantum signatures are spreading faster than they can contain them."

Blackwood's phone buzzed. His mask slipped further as he read the message, genuine fear flickering across his features. "Clever," he admitted. "Using our own quantum network against us. The encryption protocols she designed... we always wondered if there was a backdoor we'd missed. But did you really think we wouldn't have contingencies?"

He pressed a button on his phone. Alarm klaxons blared as blast doors slammed down throughout the facility. The sound reminded Mandy of ice cracking, of her grandmother's lessons about pressure and crystallization points.

"Total lockdown," he announced. "No one in, no one out. And in exactly ten minutes, this entire server complex will execute an electromagnetic pulse burst. Everything – the evidence, the broadcasts, your precious revolution – gone in an instant." His smile turned cruel. "Just like your grandmother's first attempt to expose us. History does love its echoes."

"Along with you," Mandy noted, watching frost patterns spread across nearby screens. "You really willing to die to protect your secrets? Or is this another bluff, like the contingency protocols Ghost just dismantled?"

Blackwood's laugh was hollow, echoing off servers that now hummed with her grandmother's viral code. "Die? My consciousness was uploaded to The Consortium's quantum storage years ago. This body is just a vessel." He spread his arms. "Kill me if you want. I'll simply wake up in a new one, while everything you've fought for burns. Amanda thought she could outmaneuver us too, right up until the moment we showed her how wrong she was."

Mandy's mind raced. The quantum core behind her held everything — not just evidence of The Consortium's crimes, but the key to their entire operation. Every secret, every leverage point, every digital chain they'd used to enslave people like Cobra. If it was destroyed...

"Ghost," she subvocalized, "how much has gone out?"

"Sixty percent of the files. But Mandy..." Ghost's voice carried the weight of impossible choices. "Your grandmother's location was in the last batch. If that core goes down before it transmits, we lose our only chance to find her. The quantum signatures proving she's alive will be lost."

The choice crystallized: pursue personal vengeance, try to save her grandmother, or ensure The Consortium's secrets reached the world. She couldn't do both. The ice metaphor had never felt more apt – pressure building beneath the surface, waiting for the perfect moment to transform everything.

Blackwood saw the conflict in her eyes. "Time's running out, little snowflake. What's it going to be? Family or duty? Love or justice?" His smile turned predatory. "Such delicious irony – the same choice your grandmother faced. And we both know how that ended. Twenty years in our custody, watching as everything she built was turned against the world she wanted to save."

"You're wrong," Mandy said softly, her grandmother's teachings flowing through her like winter wind. "Grandma didn't choose. She found another way." Her free hand moved to the jade pendant, feeling the subtle vibrations of quantum code awakening. "She knew sometimes the most powerful force isn't the obvious one. It's the one working silently, spreading through the smallest cracks until everything changes."

"Ghost, activate ICE Protocol."

"What are you-" Blackwood's eyes widened as new code began streaming across the quantum core's display, patterns of frost and fire dancing through The Consortium's digital architecture.

"A virus," Mandy explained, allowing herself a cold smile. "Written into the pendant's quantum structure years ago, right under your noses. The one place you never thought to look, because you were so sure you'd broken her. Right now it's replicating through your entire network. Every system, every backup, every digital bolt-hole you thought was secure."

The core's crystalline surface began to glow brighter, its hum rising to a fever pitch. Frost patterns spread across its surface, beautiful and terrible as winter storms. Blackwood lunged for a control panel, but Mandy's shot took him in the shoulder, spinning him away from the controls.

"Even if you destroy this facility," she continued, her grandmother's quiet strength flowing through her words, "the virus survives. It's in everything now, spreading through quantum pathways you never knew existed. And when it finishes its work..." She met his gaze steadily. "Every dirty secret, every hidden file, every scrap of evidence ICE ever gathered goes public. Including the location of every backup of your precious digital consciousness."

For the first time, real fear crossed Blackwood's face. "You'll die too. When the EMP-"

"Maybe," Mandy acknowledged, thinking of Cobra's sacrifice, of all the others who had given everything for this moment. "But I'm my grandmother's heir in every way. Some things are worth dying for. Some transformations require catalysts."

The countdown ticked past five minutes. Warning lights bathed the room in crimson, competing with the ethereal blue of the quantum core and the spreading frost patterns that now covered every surface. Through her earpiece, Ghost reported that Nova's team was trying to breach the lockdown, that her parents were coordinating with authorities outside.

But none of that mattered now. What mattered was the look of dawning comprehension on Blackwood's face as he realized just how completely he'd been outplayed. Twenty years of watching Amanda's daughter grow up, of thinking they understood the threat, and they'd missed the real danger entirely.

"She planned this," he whispered, something like awe creeping into his voice. "All of it. The pendant, the virus, you... ICE knew she wouldn't be the one to end it. She was just setting the stage, using your quantum networks to spread her code like frost through glass."

"For a new generation," Mandy finished, feeling the weight of inheritance in every word. "One you couldn't predict or control. One willing to sacrifice everything to tear down your house of cards." She gestured at the frost-covered screens surrounding them. "You thought quantum encryption would protect your secrets forever. But you forgot the most basic law of thermodynamics – everything changes state eventually. Everything transforms."

The quantum core's light had become almost blinding, its crystalline structure resonating with frequencies that made Mandy's teeth ache. Alerts screamed from every console as ICE's virus bore deeper into The Consortium's digital heart, spreading through pathways her grandmother had prepared decades ago.

Blackwood raised his gun, desperation replacing his usual smooth confidence. Blood from his shoulder wound stained his perfect suit, a splash of color in the blue-white radiance of the dying server room. "I can still kill you before-"

The shot echoed through the server room like breaking ice. Blackwood stared down at the spreading red stain on his chest, his weapon falling from nerveless fingers. In that moment, he looked old – not the ageless digital entity he'd become, but a man who had lost everything to his own hubris.

"That's for my grandmother," Mandy said quietly. "And for everyone else you tried to freeze in place while you played god with their lives."

She turned back to the quantum core, ignoring Blackwood's gasping breaths behind her. The countdown showed less than two minutes. Just enough time to make her final choice, to embrace the transformation her grandmother had prepared her for all along.

"Ghost," she commanded, "initiate Protocol Avalanche. Full broadcast, every channel we've got. Let it all come down."

"But Mandy, if we don't get you out-" Ghost's voice cracked with emotion, the first time she'd heard them lose composure in eight years of partnership.

"The mission comes first. The transformation has to complete." She smiled, feeling ice crystals form in the rapidly cooling air. "Just... tell my parents I love them. And I finally understand what

Grandma meant about pressure points and crystallization. Sometimes you have to be the catalyst."

As Ghost reluctantly complied, Mandy sank into a server bank chair. The quantum core's light wrapped around her like a shroud as The Consortium's secrets blazed across the world's digital networks. Frost patterns danced across every surface, beautiful and terrible as justice itself.

Blackwood's bitter laugh turned into a cough. "We're not so different, you and I. Both willing to die for what we believe in."

"No," Mandy corrected him, watching the countdown tick toward zero. "I'm willing to die for the truth. You're dying to protect lies. That's all The Consortium ever was – one giant lie about power and control. But the thing about lies..." She touched the jade pendant one last time. "They can't survive exposure. Not when the truth spreads like ice through every crack you left open."

The room's temperature plunged as systems began to overload. Through her earpiece, Ghost reported that the broadcast had reached critical mass. There would be no stopping it now, no containing the avalanche of revelations. The transformation was complete.

Mandy closed her eyes as the final seconds approached, feeling the cold embrace of her grandmother's legacy. "The frost spreads," she whispered, the words feeling right on her lips. "And everything breaks."

The world went white, and in that blinding moment of transformation, Mandy thought she felt her grandmother's presence – not imprisoned somewhere in The Consortium's facilities, but free and fierce as a winter storm, finally fulfilled in the change she'd spent decades preparing.

The avalanche had begun. And nothing would ever be the same.

27 LEGACY

Sunlight streamed through the hospital window, painting warm patterns across Mandy's bandaged hands. The quantum core explosion had left its mark – fine, frost-like scars tracing up her arms like delicate circuit patterns. Two weeks had passed since that moment in the server room, since Ghost's last-second override of the blast doors had saved her life while still allowing ICE's virus to complete its work. The world outside her recovery room was transforming, breaking and reforming in ways that even her grandmother might not have imagined.

The jade pendant rested cool against her chest; its quantum structure now dormant but still holding echoes of the code that had changed everything. Sometimes, in the quiet hours of night, Mandy thought she could feel it humming with remembered purpose, like ice remembering the moment of crystallization.

On the television mounted in the corner, another news report played: "In what analysts are calling 'The Great Revelation,' arrests continue worldwide as evidence exposed by the ICE Protocol leads to unprecedented action against The Consortium's network. Today, three more Supreme Court justices have resigned, while the European Union has frozen assets of over thirty major financial institutions. The quantum-encrypted data breach has exposed decades of manipulation, revealing a web of corruption that..."

A soft knock interrupted the broadcast. Nova stood in the doorway, looking more relaxed than Mandy had ever seen her. Gone was the rigid posture of a former operative, replaced by something closer to peace. "Your parents are handling the CIA briefing. Thought you might want to see this."

She handed Mandy a tablet displaying live security footage. In dozens of windows, Mandy watched as international authorities led former Consortium members from homes and offices. Bankers, politicians, corporate executives – the mighty brought low by the truth. Each arrest felt like another crack spreading through ice, another pressure point giving way.

"The quantum virus did more than expose their secrets," Nova explained, settling into the visitor's chair. Her fingers absently traced the scar on her neck – a reminder of her own history with The Consortium. "It unraveled their entire digital infrastructure. No more backups, no more hidden accounts, no more electronic insurance policies. They're just... people now. Vulnerable, accountable people."

Mandy's fingers traced the jade pendant, now repaired and hanging once more around her neck. "And Blackwood?"

"Maximum security wing at Florence. His digital consciousness backups were all corrupted by the virus. He's just flesh and blood now, facing multiple life sentences." Nova paused, studying Mandy's expression. "He's asked to see you."

The request hung in the air like frost crystals, delicate and sharp. Mandy was silent for a long moment, watching as more arrests played out on the tablet. Each face reminded her of the server room, of Blackwood's final moments of realization as everything he'd built crumbled around him.

"Take me to him," she said finally.

The next few days passed in a blur of medical checks and debriefings. Ghost visited daily, their usual digital presence supplemented now by cautious visits in person – a trust earned in fire and ice. They brought updates on the virus's spread, on the continuing avalanche of revelations that was reshaping the global power structure.

"It's beautiful, you know," Ghost said one evening, their dark eyes bright with appreciation. "The way your grandmother coded the virus. It's not just destructive – it's selective. Surgical. The quantum pathways she built... it's like she created a digital immune system, targeting corruption while preserving necessary infrastructure. Twenty years in captivity, and she was writing the future."

Mandy thought of the frost patterns that had spread across the server room screens, of the way ice could reshape landscapes while leaving delicate flowers untouched. "She always said the most powerful forces were the ones that worked through transformation, not destruction."

Finally cleared for travel, Mandy sat across from Marcus Blackwood in a stark concrete room. He looked smaller somehow, diminished without his tailored suits and technological advantages. Just an old man in prison orange, hands shackled to the table. The frost-like scars on her arms seemed to tingle in his presence.

"I didn't expect you to come," he said quietly.

"I almost didn't," Mandy admitted. The jade pendant felt heavier, a weight of history and choice. "But I needed to know one thing. Where is she?"

Blackwood's laugh was bitter. "After everything, that's what you want to know? The location was in the files, surely-"

"The facility was empty when authorities arrived," Mandy cut him off. Her voice carried the sharp edge of winter wind. "Where is my grandmother?"

Something like respect flickered in Blackwood's eyes. "You really are her heir," he said softly. "Always seeing the bigger picture. The facility was empty because she escaped during the chaos of The Great Revelation. All those years in captivity, and she was just... waiting. Building her strength. Planning. Like water freezing in rock cracks, patient until the moment of transformation."

Mandy's heart raced. "She's alive? Free?"

"Free," Blackwood confirmed, and for a moment, genuine emotion cracked his facade. "And still ten steps ahead of everyone. The ICE Protocol, the quantum virus... they weren't just her legacy to you. They were her escape route. While we were all focused on the digital avalanche, she simply... walked away. Just like she always said — the most powerful changes happen in the quiet moments between the obvious ones."

Tears pricked at Mandy's eyes. All this time, her grandmother had been playing an even longer game than anyone realized. The virus hadn't just been about exposure and justice — it had been a key, turning in digital locks that had held Amanda "ICE" Johnson captive for two decades.

"She'll find you when she's ready," Blackwood added, his voice carrying a strange mix of admiration and regret. "After she's made sure every last piece of The Consortium is truly gone. That was always her way — thorough to the end. Like frost spreading through every microscopic crack until the whole structure transforms."

He leaned forward, chains clinking. "You know what the worst part is? We thought we were containing her. Twenty years, watching her every move, thinking we had her under control. But she was spreading the whole time, wasn't she? Teaching through that pendant, encoding her knowledge in quantum structures we couldn't detect. Creating you — not just an heir, but a catalyst."

"You never understood her," Mandy said quietly. "You saw power as something to hoard, to freeze in place. She knew real power flows like winter streams, adapting and transforming."

"No," Blackwood corrected, "I understood her perfectly. That's why I loved her. Why I still do, God help me. She was always the perfect fusion of passion and patience, of fire and ice. I just thought..." He trailed off, staring at his shackled hands. "I thought I could control that force, direct it. As if anyone could control an avalanche."

As Mandy left the prison, her phone buzzed with a text from an unknown number. A single image: a fresh snowflake drawn in frost on a window pane. Below it, two words: "Well done."

The world was still transforming in the wake of The Great Revelation. Every day brought new resignations, new confessions, new evidence of The Consortium's reach. But it wasn't just about exposure anymore – it was about reconstruction, about building something better from the crystalline ruins of the old order.

Ghost had taken charge of securing and analyzing the quantum networks, ensuring that no shadow of The Consortium's digital infrastructure could ever be rebuilt. Nova led a task force helping former operatives like herself reintegrate, healing old wounds and building new connections. And Mandy's parents had emerged as powerful voices for reform, their years of quiet resistance finally bearing fruit.

Back in her hospital room that evening, they all gathered to celebrate her impending release. Her mother Abby brought contraband champagne, while her father Drake produced a small box wrapped in silver paper.

"We found this in the evidence lockup," he explained as Mandy unwrapped it. "It was in your grandmother's personal effects at the facility. The note said it was for today."

Inside was a delicate silver bracelet, frost patterns etched into its surface. A small quantum chip gleamed at its heart, and when Mandy slipped it on, she felt the familiar hum of her grandmother's code singing through the metal.

"It's not just jewelry," Ghost observed, their eyes gleaming with technological appreciation. "It's a key to something. The quantum signatures..."

"Are still propagating," Nova finished, checking her phone. "The virus didn't just expose The Consortium's networks – it's been rebuilding something in their place. A new kind of infrastructure, designed for transparency instead of control."

"A framework for the future," Mandy murmured, remembering her grandmother's lessons about systems and transformation. "Not a weapon anymore, but a tool for change."

"So what now?" Ghost asked as they shared the champagne. "The Consortium's finished, Blackwood's locked up, your grandmother's out there somewhere... what's next for ICE's heir?"

Mandy looked around at the faces of those who had risked everything to help her fight for truth. Her mother's strength, her father's dedication, Ghost's brilliance, Nova's unwavering support — all of it part of her inheritance, as much as her grandmother's technical legacy.

"Now," she said, raising her glass, "we make sure nothing like The Consortium ever happens again. We keep fighting for transparency, for accountability, for justice. Not from the shadows anymore, but in the light."

"To ICE," Nova proposed.

"To truth," Drake added.

"To family," Abby smiled.

"To legacy," Mandy finished softly.

Through the window, she could see snow beginning to fall over the city. Each flake caught the light differently, creating patterns as unique as quantum signatures. Somewhere out there, Amanda "ICE" Johnson was watching, waiting, ensuring that the frost she'd cultivated would keep spreading, keeping the powerful in check, preserving the delicate balance between justice and power.

The jade pendant hummed against her chest, harmonizing with the new bracelet's quantum frequencies. Two generations of ICE's legacy, old code and new, working in concert to protect the transformations they'd set in motion. Not through force or control, but through the patient power of truth spreading through every crack in the world's systems.

Ghost raised an eyebrow at Mandy's contemplative expression. "What are you thinking about, Snowflake?"

Mandy smiled, touching the pendant that had started it all. "That some inheritances aren't burdens. They're gifts. And it's what we do with them that matters." She looked at the falling snow, each flake a promise of renewal. "Grandma didn't just teach me how to fight The Consortium. She taught me how to build something better. How to be patient, to work through the small changes that add up to transformation."

"The frost spreads," Nova quoted softly.

"And everything changes," Mandy finished.

A week later, she stood in her apartment, watching dawn break over the city. The world was different now – not perfect, but clearer, like air after a winter storm. The Great Revelation had shaken every institution, exposed every shadow, but from that upheaval, new patterns were emerging.

Her phone chimed with a message from Ghost: another Consortium backup server found and cleansed, another piece of the old order transformed by ICE's persistent code. The quantum virus continued its work, not destroying but rebuilding, creating transparent systems where shadows had once ruled.

On her desk, a small indoor garden flourished – different plants growing together in careful balance, frost patterns decorating their container. A gift from her grandmother, delivered anonymously but carrying unmistakable meaning: life finds a way to thrive, even in winter. Even through ice.

The work wasn't over – it never would be. Power would always seek shadows, corruption would always try to take root. But now they had tools, frameworks, and most importantly, a legacy of transformation to build upon. Not just ICE's technical brilliance, but the human connections that had made their victory possible.

Mandy touched the jade pendant, feeling its familiar resonance with the silver bracelet. Old code and new, working together just as she and her grandmother had across twenty years of separation. The frost had spread, creating not just cracks in The Consortium's power, but pathways for something new to grow.

Outside, the morning sun caught countless snowflakes, each one carrying its own pattern of truth and transformation. And nothing would ever be the same again.

28 BEYOND ICE

The penthouse suite of the Frost International building offered a panoramic view of the city skyline. At twenty-three, Mandy stood at the floor-to-ceiling windows, her reflection ghosting against the night beyond. Her short platinum hair was growing out, dark roots showing – a physical manifestation of her transformation. The frost-like scars from the quantum core explosion traced delicate patterns up her arms, visible beneath the sleeves of her tailored black jacket.

Ghost's voice broke the silence, their presence announced by the soft blue glow of multiple screens. "The last of the Consortium's accounts have been frozen. Interpol just arrested their CFO in Geneva. The quantum virus is still working its way through their backup systems, ensuring nothing remains hidden."

Mandy nodded, her hand instinctively going to the jade pendant. Its familiar weight was joined now by the silver bracelet, both humming with quantum frequencies that seemed to resonate with her very being. "And Blackwood?"

"Maximum security. He's singing like a bird, trying to cut a deal." Ghost paused, their fingers dancing across keyboards as new data streamed in. "The quantum interrogation protocols your grandmother designed are proving... remarkably effective. Every answer he gives opens new pathways, reveals new connections."

They hesitated, then added softly, "They found her, boss. In an unmarked grave outside Madrid."

The words hit Mandy like a physical blow, despite her years of preparation for this possibility. After all this time, her grandmother's final resting place had been discovered. She closed her eyes, memories washing over her – the smell of vanilla ice cream, the sound of laughter, the warmth of unconditional love. But mixed with those memories now were newer ones: the quantum code they'd shared through the pendant, the lessons hidden in every transmission, the way her grandmother had prepared her even from beyond what everyone thought was the grave.

"Have my parents been notified?"

"Yes. They're arranging transport now." Ghost's expression softened, showing the human beneath their usual digital facade. "There's something else. We found ICE's contingency files. The ones even the Consortium didn't know about. They were hidden in quantum storage nodes across six continents, each piece only accessible with the combined signatures of your pendant and bracelet."

Mandy turned from the window, the city lights casting shadows across her face. "Show me."

The files painted a picture that took Mandy's breath away. Her grandmother hadn't just been fighting corruption – she'd been building something far more ambitious. A network of operatives, whistleblowers, and reformers spanning the globe. Safe houses equipped with quantum-secured communications. Hidden accounts containing millions in untraceable cryptocurrency, each coded with specific ethical parameters for its use.

Most importantly, a web of influence reaching into every corner of the underground world, built on trust rather than fear.

"She was creating a shadow organization," Mandy breathed, watching as map after map populated the screens. "One to counter the Consortium. To fight fire with fire, but with built-in safeguards against corruption."

"And she left it all to you." Ghost pulled up a video file, their hands almost reverent as they accessed the quantum-encrypted data. "This was recorded a week before she disappeared. The timestamp matches the creation date of the original quantum virus."

ICE's face filled the screen. Despite the grainy quality, Mandy could see the determination in her grandmother's eyes – the same look she now saw in the mirror. There was something else too, a hint of the master plan that had taken decades to unfold.

"Mandy, my beloved snowflake," ICE's voice was strong, confident, carrying the weight of carefully laid plans. "If you're watching this, then you've done what I couldn't – or rather, what I couldn't do alone. You've exposed the truth. But the work isn't finished – it never is. The Consortium may fall, but another will rise to take its place. The world needs a guardian, someone to stand in the shadows and fight for justice when the law fails."

ICE's expression softened, showing the grandmother beneath the legend. "I never wanted this life for you. But you've proven yourself more capable than I could have ever imagined. The network is yours now, built with safeguards I never had. Use it wisely. Be better than I was. And remember – the name ICE was never about being cold or hard. It was about being clear. Pure. Transformative."

The video continued, revealing detailed plans for a new kind of organization. One built on transparency and accountability, using the very quantum technology that had helped bring down the Consortium. ICE had designed systems of checks and balances, ways to ensure that power remained distributed, that no single person could ever accumulate the kind of control that had corrupted the Consortium.

A soft knock at the door preceded Nova's entrance. Despite her injuries from the raid on the Consortium's quantum core, she moved with quiet grace. "The old guard is assembled in the secure conference room. Along with some new faces. They're waiting for your decision."

Mandy gathered her thoughts, feeling the weight of legacy and future pressing equally on her shoulders. "How many came?"

"More than we expected," Nova replied, a rare smile touching her lips. "Word travels fast in certain circles. The quantum virus didn't just expose corruption – it revealed hope. People want to be part of something better."

In the building's secure conference room, Mandy found a gathering that would have seemed impossible just months ago. Former operatives of her grandmother's network, drawn out of retirement by recent events. Young hackers and activists recruited by Ghost, their skills refined by quantum computing. Even a few reformed Consortium members, seeking redemption after the Great Revelation had shown them the true cost of their actions.

They all fell silent as she entered. These were people who had known her grandmother, who had seen Mandy grow from a desperate teenager seeking answers to the woman who had brought down the Consortium. But more than that, they were people who believed in the possibility of change.

"My grandmother built this network to fight corruption that law enforcement couldn't touch," Mandy began, her voice carrying across the room with quiet authority. "But she worked alone, carried all the burden herself. That ends now."

29 REDEMPTION

The command center hummed with activity, dozens of screens casting a blue glow across the modernized space. Mandy watched the central display while absently touching the jade pendant at her throat, its quantum frequencies resonating with the silver bracelet on her wrist. The face staring back at her belonged to Viktor Petrov, a ghost from her grandmother's past that had haunted ICE's archives for far too long.

"Target confirmed in Shanghai," Ghost announced, their fingers dancing across multiple interfaces as they manipulated the holographic display. "He's not just reopening old Consortium channels – he's innovating them. Using quantum tech to mask the trafficking network's digital footprint."

Mandy's jaw tightened. She remembered the name from her grandmother's files - Petrov had slipped through ICE's fingers fifteen years ago, leaving three dead agents in his wake. The jade pendant seemed to pulse against her skin, as if responding to her rising anger.

"Nova, what's our insertion plan?"

Nova moved from her monitoring station with deliberate care, her recent injuries still evident in the slight stiffness of her movements. She brought up the building schematics, the Azure Dragon Casino materializing in shimmering blue light.

"Petrov's hosting a private auction at the Azure Dragon," Nova explained, highlighting key points in the projection. "Guest list reads like a who's who of underground royalty. He's using the casino's legitimate business profile as cover, but the real action's happening in the quantum-secured upper levels."

"Security's multi-layered," Ghost added, splitting their screens to show different systems. "Traditional armed guards, cutting-edge surveillance, and..." They frowned, fingers flying across keyboards. "Something new. They've got quantum-entangled security nodes. Try to hack one, and the others instantly know."

"But nothing's unhackable," Whisper's voice came from the doorway. The former Consortium operative had arrived silently, her natural stealth enhanced by the quantum tech now woven into her tactical gear. "Not if you know how to dance with it."

The plan unfolded like a deadly chess match, each piece carefully positioned. Whisper would work the casino floor. Ghost would hit their network. Nova would be their eye in the sky. And Mandy... Mandy would confront the past. Not just Petrov, but the legacy of how ICE had failed to stop him before.

"Remember," she addressed the team, studying each face in turn, "Petrov's expecting the old ICE playbook. He's prepared for a lone operator, a single point of attack. Let's show him how we operate now."

Hours later, Mandy stood in a private elevator ascending the Azure Dragon's upper levels. Her evening gown, a masterpiece of understated elegance, concealed cutting-edge tactical gear. The jade pendant at her throat now housed advanced communications tech, while quantum-responsive fabric allowed her to move without restriction.

The elevator opened onto a corridor that practically screamed wealth and power. Ancient Chinese art shared space with cutting-edge security tech, the past and present intertwined just like ICE itself.

Two guards stood watch, their poses casual but their eyes alert. Before they could react, tiny drones – courtesy of Ghost's tech division – dropped from ventilation ports in the ceiling. The quantum-engineered sleeping gas took effect instantly, dropping them without a sound.

"Sweet dreams," Mandy murmured, stepping over their unconscious forms. "Ghost, how's our exit strategy looking?"

"The quantum virus is spreading through their financial networks now," Ghost reported, satisfaction evident. "Billions in criminal assets, all being tracked and tagged for law enforcement. But Mandy... there's something else in their systems. Something old. Really old."

"Old like Consortium old?"

"Older. I think... I think these might be some of your grandmother's original programs. Like they've been waiting, dormant, for exactly this moment."

The revelation hit Mandy like a physical blow. Even now, years later, her grandmother's planning continued to amaze her. She reached the penthouse doors just as chaos erupted in the casino below. Right on schedule.

"Stock market crash simulation running perfectly," Ghost reported. "Their entire criminal empire is hemorrhaging money by the second. Petrov's buyers are pulling out in a panic."

"And now he'll be desperate," Mandy said softly, touching the jade pendant. "Just like old times, right, Grandma?"

She pressed her hand to the door's biometric scanner. Quantum tech lifted from Consortium labs did its work, and the lock disengaged with a soft click. The penthouse suite beyond was a study in contradictions – ancient artifacts and modern luxury, all bathed in the neon glow of Shanghai's night sky.

Petrov stood by the floor-to-ceiling windows, barking orders into a quantum-encrypted phone. He froze at the sight of her reflection, his face going pale as if he'd seen a ghost. In a way, he had.

"Impossible," he breathed, turning slowly. "You're dead. I saw the body... I made sure..."

"Wrong ICE," Mandy said, her voice carrying her grandmother's authority but her own steel. "Though I think you'll find we share similar feelings about people who traffic children."

Petrov's hand darted for a weapon, but Mandy was already moving. Her grandmother had been a brawler, relying on experience and raw power. Mandy's style was different – swift, precise, almost elegant. She disarmed him with a fluid grace that would have made Nova proud.

"The world's changing, Viktor," she said, securing his wrists with smart-cuffs that interfaced directly with ICE's quantum network. "The Consortium's gone. The old networks are dead. But ICE? ICE adapts. Evolves. Transforms."

"You think this changes anything?" Petrov spat, but fear had crept into his voice. "Cut off one head-"

"Save the metaphors," Mandy cut him off. "Ghost, you getting this?"

"Every word. Also downloading his entire server network. It's... Mandy, this is bigger than we thought. These connections go everywhere – politics, finance, even some quantum research facilities. He's been building something. Something big."

As sirens approached the casino, Mandy stood at the window, watching the city lights below. Shanghai spread out before her, a glittering maze of old and new, just like ICE itself. She touched the jade pendant, feeling its familiar weight and the quantum pulses that seemed to beat in time with her heart.

"Command, I'm ready for extraction."

The window before her shattered – precisely, controlled, each piece caught in a magnetic field generated by tech that didn't officially exist. A sleek transport hover-drone waited beyond, another innovation her grandmother could never have imagined.

"Show-off," Ghost muttered in her ear, but she could hear the pride.

Petrov called out behind her, his voice desperate: "You're not her! You'll never be what she was!"

Mandy turned, silhouetted against the night sky. The quantum tech in her suit responded to her emotions, creating an almost ethereal glow. "You're right. I'm not my grandmother. I'm what ICE has become. We don't just fight corruption anymore – we change the game entirely."

30 DEEP FREEZE

The holographic display filled ICE's war room, a three-dimensional spiderweb of connections glowing in the dim light. At its center rotated the image of a quantum computer core - the next evolution in digital warfare. The data streams from Petrov's operation had led them here, to something far more dangerous than they'd imagined.

"But the future belongs to machines, my dear. Perfect prediction through perfect computation. Prometheus will do what the Consortium never could - create absolute order through absolute control."

Mandy studied the data streams, her grandmother's jade pendant catching the blue light. At twenty-four, she carried authority in every movement, the weight of ICE's legacy balanced by her own hard-won wisdom. The pendant pulsed softly against her skin, its quantum frequencies detecting something familiar in the patterns before her.

"Who's behind it?" she asked, though she already suspected the answer. The quantum signatures were too similar to ignore.

Nova, now fully recovered and serving as ICE's operations director, stepped forward. "Former Consortium scientists, backed by a coalition of underground syndicates. They learned from our takedown of their old infrastructure. They're building something that can't be touched by traditional methods."

"Nothing's untouchable," Mandy said softly, remembering how they'd dismantled Petrov's empire. "Ghost, what are we looking at in terms of security?"

The hacker's expression was grim as they manipulated the holographic display. "That's the thing, boss. It's not just digital. They've split the quantum core across three physical locations. Multiple redundancies, failsafes. The architecture is... beautiful, in a terrifying way. Even if we hit one site..."

"The others adapt and compensate," Mandy finished. She straightened, addressing the assembled team. The war room was fuller now than it had been during the Petrov operation - dozens of specialists, each bringing unique skills to the table. "Then we hit them all. Simultaneously."

The room fell silent. Even for the new ICE, with all its resources and personnel, coordinating three major strikes at once was unprecedented. The quantum calculations alone would require processing power they'd never attempted to harness before.

"Nova, you'll take Singapore with Team Alpha. Whisper, Dubai is yours - take Beta Squad. I'll handle the Russian site with Ghost coordinating from here."

She turned to the latest addition to their inner circle - her mother, Abby, who now served as ICE's intelligence director. "Mom, what are we dealing with on the ground?"

Abby brought up energy signature analyses that made Ghost lean forward in their chair. "We've detected patterns matching old Consortium tech. They're not just building something new - they're incorporating salvaged equipment. Equipment that..." she hesitated, glancing at Mandy.

"That was used the night Grandma disappeared," Mandy finished quietly. The jade pendant seemed to grow heavier against her skin.

"They're not just trying to predict us. They're trying to understand us. To understand her."

"Then they're already falling behind," Mandy said, straightening. "Because we're not just my grandmother's ICE anymore - we're something they've never seen before."

The night of the operation arrived clear and cold, the kind of crystalline darkness that seemed to amplify every sound, every movement. Mandy stood in the final equipment check room, the quantum frequencies of her enhanced tactical suit harmonizing with the jade pendant's pulses. Around her, dozens of screens monitored the other teams' preparations, a symphony of coordination her grandmother could never have imagined.

"Execute Operation Deep Freeze. On my mark... three, two, one. Go dark."

Across three continents, ICE teams moved with synchronized precision. In Singapore, Nova's team infiltrated through the building's cooling systems. In Dubai, Whisper's squad rappelled down the skyscraper's face. And in Russia, Mandy approached the bunker alone - surrounded by a swarm of microscopic drones, another innovation that merged Ghost's digital expertise with Nova's tactical experience.

"It's not just about predicting us," she realized as she moved deeper into the facility. "They're trying to recreate that night. To understand exactly how she thought, how she moved..."

"It's a trap," Ghost confirmed. "They're not just building Prometheus - they're trying to draw you in. To finish what they started with ICE. But Mandy..." A note of fierce pride entered their voice. "They have no idea what they're really dealing with."

Mandy reached the bunker's central chamber just as the first waves of data began flowing back through their quantum network. The space was vast, carved from the living rock and filled with humming servers that pulsed with otherworldly light. At its center stood the quantum core, its crystalline structure eerily similar to the one that had been active the night her grandmother disappeared.

"Welcome, Ms. Thompson," a voice called from the shadows, cultured and precise. "Or should I say... ICE? Though I suppose that title's becoming rather complicated these days."

A figure stepped into the light - elderly but straight-backed, wearing an expensive suit that seemed out of place in the technological cave. "Doctor Heinrich Strauss," she said coolly. "I thought you'd retired. Though I have to say, Prometheus seems a bit ambitious for someone in your golden years."

Strauss smiled thinly, running his hand along one of the quantum processors. "Your grandmother had a similar sense of humor. She never did take our work seriously enough. Always relying on human intuition, on unpredictability..." His eyes gleamed in the blue light. "But the future belongs to machines, my dear. Perfect prediction through perfect computation. Prometheus will do what the Consortium never could - create absolute order through absolute control."

The core's crystalline surface began to glow brighter, its hum rising to a fever pitch. Frost patterns spread across its surface, beautiful and terrible as winter storms. Strauss lunged for a control panel, but Mandy's shot took him in the shoulder, spinning him away from the controls.

"Your grandmother..." Strauss began, reaching for something in his jacket.

"Was brilliant," Mandy cut him off, her movements smooth and practiced as she disabled his hidden weapon before he could draw it. "But she knew something you never understood. Something Prometheus could never predict." She secured his wrists with quantum-locked restraints. "The future isn't about lone wolves or perfect machines. It's about networks. Adaptation. People working together in ways that transcend individual limitations."

337

The core's light died completely, along with every system in the facility. In Singapore and Dubai, the same scene played out with perfect synchronization. Prometheus, the perfect predictive machine, had been outthought by human ingenuity and teamwork.

Later, in the war room, Mandy watched as Ghost's team began the delicate process of dissecting Prometheus's remains. The quantum technology wouldn't be destroyed - it would be transformed, repurposed from a tool of control into something that could help them protect and serve justice in ways even her grandmother couldn't have imagined.

"She would have loved this," her mother said softly, joining her at the window. The rising sun painted the city in shades of possibility. "Not just the technology, but what you've built. Who you've become."

Mandy smiled, watching her team at work. Nova was already planning improvements to their tactical systems based on what they'd learned. Whisper was developing new training protocols that merged her Consortium experience with ICE's evolving methods. And Ghost... Ghost was in their element, exploring the captured quantum cores with an excitement that bordered on reverence.

"She built ICE to be a weapon against corruption," Mandy said, touching the pendant one last time. "We've turned it into something more - a shield, a network, a force for change that keeps evolving."

As she moved to the command center, a soft chime from her quantum interface drew her attention. A message, encoded in a pattern she recognized instantly - the same crystalline structure that had protected her grandmother's secrets all those years ago.

The message contained only two words, but they made her breath catch in her throat:

"Well done."

The jade pendant hummed against her skin as she looked out over her assembled team - no longer just her grandmother's legacy, but something new. Something better. The frost was spreading, transforming everything it touched. And this time, it wasn't spreading alone.

EPILOGUE

ICE LIVES - Full Circle

Twenty years had passed since Amanda's death, and the Thompson household had changed in ways none of them could have predicted. The reading nook at the library, once a sanctuary of healing, had grown into a flourishing community center. But beneath the surface of their seemingly peaceful lives, secrets lingered like shadows at twilight.

Abby sat in her home office, surrounded by the familiar comfort of legal briefs and case files. At sixty-five, she had scaled back her practice but couldn't quite bring herself to retire completely. Her hair had silvered gracefully, and laugh lines marked the corners of her eyes - testament to a life well-lived, despite its complexities.

She picked up a framed photograph from her desk - a candid shot from Mandy's college graduation fifteen years ago. Her daughter stood proudly in her cap and gown, flanked by Abby and Drake, their faces beaming with pride. But there was something in Mandy's eyes, a glint that Abby had never quite been able to read, that now sent a chill down her spine.

The signs had been there all along, she realized. The way Mandy had immersed herself in criminal psychology after college, her fascination with cold cases, her uncanny ability to understand the criminal mind. At first, they'd attributed it to Amanda's influence - their daughter following in her grandmother's footsteps of seeking justice. Now, Abby wasn't so sure.

Drake appeared in the doorway, his once-dark hair now completely white, his face creased with the weight of shared worries. "She's here," he said softly.

Abby nodded, taking a deep breath to steady herself. Their

monthly dinners with Mandy had become a ritual, but lately, they'd taken on an edge of tension that neither parent could quite explain.

Mandy swept into the house like a cool breeze, elegant and composed in her FBI uniform. At thirty-five, she had risen quickly through the ranks, earning a reputation for being brilliant but unconventional in her methods. Her colleagues called her "ICE" - a nickname she'd embraced with an enigmatic smile that reminded Abby painfully of Amanda.

"Mom, Dad," Mandy greeted them, her voice carrying that familiar mix of warmth and something else - something that echoed from the past. She set her briefcase down carefully, and Abby couldn't help but notice how her daughter's hand lingered on it protectively.

Over dinner, they maintained their familiar dance of conversation - work updates, community news, memories of Amanda that had become well-worn with repetition. But tonight, something felt different. The air crackled with unspoken words.

Finally, as they settled in the living room with coffee, Mandy spoke. "I've been doing some research," she said, her voice steady but charged with purpose. "About Grandma's death."

Abby's hand trembled slightly as she set down her cup. "Mandy, we've been through this. The doctors explained-"

"The doctors were wrong," Mandy cut in, her eyes suddenly sharp with a familiar intensity. "Or rather, they were led to be wrong. I've found evidence, Mom. Things that don't add up."

Drake reached for Abby's hand, squeezing it gently. They'd known this day might come, had seen the signs in their daughter's relentless pursuit of truth, her unwavering connection to Amanda's memory.

"There's something you both need to know," Mandy continued, opening her briefcase. "About who Grandma really was. About who I am."

As Mandy began to lay out her findings - documents, photographs, testimonies gathered over years of careful investigation - Abby felt the carefully constructed walls of their family narrative begin to crumble. The truth about Amanda - about ICE - emerged like a shadow taking form in darkness.

"She wasn't just my grandmother," Mandy said, her voice taking on a tone that sent shivers down Abby's spine. "She was my mentor, even if she didn't know it then. Everything she was, everything she stood for - it's in my blood, Mom. I am ICE now."

The revelation hung in the air like smoke, changing everything and nothing all at once. Abby looked at her daughter - really looked at her - and saw Amanda's spirit burning bright in those determined eyes. The same strength, the same complexity, the same capacity for both love and calculation.

"What are you going to do?" Drake asked quietly, his voice heavy with concern.

Mandy's smile was gentle but resolute. "What Grandma would have wanted. I'm going to finish what she started. But I'll do it right this time - from within the system, where I can make real change."

Abby felt tears welling in her eyes - not of sadness or fear, but of understanding. Their daughter had always been destined for this path, shaped by forces set in motion long before her birth. Amanda's legacy lived on, transformed but undiminished, in the woman Mandy had become.

"We're still a family," Mandy assured them, reaching out to take both their hands. "That was real - all of it. Grandma's love, her dedication to us, her desire to change. But she was also more than that, and so am I."

As the evening drew to a close, Abby stood at the window watching Mandy drive away. The street lights cast long shadows across the pavement, reminding her of how far they'd all come from those early days of uncertainty and hope.

"She'll be okay," Drake said softly, wrapping his arms around her waist. "She's stronger than we ever imagined."

Abby nodded, leaning back against him. "Just like her grandmother," she whispered.

Later that night, as Abby lay awake in bed, she thought about the cycles of life, about how love and truth and justice could take so many forms across generations. Amanda's story hadn't ended with her death - it had merely transformed, finding new life in Mandy's determined spirit.

The future stretched out before them, full of uncertainty but also possibility. Their family bonds, tested but unbroken, would continue to evolve. And somewhere, Abby liked to think, Amanda was watching over them all - proud of the legacy she'd created, of the granddaughter who carried her spirit forward in ways none of them could have foreseen.

In the end, it wasn't about right or wrong, good or evil. It was about love, in all its complex and sometimes painful forms. It was about truth, even when it hurt. And it was about justice - not always the kind found in courtrooms, but the deeper justice of the heart, of family, of understanding.

As Abby finally drifted off to sleep, she felt a profound sense of peace. Their story - Amanda's, Mandy's, all of theirs - would continue to unfold in its own way, guided by the unbreakable bonds of love and the eternal quest for truth that had brought them all together in the first place.

The wheel had come full circle, and somewhere in the darkness, ICE lived on.

ICE RESTS - Echoes of Winter

Two years after Operation Deep Freeze, the ICE headquarters

buzzed with activity beneath a crystalline winter sky. The quantum-enhanced windows of Mandy's office shifted subtly, adapting to the changing light as she studied the holographic displays floating before her. At twenty-six, she carried both her grandmother's legacy and her own hard-won wisdom in equal measure, the jade pendant at her throat now joined by an array of quantum tech that would have seemed impossible just a few years ago.

"Latest intelligence update coming in," Ghost announced through their quantum-linked communication system. Their voice carried the easy confidence of someone who had helped reshape the world of digital security. "The last remnants of Prometheus have been completely dismantled. The quantum virus we developed from its core has revolutionized our entire network. Even the legitimate agencies are starting to adopt variations of the technology – under our supervision, of course."

Mandy smiled, remembering how far they'd come since those desperate days of fighting the Consortium alone. The ICE facility around her was a testament to that evolution – no longer hidden in shadows, but operating in plain sight under the cover of a "cybersecurity consulting firm." The quantum technologies they'd captured and transformed had allowed them to build something her grandmother could hardly have imagined: a global network of justice that worked in perfect synchronization while maintaining absolute independence.

"Nova's team just checked in from Bangkok," Ghost continued, bringing up new tactical displays. "The human trafficking ring we've been tracking tried to resurrect some old Consortium protocols. Big mistake." Their grin was audible. "The new quantum detection systems caught them before they even got their operation running. Local authorities are making arrests as we speak."

"And Whisper?"

"Currently teaching an advanced infiltration course to our newest recruits. You should see them – former hackers, reformed criminals, even a few ex-government agents. All of them learning to work together in ways that would have seemed impossible a few years ago." Ghost's fingers danced across invisible interfaces. "The quantum neural link systems are revolutionizing how we train people. It's not just about sharing information anymore – it's about sharing experience, intuition, understanding."

Mandy stood, moving to the window. Below, she could see teams of recruits training in the facility's courtyard, their movements synchronized by barely visible threads of quantum energy. The frost patterns on the glass seemed to respond to her proximity, creating beautiful fractals that reminded her of code and crystallization.

"My grandmother would hardly recognize what we've built," she mused, touching the jade pendant. Its familiar weight now carried new purpose – not just a symbol or a tool, but a bridge between past and future.

"I wouldn't be so sure about that," a new voice said from the doorway.

Mandy turned, her heart skipping a beat. Her mother stood there, but she wasn't alone. Beside her was an elderly woman, her silver hair cut short and practical, her bearing still carrying traces of the legendary operative she'd once been. The jade pendant at Mandy's throat seemed to pulse in recognition.

"Grandma?" Mandy whispered, hardly daring to believe.

Amanda "ICE" Johnson smiled, the expression carrying decades of carefully hidden pride. "Hello, snowflake. I think it's finally time we talked."

The next hours passed in a blur of emotion and explanation. Amanda had spent years in hiding, recovering from what the Consortium had done to her, but more importantly, watching. Waiting. Seeing how her granddaughter would handle the legacy she'd left behind.

"I knew you'd find your own way," Amanda said, studying the quantum displays with obvious appreciation. "The Consortium thought they could use my research to control the future. But you... you've turned it into something entirely new. Something better than I could have imagined."

"We had help," Mandy replied, thinking of Ghost's brilliant innovations, Nova's tactical excellence, Whisper's redemption story, and all the others who had joined their cause. "That's what they never understood. The future isn't about lone operators anymore. It's about networks, cooperation, constant evolution."

Amanda touched one of the quantum interfaces, her fingers moving with surprising familiarity. "You've taken everything I built and transformed it. The quantum encryption methods I developed, the tactical protocols, even my old codes – you've evolved them into something that serves justice instead of power." Her eyes met Mandy's. "I couldn't be prouder."

The facility hummed around them, its quantum networks carrying the combined experience and expertise of hundreds of dedicated operatives. Through their enhanced systems, Mandy could feel teams working across the globe – Nova coordinating a strike in Moscow, Whisper's trainees practicing infiltration techniques in Dubai, Ghost's hackers evolving their quantum virus protections.

"But that's not why you came back now, is it?" Mandy asked, recognizing something in her grandmother's expression. "Something's coming. Something big."

Amanda's smile turned serious. "There are always threats, snowflake. Always people who think they can control the future through force or fear or technological superiority. But now..." She gestured at the facility around them, at the quantum networks that connected ICE operatives across the world. "Now we have something better. We have hope."

She reached into her jacket and withdrew a small quantum storage device, its crystalline surface catching the winter light. "I've spent the last few years gathering intelligence, tracking something that makes the Consortium look like amateurs. They call themselves the Quantum Collective – a group of brilliant but ruthless scientists who believe they can use quantum technology to reshape reality itself."

Mandy took the device, feeling its subtle vibrations through her enhanced senses. "And you want us to stop them?"

"No," Amanda corrected, pride evident in her voice. "I want us to work together. The old ICE and the new, combining our strengths. Because what's coming isn't just another criminal enterprise or power grab. It's a fight for the very nature of human consciousness and free will."

Through their quantum network, Mandy could feel her team's reactions. Ghost's excitement at the technological challenges ahead. Nova's strategic mind already working through tactical implications. Whisper's quiet determination to prevent others from being victimized as she once was. And underlying it all, the combined strength of hundreds of dedicated operatives, each bringing their own skills and perspectives to their shared mission.

"Then they're in for a surprise," Mandy said, touching the jade pendant. "Because they're not just facing ICE anymore. They're facing something that evolves faster than they can predict, adapts faster than they can plan, and works together in ways they can't imagine."

Amanda's smile was fierce and proud. "The frost spreads," she quoted, her voice carrying years of carefully laid plans.

"And everything transforms," Mandy finished, but she wasn't just quoting anymore. She was stating a truth that the Quantum Collective would soon learn: ICE wasn't just back – it had become something entirely new. A force for justice that grew stronger with every challenge, evolved with every confrontation, and worked together in ways that no quantum calculation could predict.

Outside, snow began to fall, each flake carrying its own unique pattern. Through the quantum-enhanced windows, they looked like stars falling to earth, each one a promise of transformation. The world was changing, evolving, becoming something new. And ICE – both old and new, working together at last – would help shape that evolution toward justice rather than control.

The frost was spreading. But this time, it carried hope as well as justice, transformation as well as strength. And nothing would ever be quite the same again.

In her office high above the transformed city, Mandy Thompson – heir to ICE's legacy but architect of its future – smiled as she watched the snow fall. The jade pendant hummed against her throat, harmonizing with the quantum frequencies that connected her to operatives and allies across the globe. They were ready for whatever came next.

The game was changing once again. But this time, ICE wasn't just playing.

They were rewriting the rules entirely.

And somewhere in the quantum networks that now spanned the globe, in the frost patterns that carried coded messages between agents of justice, in the transformed technologies that served hope instead of power, a new kind of future was taking shape. One that combined the best of human intuition with the most advanced technology, the strength of individual brilliance with the power of cooperative action.

The frost was spreading, transforming everything it touched. And this time, it carried the seeds of something greater than justice alone. It carried the promise of a world where technology served humanity rather than controlled it, where power was balanced by responsibility, and where the future remained free to evolve in ways that no quantum calculation could predict.

ICE was back. And the world would never be the same.

ABOUT THE AUTHOR

Welcome to my corner of the literary world! I'm Kellie, writing under the pen name Cass Kellie—a moniker inspired by my beloved furry companion who's never far from my writing desk. Nestled in the heart of Northcentral Wisconsin, where the changing seasons paint an ever-shifting backdrop to my stories, I've spent most of my life discovering the extraordinary in the ordinary.

As a storyteller, I find inspiration in the vibrant tapestry of everyday life. Whether it's a chance encounter at a local café, the way sunlight filters through autumn leaves, or an overheard conversation that sparks a narrative thread, my writing draws from the endless well of human experience. Every person has a story, every place holds secrets, and every object carries a history—these are the elements that fuel my creative process.

www.ingramcontent.com/pod-product-compliance
Lightning Source LLC
Chambersburg PA
CBHW050541260626
47157CB00002B/394